Waiting for
the All Clear

L.B. Gray

LEAF BY LEAF

Published by Leaf by Leaf
an imprint of Cinnamon Press,
Office 49019, PO Box 15113, Birmingham, B2 2NJ
www.cinnamonpress.com

British Library Cataloguing in Publication Data. A CIP record for this book can be obtained from the British Library.

Designed and typeset in Adobe Jenson by Cinnamon Press.
Cover design 'Daymark on St. Martin's, Isles of Scilly', by Adam Craig © Adam Craig.
Cinnamon Press is represented by Inpress.

The story and characters in this novel are fictitious. Whilst research has been undertaken and certain institutions, agencies, and public offices are mentioned, the characters and events are the work of the author's imagination and any resemblance to actual persons, living or dead, or actual events is purely coincidental..

Waiting for the All Clear

Part One:
Don't Promise Her Anything

Birmingham, England

June 1943

Eleanor Barton peered through the cracked window at rows of empty shelves. 'M. Masterson, Purveyor of Fine Fruit and Vegetables.' The gilt letters above the window spoke of better times. She shaded her eyes as she searched in vain for fine produce. A day's teaching in the shadow of war had taken its toll. Her head and feet ached. She imagined how dishevelled she looked, with the morning's carefully placed hairpins probably scattered on the schoolroom floor, lost as she'd separated two scrapping six-year-olds.

She spotted a basket of slightly wrinkled apples and gazed at the fruit. Her mouth watered as she imagined the crunch and sharp taste. Only four other women ahead of her, waiting to be served. She gazed around, tracking every move made by anyone in the queue, any attempt to push in.

A woman gave her a sour look. 'Don't get your knickers in a twist, Missy, I'm too tired to fight you for them.'

Embarrassed, Eleanor looked at the speaker. 'Sorry,' she muttered, 'I didn't mean to…'

'Oh yes, you did,' came the reply. 'We're all like bloody wild animals now.'

Lost for a response, Eleanor faced forward, her craving quelled, ashamed of her readiness to do battle. For an apple.

As she debated relinquishing the apples, the air raid siren wailed. Thoughts of fruit vanished as she was trapped by the scurrying crowd heading for Smith Street public shelter. She couldn't even lift her arms as bodies stampeded around her. She was drowning, caught in a torrent, about to go under, unable to breathe. In her panic, she turned and fought to get back to her lodgings, away from the suffocating crowd. All she managed was to incur the wrath of frenzied citizens.

'Get down the shelter, Miss, you trying to get us all killed?' A woman shrieked.

'Move it, the shelter's this way, where d'you think you're going?' This last speaker grabbed at her shoulder but missed and caught hold of her loosened hair. He dragged her roughly in the opposite direction.

Helpless now, her feet almost leaving the ground, Eleanor could only try to keep up, to avoid being trampled by the human tide surging down the street. She scrabbled at the hand gripping her hair and felt pain as her neck twisted. She broke free and ran for her life with the crowd. Just as she reached the shelter, the first bombs dropped, close, with a terrifying crash. She was blown straight through the entrance, landing on her hands and knees at the bottom of the steps.

Eleanor didn't stop to assess her injuries. *Must find a space against the wall, away from people, mustn't be trapped…* Panic drove her to push past looming bodies until, with relief, she sank against a wall. She looked out towards the mass of families staking claims to larger spaces. Then, as if a switch was thrown, the shouting and screaming stopped. The noise was replaced by an eerie quiet as the dim yellow lights on the wet stone walls picked out pale faces, etched with fear, waiting for the next bomb to fall.

Time to take stock. Eleanor was still clutching her battered handbag. To her surprise, given the frantic crush, her string shopping bag containing her purse was still wrapped around her arm. The rough handle had scraped the skin on her forearm, which, with cuts on her hands and knees, was the extent of the damage. She wiped her wounds with a handkerchief and settled back. She felt a kind of calm creep over her, allowing her to examine her surroundings, to accustom herself to the sights, smells and sounds of the shelter.

Most of the others taking refuge were families with children. In the half light, Eleanor picked out several children who attended the school where she worked. Despite the government's efforts, many families chose not to have their children evacuated to homes in the country. As a result, Eleanor knew that the number of pupils in the school was not much below pre-war levels. In many ways, she didn't blame the families. She'd seen the terse instructions sent out by the Ministry:

1. Children should come to school at 6am

2. Each child evacuating should bring their respirator, a change of clothes, night attire and food for two days

3. Children will be taken from school to trains, and thence to their destination, which will be unknown for security purposes

4. They will be met by host parents who have generously opened their homes to evacuees, where they will be safe and well cared-for

Eleanor heard rumours of problems arising from the evacuation scheme, and although some children had settled, a good number had returned, unable to cope with the separation.

She watched as women tried to soothe and distract the children with fruit drinks and biscuits from the 'shelter bags', always ready by many back doors. She observed the constant movement to the two lavatories serving the entire shelter and tried to block out the smell of human waste overlaid with disinfectant. As she settled herself, wishing she had remembered to put a book in her bag to pass the time,

Eleanor noticed a group of about ten children ushered into a small annex by two women in identical serge suits. She couldn't quite make out the logo on their shoulders, but they appeared to be from a charitable organisation.

Unwilling to risk losing her place, she craned her neck and could just see into the room. She watched as the children were seated at wooden tables by the uniformed women, she heard the children call them 'Miss Rhoda' and 'Miss Audrey'. Paints and copybooks were laid out, two children made puppets, two more used cardboard to create a model village.

Eleanor couldn't resist. Leaving her cardigan spread on the ground as a feeble barrier against invaders, she slipped into the room and spoke to the woman the children called Miss Rhoda, who looked up with a tight smile. *Not sure she's welcoming the interruption*, thought Eleanor. *Reassurance needed. Charm.*

'Excuse me, I just had to speak to you, I teach some of these children and I'm simply amazed at what you are doing in these difficult surroundings.' Miss Rhoda's lips became noticeably less pursed. Eleanor pressed on. 'So, is this a sort of play centre?'

Miss Rhoda now favoured Eleanor with a full smile. 'That's it exactly, my dear. We are from the Save the Children Fund, and we try to make these children feel secure, take their minds off what's'—she pointed skywards—'up there.'

Eleanor did not have to pretend to be impressed as she observed the activities. 'What an excellent idea. I wonder, do the play sessions give them a chance to talk about their fears as well as enjoying themselves? They seem to clam up when we try to talk to them at school.'

Miss Rhoda looked thoughtful. 'Well, I suppose so, we certainly don't discourage talk of the war if they seem to want to. Or more often it comes out in their drawing.' She looked around the room, then beckoned Eleanor to the end of a table. A boy of about six, tongue protruding from his lips, painted with intense concentration. He had produced a stick figure family, gathered around a rock, on which the boy had drawn crude eyes, nose, and a down-turned mouth. Crooked letters at the top proclaimed: 'MY FAMILY BY WILLAM'.

Eleanor looked at the painting, then the child. 'William, could you tell me about your painting?'

The boy seemed happy to oblige. He pointed to the tallest figure. 'Well, Miss, there's my Mam.' He then indicated two smaller figures. 'That's my sisters, Maisie and Beth, they're twins.' The final figure, standing next to Mam, was identified. 'There's me, I'm the youngest, but Mam says I'm the man of the family now.' He pointed to the rock-shaped object. 'And there's Dad, I heard them say there were just bits of him, so I drew one o' the bits. See, he's sad because he can't be with us.' He turned to the two women with a half-smile, looking uncertain.

Eleanor felt her stomach contract. Her voice was soft. 'Thank you, William.' Miss Rhoda led her away. William got on with his painting.

As she returned to the main room, Eleanor saw that two women had encroached on both sides of her hard-won place. However, she was able to squeeze into the space left, gratefully accepting a biscuit from one and a hot drink from the other. She forced herself to nibble the biscuit. Her appetite and strength were deserting her.

Scraps of conversation reached her as she tried to relax: '...only recognised me missus by one of her boots...she used to read bits of the paper to me every evening. Can't read, meself...'

'...my cousin's still under there. They got his little Benji out, dog was in one of them Frank-Heaton kennels. Y'know, like a rubbish bin tipped on its side...'

'...lost my son. We had a funeral but no idea what was in the coffin...'

Finally, Eleanor slept fitfully against the rough wall, troubled by images of William's father. And the voice of the last speaker she heard as she drifted off: '...oh well, life's a short business, so it is...'

Out of the Shelter

June 1943

Broken glass and rubble crunched underfoot as Eleanor hurried back from the shelter in the warm early summer morning. *Going to be late, must clean myself up first.* Around her, buildings were sliced open from top to bottom. They looked like giant dolls' houses, some furniture in place, exposed to the air, and some scattered on the ground. She put her hand to her face, a futile attempt to block the acrid smoke. Her foot brushed a clump of dusty hair strewn above the rubble, was the owner buried beneath?

Wardens nearby dug frantically. 'Stay away, Miss, we might have someone under here.'

'Sorry, sorry. Didn't see…' She stumbled away. Looking over her shoulder, she imagined she saw the children following, running to get to the shelter. She tried to tell them: 'Go back, go home, it's that way, what are you doing, following me?' The children, looking ahead, ignored her, rushed on.

And then an explosion ripped through the taut fabric of the day, scattering the searchers. The children vanished. Stunned, Eleanor fell into a broken armchair.

Someone was pulling her arm and she fought back. An urgent voice said, 'Come on Miss, it's not safe, Jerry left a few behind and another one might go off any minute.'

Eleanor staggered back to her lodgings. Disorientated, she slumped onto her bed, trying to gather her thoughts. Despite the summer heat, she shook with cold and shock. Crawling under the bedcovers, she waited for the tremors to subside.

Eleanor could not have said how much time passed as she

lay curled in a ball. Slowly, she pushed herself up and opened the wardrobe. She pulled the nearest blouse and skirt off their hangers, then found that her fingers were shaking too much to fasten the buttons. A jumper covered the gaps. Looking in the mirror as she tried to drag a comb through her hair, she thought she'd aged ten years. There was food in the pantry, but she wasn't hungry. And the children were waiting.

Breaking Point

June 1943

She felt better after walking to the school. As she opened the door to her classroom, the Headmistress stopped her.

'Miss Barton, a word if you don't mind.'

Eleanor gestured towards the door. 'But, Miss Thomas, the children...'

'Don't worry.' Miss Thomas smiled. 'I've asked the Caretaker to keep an eye on them. They love his stories of the good old days.' She led the way into her study, closing the door behind her. 'Please, sit down.' She indicated a chair and seated herself on the other side of her desk.

Eleanor was really worried now. *I haven't been late that often. It's my first real job, I can't get the sack.* She kept silent and braced herself.

Miss Thomas took a deep breath. 'First of all, let me say how pleased we are with the work you are doing. You are a gifted young teacher with a bright future ahead of you. The children respond so well to you.' Eleanor was far from reassured. A 'but' was coming, she was sure of it.

The Headmistress continued. 'However, I have a duty to look after my staff as well as the children, and anyone can tell that you are ill.'

Eleanor opened her mouth. But Miss Thomas ploughed on.

'You've lost weight, you are as pale as a ghost, and worst of all, you seem distracted and anxious most of the time. And that worries me greatly.'

Finally, Eleanor managed to speak. 'But Miss Thomas,

everyone's been affected by the raids, the bombs, the war. I've hardly suffered at all compared to those who've lost loved ones, their homes.' She raised her head and saw a look of compassion on the usually stern face of the Headmistress.

'That's perfectly true, my dear. But I am recommending... in fact, I am insisting that you take a break. There are those I wish I could have saved...' She broke off, turning her head to look out the window.

Eleanor waited, distracted from her own distress. *How little we know of the people we see every day*, she thought.

Miss Thomas gathered herself. 'You are the future, Miss Barton. You will be making a difference to children's lives long after I'm gone, and I am quite determined that you will survive to do that.'

Eleanor's control slipped in the face of the Head's kindness. She put her elbow on the edge of the desk, head in hand, and leaked tears onto the scratched oak surface. After a minute, a cotton handkerchief appeared under her arm. Slowly she became quiet, blew her nose, and was ready to listen.

A look of what might have been relief passed over Miss Thomas's face. 'Now, am I right that you have family in the country?'

Eleanor nodded. 'My parents live in a village. But...' Seeing a quizzical brow raised, she explained. 'They advised against taking this post, but I didn't listen. I wanted the experience of teaching in a big city, teaching children who perhaps didn't have the advantages that country children do.'

'And a very good job you've made of it too,' said Miss Thomas. 'You've adapted so well to our ways. The children will miss you, I know, but get yourself sorted and you might just be able to come back.'

With this carrot dangling in front of her, Eleanor weakened. 'Well, I could contact my parents, see what they say.'

'That's the spirit. Show a bit of the courage you've shown in the bombing and face up to your own parents.'

That evening, Eleanor pushed a good supply of coins into the hall telephone at her lodgings. 'Hello, Father, it's me.' Worried noises came at her from the receiver, and she hastened to add, 'No, I'm all right. But I have a favour to ask.'

One week later, she was on her way south.

Westholme, Wiltshire

June 1943

At the end of the afternoon, Eleanor pushed open the gate to her parents' garden, and sank gratefully into the nearest frayed deck chair. It was a hot walk from Marshfield School where she had now been teaching two weeks. She loosened the buttons on her high-necked dress to let the air through. She sighed. It hadn't been a bad day. She'd only panicked once, lurching backwards and hitting her head on a shelf at the sound of a book dropping. She had managed to pull herself upright and walk on as a couple of the children passed by.

'You all right, Miss?'

'I'm fine, just knocked my head on the shelf there.'

The children lifted their gaze to the sharp corner. 'Ooh, better be careful, Miss, mind you don't knock yourself out.' They rounded the corner, giggling.

Safe in the garden, Eleanor mulled over the episode and took a deep breath. *Good effort,* she told herself. *They didn't notice anything odd, I didn't overreact, maybe I am getting better.*

The early summer sun on her face, Eleanor still couldn't believe how her life had changed. She could tell her parents, especially her undemonstrative Northern mother, were somewhat discomfited by her request to stay with them. Although they opened their village home to their damaged daughter without a murmur, she could not escape a belief that she was an unexpected burden.

She recalled her mother's tired voice when they spoke just before her return. 'Of course, Eleanor, if you need a rest. I suppose we could clear your old room; I could find somewhere else for my sewing.'

Eleanor had sensed more than resignation in her mother's words, possibly resentment at an intrusion. She was not having that. 'Thank you for the offer, but I'll be fine in the box room. It gets the afternoon sun, and I like the view over the garden.' No argument from Mother. 'And in any case, I may not be here for long, no point in creating upheaval for a short time.'

To begin, Father had offered work at Westholme Primary, where he was Headmaster. 'Now then, Eleanor, I suppose we could use some help with the Infants,' he began one day shortly after her arrival.

'Very kind of you, Father.' She tilted her head up with a slight smile. 'Actually, I understand there's a position at Marshfield School, it's not far to walk and I'd like to give it a go.'

Like Mother, Father did not argue. Eleanor was pleased. She wanted to maintain some independence from her parents, at least during working hours. With so many men away fighting, she knew a well-trained schoolteacher was more than welcome. There was always the possibility the post could be a springboard back to Birmingham and away from dependency.

Eleanor continued to bask in the sunshine, satisfied with her decisions since returning. Inside the house a door slammed in the breeze. She did not move a muscle, allowing herself a small smile. *Yes, indeed, I'm getting there. Would have jumped out of my skin a couple of weeks ago.*

At work, however, she sometimes found it hard to reconcile her new situation with the fresh memories of Birmingham. When the other teachers complained about petrol rationing, endless mending of threadbare clothes, lack of decent fruit, and aching backs from digging veg, Eleanor kept quiet. Her colleagues could not understand her patience with the evacuees now at Marshfield School, children filled with anger and unable to concentrate.

'Ungrateful little buggers, aren't they?' a teaching assistant muttered as Eleanor helped her sweep the debris resulting from a disrupted art lesson. Megan, the apparent cause of the mayhem, was seated on a high-backed chair in a corner of the room, sniffling. All that could be seen of her was brown hair frizzed away from two rough plaits. 'I simply asked them to draw a house.' She shook her head. 'Next thing I knew, Megan covered her paper with orange paint, then ripped it to pieces when I asked her about it.'

Eleanor glanced at Megan's heaving shoulders. Miss Rhoda's voice came back to her from the shelter: *Sometimes it seems that impersonal pictures take away personal horrors. And what we really hope is that if they can feel safe and happy, we can persuade them to try the country again.*

Eleanor remembered her initial reaction. 'Persuade' them? Had these well-meaning people learned nothing from the repeated returns of some evacuees? And yet, she could understand the impulse of parents and welfare organisations to prioritise physical survival over the emotional security provided by family bonds.

As they finished sweeping the debris in the Marshfield classroom, Eleanor gathered a few pieces of the torn painting. 'Mind if I have a word with Megan?'

The other woman shrugged. 'Suit yourself, but I hope you'll have more luck than I've had.'

Eleanor approached the child. 'Megan, I saved some of your painting because I thought it was interesting.' She waited, expecting another outburst.

Megan turned slowly, a wary expression on her blotched face. She took the vivid orange paper from Eleanor and smoothed it on her knees. She wiped her eyes with the back of her hand. 'Miss told us to paint a house, an' that's it. My house.' A fierce glare at Eleanor, as if daring her to comment. Eleanor simply nodded. Megan ducked her head and muttered. 'It burnt.' Another sniffle. 'An' now we can't go back.'

Eleanor sighed and relaxed back in the garden chair, letting her mind drift from Megan's distress. Although Eleanor was recovering, she still believed she had failed, should have been stronger, should not have abandoned the children. Now, she could at least offer understanding to the evacuees who, like her, had escaped the bombs but suffered in the aftermath.

Eleanor's reflections were interrupted as Father came out of the house; pipe clamped in the side of his mouth. She was just about to kick off her sensible shoes and unhitch her lisle stockings. There were spots of high colour on Father's otherwise pale cheeks.

'Don't get too comfortable. Couple of American officers coming to tea. They gave a talk at the school today, went down rather well, so least we can do is feed them before they go back to base.'

He hurried back into the house before Eleanor could reply. But she wasn't fooled. Mother's health was bad, and she knew she and her sister Annie, probably upstairs with a magazine, had about an hour to scratch together a meal to do justice to the Americans.

Ray

Summer 1943

Extracting Annie from her magazine wasn't difficult. The words 'American officers' had her shooting downstairs and into the kitchen.

As so often, she took charge. 'Right then, Eleanor, better have the best china for the Yanks.' With care, the sisters dug bone china cups and plates from the back of the sideboard.

Eleanor peered into the pantry. 'There's some of Father's wholemeal loaf here, that'll test their teeth.' Squinting further into the cool semi-dark, she picked out a small paper-wrapped packet. 'And what's this I see? We can treat them to real butter, but we might have to use the marge for our bread.'

Annie passed Eleanor a battered saucepan and a bowl containing half a dozen eggs. 'Got some eggs left from our share. I'd say Father's 'girls' are doing him proud. Boil these up, while I get some tomatoes and strawberries from the garden.'

Thirty minutes of frantic activity later, they surveyed the table. Polished oak, gleaming china and cutlery, and a wholesome spread. The vivid reds of the tomatoes and strawberries made a pleasing contrast with the warm brown of the bread and pale hard-boiled eggs. It would do.

They scampered upstairs to change. Annie pulled two matching dresses from the back of their wardrobe. 'Look, these will still fit. And it'll be a laugh to confuse the Yanks, what do you think?' She held up a flowery garment and twirled.

The twins no longer dressed identically, but these summer frocks from before the war were in good repair and would be just right for a tea party.

Eleanor wasn't so sure. 'Aren't we a bit old for those sorts of games?' But, seeing Annie's disapproving look, and not wanting to be a spoilsport, she gave in. Dressed alike, they faced each other.

Sometimes people said, 'It must be like looking in a mirror, being identical.' But they were wrong. It was true they were both of medium height, with dark curly hair and wide-spaced pale blue eyes. They had inherited their father's cool white complexion. The Barton nose, with its high ridge, stood out proudly from oval faces. Father, quite a sportsman in his youth, had also passed on his athletic, well-muscled frame to his children.

However, Eleanor knew that events in their lives had left marks that made them instantly distinguishable to those who were close. Like the lines across Eleanor's forehead and between her eyes, in contrast to Annie's smooth face. Or the protruding bones in Eleanor's hands, while Annie's were well-fleshed and smooth. And, Eleanor sometimes reminded herself with sisterly spite, the small bristly mole next to Annie's nose.

Downstairs, Eleanor heard her parents answering the doorbell. The girls joined them and were introduced to 1st Lieutenant Ray Miller and his officer pal Mac Shilton, both in their best uniforms. Small talk cloaked Eleanor's initial shyness while she studied Ray. He towered over her parents, carrying himself with strength and confidence. She supposed people would describe his features as 'ordinary': brown eyes behind round military-issue spectacles, hair Brylcreemed back to a peak in the middle above a sun-tanned forehead, a prominent nose, and thin lips. His voice was deep and resonant, turning chitchat to poetry in Eleanor's ears. He took the lead after Father made the introductions. Mac stood back, the smaller and possibly shyer of the two men.

'Pleased to meet you, Miss Barton. And, uh, Miss Barton.' Ray smiled, seeming to see the funny side as he turned from one sister to the other.

Annie extended her hand. 'I'm Annie, she's Eleanor, and now you gentlemen will have to figure out how to tell us apart.'

Ray looked at them, rubbing his chin and furrowing his brow. He snapped his fingers. 'Got it! Annie, I see you are wearing a bracelet, so as long as the two of you don't swap jewellery, I guess we'll be just fine.'

Eleanor was impressed with his confidence and easy banter with Annie, especially in front of her parents. *Maybe this is what Americans are like,* she mused. *They just assume everyone is going to be as friendly and open as they are.*

She decided it was time she spoke up and gestured to the dining room. 'Won't you come through. I imagine you are hungry after facing an interrogation from Father's top class.' She knew she hadn't quite managed Annie's breezy tone, but the men smiled and followed her to the table.

The sisters served tea, and Eleanor continued to observe the two soldiers. As she did, her heart sank. Even with the twins' near-identical features, dresses, and hairstyles, both men looked mostly at Annie. Eleanor thought she knew why. Her sister chatted with ease and wit, whereas her mirror told her that months of tension had dimmed the sparkle in her own eyes.

Annie moved around the table, lifting dishes, laughing at jokes, and looking so comfortable. Whereas Eleanor struggled at times to concentrate on the conversation. Worst of all, when she brought a dish to the table, she imagined it shattering across the polished surface, blown apart by a bomb. Her hands shook and she was sure they noticed. Being soldiers, she imagined they sensed her inner wounds and preferred the bright sunny girl on a day to match.

Over the next days following the soldiers' visit, Eleanor put the tea party, and what she perceived as her rejection by the Americans, behind her. The weather helped. Five days of chilly June rain made sunny times in the garden seem distant.

Friday afternoon and, after another sodden slog from Marshfield School, Eleanor curled up with a cup of tea. She was thankful that tea had been spared the scythe of total rationing, but the drink was not much enhanced by a tasteless sprinkle of powdered milk, all that was available. She had changed into an old pair of trousers and an itchy wool cardigan to ward off the chill. Father would be in soon, and Annie would be back from her clerical job at the Supply Depot. Then they'd have a fire. Mother didn't hold with wasting coal on fewer than four people, no matter how cool and damp the summer evenings might be.

An hour later they were benefitting from the modest warmth generated by carefully selected lumps of coal. Father reached over and turned off the Home Service, in the middle of his favourite gardening programme.

He nodded at the twins. 'Had an invitation today for you two. Those American officers want to take you to the pictures tomorrow. They seem all right, so what about it?' The girls exchanged looks. Annie gleeful, Eleanor wary.

However, Eleanor overcame her uncertainty, remembering Ray's kind face and warm, baritone voice. 'I wouldn't mind, we seem to spend the days working, and the evenings like this. It could be fun to get out for a change.'

'Right,' said Father, 'I'll get back to them.'

He switched the wireless back on. With relief, Eleanor suspected. He did his best but dealing with personal matters related to his daughters made him twitchy, and Mother tended to remain aloof. Eleanor was left wondering what on earth had possessed her to agree to yet another evening on the side lines. Although it might be worth it to hear Ray's voice again, even if he was only telling stories of camp military life to amuse Annie.

The next evening the two men, preceded by a waft of pungent aftershave, arrived to collect the girls. On the bus into town, Ray sat with Annie and Mac settled beside Eleanor. *Oh well*, she thought, *just enjoy the evening*. And she did enjoy it. The film was *No, No Nanette*, a perfect escapist comedy. The nervous chatter of the bus ride into town was replaced by relaxed hilarity over chips and a shandy afterwards.

That first evening set the pattern for the coming weeks, the four of them enjoying themselves when they could. Eleanor noticed that Ray and Annie sometimes disappeared for a short while, and she had a good idea of what was going on. Ray did his best to remove the lipstick from his face but didn't always make a clean job of it. She had hoped he might show a bit of interest in her, but she could understand that he was obviously drawn to her more vivacious sister. And after all, she could relax in Mac's quiet, undemanding company.

Gone with the Wind

August 1943

One hot afternoon, Eleanor trudged back from town, tired and aching from queuing hours at the butcher's shop. She knew that rationing of essential food meant more was available for the troops, but sometimes the shortage of meat and dairy produce was dispiriting. She didn't think there was enough time left in the world to stew the gristly meat she was carrying home into some edible form for supper that night.

As she turned a corner, a jeep passed, then executed a smart U-turn in a cloud of dust and pulled up beside her. At the wheel was Ray.

'Need a lift?' Eleanor hesitated. She knew 'frivolous' use of petrol was universally frowned on, as was the sight of an English girl on her own with an American soldier. Especially in a jeep, with her hair blowing in the breeze, her presence visible to passers-by. He seemed to know what she was thinking. 'Don't worry, I'm on an errand for the Commanding Officer, and I don't think the Army will object to the splash of gas it will take to go down your lane. In the interests of good relations with the community, of course.' He smiled warmly, opened the passenger door, and the heavy bags and her aching shoulders did the rest of the persuading.

Eleanor always felt that it was from that moment that the two of them 'clicked'. Annie had been called up to National Service. In the blink of an eye, it seemed, she was in Auxiliary Territorial Service uniform and on her way to Liverpool to help with refugee resettlement. Eleanor wasn't proud of her thoughts after Annie left: *I do miss her, but who knows what could happen with Ray now that I'm out of her shadow?*

Mac's main topic of conversation was his wonderful girl back home. When they occasionally met for coffee, Eleanor felt more like a sister, listening to the latest news of this paragon of womanhood. *A bit boring*, she confessed to herself, although she tried to be sympathetic.

Two days after the jeep ride, the telephone sounded in the hall, and Eleanor answered.

Her 'Westholme 252' was met by a brief silence, then, 'Well, hello there, am I speaking to Miss Eleanor Barton?'

No mistaking the accent, or the melodious voice. She responded, hoping her tone was suitably light. 'You are, and what can I do for you, Lieutenant Miller?'

'Well, you can let me take you to the pictures again. This time, just the two of us, what do you think?'

'I'd love to.' Was her tone overly enthusiastic? 'Although I'm not sure what's playing.'

A chuckle at the other end of the line. 'You're quite right to be cautious, I wouldn't want to take you to some third-rate garbage. Have you seen *Gone with the Wind?*'

'No, but I've been wanting to see it for ages, ever since it came out over here.' This was true, and she couldn't keep the excitement out of her voice.

'I was hoping you'd say that. Six o'clock bus into town, then? I'll come by your house, and we can walk to the bus stop.'

Much later that evening, the lights faded on the screen. Eleanor sat glued to her seat, dazed by the spectacle she'd witnessed, tears drying on her cheeks.

Ray waved his hand in front of her face. 'Hey there, anybody home? I know it was a pretty long movie, but are you still with me, sweetheart? You okay?'

Eleanor shook herself. 'I'm a bit stunned. I've never seen anything quite like that.' He stood and she took his outstretched hand, pulling herself up to join him. 'I think I'd like to walk for a bit.'

Ray pulled her hand through the crook of his arm as they strolled out of the cinema into the soft dark. Ten o'clock at night, and the summer sky still had a glow. 'So then, what's up?' he said. 'I'm no mind reader, but I can see something about that movie really hit you.'

Eleanor sighed. 'Well, it was a different time, a different war, but like them… one minute we were living a normal life, and then death, destruction, families torn apart…' She stopped, and she looked up for any sign he was mystified, or even irritated, by what she was saying.

But he nodded and stared up into the night sky. 'You are so right. Sometimes I wonder what happened to me. I used to be this happy guy, playing his music, and helping out on the farm. And how's it all going to end up?'

'That's it, exactly, and the film showed how truly awful, how stupid and pointless, any war is. I thought about Melanie, and whether being loving and loyal is enough. It didn't seem like it was, for her. Yet Scarlett, well, she was strong and wilful and didn't give up. I'm not sure I could be like that. In fact, I know I'm not, because here I am, safe in the country. Not strong at all.' She thought Ray looked slightly uncomfortable at these revelations. 'Sorry, I don't know what got me started, you must think I'm a bit feeble.' He opened his mouth, but she didn't give him a chance. *Change the subject, Eleanor.* 'And another thing I couldn't help wondering about.'

'Yes?' Ray drawled his response.

Eleanor hurried on. 'The Civil War, like we've had in England in the past. The North and the South, all part of the same country.' She lifted a puzzled face. 'But I couldn't understand, why were they fighting? What exactly were they fighting for?'

Ray stopped. 'Funny, I've never thought too much about it, it was just The War Between the States.' He frowned. 'You know I grew up in the North, what they call Yankee land. In fact, Minnesota sent some of the first soldiers to fight against the South.' Eleanor waited. She had a sense Ray was taking a new look at his own old history, and that the view was unsettling. They started to walk again. 'I had some cousins used to visit from Georgia. They always wanted to play Yankees and Rebels, us kids all shooting at each other. I remember my uncle, he told us once he kept some Confederate money, said the South would rise again and he might need it.'

Eleanor still couldn't understand. 'So, if they were called Rebels, what were they rebelling against? Why were children still fighting it out, all those years later?'

Ray blew out his cheeks. Eleanor thought she might have pushed him too far. What she'd said about the story in the cinema seemed connected to something uncomfortable for him. 'Well, far as I can tell, this is what it was about. The Southerners had big tobacco and cotton plantations. They got the best profit if they didn't have to pay the workers and kept them from running away. Slavery, basically. The government wanted to make slavery illegal, on, y'know, moral grounds. That movie made being enslaved look kind of romantic, but basically it was men owning other men.' He sighed. 'Anyway, the South rebelled, they fought for the right to own the people they'd enslaved. My dad told me that's what it was, no matter how anyone dresses it up. But my uncle from Georgia used to say it was some issue about the states' rights.' He shook his head. 'I just don't know, to tell the truth, too complicated for me.'

They walked on in silence. An old wooden bench emerged out of the gloom. Ray sat, then patted the seat next to him and leaned forward with his elbows on his knees. 'I tell you, Miss Eleanor Barton, you are something special. I reckon we hardly know each other, I thought you were a bit shy, a bit prim and proper. But there's more to you than meets the eye, and I want to spend a lot more time finding out about it.' He sat up and put his arm around her. Slowly.

Eleanor leaned in towards him and smiled in the dark. 'Fine with me,' she said. 'How about a picnic this weekend?'

Picnics, walks, tea with Eleanor's parents and village hall socials filled the lazy days of August. Ray was able to get leave at least twice a week, and they spent every possible minute together. Superficial chat diminished in favour of something more relaxed. He intrigued her with stories of life on his parents' farm.

'Got a letter from my dad today.' Ray pulled an envelope from his pocket as he and Eleanor sat on a windy hillside trying to keep the flies off their sandwiches. 'Typical Pop, it's all about the animals. Big news is, they're finally getting electricity to the farm so they can run a freezer for the sperm from their new bull. Pop's really excited about it, I can tell.'

Eleanor couldn't hold back a laugh. 'Well, I've picked up quite a bit from the farmers' children at the school, but I can't imagine insemination ever being the main topic in a letter from my father. Your dad sounds like a pretty straight-talking chap.'

'Oh, yes, and he likes to think he's Mr. Modern Farmer. But the real funny thing is, he still won't have a phone put in, I guess I'm going to have to persuade him when I get back.'

The two of them rocked back onto the blanket, laughing. Ray kissed the tip of her nose.

'Now that's what I like to see, no more shadows on your face from whatever went on up in Birmingham.'

Eleanor stopped laughing and pushed herself up on her elbow. 'Ray, I feel like I ought to tell you about that, maybe I should talk about it.'

This time, he kissed her lips and silenced her. 'Honey, we don't need to talk about bombs and war when we're together. You need to put all that out of your mind, you'll just drive yourself nuts.' He pulled her up. 'Now let's climb to the top of this fine hill, work off some of that food we just ate.'

Eleanor sighed. It was true, she wasn't as jumpy as she had been, and slept better and laughed more. Maybe Ray was right. She should put the nightmare of Birmingham behind her and live in the present. They climbed the hill together. She got to the top first.

Then, in September, just as they realised that what they felt for each other was more than close friendship, the news came that Ray was being posted to France.

A shock, but it shouldn't have been. Ray's job in the Army involved organising transport of essential supplies to frontline troops, and Eleanor had always expected that this could happen. But it was a shock that catapulted them out of their sedate courtship into something more urgent. The three weeks between Ray's notice of posting and his departure passed in a haze. In different ways, each of their lives had given them little experience of sudden passion and desperate decisions. Especially ones reaching across distance, culture, and background.

The night before he left, Ray suggested a stroll. Dusk was falling; the air in the garden was damp. He put his arm

34

around her shoulders, catching his watchband in her cloud of dark, curly hair.

Eleanor winced and pulled away. 'Ow—careful, Ray!' She rubbed her head, and a few strands of hair came away in her hand.

Ray seemed distraught. 'Oh, my Lord, now look what I've done. Sorry, sweetheart, I've got a lot on my mind.'

Eleanor's heart was thumping. *Of course, he's about to go into a war zone, no wonder he's distracted. But could there be another reason? Something he wants to ask me?*

However, the words that came weren't what she had expected. 'Sweetheart, the Army tells us to concentrate on the job of getting rid of Hitler and not to promise anything, especially to foreign girls.' Startled, and a little offended, Eleanor gave him a quizzical look. He seemed to realise he'd got off to a bad start. 'What I'm trying to say is, that advice is just too late for me, I *am* involved, I want to have a life with you… oh, hang it…' He stuttered to a halt. Eleanor folded her arms, refusing to put him out of his misery. Finally, he held her more closely and murmured: 'Darling, I'm no good at this, but I don't suppose… can I hope?' He opened his hand, revealing a gold ring with a tiny diamond.

Eleanor stared at the dainty object in Ray's large palm. Her first feeling was panic. *Wait a minute, it's too soon.* Panic was followed by euphoria. 'Oh Ray, I would be so happy.' She stopped abruptly. 'But what about your family, and your faith? I recall when we saw that old film in the village hall, about the Jewish lad who pretended to his parents that his Irish Catholic sweetheart was Jewish?'

His puzzled look vanished. He looked away, uncomfortable.

On the verge of tears, she continued. 'You said, Ray Miller, that you couldn't understand how the girl could want to marry outside her faith. Or how her fiancé could lie to his parents? And that you would never ever do that. So how,' she saw him look away, and refused to let him. 'No, look at me, Ray. How can you want to marry me?'

Ray pulled her close, whispering in her ear. 'I just love you so much, and I know my parents will too. Especially if, well, if you might think about converting.'

Eleanor wiped her eyes on the soft cloth of his shirt.

He bent down towards her. 'Hey honey, let me kiss those tears away.'

His clumsy attempt at comfort struck her as funny and brought her distress to an abrupt end. She pushed him away, sniffling, half laughing. 'For goodness' sake, Ray, I'm not six! I do love you, I do want to marry you, but converting? I will think about it, that's all I can say. Now hand over that ring, I'll keep it under my pillow. Or maybe in a drawer, safer there. Until I figure out what to say to my parents.'

Eleanor Alone

October 1943

On that hesitant note began a courtship of letters. Other than 'somewhere in France' Eleanor had no idea where Ray was or what he was doing. She could only guess at the dangers he was facing behind the lines in occupied territory.

As she went about her daily life, she sensed Mother and Father were watching her. Waiting for signs of imminent collapse, she supposed. She tried not to show her irritation at this scrutiny. She couldn't have a headache, a bad day at work, or fail to finish a meal without her sanity being questioned.

One Sunday afternoon, Father appeared at her door, holding a wooden tray. He strode into the room before she had a chance to protest. 'I've brought you a cup of tea. And a bit of toast, your mother was worried you didn't finish your meal.'

Eleanor roused herself from a pleasant doze and tried to focus. 'Oh, well, thank you, I've just got a bit of a headache.' He put the tray down and she reached for the tea. 'Didn't sleep much last night, you see.'

Father looked around, then perched his lanky frame on her dainty dressing table stool. 'Want to have a chat about it? You know they say a trouble shared is a trouble halved.' He cleared his throat. 'And if you're not sleeping...'

Now fully awake, Eleanor tried to hold back an exasperated sigh, 'Very sweet of you, Father, but you needn't worry.' She gestured to the window. 'I realise you and Mother can't hear the pigeon from your side of the house. She's raising a brood, and there's a constant cooing and shuffling from the crack of dawn.' She yawned. 'I mean, as a woman, I admire her devoted care, but it's impossible to sleep through it.' She tried to keep her tone light, but annoyance crept into her voice. 'Please stop fussing, it really doesn't help.'

Father, looking chastened, rose from the stool and made a hasty exit. 'Leave you to get some rest then.'

Eleanor regretted her sharp tone and called after him. 'Lovely supper, thank you!'

In fact, remembering the state she was in when she left Birmingham, she sometimes questioned herself. She was surprised at how well she was feeling. Missing Ray, but somehow the fear and despair she'd brought with her was gone.

About a week after Ray left, Eleanor came home to find a letter with an Army Post Office address propped against a flower vase on the hall table. Out of the corner of her eye, she spotted Mother in the flower room, shifting vases from one shelf to another. *I guess I'm still under observation*, she thought.

Eleanor called out, 'It's all right, Mother, you can stop pretending to be busy in there. It's a letter from Ray. I'm going upstairs to read it.' No reply, but Mother's lips twitched. Eleanor raced upstairs, blowing a kiss to her parent as she went.

Sliding into her favourite chair by the window, overlooking the garden, she tore open the envelope. Her first letter from Ray, and her first ever love letter. She couldn't wait to read it.

Dear Eleanor

I hope this letter finds you well, and that the weather is nice enough for you to get out on some of those walks you enjoy so much.

I want to start with an apology. I am sitting here in a field office (I'm not allowed to say where) feeling like the biggest chump there ever was. That was the most unromantic proposal a man ever made to a woman, I'm sure of it. I wouldn't blame you if you wanted to give that ring right back to me. I lie awake at night, thinking I've blown my best chance of happiness, please forgive me.

I love you so much.
Ray

Eleanor didn't know whether to laugh or cry. She'd been expecting something a bit more romantic, although she realised her lack of experience might have led her to fantasise.

She hated to think of Ray facing danger and feeling so miserable about her. *Better put him right.* She pulled out a pen and paper.

My Dear Ray

I love you, I want to marry you, and I thought your proposal was very original (although I know very little about these things, of course). I do know we are going to have to do some talking and thinking about religion, but I've always considered myself a good Christian. I can't imagine that your Catholic beliefs can be so far from mine, and I certainly want to learn more.

There! I hope you understand now how much you mean to me. I think about you all the time.

Fondest love,
Eleanor

With the letter posted, there was nothing to do but wait. Each morning, Eleanor opened the drawer on her bedside table, took out the ring and tried it on. Perfect fit, but when to tell her parents? *Let them get used to seeing letters arrive, they'll work it out, then I can tell them. And they like Ray, they'll be happy for me,* she told herself.

The following week, on Saturday morning, another flimsy US Armed Forces letter dropped on the mat. Anticipating a relieved reply to her cheery effort, Eleanor picked up the silver letter opener (always on the hall table, to avoid damage to the contents of a letter by its overeager recipient). Just in time, she looked again at the envelope. Ray's writing, but addressed to Lawrence Barton Esq.

Flustered, Eleanor returned the letter to the mat and dashed upstairs. *Good heavens,* she thought, *he's done the traditional suitor thing and I still haven't told them. What if he mentions the ring? That will just make things worse.* She pulled open the drawer, then rushed back down before Father could spot the letter.

She rounded the door into the breakfast room, breathless. Her parents looked up, slices of toast suspended mid-air.

Eleanor sat. 'I've got good news. At least I hope you will think it's good news.' Mildly enquiring looks came from across the table. Eleanor held out her left hand. A shaft of morning sunlight caught the modest diamond, and she thought it sparkled like the Koh-i-Noor. She took a deep breath. 'Ray and I are engaged!'

A stunned silence. Mother frowned. 'Really, Eleanor? You hardly know the man.' There was a movement under the table, which could have been Father's foot. Mother went on in a softer tone. 'Well, of course, you aren't a schoolgirl, I suppose you know your own mind.'

Father spoke up. 'We just need a bit of time to get our heads around this, you see. Out of the blue really. But if you care for each other, if he makes you happy, then I guess that's enough for us.'

Eleanor, aware of the letter to Father on the mat, came round the table to give them each a quick hug. 'I'll just go see if there are any eggs, the girls have been on a go-slow lately.'

She grabbed her jacket from the hall and scampered out the back door, leaving Father to make his discovery. As she went, she heard Father say, 'Madeleine, please, no point in trying to talk her out of it. Whatever you might think. You know what these wartime romances are like. Lonely homesick soldiers getting carried away. He's a nice enough young chap, but he'll probably end up with a girl back home once it's over.'

We'll see about that, thought Eleanor.

When she returned with a clutch of still-warm eggs, Father was standing in the hall, holding the letter. He peered over his glasses at Eleanor. 'Interesting letter from your young man. Funny it's come just after your little bombshell with the ring. I'll read it to you, shall I?'

Eleanor looked at him, trying to judge his mood. *Probably be wrong no matter what I say.* She nodded. Father read:

Dear Mr. Barton

No doubt you know from Eleanor that before I left, I asked her to do me the great honour of becoming my wife. You will see that I have shown my intentions by giving her a ring, and I hope you will allow her to keep it.

I also hope you will understand that, things being as they are, I have taken this liberty before speaking to you. If anything happens to me, I wanted her to have the ring for remembrance of my love.

Respectfully yours,
Raymond J. Miller

Eleanor waited. She still couldn't work out what Father was thinking.

Finally, he sat heavily on an upholstered hall chair. 'Not how we used to do things, but give the lad credit, nothing's how it used to be. I'll be writing back, saying we would be happy to have him in the family.' He sighed. '"No doubt you know from Eleanor", he says. Hmm. Say no more about that.'

Relieved and grateful, Eleanor gave her parent a proper hug, burying her face in his rough jacket. 'I'm the luckiest girl alive, that's what I say.'

Ray's next letter showed none of the tension of his first one.

Dearest Eleanor

I'm sitting here watching a full moon, just had to scribble a few lines before I get my head down for the night.

Your letter made me so happy, and today I've had a great reply from your dad. I was hoping that you—and he—would understand, but so afraid you wouldn't. Now I have peace, and I can start imagining our life together.

I might get leave in a few weeks, so I can be with you, and tell you all the things I love about you. Although there's so many I might run out of time.

I wonder if you're looking at the same moon, and what you are thinking. I wonder if you worry about me, and if you are asking yourself the same questions as other sweethearts and wives. Well, just put those thoughts out of your mind, I will keep myself safe for you

S.W.A.L.K.
Yours always,
Ray

Sealed With a Loving Kiss. Eleanor was thrilled with the warmth in this letter. And with the possibility she would see him soon.

On Ray's first leave, Eleanor was taken aback by the change in him, by the contrast with the loving letters that flew back and forth across the Channel. He had little to say, although he seemed content to sit by her side, or walk the fields and paths with her, holding hands. But he jumped at the slightest sound: a dog barking, the telephone ringing, even sudden laughter. He was barely polite to anyone who asked how the War was going. He would change the subject or leave the room.

And then she realised. When she came back to her parents' home, she existed in a private hell. Well-meaning questions, assumptions that 'it will help to talk about it', and just plain nosiness assaulted her from all sides. People were offended at her lack of gratitude, and, to her relief, eventually left her alone.

It was Ray's cheerful confidence during their early days that eased her terror then. He made her laugh and wore her into a deep dreamless sleep with relentless countryside walks. This was the shield protecting her now. She hadn't made the connection before, but the damaged part of her that Ray and Mac had once shied from was there to be used for him now.

Music was key, she decided. During their time before he left for France, she learned that the meticulous soldier who made sure that inventories were carried out and supplies requisitioned was a passionate musician. He'd paid his way through college by singing with a big band, and sometimes arranged three-part harmonies for his neighbours, who sang on local radio. He told her about his job as a high school music teacher, that he conducted the marching band, played several instruments in the community orchestra and was, as he put it, beginning to dabble in composing.

Eleanor shared his love of music, if not his talent, as she cheerfully admitted. On many occasions they danced at the village hall until their legs nearly collapsed. In fact, thanks to years as captain of the school hockey team, her legs usually held up better than his. Happy memories of Ray leaning on her as they staggered, laughing, into the blackout.

Driven by her own understanding of being shattered by war, and her belief that when words failed, music could talk, Eleanor summoned the nerve to put her ideas to Ray. On his next visit, as he sat in his usual spot by the fire, cold pipe in an ashtray beside him, staring into space.

Picking up the *Radio Times* listings, Eleanor approached and cleared her throat. 'Ray, I've been thinking…'

He turned and looked up at her. He summoned up a smile, and her heart ached as she saw the effort it took. 'Uh oh, those aren't words a man likes to hear. Everything okay, sweetheart?'

'Oh no, it's nothing bad, it's just I wanted to ask if you'd like to try, well, I just wondered about the evenings. Sorry, I'm not explaining this very well.' She stopped, frustrated.

Ray smiled, more genuinely this time. 'Well, you've made a good job of getting my attention. What's up?'

'Ray, you've told me about how much you love music, going to concerts, that sort of thing. And I know you like to dance, and sing.'

'Guilty as charged, darlin'. So?'

'Well, I know we usually sit around in the evenings, sometimes the neighbours drop in.' He nodded. 'And sooner or later, the war comes up and I've noticed, well, you find that tough.'

He sighed. 'You're not wrong there, sometimes I feel kind of bad, like I'm rude to people, but I just can't stand it, feels like I can't breathe when they start on about the war this, the war that.'

'Exactly.' Eleanor held out the week's radio listings. 'So, what if we made the evenings sort of concert time? Mother and Father would enjoy that, and maybe we could all relax a little.'

Ray was silent, looking at his hands. Eleanor held her breath. *Am I wrong? Is he offended?*

Without warning, he reached up and put his arms around her. Off balance, Eleanor toppled into his lap. There they sat, holding each other close, until he removed his glasses, wiped his eyes, and looked at her. 'Sounds perfect.'

No longer did Ray have to sit through awkward occasions when attempts at conversation were expected. Instead, he and Eleanor scoured the paper for orchestral and chamber music concerts on the Home Service. The family still gathered around the wireless in the evening, but silent enjoyment of music was all that was required. Eleanor loved to watch Ray's face as, glass of whisky in hand, he half-closed his eyes in front of the firelight.

Eleanor's other weapon in their mutual fight against fear was her father's old gramophone, which had been gathering dust in the attic for years. Ray could get records from the base, so on some warm afternoons when the windows let the breeze through, the neighbours were treated to Glenn Miller, the Dorseys, or whoever Ray could get his hands on that day. Best, a bit of furniture rearrangement meant they could sway to Bing Crosby or Rosemary Clooney, disturbed only by the occasional passage of Father through the room, clearing his throat as he went.

As the weeks and months slid by, their lives, suspended in the early months of war by the belief that 'it will soon be over', hardened around the conflict: uncertainty, death, delirious happiness, the breaking down of social conventions. Eleanor found it difficult to remember pre-war days of order and certainty and suspected that there was no end to the horror.

The Normandy Landings

June 1944

Eleanor set off to work on the 6th of June. It was a typical English summer day, with dark cloud formations scudding the sky. Not at all warm. Not awful, but requiring a cardigan and possibly an umbrella. The time between Whitsun and the end of the school year dragged. The children lost concentration, and it was sometimes hard to summon the will to help them recapture it.

Eleanor arrived at the school, savouring the moments of peace before the day began. She set out some spelling and reading exercises, and somehow managed to keep the restless bodies reasonably still through the morning.

As the children gathered their books, more than ready for the lunch break, one of the older boys stuck his head through the door. 'Headmistress says everyone into the hall!' he shouted and was off to the next classroom before Eleanor could ask what was happening.

She got the chattering, anxious children into the hall, with some semblance of the order usually achieved only at morning assembly. On the stage, a wireless hooked up to large speakers boomed the Home Service midday news. The excited audience was reduced to silence.

This is a special news bulletin. D-Day has come. The solemn tones of the announcer cut through the still air. The hush deepened.

The newsreader continued: *Early this morning, the Allies began their assault on the north-western face of Hitler's European fortress. Under the command of General Eisenhower, Allied*

Naval Forces, supported by strong Air Forces, began landing Allied Armies under the command of Field Marshal Montgomery on the northern coast of France. The Allied Armies consisted of British, Canadian, and American soldiers. Orders from General Eisenhower to his troops and those in occupied countries stated: 'The tide has turned. I call on all who love freedom to stand with us.'

That is the end of this special news bulletin.

A stunned silence was broken by a small voice from the Infants at the front. 'Is the war over, Miss?'

Eleanor leaned along the row where she sat with her class and whispered, 'No, Margaret, but it's good news. I'll explain when we get back to our room.'

She was now faced with the challenge of explaining the Normandy landings to a group of five-year-olds when she herself knew little of what was happening. However, these children had only experienced wartime, and were sadly well-informed about its harsh realities. They had listened to the adults and had learned to take everything from evening bulletins to air raid sirens very seriously. Their understanding was already far beyond what children their age would have in peacetime.

After lunch, she seated the class in a semi-circle. 'Let's start with what D-Day means.' She wrote the term on the board, then tapped on it with a pointer. 'Does anyone know?' As she expected, head shakes and blank faces greeted the question. 'Well, the "D" simply stands for "day", the day of an attack. So, D-Day means Day-Day, which is a bit strange, don't you think?' The children exchanged slight smiles. Eleanor guessed they were enjoying the relaxation of giggling at a silly idea.

Eleanor turned to the large map of Europe next to the blackboard. The school caretaker had fastened this to a thin metal sheet on the wall, and she could move arrow magnets around to show the children what was happening. She picked up a handful of arrows.

'Now watch closely, and I will show you what's been happening today.' She pointed to the arrows already on the map, showing the advance of German troops through France towards the English Channel. 'What do these arrows show?'

This time, a small forest of hands rose, and as Eleanor called on each one, she could see that they understood. 'It's the Nazis, Miss, coming to get us.' 'They are trying to stop them in France, but it's not working.' 'My dad will stop them; he won't let them come in.' Eleanor let the discussion continue for a few minutes, then placed new arrows on the map. The children watched intently.

Eleanor spoke as she put arrows crossing the Channel and touching the coast of France. 'You can see that our troops are going in the other direction, trying to push the enemy back.' Twenty small heads nodded in unison. 'We heard on the wireless that British, Canadian, and American soldiers landed in France, here.' She indicated the Normandy coast. 'And if they keep going, and manage to push the enemy back, then things might start to get better for us.' She was conscious of not raising their hopes, so she chose her words carefully. 'We don't know yet exactly what happened, or how it's going, but each day we will learn a little more, and we will talk about it in class.'

Silence. Eleanor hoped the children were digesting this more complex version of win/lose. *Have I made sense of it for them?* She wasn't sure.

After a few minutes, a quiet voice asked, 'So I s'pose the war's not over then, is it, Miss?'

'No, Frank, but it could be a big step in the right direction.'

A sigh, and a slight tremble of Frank's lower lip. 'We just get a bit fed up, sometimes, Miss.'

'I know, but we have to carry on and do our bit. And trust our leaders and our brave soldiers to win through in the end.' Eleanor heard herself using the familiar words of encouragement and wasn't sure she always believed them herself. But the little faces in front of her brightened, Frank's chin came up, and that was enough for now.

Anxious waiting followed, as the Allies struggled against enemy resistance to turn their foothold on the shores of France into a march across Western Europe. However, Eleanor was able to use the emerging facts of D-Day to keep focused on what was a costly, but ultimately solid success on the beaches of Normandy. The children were absorbed in topics such as: 'How the Allies fooled the Germans into thinking they were landing somewhere else' and 'What actually happened on Omaha Beach?'

There was hope, and a growing sense that everyone could feel it.

Part Two:
Moving Forward

Destination Carn Friar's School

July 1944

As the summer weeks crept by after Ray's last leave and the D-Day landings, Eleanor sensed a change. She slept well, the nightmares were less frequent, and she woke each morning ready, if not eager, to face the school day routine. She wouldn't have admitted it to anyone, but she was increasingly stifled. Ray's letters and visits were cherished, but infrequent, and her parents' loving surveillance was oppressive, especially as they didn't recognise her growing strength.

She also missed Annie's lively presence. Her sister had fallen for a Polish officer who had escaped a Nazi camp. She wrote of meeting him off the ship in Liverpool, helping with his resettlement papers, and 'showing him the ropes.' Ensuing letters spoke of having met 'the man of my dreams'. Eleanor assumed the chance of seeing Annie anytime soon was remote.

Towards the end of term at Marshfield School, Eleanor took a last look at the staff notice board. It was pretty much cleared for the summer, but a crookedly pinned notice in the corner caught her eye:

Junior mistress (Certificated preferred) wanted urgently for Primary School. Island community.

Contact in the first instance:

Mr. J. H. Chalmers

Headmaster

Carn Friar's School

St. Mary's, Isles of Scilly

Eleanor paused, struck by the image of faraway isles, and

a new challenge. If she married Ray, they had talked about living in America, which was far more remote and alien than these offshore British islands. She thought to herself: *This would be a chance to prove I could cope with living in a strange place, miles from my parents. Paris has been liberated; they say the rest of the continent will follow soon. It's a good time to go.*

Throughout August and September letters were exchanged with Mr. Chalmers and references sent from the Head at Marshfield. Eleanor was successful and gave in her notice.

She braced to placate her parents, who had still not come to terms with a vision of their daughter as the wife of an American soldier. She needn't have worried.

'Quite a challenge for you,' said Father. 'Beautiful islands, plenty of sunshine, build you up.'

'Thank God you're not going back to Birmingham,' was Mother's view.

The Carn Friar's school secretary provided her with the name of a local landlady in Hugh Town, St. Mary's, who responded quickly to Eleanor's letter of enquiry.

Dear Miss Barton,

We have a room available which may suit. Rent 4s6d, all in, payable weekly in advance.

If interested, reply immediately.

Yours faithfully,

A. Crawford (Mrs.)

Eleanor mused to herself: *Clearly not a woman to waste words, I don't envisage any cosy chats over tea and biscuits.* Still, a life lived with her taciturn mother had left her able to deal with what some might call 'plain-spoken' women, so she replied.

Dear Mrs. Crawford,

I would like to take the room. I enclose a postal order in the sum of one week's rent.

I will be arriving on the Scillonian 31st October.

Yours faithfully,

E. Barton (Miss)

By return of post came:

Dear Miss Barton,

We look forward to seeing you 31st October. You will find us at the newsagents, top of Hugh Street. Will you require hot water on arrival? Your rent includes one bath per week, extras charged at 6d.

Please remember to bring your coupons.

Yours faithfully,

A. Crawford

Reading this letter, Eleanor sighed. A fusty waft of newsprint rose to her nostrils. She pictured her landlady as a stern, reserved woman, who probably had to work all hours and had no time to spare for niceties. Undoubtedly with tightly permed hair and an ink-stained apron.

She responded:

Dear Mrs. Crawford,

I will not require hot water 31st October. I will be happy to discuss bathing arrangements when we meet.

Yours faithfully,

E. Barton (Miss)

The 30th of October arrived. Eleanor and Father approached

the train station at Westholme. She had limited her packing to one over-stuffed suitcase and a vanity case, but was glad of Father's assistance on the walk to the station. Her gas mask on its strap thumped against her chest as they hurried along. The overnight train to Cornwall was waiting, so together they heaved bags through an open carriage door.

The train gave its pre-departure shriek, father and daughter turned to each other in the evening gloom.

Silence fell between them, then he put his hands on her shoulders. 'Eleanor.' He stopped, seeming unsure what to say. 'I hope you are doing the right thing; you know we would want you to stay as long as you need to.'

On tiptoes, Eleanor gave him a peck on the cheek, then stepped back. 'Don't ever, *ever* think I'm not grateful, I owe my survival to you, and that's the truth. And thanks to you, I am definitely ready for this new challenge.'

Father dropped his hands. 'Go on then, it'll be moving any second.' He reached into his pocket, pulled out a battered book, and pressed it into her hands. 'I took this with me to Scilly as a boy. You might find it useful.'

And with that, the engine gave a final warning puff as the guard walked the length of the train, slamming doors as he went. The heavy crunch of the doors sent Eleanor into a panic, and she scrambled up the steps, nearly falling over her luggage, but managing not to drop Father's book.

Recovering her dignity, she staggered down the corridor, shoving her large case ahead, and hauled open the stiff sliding door to an empty compartment. The smell of stale cigarette smoke and a lingering scent of a previous occupant's egg sandwiches assailed her. She couldn't face looking for another compartment, and at least this one was empty. She heaved her cases onto the rack above a window seat and settled in as the train pulled away. She wanted to appear an experienced and confident traveller, so she leaned back against the seat and prepared to sleep upright for the best part of eight hours.

En Route to Scilly

October 1944

The overnight train juddered ponderously into Penzance station. Huddled in the scratchy corner of the third-class carriage, Eleanor stirred from a half-doze and peered out of the window. Pointless. The blackout and fog obscured what little could be seen in the dawn light. On her own in the chilly space, she yawned, tasting the lingering steam and grit blown into the carriage as they sped through the last tunnel. She tried to straighten her worsted skirt. It had twisted up, probably revealing a gap between stocking top and girdle bottom, bridged by her utilitarian garters. No-one to see, of course, but the chill on her upper thighs added to her misery.

The train executed a jerky forward-and-back stop. Her first attempts to retrieve her coat and bags failed as the movement forced her back into her seat. She waited until she heard the carriage doors slamming and then hauled her coat, hat, gas mask and two cases from the rack above her head.

Eleanor stepped onto the platform and joined the few other passengers heading towards the exit. A quick glance at her watch; just gone 7am, probably another hour until dawn, and two hours to wait until the boat sailed.

A murky covered light pointed the way to a Women's Voluntary Service kiosk, there for the soldiers but also serving other weary travellers. Eleanor bought a tea, then peered around for somewhere to sit. Some old packing crates piled against the wall provided a rough resting place. Dropping her cases, Eleanor shifted back until she could lean against the wall. She sipped the strong tea, scalding her tongue in her eagerness for warmth. The damp dawn soon enveloped her, cutting her off from the shrouded figures waiting for the boat to the islands.

As the morning lightened, Eleanor could pick out what she assumed was the Scillonian, the ferry her ticket indicated would take her to the islands. It was an eerie sight, painted wartime black, with extensions either side of the bridge holding bristling guns. With the bridge still blacked out, the ship looked like a giant insect from a science-fiction film, silhouetted against the steely dawn. The sight of the guns brought home to Eleanor that there was real danger in the four-hour crossing to Scilly. *Still, nothing compared to Birmingham*, she told herself.

She pulled her coat around her and dragged her cases towards the 'Embarkation' sign. On board, she settled by a porthole in a row of seats amidships and gazed at the oily waters. Her fellow passengers were mainly military, with a few families and couples, perhaps returning home after visits to the mainland. She sat, solitary, listening to the clanks and creaks, smelling the oily smells of maritime departure.

The sturdy ship moved out of the harbour, and Eleanor felt the beginnings of a swell that rolled, unhindered, straight from North America. Before she left, she had spoken to a few friends who had made this journey on holidays before the war. Unhelpfully, they passed on stories of stomach-churning seasickness, voyages spent doubled over the railings wishing for death, and one parent's false teeth disappearing into the deep along with breakfast. Brown wax-paper bags were prominently displayed in the seat backs, and Eleanor helped herself to a few.

The voyage wore on. Eleanor relaxed and almost enjoyed the ride as they breached each swell. She noticed that the soldiers' raucous conversation quietened as one after the other disappeared out onto the back deck. A sideways glance revealed khaki-clad legs, torsos doubled over the railing. On their return, they slumped in their seats, no doubt waiting for deliverance.

In an exhausted daze, she tried to make sense of the past weeks. Somehow, she felt she had been thrust from a contented, if becalmed, life with her parents to this chilly dawn, being transported to the windswept Isles of Scilly. A job in what she imagined would be a bleak one-roomed schoolhouse awaited, and she would be spending her time off in a lonely bedsit, on the margins of an insular community. How had this happened?

Sinking into self-pity, she stopped herself. In fact, no outside force had propelled her. She had made considered, if rapid, decisions for what seemed good reasons. *You're heading on an adventure to a beautiful part of the world,* she reminded herself. *No time or need to wallow.* Looking around for distraction, she remembered the book Father had given her and settled down to read.

Tourist's Guide to Cornwall and the Isles of Scilly, author W. Tregellas, published 1891. Eleanor chuckled. Only Father would think that a fifty-year-old guidebook was just the thing for a young woman to take on her travels. *Or maybe it was his way of travelling with me?* In any case, she hadn't time to get her own guide before she left, and this could spare her the embarrassment of displaying her ignorance to her new pupils and colleagues.

In particular, she wanted to find the meaning of the school's name. What on earth was a Carn? A quick glance through the Table of Contents pointed her to the answer, and she was soon absorbed in a chapter about the Bronze Age carns of Scilly. Tregellas informed her that Scilly was the site of numerous burial chambers, thousands of years old, marked by mounds of stone: the cairns, or carns in local dialect. Fascinated, her imagination followed the Victorian writer into the torch-lit underground burial chambers, their floors scattered with cremated human remains.

However, after reading for a short while, Eleanor couldn't keep her eyes open. Worn out from her journey, she sank into an uneasy sleep, beset by eerie images of sheltering from the Blitz in the ancient tombs of Scilly.

Despite these disturbing dreams, Eleanor dozed for the rest of the journey, only to wake with a painfully stiff neck as they neared the harbour at Hugh Town. The salted-over porthole revealed the approaching dock, with houses straggling up the hill to a forbidding castle. What struck her at first was the darkness of many of the buildings. Those that weren't washed white were of blackened granite. After the golden stone of the West Country, the stern granite weighed on her spirits, taking her confidence with it. She struggled to tidy her blown away hair, and wondered how she would find her lodgings, dragging her luggage and having little idea of where she was going.

St. Mary's

October 1944

As she descended from the ship onto the dock, behind the families and soldiers, Eleanor noticed clusters of people waiting to welcome arrivals. Envious tears filled her eyes as she plodded on. Her vision blurred, she didn't at first see the blooms thrust towards her, held by a young boy, his socks at half-mast and a beaming smile splitting his face.

A prod in the back from a man behind him and the boy said, 'Welcome to Scilly, Miss!'

Eleanor recovered herself enough to smile back. 'Beautiful flowers in late October, how lovely!' At this point the boy's grin broadened, although his powers of speech deserted him.

The man stepped forwards, extending his hand. 'Harvey Chalmers, Headmaster, delighted to see you. And this is Simon, one of the lads in our top class. Survived the journey all right, then?'

Eleanor returned the handshake with a hesitant smile. Her first impression was of a middle-aged man with thick salt-and-pepper hair. Brown eyes inspected her through round spectacles. A trim, youthful figure was belied by his most striking feature: the deep creases that lined his face, lines that would not have looked out of place on a much older man. From her experience teaching in wartime, Eleanor had some idea of the strain he must have been under. Trying to find and keep staff, coping with bombing raids and the horror of death. Difficult enough in mainland schools, what must it have been like on a remote island? His brisk voice broke into her musings.

'First things first, let's get you to your lodgings. Give you a chance to settle in.'

Eleanor's hesitant smile became a grateful beam. 'That would be lovely. Thank you.' Clutching the flowers, she attempted to replace her gas mask around her neck and pick up her cases.

Mr. Chalmers motioned to the boy. 'Simon, give us a hand with these.' Simon was only too happy to oblige.

Eleanor turned to him. 'Thank you, Simon, that's such a help.' She could tell from his flushed cheeks and wobbly grin that he probably thought the new teacher was 'all right', and she hoped he would pass this opinion on to the others.

The little procession headed up into Hugh Town towards Crawfords' newsagents. Mr. Chalmers knocked on a door set back beside the shop entrance. It was opened by a small, spare woman wearing a navy pinafore.

A welcoming smile, followed up with, 'A pleasure to have you with us, Miss Barton, I'm Audrey Crawford.' Eleanor was rapidly revising her assumptions about a tight-lipped landlady and an insular community. The woman continued, 'Thank you, Mr. Chalmers, we'll be fine now. I'm sure Miss Barton would like a chance to unpack and rest before she even thinks about work.'

'Right then,' he responded, 'we'll leave you to it.' He headed off, straight-backed, with Simon jogging to keep up. As they reached the corner, Mr. Chalmers turned and waved. 'See you Monday morning, eight o'clock sharp!'

Eleanor watched him go. A stern headmaster, with a gruff exterior concealing a kind heart. A man of few words who took his responsibilities seriously and did his best. *Now who does that remind me of?* He could be a younger version of Father. She was feeling better by the minute.

Mrs. Crawford indicated a door off the entrance hall, which led to a staircase. 'I hope you don't mind, the room's above the shop. It's quiet in the evenings, and people don't come for their papers till the boat gets in midday, but there's a steady stream before that, picking up bits and pieces.'

Eleanor shook her head. 'It's fine, I'll be up early most days, and I think I will actually like hearing the shop bell as people come and go. I won't feel so, sort of, alone.'

Mrs. Crawford's face softened, but she didn't immediately respond. Instead, she picked up the cases. 'Well, then, up you go. First door at the top, I'll follow you up.'

Eleanor opened the door and was struck by the room's warmth. It was surprisingly large, big enough for a selection of solid wartime 'utility' furniture. She could have been in her parents' spare bedroom. On one side of the narrow space was a bed, a small writing table, a wardrobe, and a dressing table with a tall mirror. A single window looked over the street below, and next to it was a curtained area containing a sink and cupboard. Eleanor's attention was caught by the gas fire in the tiled fireplace. Even on low, it filled the room with warmth and comfort. On one side of the fire was a high-backed armchair, and on the other a small cupboard topped by an electric ring.

Mrs. Crawford appeared in the doorway. 'You might not want to come all the way downstairs to boil a kettle, so we thought you could keep a few bits in the room. Oh, and the blackout's here, don't forget.' She indicated a heavy dark cloth attached to the window. 'Turn right out of your door for the lavatory, the bathroom's downstairs. Would Sunday evening suit for a bath?' Eleanor nodded, still staring at the glowing fire.

Mrs. Crawford followed her gaze. 'We can't get much coal

or wood, so I hope you'll be all right with the gas. Just keep it on low, we have to economise where we can.' Eleanor nodded again. 'Well, Miss Barton, if you've no questions, I'll leave you to unpack. I've made some soup when you're ready. You'll take your meals with us, of course?' She gave Eleanor an enquiring look.

'Oh, sorry, I forgot.' Eleanor dug in her bag and passed over her ration book. She knew it was essential for provisions, now that the Crawfords had another mouth to feed.

'Thank you, and I hope you'll be happy here, I know they need you at the school.' Mrs. Crawford left, shutting the door gently behind her.

'And thank *you*,' breathed Eleanor, sinking onto the bed and staring into the fire. How wrong she had been in her assumptions. Friendly chats over a cup of tea were definitely on.

A short time later, she heard a shout of, 'Soup's hot!' from below, and jumped. As she left the room, she turned back and opened her smaller case. Carefully she took out photos of Ray in a variety of settings and poses; in the countryside, in uniform, walking on the sand on a day out at the seaside. She lined them on the dresser.

Pausing, she fished out her favourite photo with Annie and added it to the display. A chilly August day on a North Yorkshire beach, the two of them about ten years old. Wearing homemade knitted swimsuits that sagged almost to their knees with the weight of sea water, their hands were raised in triumph. Eleanor remembered that summer, just a few years after Gertrude Ederle swam the English Channel. The first woman to do so, beating the fastest time of the men before her. Eleanor and Annie were strong girls who normally preferred team sports, but Gertrude's individual achievement captured their imagination. In the cold North Sea off Whitby, 'Girls Swim the Channel' was their favourite holiday game. *I wonder*, she thought, *some lovely bays and coves here on Scilly, wouldn't it be great to swim again?*

Daydreaming of powering through waves, Eleanor's eyes travelled from the uninhibited joy of the sisters on the beach to an unsmiling photo of Ray, stiff in his uniform. She touched his solemn face. *So, where's your laughing child, my fine soldier?*

Then the clatter of china below brought her back to the little room.

'I'm just serving out, Miss Barton!' A slightly more insistent tone.

'Coming, Mrs. Crawford!' she called, as she followed the delicious smell down the stairs.

First Days at Carn Friar's School

November 1944

Eleanor woke early, contracting her muscles against the fingers of cold that had crept under her sheet, pulling her feet up into her flannelette nightgown. She reached over to switch on the frilled bedside lamp, peered at her clock, and groaned. Six-thirty, and she was due at the school at eight am. There was a satin comforter covering her bed. She rolled herself up in it, waddled over to the gas fire, and sent some blessed heat into the room. Still too cold to move, she sat burning her front and freezing her back until her bladder sent her out of the room and into the lavatory. Once she got moving, she kept going. Woolly dressing gown, knitted socks and worn slippers, then over to the sink for a cold-water wash. Using her dressing gown against the chill, she dressed her bottom half first, grateful for her thick lisle stockings as they encased her goose-pimpled legs.

The room was starting to warm, so the final ordeal of putting on her satin brassière was lessened. The creamy fabric felt lovely on her skin, just as it must have in its previous incarnation as her mother's wedding dress. When clothing coupons came in, her unsentimental parent had created numerous undergarments from that dress, and Eleanor thought this was the most beautiful. An essential wool vest eclipsed its beauty. She topped off this garment with a pastel jumper and a more-or-less matching worsted skirt and jacket. Last of all, she tamed her flyaway hair into side and back rolls. Ready for anything.

Breakfast at seven, and she was right on time. Mrs.

Crawford gave her an approving nod. 'We've managed an egg this morning for you, and a bit of toast.' Eleanor's face lit at the prospect. She spotted a pan of porridge on the stove and homemade jam by her plate. Mrs. Crawford indicated a place set for her new guest. 'And I'm pleased to say your rations added a jug of milk to go with our pot of tea.'

It was still pitch dark outside, so Mr. Crawford wasn't yet back from his Air Raid Protection duties. Eleanor had enjoyed meeting him after he'd closed the shop on Saturday; another care-worn, gentle man, deemed too old for service but dutifully patrolling the blackout at night and digging his garden by day. Like his wife, he rationed his words. 'Hope you'll be happy with us, Miss Barton, and up at the school.' It was the sum of his greeting, before, 'Well, if you'll excuse me, I better have a wash.' At that he made a quick exit.

Fuelled by food and kindness, Eleanor set off. Dawn was just turning the edges of the sky milky. She walked carefully in the near dark, cutting across from Hugh Street towards The Strand. She was glad she had already practised the walk during daylight and found that she could pick out the silhouette of the school on its rocky outcrop above the lifeboat station. Waves sloshed and sucked against the rocks below, and she stopped to look up before opening the school door. The open granite tower housing the school bell was now visible; the bell that would soon call the children who would become part of her daily life.

She was early, but Mr. Chalmers was ahead of her. 'Good morning, Miss Barton. Your first day. I'm sure it's going to be a good one.' Two women stood behind him in the passageway leading to the main school building. 'Let me introduce Miss Elmore, who's kept the ship afloat against all the odds.' A tall woman, possibly in her thirties, wearing a grey suit that set off her blond hair, stepped forward. Eleanor could see that a flush had mounted her neck at the Head's words.

'Mr. Chalmers, I only did my part, as you very well know.' She extended her hand to Eleanor.

'Miss Elmore, I won't have it.' Firm words from the Head, said with a smile. He turned to Eleanor. 'With my deputy on active duty, there's only been the two of us. One hundred and thirty-seven children aged four to eleven, we've had to do just about everything. There's been a bit of help from some of the parents, of course. But as for the rest… we've both had a crash course in office skills, I've tried not to kill everything in the vegetable garden, while Miss Elmore has coped with our antique plumbing.'

He stopped, as if surprised at the length of this speech. *I was right*, thought Eleanor. *There's a kind, generous heart under that stiff exterior. He's made her day.*

Mr. Chalmers took a few steps along the passageway. 'Now I'd like you to meet the second miracle worker of Carn Friar's. Mrs. Thorne, our cook.' He indicated a tiny, spare-framed woman of fifty.

Eleanor knew that the cook was often at the heart of a school. 'A pleasure, Mrs. Thorne, and I imagine those miracles come from stretching rations to feed the school. It must be an enormous task.'

'Yes, indeed, Miss, but I like the challenge. At home it's just me and Mr. Thorne, where's the excitement in cooking for two?'

Mr. Chalmers broke in. 'Mrs. Thorne's Lord Woolton Pie is legendary, Miss Barton, there's a treat in store for you.'

The cook ducked her head. 'It's nothing special, Sir, we're lucky to have the veg. And my secret ingredient, of course.'

She tapped the side of her nose with a smile. 'Not at liberty to say.'

Miss Elmore leaned towards Eleanor. 'Beetroot peelings,' she whispered. 'Supposed to add a bit of extra sweetness.'

Smiles all round, and relief for Eleanor at this positive start to her leap into the unknown. *It feels like we're a team already*, she thought. She turned to find Mr. Chalmers looking straight at her. Catching her glance, he seemed embarrassed and dropped his gaze. Eleanor wasn't sure why, but she sensed he felt the need to reimpose order on the troops.

Mr. Chalmers laid out his plan for Eleanor to meet the children. 'Miss Barton, I am going to suggest you wait here.' He indicated a seat on a raised platform at the far end of the hall. 'We will get the children ready to march in for assembly and, when they are seated, I will introduce you. After that, you could then go to the Infants' room and take it from there. Does that sound all right?'

From the Head's tone, Eleanor had a feeling that the answer had to be 'yes'. 'Of course, although I did wonder… would you like me to help, getting them in?'

'Quite frankly, Miss Barton, that would be a recipe for chaos in the playground.' Perhaps he realised he sounded a bit dismissive, and his voice softened slightly. 'Let's have a bit of drama, with you as the focus on the stage, shall we?'

So Eleanor waited, alone, for the double doors to open. Muffled sounds came from the playground, but she was wrapped in silence.

The silence continued when the doors were opened. Youngest to oldest, the children filed in and took their seats. Eleanor filled the time watching their reactions to the stranger on the stage. Attempts to catch her eye, silly faces, sideways glances, neighbours nudged, the children began to show their individual characters before a word had been spoken.

Mr. Chalmers stepped onto the stage. Instant hush. 'Good morning, everyone. I think you may have noticed that there is someone new with us today.' A few younger children pointed at Eleanor. The Head continued. 'That's right, we have been waiting for a new teacher for a long time, and now we can say hello to Miss Barton, who will be in charge of the Infants' class.' He motioned to Eleanor to stand, then turned to the children, arms outstretched in the manner of an orchestra conductor. 'Welcome to Carn Friar's, Miss Barton.'

'Welcome to Carn Friar's, Miss Barton,' came the ragged chorus in response.

Eleanor hesitated, but quickly decided that she was expected to respond. 'Thank you for that lovely welcome, I'm very glad to be here, and I'm looking forward to getting to know you all.'

She sat to a round of applause. *Drama indeed, Mr. Chalmers*, she thought.

Eleanor and her new class then settled into familiar routines of assembly, gas mask drill, lessons, lunch, and break times, played out for her against a backdrop of a strange setting and new faces.

With the flurry of the first day behind her, Eleanor spent the rest of the week observing and trying out small changes to the daily routines. She was in sole charge of the Infants, all aged between four and seven years. They had their own granite-walled classroom, cloakroom and play area. Apart from daily assembly and prayer in the hall, these very young children were somewhat insulated from the rough and tumble of the main school, except during visits to the school lavatories set against a far wall. These had apparently been a factor in a recent, damning School Inspection Report. A quote provided in resigned tones by Mr. Chalmers told her all she needed to know about the state of the boys' facilities. 'Arrangements for flushing the boys' offices are totally inadequate.' According to the children, by the end of the day, 'It stinks in there, Miss, and you slip on stuff.'

Eleanor was told that there was nothing in the budget for plumbing, as it had all gone on boarding up and putting mesh on the windows and installing blast walls around the school to deal with the heavy bombing of three years ago. Despite these efforts, the school had been damaged, and two children killed in a raid. Eleanor suspected a few of Mr. Chalmers' deepest facial lines had been carved during that time. Suggestions from a new teacher about improvements to plumbing would probably be unwelcome.

However, many of the Infants would wet themselves rather than venture into 'The Block' after lunch, so Eleanor persuaded Mrs. Thorne to leave the kitchen door open and 'keep an eye' on the classroom while she escorted the agonised children back and forth in groups. Even in one day, the children seemed to relax into the security provided by a firm and experienced hand. She told them not to move from their seats and, to her satisfaction and Mrs. Thorne's expressed surprise, they did not.

Towards the end of the week, Eleanor was beginning to find her feet. She enjoyed the novelty of being responsible for a class, without the dead hand of a senior teacher inhibiting her ideas. The School Inspectors had noted that most of the children were behind in their reading, so Eleanor decided to offer story time after lunch, with the children in a circle around her. This worked, as the children applied themselves energetically to their own reading afterwards. *Early days,* thought Eleanor, *but I will find a way. Reading for fun, not as a chore.*

When the last child had waved goodbye at the end of Friday afternoon, Eleanor started back to Crawfords', appreciating the wartime extra hour of afternoon daylight. Even in the short November days there was enough light for her to make it back to her lodgings, without getting mown down in the blackout by a cyclist in a hurry for tea. She did not even have to use the clumsy blackout torch, the downward beam from which always seemed to lag just behind where she wanted her feet to go.

Mrs. Crawford greeted her at the door. 'Hello, I thought you'd be ready for a cup of tea and a sit down.'

Eleanor hung up her coat, put her bag on the hall table and followed her landlady into the cosy kitchen. 'Sounds wonderful,' she said, 'it's been a long week.'

The Letter

November 1944

She eyed the table before her, touched Mrs. Crawford seemed to have set out her best Brown Daisy tea service for her new lodger. The teapot was hidden under a knitted cosy, but the milk jug, sugar bowl, cups and saucers showed the fluted edges and tiny brown flowers familiar to Eleanor from her mother's Women's Institute meetings.

'Oh, this does remind me of home!' Eleanor said. 'What beautiful china, and so lovely to see it set out like this.'

Mrs. Crawford's cheeks reddened. 'We've been keeping it wrapped away. The bombs, you know… but I suppose it's a bit of a special occasion, your first week with us.' She cleared her throat. 'Milk and sugar?' she went on briskly.

Mrs. Crawford poured, and Eleanor wallowed in the bliss of hot tea. As she replaced her cup on its saucer, she noticed a brown envelope by her plate. 'Miss E. Barton', it read, and the APO887 postmark set her heart thumping.

Her landlady stood behind her. 'Came this morning, might be from that young man you were telling us about.' With hasty thanks for the tea, Eleanor flew upstairs, turned on the fire, and settled down to read the letter.

My dearest beloved one,

If you aren't sitting down now, please sit down. There may be just a bit of a jar connected with what I have to say now, and I want so badly to say it.

Eleanor felt her hands go cold. She thought she knew what

was coming next, and she shut her eyes for a moment against the looming rejection.

What I'm driving at is this: would you be willing to get married just as soon as things can be arranged? I know we said we'd wait, and I had my objections to getting married in uniform, but all these have disappeared under the impact of loving you so much, missing you so much, and wanting you so desperately. Over and above all is the feeling that I can't submit to practicality. I love you, I want you for my wife, and the sooner I can have you for my wife the happier I'll be.

She felt a mixture of relief and something like fear. *Hold on a minute*, she thought, as the strength of his feeling hit her with almost physical force. Taking a deep breath, and wondering what was coming next, she continued reading.

I know full well that the biggest angle as far as you are concerned is the subject of religious instruction, and that point has made me hesitate to write as I am. If you would rather not go through the instructions without me, and with only the priest to help you, I will accept a negative answer. If you can get the instruction completed, we could go ahead with the wedding at the time of my next leave. I'm not sure if you have to be baptised, as I assume you already have been, but wouldn't it strengthen your welcome into the Catholic faith? As I understand it, Baptism could be done shortly before the marriage service.

Please write soon and make me a happy man.
All my love to my darling girl,
Your Ray

The Decision

November 1944

The letter rustled in Eleanor's hand as her shaking fingers placed it beside her on the table. She would re-read it in a calmer moment. The distant dream of a life in America with the man she loved was right in the room with her. The softly lit picture came into focus with some harsh edges. Leaving her home and family within months, or even weeks. More immediately, finding a priest and undertaking instruction in a faith that, for all its apparent Christian similarities, felt alien and mysterious to her.

For the first time, Eleanor doubted their future. Ray had made it clear she must convert, as he simply could not marry a non-Catholic, so Eleanor had a decision to make. And she had to make it alone. She paced, then paused. Wait, was she ever entirely on her own? She could hear her twin's cheerful voice as clearly as if they were in the room together. *'Well, my dear sister, you might as well give it a go. Who knows what will happen to any of us? And if you can't find a priest, it will all have to wait anyway.'* Eleanor was sure this *Qué será será* attitude would be behind any advice Annie would give. After all, her sister had quickly become engaged to her Polish officer, relying on love and osmosis to overcome language and cultural barriers.

Inspired, Eleanor hurried down the stairs and grabbed her coat, calling out, 'Just going for a walk, Mrs. Crawford, won't be long!'

'Be careful in the blackout,' came the reply, 'and they're saying there are gales on the way.'

The wind whipped Eleanor's coat around her as she padded through the pitch-dark streets towards the school. She had a plan, and if it didn't work, she would have to try again in daylight. Somewhere along the Strand, on her way to Carn Friar's, she had noticed the imposing bulk of St. Mary's Church of England. In her experience, places of worship were sometimes clustered, so if there was a Catholic church nearby, she might be able to pick it out. In any case, far better to be out in the salty air than fretting in her room.

Eleanor passed a row of cottages, some whitewashed and giving off reflected light as the clouds scudded past the moon. One cottage, wider than the others with a small cross on the roof, displayed a plaque by the door. Eleanor was just able to read it in the intermittent moonlight:

Our Lady, Star of the Sea

Catholic Chapel

And a notice beneath:

Mass celebrated by visiting priests

Sundays 10 a.m., Mondays 5 p.m.

(Subject to weather and transport)

Please enter. DON'T SHOW A LIGHT

Eleanor tried the door, and, to her surprise, it opened into a dark space, with a further door ahead, outlined by the faintest glow. Hastily she closed the first door behind her and felt for a handle on the second. She opened it onto a scene that reminded her of illustrations in the Peter Rabbit books that she read to the children at story time. Steps led down to a vaulted low-ceilinged room, lit by the glow and flicker of dozens of candles and votive lights. There was a small altar, cushioned benches, and several statues. The most prominent of these was a woman in a blue and white robe, head encircled by stars. 'Our Lady, Star of the Sea', presumably.

Instead of a family of rabbits, this burrow was inhabited only by a male figure in white woollen robes, topped by a green embroidered chasuble. She had found a priest.

He was collecting hymn books and, without turning, said, 'I'm afraid you're too late for Mass, we've just finished.'

Eleanor cleared her throat. 'Actually, I just wanted a quick chat.'

He spun around. 'I'm so sorry. We have a Friday evening service for the farm workers who can't come in the daytime, I thought you were someone who'd got the time wrong.' He held out his hand. 'Father Lionel Simmons, and I don't need to ask your name. Everyone on St. Mary's knows the new teacher. What can I do for you, Miss Barton?'

Eleanor's plan had worked almost too well, and she was momentarily speechless. She considered the man's bright blue eyes, short red hair, and kindly smile, and took a deep breath. The urgency of Ray's letter was still with her, compounded by the uncertainty of war. *There really is no point waiting, putting things off. We could be dead tomorrow.* These thoughts had sent her rushing into the night, and spurred her on.

'I'm engaged to a Catholic,' she said, 'and I'd like to take instruction so that I can join the Church.'

Walking back to Crawfords' having planned to meet Father Simmons the following Sunday evening, Eleanor realised the decision had been made. The letter to Ray 'making him a happy man' was on its way the following day.

St. Mary's: Settling In

Winter 1944

The November gales drove the islanders indoors. Eleanor was more than happy to follow their lead most of the time, however, her connection with the taciturn Mr. Chalmers was forged in the cold outdoors. The school vegetable garden provided the unlikely catalyst.

Looking from the window during her break on a blustery morning, she picked out the figure of the Head, digging rhythmically in the small vegetable patch. His battered hat was just about staying on his head in the wind. *Hmm*, thought Eleanor. *Two could get that done in half the time.*

A quick glance at her watch; she could make use of the twenty minutes left of her break. Winter coat, gloves, hat and boots on at speed, she strode to join Mr. Chalmers in the scraggly patch.

'Your new Land Girl, reporting for duty, Sir.'

He jumped, spun, raising his elbow slightly, his eyes unfocused. *Uh-oh, shouldn't have crept up on him.* Eleanor realised she might have triggered a response from his military past. 'Sorry, Mr. Chalmers, I saw you out here, I thought maybe another pair of hands might shift some of this soil.' Still no reply. 'I mean, I like gardening, it was an impulse, to get out of the stuffy room and in the fresh air, I've got a bit of time still, on my break.' *You're babbling, Eleanor, just leave it.*

Mr. Chalmers shook himself with a laugh that sounded a bit forced. 'Wasn't expecting to see anyone come out in this.' He took a few steps towards a ramshackle shed, reached in, and handed her a spade. 'If you must, then. This looks about right for you.' He pointed to a row of swede. 'Maybe just turn the soil around these a bit, they seem to be gasping for air as well.' The smile that went with the words looked a bit less forced.

Glad to have something to do, Eleanor followed his gesture and loosened the earth, lifting the weeds. She'd always loved the deep purple curve peeping out as the swede ripened. *Three-root mash, lovely*, she thought, and stepped up her efforts.

After this initial success, all-weather gardening was soon added to Eleanor's list of duties. With a Land Army coat over her tweeds and a bandana around her head, knotted at the top, she hoped that she convinced the Head of her commitment. The two of them spent time in the wind and rain coaxing every last winter vegetable out of the chilly soil, while Miss Elmore and Mrs. Thorne supervised break time. Mr. Chalmers took photos for the school notice board, and she sent one to her parents. They had evidently seen posters urging women to take up 'men's' jobs, unfilled after so many enlisted, and replied asking if she now wanted to be called Rosie the Riveter. Or Lettice the Land Girl. At least they saw the funny side of the direction her career had taken.

As November moved on, some of the sturdier children were emboldened to offer 'help' and were put to work shifting the harvest to the school cold store. Eleanor believed this community effort to be as much a part of education as sums on slates, and her view was obviously shared by the Inspectors. To Mr. Chalmers' incompletely concealed delight, the 'Garden Project' received high praise in another otherwise disappointing Inspection Report that year. So it made perfect sense he and Eleanor should celebrate with a quiet drink after work. Thus began a weekly tradition.

Inside the school, the rhythm of the classroom pulsed surprisingly smoothly considering the ever-present shadow of war. Although there were reminders. Air raids targeted at Scilly ceased in 1942, possibly because the battery belatedly set up on St. Mary's had success in shooting down Luftwaffe aircraft. Mr. Chalmers gave his opinion that the islands were not important enough for the Germans to risk losses after that.

However, the children were still required to undergo regular gas mask and evacuation training. The former activity proved a trial for the exasperated teachers. With the threat of annihilation diminished, and the continuing shortage of toys and play equipment, it was hard to prevent the children from finding alternative uses for their masks. They discovered that the rubber mouth seal made a delightfully rude noise when air was blown through it. Competitions for 'loudest trump of the day' resulted in discipline breaking down into suppressed giggles. But for Eleanor, it was good to hear the laughter. She had to struggle not to join in.

As the weeks went by, Eleanor and the Infants settled into a routine: lessons, school dinners (naturally featuring quantities of winter vegetables from the school garden), assemblies, and playtime regardless of protests about the weather. No child was denied the health benefits of the Scilly air.

There were snags, and nothing was idyllic about the children's lives. At some point Eleanor found herself in the role of Chief First Aider. From the youngest upwards, children would peer round her door with scraped knees and various bumps and bruises. And splinters, endless pierced fingers requiring her delicate touch with a sterilised needle.

Eleanor was puzzled by the sheer numbers of this injury,

and finally questioned young Simon when he came needing his third extraction. 'It's the slates, Miss.'

The light dawned. With little available paper, the children wrote on slates framed by rough wood. As they moved the slates to write or draw, splinters pierced their hands. The younger and softer the hands, the more deeply the splinters embedded, yet Eleanor never heard a child complain or refuse to use the slates. She realised that, even in wartime, her previous school had been well resourced by mainland suppliers, and that these tiny islands suffered even more because of their isolation.

Eleanor's first aid skills, learned on the job, helped her get close to some children who were described to her as 'hard to manage'. Her breakthrough with Jackie, generally considered by colleagues and pupils alike to be 'the naughtiest boy', brought particular satisfaction.

Five-year-old Jackie was the oldest of the three Whatmough children, whose mother was struggling to hold the family together on a small income while her husband was away fighting. Eleanor, along with other school staff, had struggled in turn to get this angry boy to learn at all.

One afternoon, Eleanor was supervising breaktime in the school yard when a scream rang out. She ran to the source of the outcry to find Jackie rolling in the gravel.

Another lad, eyes wide and face chalk white, stood seemingly frozen beside him. 'We were just having a laugh, Miss, he nicked my cap and threw it up that tree.' He pointed, and the evidence could be seen in an old oak overshadowing the yard. 'I just kicked his bum a bit, and honest, I hardly touched him.'

Eleanor glanced at the writhing Jackie and then turned

back to the other lad. 'Oliver, you go on into class, I'll see to Jackie.'

She hurried over to the sobbing boy, more worried than she had let on to Oliver. An earlier glance had revealed what appeared to be bloodstains on the seat of Jackie's trousers.

Expecting him to lash out, she was surprised when, without looking at her, he pulled down one side of his trousers to reveal an angry, bleeding wound. 'It's a boil, Miss, Mum said she'd see to it with a needle, but I wouldn't let her, now he's kicked it and it's killing me.'

Eleanor kept a concerned look on her face as she viewed the white buttock, an oozing lump standing out from the pale skin.

'Go on, laugh, Miss, that's what they'll all do. "Dirty Jackie's got a boil on his bum", that's what they'll say.' He hastily pulled up his trousers and glared at her with defiance.

Eleanor didn't flinch. 'That must have been hurting for a long time, but it should heal up once it's properly burst. Just needs bathing with a drop of antiseptic.' No response from the boy, so she continued. 'I've got an idea; we don't have to make a big fuss about this. Do you think you can walk?' Jackie let her lead him to a bench that was out of sight behind the back wall of the school. 'Now, lie down on your stomach, don't move, and I'll be right back.' He looked at her, his sobs quietened, and nodded.

Eleanor slipped through the back of the school kitchen to the nurse's room. Mrs. Garrick was nibbling a biscuit, looking over notes. The nurse was coming up to retirement, and Eleanor was sure there was little she hadn't seen. 'Do you fancy a mission of mercy, Mrs. Garrick?'

The two women approached the prone sufferer, Eleanor holding out a pair of trousers from the school spares. 'Pop these on after Nurse has treated you, Jackie. I'm pretty sure they're your size.' Silence from the bench. 'Then you can stroll back into class, sitting down might hurt a bit, but no one will know.'

He lifted his head, and it was the first time she'd seen Jackie's face without its customary sneer. 'Thanks, Miss,' he muttered.

Eleanor seized the opportunity. 'I'll see you back in class then, all right?' A mere suspicion of a nod from Jackie. She pressed the advantage. 'We're starting a new numbers workbook, you're quite good with numbers, so you won't have to concentrate too much if you are feeling a bit rough.'

The twist in Jackie's half grin suggested he knew he was being manipulated, but perhaps he didn't mind.

The November gloom was lifted by the approach of Christmas, and Eleanor continued to lead what she believed (mistakenly, she soon discovered) to be a secret life. Every Sunday evening, she crept through the dark to ring the bell connected to Father Simmons's flat at the chapel. The Scillonian was prevented from sailing in the winter and the flights were subject to numerous delays and cancellations due to weather, so the priest was effectively marooned for weeks. This gave Eleanor, and the few Roman Catholics on the island, the benefit of his nearly full-time presence.

Traces of the chapel's former life as a school lingered in the flat, which had been attached to the school: blackboards fixed to the wall in the priest's sitting room, desks stacked in the corridors, and a lavatory more suited to smaller users. At times, when Eleanor's attention wandered from Father Simmons's earnest efforts, she entertained herself by speculating on the contortions the tall, slender man might have to make as he attended to his personal hygiene.

She was also amused by her own behaviour as she undertook these clandestine visits. Looking over her shoulder before ringing the entrance bell and skulking in the shadows until the moon was hidden by clouds. On one occasion, when she had a rare encounter with someone else in the dark, she responded to his, 'Evening, Miss,' by walking briskly past her destination until she was sure he was gone. Anyone would have thought she was carrying on an affair, rather than pursuing spiritual knowledge.

However, her illusions of secrecy were soon shattered. She and Mr. Chalmers continued to take their afternoon tea in his study, as it was an opportunity to review her progress and that of her pupils. One Monday afternoon, following a companionable silence and a bit of throat clearing from the Head, he asked, 'So, how are you finding your sessions with the good Father?'

Eleanor's sip of tea turned into a light spray. It was her turn for some throat clearing, as Mr. Chalmers hastily passed her a clean handkerchief.

'So sorry,' she spluttered, '…had no idea.'

He leaned towards her with what almost looked like a rueful grimace. 'No, in fact I'm sorry. It's none of my business. I suppose I thought that by now you would have had some experience of the St. Mary's telegraph and wouldn't mind.' Eleanor frowned slightly to let him know he hadn't been quite right about that, but he persevered. 'Your American chap… I presume he's a Roman Catholic, and you need to convert so you can marry?'

Eleanor sighed. She supposed it would be a relief to talk to someone and, in fact, Mr. Chalmers had quietly become more of a friend than merely 'The Head' as they worked side by side in the garden.

'That's about it,' she said. 'We love each other very much, of course, but he can't, or should I say won't, marry a non-Catholic. So I'm taking instruction.'

She rubbed her forehead, aware she must sound as confused as she felt. 'It's all happened so quickly...' And at that moment the bell clanged to drag them back from the cosy study to the bustling school.

The topic was closed, but as Eleanor reflected later, their relationship had somehow changed. *Why on earth was I so flustered?* she thought as she plodded back to Crawfords'. She took a slight detour to gaze over the darkening winter sea. As she had looked into the calmly sympathetic face of Mr Chalmers and tried to explain her situation, she realised that she felt uneasy in a way that did not make sense. Thinking it over, she considered that the content of her sessions with Father Simmons had recently moved into areas that left her similarly uncomfortable. The topics concerned doctrine relating to what the priest called 'the more physical aspects of marriage, and the creation of new life'.

Eleanor's experiences in Birmingham had left her well able to enter into a robust discussion on this subject. She challenged the priest: 'But Father, why is it a spiritual wrong to prevent conception?' As a primary teacher, she had seen the mothers of some charges worn out by consecutive pregnancies. And in the shelters at night, with the bombs whistling overhead, couples around her had responded to the danger in many ways, successfully using the distraction of sex. The scuffles, sighs and moans made her think that yet more 'new life' was being created, not always by families who could afford to support it, and sometimes, she knew, to the despair of women whose husbands were away on active duty.

In Eleanor, these memories awakened considerable alarm,

as she imagined herself producing one child after another, with no choice in the matter. She turned from the cold wind blowing off the sea, gave herself a shake to dispel what were probably groundless fears, and hurried towards the warmth of the Crawfords' kitchen.

As the wind blew her into the room, both Crawfords looked up at her.

'There you are,' wheezed Mr. Crawford, suffering from too many cold nights on watch. He heaved himself up to help her with her coat. 'Thought you'd been blown out to sea.'

'Oh, I just stopped to clear my head a bit. Busy day.'

Mrs. Crawford passed her a cup of tea. 'It's fine, my dear, we just wanted to ask you something.' Eleanor raised her eyes. *Not more about her 'secret' sessions with the priest.*

The Crawfords looked at each other, and then Mrs. Crawford spoke. 'We wondered… well, we just thought we'd ask… your young man being on active service, and our Clive out in the Pacific… and you said your Ma doesn't want you to risk the travel.' She took a deep breath. 'We would love it if you would join us for Christmas dinner.'

St. Mary's Christmas

1944

Finally, the long term came to an end, and the excited children descended on their homes for the holidays. On Christmas Eve, Eleanor was staring at the brown paper-wrapped package Mr. Chalmers had pressed into her hands. He had invited her for afternoon tea, and she was already uneasy, visiting his home for the first time.

'Open it, please.' He gestured to a fireside chair, and she sat abruptly.

'I'm so sorry, I haven't… I mean, I didn't think to get you…' she stammered in reply, hoping the glow of the fire would camouflage her red face.

'Don't be daft,' he smiled. 'Just a little thank you for everything you've done.' A dismissive wave of her hand was meant to convey 'just doing my job', but he ignored it.

His smile receded, and he leaned towards her. 'Have you really no idea how much difference you have made? To the school… and to me? Now open your gift, then we'll have some tea and some of Mrs. T's Christmas biscuits, guaranteed to strengthen your jaw muscles.'

Eleanor peeled back the paper to reveal a mauve and cream cashmere scarf. 'It's beautiful,' she gasped. 'How on earth did you get…'

He interrupted. 'Naturally, I don't get wool coupons, but I did manage to find a couple of Mother's cashmere jumpers. I never got round to giving them away after she died. She'd hardly worn them, so a bit of unpicking, and here we are.'

'But then who…' Eleanor managed to stutter.

'Actually, I made it.' She thought he looked pleased with himself as he said it. And he definitely seemed to be enjoying her astonishment. 'Well, I was confined to bed for months after the Somme,' he continued. 'The missing leg, you know.' Eleanor's eyes widened. In fact, she hadn't known, had just thought he walked a bit stiffly, might have a touch of arthritis. She hadn't realised that, like so many others, he had lost a limb. Possibly in the stinking mud and cold of the battlefield, possibly to save his life. She held back from probing, there was a feeling between them she couldn't bear to break with intrusive questions.

He continued. 'I started to feel better, but couldn't get up, so Matron said I might as well make myself useful and taught me how to knit. At first it was mainly scarves, and bed shawls so the chaps didn't get chilled sitting up.' He paused, as if deciding whether to go on. Eleanor waited, watching shadows play across his lined face. Finally, he spoke. 'I got quite good, went on to making amputation stump covers.' He looked up, as if checking her reaction, but by now Eleanor was more fascinated than surprised.

'I guess those were a bit more complicated,' she said, keeping her tone matter of fact.

Mr. Chalmers took a deep breath. 'Made one for myself. Regulation Khaki wool, very smart, still use it when the skin gets a bit raw. So that,' he pointed at the scarf, 'was a doddle.'

He looked at her intently, and this time she gazed back calmly. She held the scarf to her cheek. She could feel that her normal colour had returned, but some unease remained. *What was happening here?* she wondered.

'Mr. Chalmers, I don't know what to say.'

He turned and slid the tea tray gently towards her across the table. 'Please call me Harvey, say thank you, and pour us a cup of tea.'

After a brief hesitation, Eleanor straightened up in her chair. 'Thank you, Harvey.' She reached for the teapot.

The next day, Eleanor and the two Crawfords pushed themselves back from the table and sighed with satisfaction as they surveyed the remains of their Christmas feast. The bird had almost certainly died of old age, but the vegetables were fresh. Eleanor didn't want to know the full origins of the ingredients for the solid Christmas pudding, fearing some may not have come through 'official' supply channels. Although the seemingly upright characters of her hosts made contraband activities unlikely, she would not want to risk making them uncomfortable with any reference to the black market.

Mr. Crawford stood slowly, hand to his back as he rose. 'Right, ladies, let's clear, he'll be on in a minute.' As they bustled back and forth to the kitchen, Eleanor remembered how she had dreaded this Christmas. Away from her family, and especially from Ray. How wrong she'd been.

Half an hour later, all three were settled around the wireless, tuned to the Home Service for the King's Christmas Speech. Eleanor leaned back and closed her eyes, the better to concentrate on the soft, clear voice. Listening carefully, she could only catch the slightest hint of a stammer on 'loved ones far and n-near'. Along with the rest of the country, she was willing this quiet, slightly awkward man to get through the speech, as he had battled through so many since the beginning of the war.

As the King got into his stride, Eleanor was able to relax and focus on his message. Glancing sideways, she could see that the Crawfords were touched by his mention of 'our brave soldiers on the battlefield' and had tears in their eyes at his reference to 'the grief of separation'. The speech ended with optimism, referring to the successes since D-Day: 'We rejoice in victories that bring us nearer to the time when we can all be together again.'

At this point, Eleanor too was overwhelmed with emotion. She rose hastily. 'Shall we all go for a stroll to walk off that delicious pudding? I'll just freshen up first.'

Mrs. Crawford pulled herself up from the chair and nudged her husband, who had fallen into a gentle doze. 'Lovely, perhaps we could go to…'

Eleanor didn't wait for Mrs. Crawford to finish. She scampered upstairs to her room, shutting the door before flinging herself onto the bed and giving in to tears. Rolled in a quilt and sunk in misery, she didn't hear the soft knock.

Mrs. Crawford was halfway across the room, holding out a package and studiously ignoring her lodger's swollen face and dishevelled state. 'Miss Barton, this came for you, but I thought you'd rather open it in private without us gawping at you. Maybe I was wrong? I'm so sorry, I should have given it to you sooner.'

Eleanor sat up, brushing away strands of hair that were glued to her face with salt from her tears. She reached for the parcel. APO postmark. So he had managed to get something through. 'That's all right, Mrs. Crawford, I'll just open this and I'll be down in a minute.'

On her own, Eleanor tore away the Army-issue paper. Inside was a card, a winter scene with angels hovering over a rough wooden manger. The message read:

My Dearest,

The cruelty of being apart from you at what should be a joyous time is almost unbearable. I can only imagine how these small gifts will look against the softness of your skin and wait impatiently for the day when I can see for myself.

Your loving Ray

With shaking hands, Eleanor pulled out a cream silk blouse. *Hand-embroidered,* she thought. *I haven't seen anything like this in years.* And nestled underneath was a pair of sheer nylons. They weighed nothing, and she could not imagine putting them on her legs. Silk. Nylon. Both rationed, she knew, available mostly to American soldiers and their girlfriends. She started to pull her jumper over her head to try on the blouse, and then looked up at the window. The driving rain was trying to perforate the panes, and she could hear the howling wind. Suddenly she couldn't bear to look at the blouse. Filled with exasperation, she thought: *What use does he think I will have for these flimsy things? Maybe to pop on whilst digging potatoes? Or teaching in a classroom filled with drafts? Wiping the dripping noses of crying children? Or even for the benefit of Father Simmons during our fireside instruction?*

Strangely disappointed at what she thought were frivolous, impractical gifts, she pulled her jumper back on, opened the bottom drawer of her chest and gently laid the delicate items underneath her light summer frocks. As she did so, another reaction surfaced. Something about his words. Imagining how these will look against the softness of her skin. An unwelcome thought pushed itself into her mind. The gifts weren't for her; they were to build a fantasy for him. She was not such a prude that she would judge him for reaching out for something away from the horror of war. And, of course, she was flattered and yes, a bit excited, by the pleasure they could have together. So what was the matter with her? *Pull yourself together, Eleanor, and stop making such a drama out of it.* She left the room, and her niggling doubts, behind her.

She descended the stairs with a brisk tread, stopping at the bottom to put on her coat and wrap the soft mauve and cream scarf around her neck. A scarf that had been painstakingly made by Harvey, with evidence of his efforts in the presence of dropped and caught stitches. The luxury of cashmere wrapped her in warmth and security. A lovely, thoughtful, gift. Beautiful, and so practical.

She popped her head around the sitting room door. Mr. and Mrs. Crawford looked up nervously. Eleanor smiled brightly. 'Anyone ready for a walk?'

To St Martin's

February 1945

Late February, Christmas a distant blur already, and spring came early to Scilly. One Friday afternoon, Eleanor was peering through the window of the store cupboard that doubled as a staff room and watching drifts of daffodils waving in the sunshine. The sea sparkled, the air was clear, and some of the off islands were visible across the water. She sighed, imagining how the sea would feel in the warmth of spring. *How lovely it would be to stretch my arms and swim to one of those islands. Just for a bit of quiet time.* She stopped herself. Quiet time? There was plenty of that on peaceful St. Mary's, but all the same she felt under relentless scrutiny, more so than in the anonymity of Birmingham.

The week before, Mrs. Nelson, whose family lived next to the newsagents, had approached her as she let herself in to Crawfords'. 'How are you settling in, Miss Barton?'

'Very well, thank you, everyone's been so kind. And the children are delightful.' Eleanor turned the handle to go in, then saw that the other woman was hovering.

'We all think a lot of Mr. Chalmers, it's a pleasure to see him happier. Like a weight's been lifted off, you could say.'

'Yes, it must be a relief to him, and to Miss Elmore. To have another pair of hands to share the load,' Eleanor said, smiling, keeping her tone light.

Mrs. Nelson didn't give up. 'Um. Yes. Well, I was also thinking, nice for him to have a young lady around, someone to chat to. He's such a fine gentleman, but never seems to have anyone to keep him company.' She stared at Eleanor. 'Of course, we would hate for him to be let down, if someone already had a sweetheart, I mean.'

At this point, Eleanor's cheeks were burning. She sensed she was being warned, but it was hard to summon righteous indignation when there was more than a hint of truth in the statement. She pushed open the door. 'I couldn't agree more, Mrs. Nelson, I must get this shopping to Mrs. Crawford.'

She may or may not have convinced her neighbour, but she could no longer fool herself.

Furthermore, Eleanor was uncomfortably aware she hadn't written to Ray for weeks. She couldn't blame the pressure of work for this lapse. In fact, there were things she wanted to say to him, difficult things that would require considerable thought to find the right words. But she must. Her future with Ray depended on it.

The door to the tiny staff room banged into the back of her chair as Harvey breezed in, interrupting Eleanor's reverie.

'Oh, sorry, didn't know you were in here. Been looking everywhere for you.'

Eleanor stood and slid her chair from the door so he could squeeze in. After a bit of shuffling, he perched on the table, she went back to the chair, turning it to face him, and their knees did not quite touch. She looked up to see Harvey framed by lopsided clay chickens, stored on shelves until dry enough for the Infants to paint. It was a funny sight, and she relaxed a bit.

'Is anything wrong?' Eleanor thought that Harvey was showing uncharacteristic agitation. His knee jiggled slightly, and he stared over her shoulder.

'No, no, of course not,' came the hasty reply, followed by a pause. 'Well yes, but not with us... that is, not with Carn Friar's.' Eleanor waited for him to get to the point. 'You remember Miss Billings? She came to the last Island Education Committee meeting.'

Eleanor nodded, recalling a woman probably in her mid-fifties, with a pleasant manner. 'You mean the Head Teacher on St Martin's?'

Harvey continued: 'Actually, the only teacher at the school there. And that's the problem. She has elderly parents on the mainland, seems they've both gone down with the 'flu and there's no one to look after them.'

Eleanor thought she could see where this was going, so she tried to make it easier for him. 'Is there any way we could help?'

Harvey seemed to breathe a sigh of relief and, for the first time, shifted his gaze away from the view to look directly at her. 'It's a lot to ask, you've only been with us a short time, but what would you say to taking over on St Martin's while Miss Billings is away?'

Eleanor's eyes widened and she opened her mouth, but Harvey held up his hand and continued at speed. 'You would be in sole charge, but there's a caretaker to help out. And only eleven children. All ages, though. Maybe an opportunity to test yourself a bit? Miss Billings has her own little cottage, she's offered her spare room, so you would have a place to stay. Churchtown Farm could keep you supplied, there's a bakery, some super walks. It probably won't be for long, they're sturdy folk, the parents, expect they'll recover soon. Miss Elmore and I will be fine. I… we… will miss you of course, but we can manage….'

Eleanor's first instinct was to refuse. A wave of anxiety swept over her as the reality of the request hit. To be solely responsible for the school and for the safety of the children. *What if the bombing started up? How would she cope? Would she fall apart again?* But times were different now, and so was she. Harvey was watching her, waiting, perhaps sensing that more pressure was not what was needed.

Eleanor used the pause to gather her thoughts. She took a deep breath. 'Harvey, I really do want to help, but could I take a little while to think about it?'

He reached out and took her hand. 'Of course you can, but you would have to leave Sunday at the latest, you understand? And you know I've got absolute confidence in you?' A quizzical look from Eleanor. He went on: 'You've done so much since you've been here, the Infants were lost little souls and now I see them run in laughing, glad to be at school. And that's all down to you.'

He hastily let go of her hand, blushing, turning to straighten a couple of chickens on the shelf. 'Maybe we could meet at The Atlantic tomorrow, have a bite to eat and a chat?' he suggested. 'I'm sure we could find a quiet corner away from the Army lot, what do you say? I'll call for you, say around noon?'

Eleanor reached down and gathered her things, ready to depart. 'I really will think about it, it's just a bit sudden. I've never been in sole charge before.' She wasn't about to tell him about Birmingham. 'I'll see you at lunchtime tomorrow then.'

Eleanor took the long way back to her digs, walking slowly, hardly observing the spring beauty. Semi-coherent thoughts buzzed in her brain. *Was it really my fault, what happened in Birmingham? Was I wrong to blame myself, to be ashamed of weakness? I did everything I could then, did I seriously think I could single-handedly save every child against the might of the Luftwaffe?* It was the first time she had questioned her assumptions about that time, and the burden she had carried so long. *Or wasn't I a coward after all? I coped then, for as long as anyone could, and I could cope now if I had to. But can I forget Betsy?* She sighed, squared her shoulders, and headed back for her tea.

Despite this surge of confidence, Eleanor passed a restless night. In half-waking dreams she was marooned on a lonely beach, unable to escape. Ray stood on a far island, stretching out his hand, which she tried and failed to reach as she swam across the choppy sea. She was cold and frightened.

She woke with a start. *I really must write to Ray*, she thought. A remote island with a tiny population might be just the place to do it.

Just after noon the next day, Harvey and Eleanor strode silently towards the Atlantic Hotel. It was a former smugglers' inn, bigger than it appeared from the street. Its size made it suitable as a Mess for the Garrison, but there were plenty of tucked-away spots in the lounge bar. Harvey, true to his word, found one of these: a cosy table, with a crackling fire to banish the chill.

'I'll do it,' Eleanor said firmly as they sat with a drink and a plate of local fish.

She was treated to one of Harvey's rare full-beam smiles. Then it faded. 'Are you sure?' he asked, 'I did get the feeling yesterday that the idea rather... alarmed you.'

Eleanor was tempted to tell him he was right, and to explain. He was becoming a friend, and she could see a sensitive and understanding man under that crusty exterior. But she was not ready. 'Yes, yes, it's fine, I'm looking forward to it.' At least partly true. 'Now, how am I going to get to this paradise? I'm a strong swimmer, but it's still a bit cold this time of year.'

With a straight face, Harvey replied: 'Actually, it's not even three miles away, so it's certainly possible to swim there.'

A sceptical look from Eleanor. She wasn't sure if Harvey was joking. She knew some of the islanders thought nothing of a swim across the channels.

'Maybe when it warms up a bit,' he went on with a chuckle. 'For now, I've made better arrangements for you. The St. Mary's Boatmen won't be going out, simply not enough people to fill a big Association boat. But Mrs. Thorne's husband, Fred, has a 12-seater; I've got some marine diesel the Ministry gives the school for emergencies, and if we put the two together, you'll travel to St. Martin's in fine style.'

Eleanor was reassured. 'That sounds fine, and another new experience for me.'

'Meet Fred at ten fifteen, then, back of the hotel.'

The next morning Eleanor, shivering with nervous excitement, shoved her nightdress into the case she'd packed the night before, then dressed quickly. Trousers and a warm jumper for the open seas, she decided. At the last minute, she snatched her favourite photo of Ray and placed it on top of the nightdress. Calling a cheerful goodbye to the Crawfords, who had congratulated her on getting what they saw as a career opportunity, she received a 'Good luck!' in return. She hurried out into the street, head down in a stiff breeze, and nearly bumped into Harvey. They stopped, facing each other, both slightly out of breath.

Harvey spoke first. 'Thought I might pop across with you if that's all right?' Eleanor nodded agreement, pleased she would have his company. He took her bag. 'I'll be your porter, then get you settled at the cottage over there. Fred and I will catch the tide back.'

As they made their way around the back of the Atlantic Hotel to the small boat docks, Eleanor caught sight of what she assumed was Fred and his boat. To her dismay, she saw that the boat was almost completely open, apart from a small wheelhouse towards the stern. However, it looked well cared for, and she was happy to be shown to a comfortable cushioned seat. Harvey settled in beside her, and they were off. The sun glistened on the turquoise waters, which turned choppy as they left the shelter of the harbour. The little boat pitched forward, and Eleanor matched its movement, feeling precarious until she felt a strong arm anchored firmly around her waist. Unsure about this physical contact, Eleanor shot Harvey a sideways glance. He caught her look. 'You did say you didn't fancy a swim, and I don't fancy going in after you,' was his only comment. As they ploughed on, a long, flat piece of land came into view, seeming at an angle to the other islands.

'Is that it?' asked Eleanor, trying to keep a doubtful note out of her voice.

Harvey replied, 'It's the only one lying north-south; we'll be coming into the harbour on the south side, at Higher Town.'

At first Eleanor thought she was looking at nothing but a bleak slab of granite, but as they drew nearer, she could see wide sandy beaches, meadows full of early spring flowers, and a few houses here and there.

She turned to Harvey. 'It's so beautiful, why didn't you say?'

'Well, I did say there were some nice walks.' He sounded defensive.

Eleanor grinned. 'Indeed you did, and I can't wait to do some exploring.'

Fred pulled up to the little jetty. He hopped off, tied up, and turned to give Eleanor a hand. Without thinking, however, she used her strong legs to launch herself neatly onto the jetty. *Good thing I've got trousers on,* she thought smugly as the men gaped. She then turned to Harvey and held out her hand, smiling sweetly. He grinned and took it.

Fred offered his opinion. 'A good start, that, Miss.'

Eleanor looked around. 'Thank you, Fred. Now, which way?'

Harvey spoke up. 'It's about a mile to the cottage, and there's certainly no taxis, so we'd better set off if Fred and I are going to catch the tide. When the tide's out, it's all rocks, even a small boat would have a job to get through.'

A short while later, Harvey and Eleanor stood at the low wooden door of Miss Billings's cottage, which was at the end of a terrace of three. Like many on the Isles, it was solidly built of granite, with deep-set windows and an overhanging roof.

'Where do you suppose she's left the key?' whispered Eleanor, not sure why she felt the need to lower her voice. Harvey looked at her quizzically, twisted the doorknob to open the door, and motioned for her to enter.

'Oh,' said Eleanor. 'Not the custom to lock up, I guess.' This would take getting used to. The cottage was small and simply furnished, but cosy. A huge stone fireplace reached to the ceiling. This edifice dwarfed a two-bar electric fire on the hearth, but she supposed it would be more than adequate in this low-ceilinged room. Two high-backed armchairs were pulled up around it. They didn't match and were of the government's war-time Utility design, but she gave one a try and felt wrapped in comfort.

There were doors off the main room, one of which led to Miss Billings' bedroom, and the other to what would be Eleanor's room. She was touched to see a small vase of daffodils on the bedside table, along with a rubber hot water bottle in the shape of a cat.

Eleanor wandered into the kitchen, pleased to see a Baby Belling on the counter. Its tiny oven and two electric rings would be more than sufficient for any cooking. There was an Ascot water heater over the sink. A relief, she wouldn't have to light fires for her basic needs.

Off the kitchen was another door, leading out to a small but thriving vegetable patch. *Clearly Miss Billings is 'digging for victory,'* thought Eleanor with approval. She followed a path through the garden to a wooden door set into a thick wall, embellished with a cut-out circle near its top. Eleanor's heart sank. She'd found the lavatory, and it was a fair way from the cottage. *That's one trip I won't be making in the middle of the night*, she declared to herself. She peeped inside to find the tiny room clean, reasonably sweet smelling, and free of wildlife. No worse, in fact, than her parents' WC, before they got indoor plumbing.

Harvey came up behind her. 'Oh sorry, did you need to use...'

'No, just exploring, we used to have an outside lav, so I can certainly manage with this.'

'Right, I'm off to meet Fred, I'll leave you to get sorted.' He gestured down the slope to a similar granite building about a hundred yards away. 'The school is just over there.'

'Thank you, Harvey, I'm so grateful for this opportunity.' Eleanor had to resist hugging him.

He ducked his head. 'Anyway, keep in touch. There's a telephone at the school, or you can go up to the post office. Let me know when you're coming back, I'll arrange things.' She watched him disappear down the track to the harbour.

On her own, Eleanor's priority was warmth. She switched the fire on, then pulled her slippers from her case and padded into the kitchen. As she filled the kettle, she spied a scrubbed wooden table, dotted with handwritten notes. She waited for the kettle to boil and read through Miss Billings's messages.

Dear Miss Barton,

Tea in the caddy, milk in the pantry, couldn't get sugar, I'm afraid.

Eleanor found a teapot and brewed the tea. She stepped into the chilly pantry and brought out the milk in a Cornish blue jug, protected by a weighted crochet cover. As she sipped her tea, she read Miss Billings's suggestions for her guest's supper:

There's part of a loaf in the bread bin, should be all right toasted. Cheese and margarine in the pantry, you can open a tin of pilchards if you wish. Other tins in the cupboard. Help yourself to veg. They will deliver a box of essentials from the farm on Monday, leave a note if you'd like eggs, or a boiling bird. Might be fish during the week. School keys in the drawer.

This last piece of information was scribbled in the margin; Eleanor could imagine Miss Billings, worried about her parents and rushing to catch the flight from St. Mary's, still doing her best to provide a welcome.

Eleanor picked up a stack of files labelled 'CLASS NOTES' and took them to read by the fire. She was pleased to see a wireless on a shelf by the chair and found some soft music on the Light Programme to break the silence. There was a file for each child, with notes about their progress and current work. From four-year-old Pam ("Working on her letters and simple sums") to eleven-year-old Brian ("Preparing for the Scholarship test next week, we have high hopes for him"), there was a complete pen picture of each child.

Eleanor breathed a silent 'thank you' to Miss Billings for

her meticulous record keeping. According to Harvey, she had been at the school for more than twelve years, with never even a day's illness. Eleanor realised that these children, who lived in such a remote place and had never known any other teacher, might not readily respond to someone new. Her plan was to be guided by Miss Billings' notes and by the children themselves. Now was not the time to unsettle them with any of the bright ideas she had gradually introduced to the Infants at Carn Friar's. In any case, it would be hard enough to juggle the needs of such a mixed group. That would have to be the focus of her efforts.

Setting the notes aside, Eleanor thought back over the day. Remembering her conversation with Harvey about Miss Billings led her thoughts directly to the feeling of his arm around her waist. Was it just a gesture of concern? A ring of warmth encircled her body at the thought that there might be something more between them.

Horrified at the ease with which she had accepted touch from another man, even if through layers of winter clothing, Eleanor put a mental block on thoughts of any attraction between Harvey and herself. She picked up a sheet of paper and headed it: *St. Martin's School Lesson Plans*. A perfect distraction.

The next morning, she hurried down the track to the school. Another strong-built granite building with chimneys at each end over the gables, surrounded by rough stone walls and with the cold glint of the sea beyond. It was not long after dawn, and the children would not arrive for another hour, but she wanted time to make sure everything was ready.

She was surprised to find the door unlocked but delighted when a blast of warm air greeted her entry. The heat was coming from an iron stove at the far end of the room.

All was explained when Mr. and Mrs. King, the caretakers, came up to greet her. He spoke first. 'Hope you'll be all right, Miss, we thought you'd like it warmed up a bit. Being from St. Mary's, you won't be used to what it's like here.' Eleanor was amused at the implication that St. Mary's, only about three miles across a channel, was some sort of soft urban metropolis.

'Wonderful,' she replied, 'it's a bit chilly this morning, so nice to step into a warm room.'

'And I'll pop in after school each day, just to put things right for you. We're just behind the schoolhouse there if you need anything,' added Mrs. King.

Eleanor smiled as she walked with them to the door. 'Thank you so much, you've really made me feel welcome.'

Eleanor hung her gas mask and coat on a hook in what passed for the 'staff room': a windowless cubbyhole containing a telephone, an electric hot plate, a sink, and a well-organised stationery cupboard. The Carn Friar's staff room was luxurious by comparison. Her next thought was of safety. It had been three years since the last air raid, but Eleanor didn't think she was being overcautious, wanting to be prepared. *Or is it my own fear?*

A door at the back of the room led to a porch-like enclosure. Three wooden boxes caught Eleanor's eye. Labelled "In Case of a Raid", they contained necessities for survival. Books, decks of cards, paper, drawing materials and a battery-operated wireless filled one box. Crammed into the others were a supply of batteries, tins of biscuits, lanterns, torches, bottled drinks, a first aid kit, Elsan tablets and a mouth organ. Eleanor tested the weight of each one and decided she would need help from the older children to get all this into the shelter quickly.

Grabbing a torch, Eleanor lifted the hatch stamped "To the Shelter" and descended the steps onto an earthen floor. Considering its underground location, the air was surprisingly sweet and dry. Taking a deep breath, she stepped further into the room. As far as she could see, it was big enough for twice the number using it, lined with wooden seats, and providing shelves higher up for the lanterns. Small tables were stacked against one wall. Her torch picked out a heavy green curtain at the far end. Walking carefully on the uneven surface, she explored.

Behind the curtain were two small cubicles. A length of fabric, which looked as if it would not quite shield the occupant from prying eyes, enclosed the first. A crudely labelled sign: 'boys ONLY' was pinned to the cloth. Peering in, Eleanor saw a sandpit dug in a precise square. A paving stone was pulled up to one side, and she could see the shadow of footprints worn into the surface. White pebbles and shells that glowed in the dark like runway landing lights neatly edged the sandpit. Presumably to assist with hitting the target.

The other cubicle, made of wood, looked more like the garden privy outside Miss Billings' cottage. In childish letters, it was labelled: 'GIRLS ONLY boys SOMETIMES'. Eleanor tugged on the creaky door, which flew open to reveal a stone plinth, on which was displayed a shiny Elsan. Eleanor's torch travelled over the enamelled green exterior, highlighting the regal red and gold raised emblem on the front and the black Bakelite seat. In a better light, it would have resembled a miniature green post box. To Eleanor, the near darkness of the shelter gave it a slightly sinister air, with its slash of red gold mouth, green skin, and black hat. She shook herself and climbed back up the stairs. 'Better than a bucket in the corner, I guess,' she muttered.

Satisfied, her butterflies stilled for the moment, Eleanor hastened into the schoolroom, found each child's work on named shelves, and was pleased to uncover a piano hidden under a dusty cloth. She tried a few bars of 'God Save the King', cringing once or twice at sour notes. *Could do with tuning.* She approached the front of the room, took a deep breath, and wrote "Miss Barton" in large letters on the board.

At this point, the door creaked, and Eleanor spun, greeting the arrivals with a smile. A thin-faced girl of about eight was trying to drag a younger one, aged no more than four, into the room.

'Good morning, children.' Eleanor approached slowly, taking care not to overwhelm them. 'You must be Peggy, and this is your little sister. Pamela, am I right?' Wide-eyed nods from both. 'Now, Pamela, would you show me where you hang your coat?' Still wordless, the tiny blond girl slowly let go of her sister's hand and stepped towards the lowest coat hook at the end of the row. As she did, nine more children of varying sizes shuffled into the room in fairly good order. Eleanor kept a straight face. Apparently the sisters had served as the vanguard.

Eleanor introduced herself and, once seated, the children complied readily with her request for the Lord's Prayer, stood for 'God Save the King', and rounded off the assembly with a decent attempt at 'Morning Has Broken'.

The class then settled to work. After an initial panic, Eleanor found she could move among the eleven, helping one or two as she kept an eye on the others. Her head was spinning, however, and respite came in the form of 'school dinner': a hot meat and vegetable pie brought over by Mrs. King. This was served family style, with Eleanor at the head of two tables pushed together. The children had relaxed a bit, so Eleanor found she was gobbling her food while sorting squabbles. 'Miss, he's got more mash than me.' 'Miss, I *hate* cabbage, do I have to eat it? I'll be sick, I will!'

At the end of the day, Eleanor was exhausted by the effort of being in sole charge. There was no one to give her even a five-minute break, including for a lavatory visit. Her 'comfort breaks' were shadowed by Pamela and her five-year-old friend Helen, who waited by the door. They seemed determined to make sure she would not disappear and leave them alone.

Back at the cottage, Eleanor revived herself with beans on toast, and utter stillness. It occurred to her that she was getting a mere glimpse into the life of a mother of eleven children. And this was without bedtime tantrums, middle-of-the-night wakings and childhood illnesses. This thought spurred her to pick up pen and paper and begin the delayed letter to Ray:

My dearest Ray,

I'm writing to you from my temporary posting to a tiny school on the island of St. Martin's. It is very quiet here, and so I've got a good chance to think, and write. I want to let you know about some doubts that I have.

You can be sure that these doubts have nothing to do with my love for you, or my wish to spend my life with you. Rather, it is some of the Catholic teachings I am having great difficulty understanding and accepting. I know how much the Church means to you, so my conscience simply won't let me keep silent.

Writing this letter is even more difficult because my concerns are about the delicate area of contraception. Of course, I want children, as I know that you do, but I will be very honest and say that the thought of having one child after another as the years go by fills me with horror. I am sorry to put it so strongly, but it is how I truly feel.

I do not know if there is any solution, but I do know that I love you with all my heart and pray that God keeps you safe.

Yours ever, Eleanor

She put down her pen, hand shaking. Relieved, though, that she had finally written the truth. She read over what she had written. As with even her most intimate letters, she had tried to pay attention to grammar and sentence structure. Not something she could shake after all her teacher training. But was it too stark? Unkind? Should she include a few amusing anecdotes about St. Martin's to lighten the tone and perhaps make him smile? No. *If I hide the message in a froth of chat, he might not hear it. If we are going to spend our lives together, we must face the differences between us, the hurt that they can cause.* She sighed. *Best not send it just yet, might have to change a few words. But it's a start.*

The next day, Eleanor broke up the routine of lessons and play with an air raid drill. Some of the children were too young to have clear memories of the last raids three years ago, but Miss Billings had obviously drilled them regularly since. They all knew their jobs: carrying the supply boxes, holding the torches to light the stairs and, above all, remembering their gas masks.

At Eleanor's signal, all eleven sprang into action. Like clockwork toys, they grabbed their masks and marched to the back door. Eleanor lifted the hatch and went first, so she could help them with the steps. Next came William, a tall lad who carried a torch. He turned to light the way for Rosemary, Freddie, and Billy, each carrying a box. Silent and subdued, the rest followed and assembled on the wooden seats below.

Eleanor placed lanterns on their raised shelves and then faced the children, whose ghostly faces were turned up to her in the gloom.

'Do you know, children, I think that was the best drill I have ever seen. Well done!' They beamed, seeming to forget that they were in a dark underground cave, preparing for the possibility of death from the sky.

Eleanor thought she had better make sure of the essentials, so she went on, shining her torch towards the back of the shelter. 'Now then, who can tell me what's back there?'

The beaming smiles turned to titters as the children looked at each other.

Terry, described in Miss Billings' notes as 'sensible', spoke up. 'It's the lavs, Miss. Girls that side, boys that side. Most of the time.' In response to Eleanor's puzzled look, he leaned towards her and whispered: 'Us lads can do Number Ones in the sandpit, Miss, but if it's Number Twos…' He broke off, blushing.

Eleanor succeeded in keeping a straight face. 'Thank you, Terry, I can see I have so much to learn from you all.' *Of course,* she thought, *there were flushing toilets in the Birmingham shelters, I should have realised.* 'Now, I think it's time for elevenses, so let's go carefully back to the classroom.'

Return of the Raids?

February 1945

Friday morning, and a bleary-eyed Eleanor sat hunched over at the kitchen table, sipping her first cup of tea of the day. She was shattered, and the weekend couldn't come soon enough. Her letter to Ray reproached her from its place by the teapot. She tried to convince herself there simply had not been time to post it. But Mrs. King would have been happy to do so. In truth, Eleanor knew she was taking a huge risk in writing about her doubts. Once sent, it was irretrievable and could change the course of her life.

The short walk to the school revived her. A breeze caught her hair, and silvery waves sloshed onto the sand just below the school gate. After morning assembly, Eleanor passed out workbooks, gave Brian some past Scholarship papers to practise, and sank gratefully behind her desk to catch up on the logbook she was leaving for Miss Billings.

Peace was shattered by the sound Eleanor least expected and most dreaded. The undulating rise and fall, the terrifying wail of the air raid siren. Eleanor looked up at the children, and they stared back. The older ones were frozen in shock by a sound they could never forget, the younger ones confused and frightened by a deafening noise they could barely remember.

No one moved a muscle.

'Well, children, we'll have to leave our work for now. That's the air raid signal, so grab your masks and straight down to the shelter. Let's see if you can make this even better than our drill.' Eleanor managed to keep her voice steady.

Still in stunned silence, the children collected their masks, formed a queue at the hatch, remembered their tasks, and were assembled in the shelter in less than two minutes.

Eleanor lit as many lanterns as she could find. 'Goodness, that was quick. Well done, now let's get settled. Rosemary and William, could you help me set the tables out, everyone else find a seat.'

The chosen two, brother and sister from a large family, were obviously used to doing chores together. Soon every child had a seat and a low table, and Eleanor was ready to start.

For just a minute she hesitated, straining to hear the familiar 'woo-woo' of the Luftwaffe twin-engine bombers. Still nothing.

Unexpectedly, she remembered Miss Rhoda in the shelter. Recalling the calm and ordered environment created for the Birmingham children, she steeled herself to do the same. She rummaged in the supply boxes. 'Well, it looks as if we might be here for a little while, so we don't want to go hungry, do we?' Solemn shakes of small heads, then Eleanor raised her arms, a bottle of Tizer in one hand, a packet of digestive biscuits in the other. 'Special treat?' A smattering of applause greeted this performance, and the atmosphere lightened.

Eleanor then found some Salt and Shake crisps to add to the feast. *That will keep them occupied, fiddling with those packets,* she thought, remembering how she loved to carefully shake the salt from the blue paper, still managing to spill quite a bit. *Not nutritious, but morale boosting,* she decided.

She lifted her head to listen again for any sounds that might penetrate underground. Could she just hear a faint drone coming through?

Once the snacks were consumed, Eleanor encouraged the

children to choose a book, or other absorbing activity from the boxes: card games, drawing, or knitting.

The humming grew louder. Eleanor felt her palms grow damp. She was getting anxious, but so far, a long way from terrified. In the Blitz, most prided themselves on being able to pick up the ominous two-toned sound of the Luftwaffe. However, the closer it came, the more she thought the steady hum could even be the four-engine American Liberator. Funny looking bird, Ray had said, straight sided, more like a cigar box than a plane. But why over Scilly? If only there was a way to look outside.

The children glanced fearfully upwards.

Eleanor's mind was dragged back to the shelter by little Pamela tugging at her skirt. 'Miss, I really need to go. It's a Number Two!'

Eleanor stood and held out her hand. 'All right, Pam, do you want me to take you?' Emphatic nod.

As Eleanor opened the door, Pamela took one look at the Elsan, and cried out, 'No, Miss, no! I'll fall in, it will eat me!'

As she pulled away from Eleanor, one of the buttons on her hand-knit cardigan flew off in the struggle to escape. Eleanor put her arms around the sobbing child and looked for assistance. The children had stopped what they were doing, and at least no longer seemed troubled by the approaching aircraft. Eleanor had an idea.

'Don't worry, Pam, Peggy will show you it's not scary.'

She motioned to the older sister, who protested, 'But Miss, I don't need to go!'

Eleanor, still holding Pam, who by now was clutching herself in desperation, said 'Please, Peggy.'

The older girl sighed and approached the gleaming green appliance. 'All right, but I'm not taking my knickers down.'

She stomped up onto the plinth, raised the lid and sat, glaring at Pam.

The smaller child stopped struggling, but still refused to approach. Her face was twisted in agony, and her control was obviously stretched to the limit. Eleanor knew that, apart from any threat from above, she was seconds from having to clean up a mess, comfort a mortified child, and live with the consequences until the All Clear. 'Look, Pam,' she said cheerily. '*I'm* not frightened.' And to the astonishment of the children, she marched up to the Elsan and sat, trying to look relaxed and unafraid.

Giggles spread through the group, starting with Pam, who broke into a run and hauled her short legs up the steep step. Eleanor kicked the door shut and helped the frantic child onto the seat. Pam clutched Eleanor tightly as the expression on her tear-streaked face changed from agony to blissful relief.

As teacher and pupil stepped back into the main room, Eleanor heard distant booms above the loud drone of what she was now sure was a Liberator. More puzzled than afraid, she looked around for a distraction to keep the children from picking up her uncertain feelings.

She spotted the mouth organ at the bottom of a box and picked it up. 'Now, can anyone play this? We could have a sing-song.'

Terry, the smallest boy in the class, raised his hand halfway and stammered, 'I can, Miss, my dad taught me. I only know one song, though, 'coz then he had to go away to fight.'

'Splendid, Terry, we only need one verse.'

She passed him the instrument, and, true to his word, Terry led them in a rousing, if somewhat repetitive, rendition

114

of 'Knees Up Mother Brown'. Their voices got louder and louder, and just as they shouted 'Don't let the breeze up!' for the third time, the music was drowned by a far sweeter sound: the steady, harmonic moan of the 'All Clear' siren.

Eleanor looked at her watch. Just gone noon. They had been in the shelter for more than two hours, she had no idea what had happened outside, but instead of shaking with panic, she simply felt drained.

After the siren died away, the children made their way back into the schoolroom. Mrs. King appeared at the back door, her entrance preceded by a tantalising smell from the shepherd's pie she carried. She was bursting with excitement.

'Oh good, you're all right. It was one of those U-boats, Miss Barton, the Yanks bombed it, right off Mincarlo, bodies in the water, you wouldn't believe it, the divers are going in…'

Worried that the children were about to be regaled with too much graphic detail, Eleanor hastily took the dish.

'Thank you so much, Mrs. King, so glad it wasn't the Luftwaffe.'

After lunch, Eleanor broke further with routine and took the children on a ramble to the highest point on the island, up to the Daymark. As they reached the top, Eleanor looked up at the striped conical tower. She knew it was built in earlier times as a guide for shipping and wondered if the U-boat had tried to sight off it. She might get the full story on the evening news.

The walk served the dual purpose of getting fresh air after the stuffy shelter and giving the children a chance to chat about what had happened. Eleanor was sure each child would take home stories of their individual bravery and spirit. But she was equally sure that, by tomorrow, there would be no one on St. Martin's who hadn't heard about 'Miss' sitting on the Elsan.

Revived, Eleanor sent the children on their way and gathered her hat and coat. Just then, the school phone rang, stopping her with one foot out of the door. She dashed back into the building, and gasped 'St. Martin's School, Miss Barton speaking,' into the receiver.

'Oh good, just caught you.' She was pleased to hear Harvey's clipped tones; she had been meaning to ring him before the day's events overtook her. 'I hear you've had a bit of excitement today; thought I'd see if you were all right.'

Eleanor wondered if she was imagining a note of anxiety in his voice. 'Oh yes, thank you, the children were marvellous, I was so proud of them.' She hoped she was striking a brave and breezy tone. 'The only damage was to the shelter supplies; I will need to re-stock biscuits and crisps before Miss Billings gets back.'

'Excellent. Well done, all.' A brief silence at the other end of the line. Was the connection broken? But then she heard a sigh, and Harvey was back. 'By the way, Miss Billings rang yesterday, her parents are on the mend, she thinks another week will do it. She's booked a flight for a week Sunday. Think you could manage to stay till then?'

'Of course. Actually, I'm quite enjoying myself. Hard work, but plenty of time to relax… and think.' She remembered the unsent letter to Ray. *Must post it tomorrow,* she thought.

Harvey's voice brought her back. He spoke briskly. 'Right, I'll get Fred organised, and we'll pick you up next Saturday, high tide at the jetty.' Another silence, and throat clearing. 'Maybe dinner and de-brief Saturday evening, if you fancy?'

Eleanor was amused at the quasi-military image of Harvey conducting a de-brief with her. 'I'll look forward to it, thank you.'

That evening, Eleanor was glued to the Home Service at 6pm. The pips went, sounding the hour, and then the voice of the BBC. 'This is London.'

Since D-Day, the 'Progress of the War' bulletins were hopeful, as the enemy was pushed back further into Europe. Details were sometimes scarce due to national security, but Eleanor was proud to think of Ray in Free France, doing his bit. She wondered if the incident on Scilly would even be reported, but near the end of the broadcast, she heard:

And now, news from the Isles of Scilly. At 0930 hours today, Friday 10 March, an enemy U-Boat (designation U681) was reported on rocks off Mincarlo. It appears she had been lying off Scilly for several days. Having sustained damage in the channel, she was forced to surface and tried to run for Ireland. She was located by an American Liberator. Depth charges were dropped, and she was sunk with the loss of eleven lives. Twenty-five crew were rescued and taken to the mainland for processing as prisoners of war.

Eleanor leaned back in her chair. So that was it. Even though the war in Europe was supposed to be nearly over, some U-Boats still prowled nearby, refusing to accept defeat. The predatory wolf of the seas had been lurking in Scilly waters as the islanders went about their daily lives. The fear she had kept hidden from the children, and from Harvey as she chatted calmly to him earlier, came flooding over her. The cup and saucer in her hand rattled as she set them on the table. Her heart thudding, she glanced up and spotted a sherry decanter in a cabinet. Surely Miss Billings wouldn't mind, in the circumstances?

Eleanor managed to pour herself a drink without spilling the sherry or dropping the cut glass decanter. It went down well, so she poured another. Her heart started to return to its normal rhythm. As it turned out, the Allied defences had done their job, and she had done hers. In some ways, it was more difficult than the Birmingham raids. Here, she was alone, and hadn't known what was happening. *Depth charges, hmm?* She mused. *No wonder I didn't recognise the sound, nothing like bombs hitting the ground, or the whoosh of a building collapsing to dust.*

She had a comic image of Pamela dropping her own 'depth charges' into the Elsan as the Yanks dropped theirs, to much more deadly effect. She reached for the unsent letter to Ray. *That would give him a laugh.* But then stopped. She must make sure he understood the seriousness of her concerns, that he knew how worried she was.

Eleanor sighed. She so wanted to talk to someone about the events of the day, and their effect on her. *I know,* she reminded herself, *Harvey works late on a Friday, I should really give him more details to pass on to Miss Billings.* Weaving slightly, she made her way back to the school and picked up the telephone. He answered on the first ring, which meant she had been right about him working late.

'Carn Friar's School, Headmaster speaking.'

Eleanor suppressed a hiccup. She must have rushed over too quickly. And perhaps she should have had a bite to eat to soak up the sherry. And what would Harvey make of her call, so soon after he had rung her? She had a fleeting thought maybe he was trying to suppress his feelings for her just as she was doing with hers for him.

Eleanor hesitated. She couldn't just plunge into the Elsan episode, he might think her terribly unprofessional. She gathered her wits and tried to adopt a brisk tone of voice, preparing to model her summary on the BBC news bulletin.

'I thought, as you made the original arrangements with Miss Billings, it might be appropriate for you to have a fuller report of the events of today.'

There was a brief silence. 'Of course, but I am happy to wait until we meet next Saturday evening.'

Eleanor felt her face redden. *You fool. Completely forgot about the dinner invitation. Oh, blow it, I can't think straight. Too late not to look silly.* 'Harvey, actually I simply must tell you a story, it won't be going in my report, but I hope you will see how funny it is.'

Harvey showed no surprise at her abrupt change of subject. 'Right then, tell away, I'm listening.'

She launched into her tale, which soon had them both doubled over their phones with laughter.

The next morning, fending off a slight headache with a couple of aspirin, Eleanor rested her head in her hands. She wondered what Harvey must be thinking. His opinion of her would have taken a nose-dive, especially as she had presented him with the unseemly image of her balancing on a chemical toilet in front of an audience of children. The meal in a week's time was more likely to involve a dressing down than a celebration of her courage and resourcefulness.

She groaned and looked around the room, spotting the unsent letter to Ray on the table. *Might as well drop another bombshell while I'm at it.* Allowing herself no time for second thoughts, Eleanor sealed the letter, walked the short distance to the Post Office, and handed it to the postmaster. He didn't appear to look directly at the address, but she wasn't fooled. 'Miss Barton's written to her American sweetheart, expect he'd be worried about her, with this U-boat business,' he might tell his customers. Eleanor didn't mind. The people of this tiny island had welcomed and supported her. She had no illusions that, even more than on St. Mary's, her life was an open book.

The letter was on its way. She might have just destroyed any chance of happiness with Ray, and Eleanor needed a distraction. Keep walking, that would do it. She was never without Tregellas's *Tourists' Guide*, and a quick search revealed it was only a short stroll to Knackyboy Carn. *Wonderful name*, she thought, *and the book says it's a "rare British site which held the remains of around sixty cremated bodies from the Bronze Age".* Unmissable.

Striding up the south slope of the island, she came to a rocky mound and a half-cleared entrance to a tunnel underneath. She shone her torch into the tunnel and imagined ancient people bringing their dead through it. Pushing through the overgrown entrance to the burial chamber, she stopped when a small trickle of rubble cascaded beside her. *Don't want to be the next body buried here.*

Eleanor sat and half closed her eyes, adjusting to the dim light. She visualised shadows cast by the mourners' flares as they brought remains to join those already in the chamber. It was not a frightening place. The sense of being a tiny part of thousands of years of human life was soothing. *I don't suppose anyone resting here spent a minute worrying about preventing pregnancy. And thousands of years from now, no one will care that I did.*

Now serene, Eleanor backed out of the entrance, congratulating herself again on bringing her gardening trousers. She looked around, catching a flash of brilliant turquoise to the north. Great Bay, according to her guide. *Father would be pleased to see me consulting Mr. Tregellas. I'm certainly not alone out here, with the spirits of Knackyboy around me and Father by my side.*

Eager to see more of the beach, she proceeded across School Lane and Telegraph Road. Then edged more slowly through heavy gorse and bracken to a scene that would not have been out of place in the Caribbean. A crescent of white sand, sparkling in the cool March sun, lapped by bright blue water.

Shoes and socks off, trousers rolled up, Eleanor made a dash across the sand, feeling like a ten-year-old again. Two steps into the water and she came to a halt, gasping. Great Bay might look like the tropics, but the temperature of the water had more in common with the North Sea of her childhood.

A flash of memory, the thrill of sea swimming at Whitby. *I know what to do. Up to the ankles then wait for the pain to go, then the numbness sets in. Then a little bit further, and it starts to feel good.* Eleanor stopped with the waves at her shins, looking at the horizon. *I'll be back here one day,* she promised herself.

Return to St. Mary's

March 1945

Eleanor teetered on the edge of the tiny jetty, suitcase at her side. It was Saturday morning, just coming up to high tide. Her case bulged with presents from the children and their parents: homemade preserves, a whole chicken carefully dressed and wrapped in greaseproof paper, plus a selection of drawings of ships, submarines, and stick figures representing classmates.

Her favourite gift was a framed photograph, taken by Mrs. King, of Eleanor surrounded by the class. All the children were lined up, smiling at the camera. Except for Billy. 'Tuck your shirt in,' she'd hissed at him, just as the camera clicked. A blurred image of Billy, with his cheeky face and hand halfway down his trousers was preserved, forever in disarray.

Peering through shreds of mist, Eleanor spotted Fred's boat. She could see that Harvey, who could have been relaxing on his day off, had come to meet her. She hoped this meant her giddy behaviour on the telephone was consigned to history, but it might be that he wanted to have a serious talk rather sooner. The thought filled her with dread.

Fred tied up to the jetty and reached for Eleanor's suitcase. Harvey held out his hand, which she ignored, feeling awkward. She settled for the journey, ensuring that she held onto her side of the boat at a distance so that no encircling arm was needed.

As they chugged across the short stretch of water, Harvey gazed out to sea. 'So, all well when you left? Everything in order for the return of Miss B.?'

Eleanor looked out over the opposite horizon. 'Yes, of course, I hope I know what's expected.'

Her voice sounded stiff to her own ears, and perhaps to Harvey as well. He subsided into silence for the rest of the short journey. As they docked at Hugh Town, Harvey stood back for her to disembark, perhaps expecting she would reproduce her previous athletic form. However, Eleanor lost her concentration and balance, stumbled, and would have taken an ignominious dip had Harvey not grasped her arm and kept her upright. Embarrassed, she shook him off and sloshed back up to the path to start the walk back to Crawfords'.

He called out. 'Miss Barton! Eleanor!' She pretended she hadn't heard. He stepped off the boat and caught her up, limping slightly. 'Your suitcase.'

Eleanor stopped abruptly, catching his exasperated tone, ashamed of her petulance. She'd forced him to almost run. She reached for the case. 'Harvey, I'm so sorry.' Her voice wobbled. 'I can't explain, it's what happened on St Martin's. Really important, but I've never told anyone… hard to put into words…' She gave up.

His eyes were obscured behind his glasses, but the tone in his voice was warmer. 'How about you give it a good try over a meal and drink tonight?'

Not trusting herself to speak at first, and feeling like a sulky child, she nodded, then shot him a sideways glance. 'So you're not going to give me a stern talking-to about, you know, the Elsan, and acting like a fool when I rang you?'

Harvey chuckled. 'Now you *are* being ridiculous. I thought it was a hoot, best laugh in ages. Couldn't you tell?'

Another nod from Eleanor, and the beginnings of a smile.

'Um, yes. I hoped you'd seen the funny side. Thing is, I'd had a glass or two of sherry and, well, it was all a bit hazy.'

'That's cleared that up then,' he replied. 'Seven o'clock, I'll be waiting outside the Atlantic. We'll try to get our same table.'

She took the case from his extended hand. 'See you then, Harvey. I'll be all right from here.'

When she arrived at Crawfords', Eleanor was relieved to see Audrey was busy in the shop, and her husband was nowhere to be seen. A quick wave, 'Lots to tell you!' and she was able to escape to her room, unpack and sink into her bed, unconscious in a minute.

Sometime later, there was a soft knock at the door. In response to Eleanor's mumbled invitation, her landlady stepped into the room, teacup in hand. 'It's nearly six, I thought you might like to come down for a bite to eat.'

Eleanor sat bolt upright. 'Oh gosh, I'm meeting Harvey, um, Mr. Chalmers at seven.' There might have been a slight lift of her landlady's eyebrow. 'To fill him in on how things went on St. Martin's. Very eventful, quite unexpected.'

Audrey set the cup of tea on Eleanor's bedside table. 'Better get your skates on, then.'

Eleanor swivelled her legs onto the floor and gulped the tea. 'Thanks so much, this is a lifesaver. Oh, I almost forgot…' Crossing the room, Eleanor carefully lifted the chicken from its resting place atop the cupboard and presented it with a flourish.

'This is going straight into the cool box. Sunday lunch and a good chat tomorrow, then?' said Audrey.

Breaking the Silence

March 1945

Eleanor looked at the empty glass, wondering if it was wise to accept a second sweet sherry, considering the results of her recent raid on Miss Billings' decanter. Too late, Harvey was already at the bar, ordering.

He joined her and spoke gently. 'Now, tell me about St. Martin's.'

At first, Eleanor hesitated, then thought, *I must speak. It's got to be now*. Harvey waited, glass in hand.

As she tried to find the words, an unwelcome image drifted into her mind. She half-closed her eyes as the room seemed to recede. Harvey became merely a blurred outline. She murmured in a dreamy monotone, 'You see, the school didn't have its own shelter, we had to take them to the public shelter. Twenty in each class. So many children. Running through the streets, a daytime raid, the bombs getting nearer.' As she spoke, she was no longer telling Harvey about the raid, she was living it, hearing the screams and explosions, smelling the smoke, shaking with fear.

Caught in the past, she tried to drag herself back to the warm room in the Atlantic. She reached for her drink, then pushed it away as, once again, she tumbled back through time. '*The children trust me to protect them,*' was her frantic thought as she raced through the streets. Desperate to find out if all the children were with her, but unable to see them in the haze.

In the pub with Harvey, but now unaware of his presence, her breathing quickened. Her head tilted back, eyes fully closed now. St. Mary's in 1945 ceased to exist as she relived the death and devastation of the early raids. Back in the dusty streets of Birmingham, she was overwhelmed with terror but trying to hold herself together. Once again, the young, inexperienced teacher feeling she had to impose her authority and save the lives of the children in her care. 'Now then, don't dawdle, you'll soon be safe,' she called to the children. Children no one else in the Atlantic could see. Some drinkers turned to look as Eleanor's best schoolmistress tones rang out incongruously.

Then Eleanor's voice dropped. She was counting to herself. The onlookers turned back to their drinks as Eleanor whispered, 'Seventeen, eighteen, nineteen…. seventeen, eighteen, nineteen.' Her voice rose in panic. 'It should be twenty, why isn't it twenty?' She twisted in her seat. 'Where's Betsy? I can't see her, why isn't she here?' Before Harvey could stop her, Eleanor made a dash for the door. She stumbled out into the pitch black, calling for 'Betsy,' then froze, eyes squeezed shut.

Harvey caught up, gently but firmly seized both wrists, and pulled her round. 'Eleanor, look at me. Open your eyes, look at me.' At first, she tried to free herself, but finally gave in to his repeated commands. She opened her eyes. She focused back on Harvey's face, leaving the air raid behind. Slowly, he released her wrists and carefully, delicately, folded his arms around her. She leaned her forehead against his chest and cried.

Sobbing, she mumbled into the rough wool of his jacket, 'She went back for her mask. I know she did. She didn't have it when they found her. We always told them, "Don't forget your mask," and she would never go into the shelter without it.' Eleanor couldn't catch her breath, she just managed to blurt between sobs, 'It was my fault, I was responsible, I should have seen her, should have stopped her. It wouldn't have happened.'

They stood in the road in the blackout, entwined, until she was quiet. 'A walk by the sea?' Harvey's suggestion seemed so banal and brought her gently back to the present.

Stepping carefully in the dark, they headed towards Porthcressa beach. 'Harvey, what's the matter with me? I get these images, and then I seem to, well, go away. Back to the bombing. I sometimes wonder if it's my punishment; I'm doomed to repeat this over and over until I die.'

At first, Harvey didn't respond, and they walked on slowly, the black, restless water with its silver trail just ahead. The concrete defence blocks on the beach were silhouetted by the moon.

Tightening his arm around her, Harvey took a deep breath. 'I think I've got a pretty good idea what's happening to you, actually. Seen it in the first war, after the Somme. No one understood it, people thought the chaps were putting it on.'

Eleanor frowned. *Bit of a difference between a battle and an air raid. Or was there?*

Harvey carried on. 'Have you heard of shell shock?'

Eleanor was doubtful. 'You mean soldiers breaking down in battle?'

He nodded. 'Well, sort of. I think they call it combat stress or combat neurosis these days, something like that.'

Eleanor protested. 'But Harvey, I'm not a soldier. I've never been in battle, so how can it be?'

'All I'm saying is, what's happening to you sounds the same—and I mean exactly.'

She looked at him. *He's trying to be kind, but what does he know?*

'Tell you what, maybe see the doc? I think there's ways to treat it these days, maybe you don't have to suffer.' He faced her that they could see each other in the fitful moonlight. 'And you know, I really, really, hate to see you suffer.'

Eleanor stood quietly as his hand rested on the side of her face. He remained completely still. The moon disappeared behind a cloud, leaving them in darkness on the edge of the sea. Then, shaking himself, Harvey guided her gently back up the beach towards the path.

On firmer ground, Eleanor spoke. 'All right.' She sighed. 'It's been nearly three years now, I keep thinking it will go away. I can never relax. There's always the fear, it can happen anytime. A sound, a smell,' she broke off. 'So yes, I will make an appointment, but whatever happens, do you know the best thing you've done for me tonight?'

A quizzical look from Harvey. 'Made you talk about something you don't want to talk about? Made you cry?'

She shook. 'No. And anyway, I did want to talk about it. I just didn't know how. What you've done is, you never once tried to argue me out of how I felt or told me I shouldn't feel that way. Or worse, that I'm silly, or even crazy.' They had reached Crawfords' now, and she pulled out her key and turned back to him. 'And for that, I think I might just have to love you.'

At this, they stood immobilised by her words. Harvey spoke first. 'Well, thank you, dear girl, but you might not think so if you really knew me. You've let your demons out tonight, it'll be my turn another day.'

With that, he vanished into the blacked-out silence. Left alone in the chilly dark, she shook her head. To think she'd been worried he would chastise her over the 'unprofessional' phone call.

As Eleanor tried to creep up to her room, the kitchen door opened. 'You're a bit early, is everything all right?' Audrey paused in the doorway, then seemed to brace herself to continue. 'Mrs. Nelson next door popped in for her paper earlier, she thought she saw you and the Head, um, arguing. Or something. Outside the Atlantic.'

Eleanor tried to fix a bright look on her face, but judging by Audrey's furrowed brow, she didn't entirely succeed. 'I'm just a bit tired still, I'll have an early night, I think, if you don't mind?'

Audrey looked slightly offended. 'Sorry, didn't mean to pry.'

'Oh, we just had a quick drink, and discussed events. How the children reacted to the U-Boat episode, that sort of thing. As you can imagine, it was a bit of a shock after no raids for such a long time. A shock to the children, and to me.' Her landlady nodded, mollified. Eleanor added, 'I'm looking forward to a roast dinner tomorrow. That chicken was from Churchtown Farm, should be a treat. I'll volunteer for veg peeling if that would help.'

Audrey reached out and patted Eleanor's hand. 'It certainly would. You have a good rest and a bit of a lie-in, and we'll go from there.'

As Eleanor turned on the gas fire and sank into the little armchair, Ray's photo on her dresser accused her. '*I think I'll just have to love you.*' Where had that come from? It would be easy to tell herself that tearing the scab off her deepest hurt had resulted in an emotional firestorm. Perhaps she'd mistaken release for something stronger? No. Eleanor made an effort to confront herself honestly. The truth was that feelings for Harvey had been creeping up on her since... was it the vegetable garden? The scarf? The trip to St. Martin's?

All of those. So different from the whirlwind generated by the scant time that she and Ray had shared. She had been able to ignore the tiny increments of her growing affection for Harvey. Until now.

Something warm and solid had taken root, nourished by daily contact, shared interests, mutual concern for the children. And more. Up to this point, she told herself that she was lucky to have such a warm and supportive friendship. A friendship that had help to turn the potentially bleak and lonely early days on Scilly into a happy and fulfilling existence. But she realised that the power of touch had wiped away that illusion.

Eleanor recalled the spark of physical desire as Harvey put his arm around her on the boat to St. Martin's, a desire that flared, and then died in the face of her determined refusal to acknowledge it. Tonight, despite her distress, or because of it, all she wanted was to curl up with Harvey somewhere calm and quiet. Thinking about the studied and careful way he held her face made her body ache. In many ways, she was probably closer to the quiet, reserved headmaster than to the man she was going to marry.

However, she was going to marry Ray. She loved him and, in any case, she had given her word. She knew a special disgust was reserved for women who betrayed the men to whom they had made a promise. Men who were fighting and dying, who were maybe getting through the horrors of the fight with the thought of joy to come. Or dying with the names of their sweethearts on their lips.

Eleanor shuddered. *Too awful to contemplate, I couldn't do that to Ray.* Another thought occurred to her. Perhaps the age difference between them had led her to misread her feelings for Harvey. What she might be experiencing was the warmth of fatherly comfort from a kind older man. That could make sense. *But the sexual feelings? Towards a father figure?* Also unthinkable. And anyway, she didn't believe it. Worn out and uneasy, she managed to sleep that night. Nothing was clear, and she had no idea what she would do.

Back to work on Monday. Each step towards the school felt as if her feet were weighted with stones. She was dreading their first contact, but she should have trusted Harvey, should have known he wouldn't make it awkward for her. He and Miss Elmore were there to meet her.

Harvey spoke first. 'Good morning, Miss Barton, and welcome back to Carn Friar's. Cup of tea to celebrate your return?'

Eleanor flashed him a grateful smile. 'I've missed you all, I seem to have been away for ages.'

Harvey opened his study door and gestured for them both to enter. 'How about if I make the tea, and then we'll fill you in before the children arrive.'

Later that day, she kept her word and rang the doctor. She was up to date with her Provident payments and would be able to pay his fees. It would be worth it to find out if Harvey was right, and maybe even get help. But she wasn't hopeful. She was a fit and healthy young woman, with no signs of physical illness, and she suspected that newer ideas in the treatment of emotional problems might not have reached the Isles.

Trying to make sense of it all

April 1945

Most doctors on Scilly were away on active service. Dr. Williams was one of those who had come out of comfortable retirement to tend to the health needs of the residents left behind. He still saw patients in the former front parlour of his home. Ill at ease in this cosy environment, Eleanor sat opposite the thin, ascetic man of about seventy. She tried to explain her experiences, how deep and pervasive her fears were, and how she was exhausted from years of fighting them.

When there was no response, she stopped, twisting her fingers, seeing no comprehension in the chilly blue eyes looking over wire spectacles.

He leaned forward. 'So, tell me, Miss Barton, are your monthlies fairly regular?'

Eleanor opened her mouth, but at first nothing came out. After a pause, in which she gaped like a fish, she managed to say, 'I'm sorry, what was that?'

He steepled his fingers, and spoke more slowly, as if to a child. 'Well, Miss Barton, sometimes the monthly flow can become a bit irregular for young ladies like yourself, who try to work perhaps a bit too hard. This can affect the brain, and I'm thinking this may be your problem. Does that make sense to you?'

Eleanor drew herself up in the straight-backed wooden chair, which could have come from her own schoolroom, and looked at him across the broad expanse of sturdy oak. 'No, actually it doesn't. My periods are regular, since you ask, and I don't see what that has to do with the awful episodes I'm experiencing.'

He paused then cleared his throat. 'Shall we just have a look?'

Eleanor stared. *Look at what?*

'If you would kindly remove your undergarments,' he continued, 'I'll just ask the nurse to pop through.' Eleanor gave serious thought to sprinting out of the room, but deference to a member of the medical profession won the day.

The doctor motioned her to the raised couch. She lay back, legs spread, as the nurse covered her below the waist with a rough sheet. From his considerable height, Dr. Williams bent between her knees. She could feel his fingers probing, and some sort of instrument parting her tender flesh.

After an eternity, he stood and went to a basin to wash his hands. 'Please dress yourself, and we'll have a chat.'

Eleanor rolled onto her side, burning with humiliation. And anger. She pulled herself upright and stepped back to the chair.

Dr. Williams resumed his position behind the desk, looking down on her. 'Miss Barton, am I correct that you are engaged to be married?'

No secrets on Scilly, she thought. She replied tersely. 'I am. Sort of.'

He seemed to be waiting for something more but continued when she remained silent.

'I can see that, to date, you and your fiancé have not had relations.'

'I can't see what that has to do with these incidents,' she almost snapped.

He seemed a bit taken aback but ploughed on. 'Well, it's my opinion that you are suffering from what we call "civilian

133

war hysteria". We see it in ladies who have experienced bombing or other traumas of war.'

Hmm, thought Eleanor, unconvinced, and her face probably showed it. *You mean a sort of special shell shock, for feeble females only, not brave soldiers?*

The doctor continued, seemingly unaware of her scepticism 'It may be that until your, um, bodily rhythms have a chance to benefit from marriage, a strengthening tonic might help your brain to cope. The nurse will get you something from the dispensary.'

As she left Dr. Williams' surgery, Eleanor looked at the dark brown bottle, labelled 'Dr. Smith's Tonic for Women'. Furtively, she slipped it into her bag as she walked back into the town, wondering about what had just happened to her.

Back again in the refuge of her room, Eleanor seethed. Maybe she should be furious at Harvey for suggesting seeking what passed as medical advice from Dr. Williams. But the examination had left her even more certain that she knew her own mind and body better than anyone. She stood, went to the little sink in the corner, and emptied the contents of the brown bottle down the drain.

Picnic at Lower Moors

April 1945

Two weeks went by, three weeks, and still no reply from Ray to the letter she had sent from St. Martin's. All the news was of Allied victories and the hoped-for end to the war in Europe. Eleanor told herself her letter may not have caught up with him, or his reply with her. But had he been so devastated, or angry, about the contents that he wanted nothing more to do with her? His Catholic faith was so important to him, maybe he could not tolerate even a hint that she might question its doctrine.

Having no option, she pushed her anxiety as far back in her mind as she could, where it nestled alongside the memory of her blurted declaration of love to Harvey and the embarrassing visit to Dr. Williams.

Alongside the burgeoning of spring on Scilly, the islanders were seized by an upswell of anticipation and hope that their suffering might soon be over.

Eleanor was passing the open door to Harvey's study at Carn Friar's late in April when he called out, 'Excuse me, Miss Barton, could I have a quick word about next term?'

She entered, shutting the door behind her in response to his gesture. He looked a bit sheepish, she thought. In addition to the usual paraphernalia on his overflowing desk, a large wicker basket teetered on top of a pile of papers.

'How about a picnic tea? Nothing fancy, I've got cheese sandwiches, ginger beer, an apple or two.' His expression did not match the confidence of his words.

Eleanor had the suspicion she was on the receiving end of

a carefully crafted plan. She hesitated. 'Well, the children are just finishing their work. I couldn't…'

Another uncharacteristically breezy response from Harvey, 'Quite all right, why don't I cycle to Lower Moors and meet you by the pond? It's mostly wetlands up there, but there are dry bits, we can put the rug on the bracken. I've left mother's old bicycle for you by the shed. Save anyone getting the wrong impression seeing us ride out together, hm?'

Eleanor understood and felt excited by the possibility of private time together. And then ashamed for being excited. 'Well, right then, I'll be along as soon as I can.'

Over an hour later, picnic eaten, they lay semi-reclined on a moth-eaten blanket. Eleanor was acutely aware of Harvey's body alongside her, inches away.

Leaning on his elbow, he tilted his head back in the late-afternoon sun. Without looking at her, he spoke. 'Been wanting to have a good talk ever since you got back from St. Martin's.'

Eleanor's heart sank. *He'll want to know if I've seen the doctor, what am I going to say?*

But he was on another track. 'You trusted me that night at the Atlantic.' He paused, she waited. 'I've never told anyone what happened, how I got through the last war. You're the person who will listen, who might even understand.'

Eleanor wished he would look at her. 'Harvey, I will, you know I will.'

But he kept his face averted, his voice turned harsh. 'Maybe so, but you won't be talking about love when I've finished, I'm damn sure of it.'

There was another long pause. Harvey pulled himself up some difficulty and sat hunched, head down, hands dangling. He began to speak, almost as if he were talking to himself.

'Nineteen-seventeen, on the Western Front. We were in the trenches, just over the Belgian border, near Ypres. Poperinghe, not famous, not special, just bloody, muddy, stinking...' He paused, then began in a stronger voice. 'I had letters from home, kept them stuffed in my pockets so I could read them, sitting in the dirt and shit. Like some sort of evil soup.'

Eleanor had never heard Harvey use anything but the most correct language. He seemed to be opening some well of agony that had been capped for years.

Cautiously she touched his hand, but he seemed oblivious to anything except his own thoughts and did not respond. 'My Pa wrote that he prayed for me every night. I used to listen to the screams of the chaps who were hit, dying... wondered if anyone prayed for them. Told Pa to keep up the prayers.' Harvey looked up briefly, shook, then went on. 'Anyway, one afternoon in the trench there were four of us: Gunner Sydney Crowther, me and two orderlies—don't recall their names. Word came that more ammunition was needed up the line, so the four of us and Marley the pack horse headed out. We didn't even see the incoming shell, but next thing I saw pieces of Marley and the orderlies fly up, like some bloody awful firework display. I saw part of Syd's thigh sliced off by a fragment, felt a pain in my leg. Then it was good night.'

The afternoon sun was sinking, the air cooler, but Eleanor noticed that Harvey was sweating.

He inhaled shakily. 'Next thing, I woke up in the Casualty Clearing Station, felt like I had spikes driven into my head and leg.'

Another long pause, and Eleanor was sure he wasn't seeing the dappled sunset across the moor, but the hellish cramped and blood-soaked clearing station.

Finally, he spoke. 'Anyway, I think I was there for a day or two, some routine with dressings, wound cleaning, and trying to hold on till the bedpan got to me. Didn't always make it. After a while, you don't care.' He pressed his hands to his eyes. 'I got to the third morning, still alive, feeling well enough to wonder about Syd. I knew we'd been hit together; couldn't understand why he wasn't there with me.'

He broke off, rummaged in the basket, and offered Eleanor an apple. 'Want one? Shame to carry them back again.'

Noting the abrupt change of subject, Eleanor took a chance. 'No thanks, Harvey. And it's okay to keep talking, I don't mind. Remember what you did for me that night, so give me a chance to hear the worst, if that's what's coming.'

He looked at her for the first time. 'You're right, it gets really tricky here.' A nod from her, and he continued. 'A few more days in, and there was Syd, next bed. Never so glad to see anyone, but all I managed was "Where the hell have you been?"'

After a deep breath, Harvey continued. 'Syd turned his head slowly, seemed like an effort to speak, I had to lean over him to hear. "*The stretcher bearers got us both out,*" he told me. "*But you were out of it, bleeding head wound, so they took you straight to the CCS to clean you up. I didn't look so bad, so they told me they'd be back shortly. There was mud everywhere, and by the time they got back to me, there were bugs crawling on my leg…*"

Eleanor watched Harvey steadily, then sat up and cautiously extended her hand.

This time he gripped it and went on, 'By then, he was half out of it with fever and infection. We chatted a bit that first hour. He told me about his 'bairn' back home. He was only nineteen, same as me, but he had a wife and child. I remember him saying, "*Write to my Em, Chalmers, her I love her, love the bairn. When this is all over, I'm going to be a good husband, father...*" His voice faded; I saw his eyes close. Then, he said, "*look in my pocket, please, there's a card from her in there, got her address on it. Never got around to answering it, you can do that for me.*" So I did, I took out the card from his wife. He whispered, "*thanks, pal*", and those were the last words I heard him say.'

Eleanor's eyes filled with tears, but Harvey's voice sounded flat and emotionless. 'They came round to dress his wound; you could smell the gangrene. I heard them say there was no point in amputation, it was too late. He died that morning, 23 October, and do you know what I did, Eleanor?' He released her hand and turned to her, grasping her arms. 'There was only a tiny space between the beds, I reached over, and, and I put my fingers into his wound and wiped the pus back into mine. I made myself a dirty wound.'

For the first time, Eleanor was too stunned to speak or move.

Harvey looked at her quickly. 'Don't think I was trying to commit suicide or couldn't bear the thought of one more pal dying. Oh no.' His grip tightened, as he forced out the words, slowly and deliberately. 'I wanted to live. To get out of it all, to go home.' His tone became bitter, and he leaned back, finally releasing her. 'There you are, my dear Miss Barton. A week later, Sydney was in the ground at Lyssenthoek Cemetery, my lower leg was clinical waste, and I was on my way home. It wasn't too late for *me*, was it?'

Eleanor found her voice. 'So you deliberately used Sydney, you made your wound worse, to get away?' She scrambled to her feet. 'I'm sorry, I can't take this in, it's getting late…'

He continued as if she hadn't moved. 'Yes, that's it exactly. And I wasn't the only one. Saw one officer put his hand under a helmet, stick a grenade in there and pull the pin. No hand, back to Blighty. But I also heard of a few chaps who shot themselves in the hand or foot, got court-martialled, then executed for cowardice. They had execution rooms, right in the Town Hall at Poperinghe.' His mouth twisted. 'Clever chap, me, I tried the subtle approach.'

Eleanor put her hands over her ears, then brought them down again. She owed it to him to hear this. She'd had three years of torment and guilt, he'd had decades.

'You might judge me,' he said, 'but you can't imagine the weariness, the fear, the despair. My crazy thinking was that Syd wouldn't know or care, no one was looking, and so I thought taking the easy route, a bit of guilt, was a small price. But the price was enormous, and I'm still paying it.'

Eleanor sank back down onto the thick picnic rug, turned from him. 'Harvey, I don't know what to think, I don't know how I feel…' She dropped her head onto her knees, trying to deal with a blizzard of thoughts and emotions. Her voice was muffled as she said, 'I suppose I should judge you, there's many who would condemn you as a coward, maybe even would say you should have been shot.'

Harvey sighed. 'And are you one of them, dear Eleanor? Because I certainly am. If I'd known what my life would be like, the life I saved by losing my leg, all these years keeping up the deception, weighed by shame at deserting… well, I'd have probably shot myself.'

Eleanor thought about the young men, some barely out of childhood, as Harvey had been when he reached across to Sydney's bed. She knew men who had survived that terrible conflict, her father among them, and she'd never heard a word about it from any of them. 'So tell me what your life has been like, Harvey.'

No reply, and for a minute she thought there wasn't going to be. Then, he said, 'I had a sweetheart, of sorts. We met playing tennis, she promised to be there for me when I came back.' He stopped again.

Eleanor had a feeling this was going to take a while, but she would wait him out. *He's lumbered me with this awful secret, he owes me answers.*

Harvey took a deep breath. 'When I was in the convalescent hospital, I wrote to this girl. Told her tennis was probably out for the foreseeable, and she'd be better off finding someone else.' He bit his lip. 'Anyway, she was probably relieved.' Eleanor waited. After another lengthy pause, he continued, 'I couldn't stand being around family, all sympathetic about something I'd done to myself, the shame, the nightmares, were terrible. The Army offered training. Rehabilitation, you know. Went into teaching because I couldn't think of anything else, then got myself a job as far away from home as possible.'

All those years, Eleanor thought, *no family, few friends, no...*

Harvey seemed to read her mind. 'Never married, in case you're wondering. Used to have a lady friend in Penzance, on the mainland, very discreet. Apart from that, I guess I just shut down.' His hand brushed her fingertips. 'But then along came Miss Eleanor Barton, turns out I'm not as shut down as I thought I was.'

Eleanor was beginning to understand. But there was one more question. Her voice was insistent, her gaze steady as she asked, 'So, Harvey, did you write to her?'

Harvey looked puzzled. 'I've just told you, I wrote and ended it.'

'No, I don't mean your girlfriend. Did you write to Sydney's wife, like he asked you to?' Eleanor imagined the dead soldier's wife, getting the telegram from the Army. Perhaps she would have been given access to his medical reports, which might have added to her distress. *If it was only a flesh wound, how did it kill him?* Emma might have wondered. Worst of all, never knowing that his final conscious thoughts were of her and their baby. Precious information, that only Harvey knew.

Harvey shook his head. With that, Eleanor felt the slow rising burn of fury. She had been brought up with traditional ideas of service to God and country, and doing the right thing, no matter how difficult. And yet this man, who had roused such powerful feelings in her, had betrayed the trust of a dying comrade and denied a young widow the comfort of knowing her husband's last thoughts.

Could I have been so wrong about him? Eleanor's fists clenched, and she found herself wanting to lash out, swamped by the force of her rage.

When he shook his head, Eleanor attacked him, furious, punching and pushing. 'Coward! You could have let her know what he said about the baby, about her, nobody else knew, you bloody, bloody coward.' All her confused feelings spilled out in a torrent as she pelted him with that most terrible insult.

At first, he held his arms rigid, taking the blows, but then he pulled her over onto the rug with him, the two of them rolling in a tight embrace. 'I'm sorry, sorry, sorry,' he whispered into her shoulder. 'You're right, I am a coward. I couldn't face writing to her, just wanted to forget it all, like a nightmare that never happened.' Eleanor was silent, and he continued, 'I did warn you that you'd regret talking to me about love.'

She tried to picture the traumatised youth that he was then, tried to find a reason for his failure to write to Syd's wife. She held him tightly, knocking his spectacles to the ground. Gradually, they came to rest, panting and facing each other.

Eleanor spoke, voice almost inaudible. 'I don't know how I feel. I don't hate you; I can't imagine what it was like for you. But it seemed such a small thing to do. And yet...' She hesitated. 'I still have these feelings for you, and I don't know what I'm going to do with them.' A silence, then he started to move in her arms.

Eleanor staggered to her feet. Harvey was crawling, feeling about in the near darkness.

He held up his specs, one lens smashed, and the frame bent. 'Could be an interesting trip back in the blackout. We'll have to push the machines; you'll have to lead.' He attached the picnic basket and rolled up the rug. Reaching into his rucksack, he said, 'But luckily for us, if I can find it, I have my trusty blackout torch.'

Guided by the almost non-existent light from the heavily shielded torch, they made their way slowly onto the path, occasionally sinking as they misjudged the marshy ground. Then they moved more quickly back towards Hugh Town. Not a word was spoken.

Eleanor was preoccupied with her thoughts, and she assumed Harvey was with his. Even more than after their evening at the Atlantic, she was confused. She now realised that the lines on Harvey's face were probably there for a much more deep-seated reason that the struggles of running a school in wartime.

They parted near the turning to Crawfords'.

'Goodnight then,' said Eleanor.

'Just a minute.' Carefully lowering both cycles to the pavement, Harvey scrutinised her face. Eleanor wondered nervously what this man, whom she previously thought of as quintessentially conventional, was going to do next.

He reached out and removed a few hairpins from her tousled hair. Peering somewhat near-sightedly at her face, he skilfully adjusted and pinned her straggling curls. 'That will do for Mrs. Crawford,' he said, and went on his way.

Caught Between

April 1945

After the picnic, Eleanor had the weekend to steady herself, to separate her dismay at what Harvey had failed to do from her affection for the man who had been the steadiest of friends to her. And to remind herself of the future she and Ray had planned, a future which might already have been wiped out by her doubts. Her doubts. Were they really about Catholic teaching? Or, even as she wrote to him about contraception, was there the tiniest part of her that would have felt something like relief if he changed his mind and headed into his future without her?

If there was no wedding, no life in America, then what would there be for her? She could stay on at Carn Friar's, find a way to be with the haunted man whose lived-in face and still-youthful body left her baffled.

As she watched the clock turn Saturday into Sunday, shut away in her room, Eleanor pushed her well-thumbed copy of *A Tree Grows in Brooklyn* aside. Ray informed her that US soldiers had been sent this book by the army as a morale booster to remind them of the joys of home.

He then passed it to her. 'You'll enjoy this, my darling, it will give you an idea of what it was like for me, growing up in America. And what it will be like for our children, lucky enough to grow up there too.'

Normally, she found the book absorbing, but her concentration was gone. She needed to feel calmer to see her predicament with detachment. Not since a passionate crush on the Head Boy at a neighbouring school had she felt such a storm of emotions, a lack of control, and an inability to think straight. A wry grin lifted her face. *That tells me all I need to know about what's happening to me. How embarrassing.*

Worn out, even though she had hardly moved a muscle all day, she put on old clothes and crept downstairs. A walk in the cool night should send her off to sleep if she could get out of the house without waking the Crawfords. She couldn't think of any reason she could give them for a midnight ramble, and she didn't want to have to try.

As she left the house, a stiff breeze blew damp sea air straight into her face. Beginning to revive, she chose a steep path, up Garrison Hill towards Star Castle. She felt lighter with every step, and would have loved to continue to the top, to face the wild western Atlantic. However, she thought there might be a risk of being shot by sentries guarding the officers in their quarters at the Castle. She stumbled back down to Crawfords'; her path lit by moonlight above the pitch-dark town below. She was concentrating on keeping her footing as she approached the door, and failed to see Audrey's pale face, just visible at the edge of the blackout.

Monday morning. Eleanor strode into the school, head up and determined to bring normality to what was beginning to feel like a melodrama. She called out a brisk 'Good Morning, all!' to her colleagues as she sailed into the staff room, catching a wary look from Harvey. Hat and jacket off, cup of tea in hand, she settled at her table, only to deflate like a punctured tyre as she saw an envelope in Harvey's writing. She lifted it slowly and read his note on the front.

I can't change what I didn't do then, but I'm going to try to do something now. I found the card to Syd from his wife, funny I still had it. Of course, the address may be long out of date, but I'm going to write to her, to write that letter Sydney asked me to as he was dying. I'll let you know what happens.

Eleanor opened the envelope and drew out a tattered greetings card. A spray of pansies against a pastel backdrop, with the printed inscription, 'My Thoughts are all of You'. She opened it and read Emma's spidery calligraphic script.

Dear Sydney,

I have been on the lookout for a letter from you today, but I have not received one. I hope I get one in the morning. Mother and I are just sitting by the fire. We have been talking about you and planning for your happy homecoming. Well, ta-ta my love, and be as cheerful as possible and don't forget I am always thinking of you and will till the end.

Kisses from baby Frances, and from
Your loving wife, Em xxxx

Eleanor turned her head to stop a tear dripping on the fragile document, with its shattered hopes.

Harvey spoke behind her. 'Twenty-eight years. She'll probably be long gone.' He sighed.

Eleanor thought for a minute, looking at the card. Then, her voice steady, she said, 'You do it, Harvey, you go ahead and try. If she's still alive, her memories certainly won't be long gone, and a letter just might find her.' Twisting in her chair, she passed the card to him, and turned back to her preparations for the day.

A pause, then he spoke to her back. 'You got through to me, you know. And what you think, what you say, matters. It really does.' He slipped out of the door before she could reply.

All Clear?

May 1945

The shocking news spread across the newspapers as they arrived off the Scillonian and were laid out in the Crawfords' little shop. Headlines screamed: *HITLER DEAD? THE NEWS WE ALL HOPE IS TRUE!*

In the breathless week that followed, Europe gradually absorbed the facts. Hitler had committed suicide, his successor Doenitz vowed to fight on. Then a few days later, 'GERMANY CAPITULATES' erupted on the front page of the *Daily Telegraph*. The 8th of May 1945 was declared a day to celebrate, to mourn the losses, and to come together in relief at the end of the war in Europe.

Carn Friar's closed for two days in celebration. Celebrations that were muted for some. For Eleanor, the end of the war meant the beginning of a reality that had, until now, seemed distant. Ray would be on his way back to America and, as far as she knew, expected her to be with him. There had been no response to her letter from St. Martin's, but perhaps he hadn't received it and was still blissfully unaware of her doubts. And he was certainly unaware of her closeness to Harvey. Either of these could prove insurmountable barriers to what not long ago had seemed a straight path to a happy future.

Eleanor joined the Crawfords for a quiet drink of celebration on VE Day. However, for them, any joy was for other people. Their son Clive was still in the Pacific, and it had been some time since they had heard from him. As they talked quietly and listened to the wireless for the latest news, there was a loud knock at the door. Eleanor was nearest, and as she went to answer, all three froze as they saw the unmistakable outline of the GPO messenger boy's cap at the door.

Audrey Crawford cried out, 'Oh God, no, please no, not Clive.'

Eleanor gripped the back of a chair thinking, *please, not Ray, not now.* 'I'll go.' She tried to hide her fear. 'Stay there.'

The boy, who couldn't have been more than fourteen, held out a yellowish envelope.

'Telegram for Miss Barton.'

Relief washed over Eleanor as she stared at the envelope. No black crosses. She called to the terrified couple in the kitchen. 'It's all right, it's not the War Office. It's from Ray.' She tore at the paper, almost ripping the message within, which read:

JUST GOT YOUR LETTER. STOP. COMING TO SCILLY ON LEAVE 12 MAY. STOP. FLIGHT BOOKED. STOP. PLEASE WAIT FOR ME. STOP. ALL LOVE RAY

Eleanor's first reaction was anger. *How could you give us such a fright? Don't you realise what a telegram usually means?* But then, she reread the message. There wasn't time to write a letter, she supposed, and he couldn't be sure it would arrive. And behind the staccato message, she sensed his response to her letter, his fear that he would lose her. Her anger was replaced by panic. Three days to prepare for a visit that would have filled her with joy months before.

She rejoined the Crawfords, placing the telegram on the table. 'I think I need another drink.'

Preparations

May 1945

The next evening, Audrey knocked softly on Eleanor's door. 'Please say if I'm speaking out of turn, but you've seemed in a bit of a state just lately.' This hesitant approached earned her a blank look, but she persevered. 'Eleanor, when I saw you rushing in last night, gone midnight, you looked, well, *wild*. And there was the other night outside the Atlantic. It's none of my business, I can imagine how hard it must be, away from home, but you seemed more shocked than happy about seeing your Ray…'

Eleanor sighed, then uncurled herself from her chair and gave her landlady a hug. The older woman hesitated, then gave her a tentative pat on the shoulder.

Eleanor stepped back. 'That's just it, there's so much going on… and now the war is nearly over, Ray will be here in days, and I don't know what to do.' She ducked her head. 'You must think I'm a terrible person.'

Audrey moved forward. 'Nonsense, these are terrible times, all we can do is see what comes.' She carried on briskly. 'Now, let's get this visit sorted.'

With Audrey's help, Eleanor arranged the practical details. Her landlady knew the owner of the Regent Hotel, a room was booked, and the flight times confirmed. That was the easy bit. The next day, Eleanor braced to approach Harvey for permission to take leave during the week of Ray's visit. Their custom of meeting privately in his office after work made the request's timing, if not the execution, easy.

Nervously, Eleanor poured tea for them both, but before

she could speak, Harvey reached in his pocket and passed her a sheet of paper. 'I've put together a few words for Syd's wife. I could do with a bit of help, cast your eye over it? Damnedest thing I've ever tried to write.'

Feeling trapped in the wrong conversation, Eleanor read over the single sheet. Judging by the blottings and crossings-out, producing it had been an excruciating exercise for Harvey. And was there a slight whiff of whisky from the stain in the middle?

Dear Madam,

I am writing because I served with Sydney Crowther in October 1917, and I was there when he died. I realise I should have written to you many years ago. I apologise if doing so now causes you distress. Circumstances in my own life have brought back vivid memories of the battlefield, and my brief time with Syd in the CCS, and reminded me of a promise I made to him. A promise I am now attempting, in my clumsy and belated way, to keep.

You will have been told at the time of the incident in which we were both wounded, his wound ultimately proving fatal. I will spare you the hurt of going over those details again. However, I am not sure if anyone will have ever told you that the last words I heard him speak were to me as I lay in the bed next to him: 'Write to my Em, tell her I love her, I wanted to be a good husband and father to the bairn.' He had a card that he had received from you in his pocket. This had your address on it. I took it, as he requested, so that I could write and convey his final words to you.

However, in the haze of illness, death, and repatriation, I did not keep my promise. I am doing so now in the hope that the knowledge that he thought of you and the baby would be comforting, even after so much time has passed. Perhaps you will wish to share these facts with your daughter, she must be a young woman now.

Yours truly

J. Harvey Chalmers (Former Gunner, "D" 189 RFA, B.E.F.)

Eleanor tried to collect her thoughts. 'Harvey, I wouldn't change a word. I guess "Dear Madam" sounds a bit stiff, but you can't risk "Dear Mrs. Crowther". After all these years, she might have a different name. And "Dear Emma", well, that's too familiar.'

Harvey nodded. 'There's only a small chance, of course. Funny thing is…' He stopped. In the midst of her own turmoil, Eleanor forced her face into what she hoped was an encouraging look. 'I felt, well, peaceful after I'd written it. As if I'd kept the promise somehow, no matter what happens.' He folded the battered paper into his pocket. Silence fell between them.

Eleanor took a shaky breath. 'Harvey, I need to ask for a week's leave. From Monday.'

'Here's me, blathering on. Are you all right? Has something happened?'

Eleanor felt even worse. 'No, no, I'm fine. It's just…' She braced. 'Ray's got leave, and he's arriving for a visit on the twelfth.'

Harvey stiffened, his face now blank. 'Of course, no problem at all, you're allowed compassionate leave for the visit of a fiancé on active duty. I'll see to it.' He moved to the other side of his battered desk and started to write.

When Eleanor remained seated, he looked up. 'Will that be all?' She nodded, miserable.

'Well, I must say, you don't look very pleased, considering

you are about to have a reunion with your fiancé at the end of a terrible war.'

Eleanor shifted uncomfortably. 'Strictly speaking, he's not my fiancé. Well, I don't wear the ring he gave me. We have an understanding, I guess you would say, and we do care for each other. But I did mean what I said to you…'

It was all too much, and she gave up. She couldn't understand her own feelings, there was no point even trying to explain them to Harvey. She left abruptly.

Visit to St. Mary's

May 1945

Eleanor watched as the little eight-seater wobbled towards the landing strip. She saw the tall man in khaki duck as he left the plane, then twist until he spotted her. She was shivering outside the draughty Nissen hut that served the arrivals. Shouldering his kit bag, he strode towards her. He was almost running as they met. She was wrapped in a tight embrace and could hear him whispering, 'Sweetheart, you came to meet me. Thank God, I was so scared.'

The other passengers, arriving on possibly more mundane business, openly gawped at the pair. 'That's the schoolmistress, that'll be her fellow, a Yank, you know, isn't it romantic?' The whispered commentary pursued them down the path into town.

Eleanor chattered brightly. 'We've booked you into the Regent, it's nice, a lovely garden. Shall we go straight there? You can get settled, then meet everyone, and have a look round the island…'

Her nervous outburst ended abruptly as Ray stopped and put his finger to her lips. 'Honey, hush. I got your letter, and I don't want to do anything but find a nice private place and have a good long talk. Okay?'

Eleanor relaxed. On this occasion, his typical American directness was what she needed. She leaned against him. 'That's fine with me. But finding a private spot could be tricky. I'm not sure you realise how small this island is, and you are possibly the only American soldier most people have seen. Let's go to the hotel, and I'll have a think about where we can have a quiet chat.'

Less than an hour later, they were seated in the garden at the Regent. There were no other guests, and the sun created dappled patterns from the shrubs surrounding their table. A beautiful display of Scilly flowers in tubs made it an idyllic setting for a romantic encounter. *Not such a great place to talk about the mechanics of sex. Or for saying goodbye, if it comes to that,* thought Eleanor as she poured the tea they had ordered, wishing it was something stronger. Ray reached into his canvas shoulder bag and pulled out a book, from which he extracted a letter. Eleanor could see it was the one she'd written from St. Martin's.

He cleared his throat. 'Now then, sweetheart, I hope we can be totally frank with each other now, just as you've been in your letter.' He looked up at her, the sun glinting on his spectacles so she couldn't judge his expression.

She responded briefly. 'Naturally. That's what I was hoping we would do.'

Ray relaxed back in his chair, easing his stiffened muscles. 'Whew, that's a relief. You know, my love, I completely understand your worries.' He ran his finger over lines from her letter. 'I bet no woman wants to be weighed down, made old before her time by too many pregnancies.'

Eleanor waited. A promising start; he wasn't dismissing her concerns.

'But of course, the Church teaches that God's purpose for sex in marriage is procreation, and any mechanical interference with that is a sin.' Eleanor's heart sank, but she kept listening. It was like being on the receiving end of one of Father Simmons's more awkward sessions, when she sensed that he just wanted to get through it without discussion.

Ray riffled through the pages of the book he held and

shook out a photograph. 'Take a good look,' he urged.

Eleanor scrutinised the photo, perhaps dating from the 1920s, judging by the fashions and haircuts on display. It looked like a family scene, with an assortment of adults and children lined in front of a splendid Model T Ford. A stern-faced grey-haired couple sat at the centre, and just behind stood what was unmistakably a young Ray, already wearing the wire-rimmed spectacles she knew well. As far as Eleanor could see, he was the only boy. And the only child wearing shoes, she noted with amusement.

She looked up from the picture to find Ray watching her intently. 'There's my Ma and Pa,' he said, pointing to a smiling younger couple, perhaps in their thirties. 'And there's me, aged twelve.'

Eleanor smiled. 'I'd worked that out.' She traced his face on the photo. 'I think you have the same spectacles and the same forehead.'

He grinned, pointing to three girls with identical bobbed hair, slim builds, but varying heights. 'And here's my sisters: Milly, aged ten, Dot, aged eight, and little Abigail, aged six.' His thumb stroked the photo of Abigail. 'Our little angel, didn't survive diphtheria the next winter.' He sighed. 'Anyway, what do you see?'

At first, Eleanor peered curiously. It was the first she had seen of his family. Then she realised what he wanted her to see. 'No babies,' she said. 'No children after Abigail. But you told me your parents were such devout Catholics.'

'They were,' said Ray. 'They still are.' With something like a flourish, he handed her the book he was holding. 'I've brought you something to put your mind at rest.'

Eleanor examined the ornate script on the cover: *The Rhythm of Sterility and Fertility in Women* by Dr. Leo J. Latz.

Baffled, Eleanor looked to Ray for an explanation.

He obliged, with enthusiasm. 'He's a Catholic doctor, and he's worked out a scientific way to limit the number of children without using contraception. He calls it "The Rhythm Method" because it goes with the body's natural rhythms.' Eleanor's expression changed to sceptical.

Ray persevered. 'It's a bit controversial for Catholics, you might not have heard of it. But take time to read through it, my darling. Basically, you will see that all we must do is refrain from, um, marital relations for eight particular days each month. We can keep to the teachings of my—that is our—faith *and* limit the size of our family. As I'm sure my parents have done.'

Eleanor held up the book. 'So, you just happened to have this with you?' she said, with a suspicious note in her voice. 'On active service?'

Ray was uncomfortable. 'In fact, a married buddy of mine let me have it. You won't believe this, but they were giving them away as prizes at his parish bingo night back home.' He paused. 'I guess he thought it might come in handy over here, so he brought it. None of my business why.' A wry smile was all he got from Eleanor in response. *Unlikely tale,* she thought.

Eleanor slowly put the slim volume into her handbag, conscious of Ray's gaze. 'I will read it, Ray. I've been so frightened; you can't begin to imagine.' He tried to interrupt, but she went on. 'You see, I felt torn apart. I couldn't bear the thought of losing you over this.'

He reached for her hand, but again she ignored him. 'But just the same, I couldn't live as I've seen so many women live. And then perhaps die of sheer exhaustion before my time. So, if this, this, *Rhythm Method* can save me from that…' Their eyes met; a spark of hope between them.

Eleanor had no personal knowledge of marital relations. However, like everyone in Britain, she had extensive experience of rationing. She had no worries about doing without for a greater good, and no doubts that she could abstain as Dr. Latz prescribed.

She reached for her cup. 'This tea's cold. Let's order another pot, then I will show you a little of Scilly.'

When they had finished the second pot and were awash with what Ray referred to as 'the Regent's finest beverage', Eleanor had an idea. 'Now we've cleared the air on this subject, would you like to meet Father Simmons? He's been so helpful.'

Ray was delighted at the prospect, so the next morning found them perched on the priest's Lilliputian schoolroom chairs, trying to balance cups of milky Camp Coffee, listening to Father Simmons's enthusiastic praise for Eleanor's efforts.

Addressing himself to Ray, he said, 'I really am quite satisfied, Lt. Miller, that Miss Barton has achieved a true understanding of the teachings of the Church, especially regarding the sacrament of marriage.'

Ray turned to beam at Eleanor. 'I am so proud of you, sweetheart, it can't have been easy.'

Eleanor squirmed, feeling like a star pupil at a school parents' evening. 'Well, Father, you've been such an excellent teacher. And really, I've quite enjoyed our discussions.'

The priest waved a deprecating hand, reached into his cassock, and drew out a cream vellum envelope. 'Here you are, this will confirm to the officiating priest at your wedding that you are ready to be received into the Church.' He hesitated. 'I do want to say that meeting you has been a real pleasure, and I wish you both all the joys that married life can bring.'

Ray stood, gently pulling Eleanor to her feet. 'Will you

give us your blessing, Father?' He bowed his head, and nudged Eleanor to do the same.

The priest made the Sign of the Cross, saying: 'May the Lord bless you and keep you. The Lord make his face to shine upon you and be gracious to you. The Lord turn his countenance towards you, and give you peace.'

'Amen,' murmured the two.

Hand-in-hand, they walked from the tiny chapel. Not a word passed between them. Eleanor's Anglican faith had formed a reassuring backdrop to daily life, but her approach to its expression had been merely dutiful. However, listening to the beautiful words of the blessing, she felt as if she had been drenched by warm, shimmering light. *How strange*, she thought, as she drifted to sleep that night.

Her mind at rest for the moment, Eleanor was free to enjoy a more relaxed few days wandering the beautiful back areas of St. Mary's in Ray's company. However, on the fourth day of his visit, everything changed.

They were finishing their evening meal of Spam fritters in the damask-bedecked dining room of the Regent, when Ray said, 'Hey, sweetheart, I'd really like to see the place where you work, meet your boss, maybe talk to the kids?'

Eleanor's brain went into overdrive, trying to think how she could head off this unwelcome prospect. 'I know what would be terrific, we could go to St Martin's, and you could see the school where I took over for a few weeks. People there are still fascinated with the U-Boat incident, how the American Liberator sunk the sub.'

A frown creased Ray's forehead. 'You know, I reckon I'd rather see where you really work, day to day. And I'm good with talking to kids, your dad said so.'

Eleanor realised it would be strange if she resisted further, but before she could speak, Ray said, 'Let's go talk to your boss first thing, tomorrow, before school starts. I've only got a couple more days, and it sure would mean a lot to me. Then I could imagine you in the place where you spend most of your time.'

Eleanor gave in to his pleading look. 'All right, Ray, we'll need to meet at the school at eight tomorrow morning, before the children arrive.' As she spoke, her anxiety rose at the image of Harvey and Ray meeting. She imagined Ray somehow knowing about her confused feelings, and the hurt in his eyes.

They approached Harvey's study early the next morning. His head was bent over papers. There was an empty chair beside his desk where Eleanor usually sat as they discussed plans for the day. Eleanor felt a wave of sadness and hastened to speak before her feelings showed. She cleared her throat and, when Harvey raised his head, blurted: 'Mr. Chalmers, I'd like you to meet my, that is, I'd like you to meet Lieutenant Ray Miller of the US Army, he's offered to talk to the children, I know you like them to hear about the experiences of serving soldiers…'

Harvey rose from his chair and interrupted her flow, extending his hand to Ray. 'Delighted to meet you, Lieutenant Miller, I hope you are enjoying your visit.' If he was disturbed by the unexpected visitors, he didn't show it.

Ray beamed. 'I sure am, it's a great little place, and I'm getting to see it with my beautiful girl at my side. Couldn't be better.' He turned his smile on Eleanor, but she was staring straight ahead.

There was a brief pause, broken by Harvey. 'Could you perhaps come in for afternoon assembly, about three? Nothing formal, maybe a few anecdotes, the children usually like to ask questions once they warm to you a bit.'

'It's a deal,' said Ray. 'And I want to say I really appreciate the chance to see where Eleanor works and meet all the folks who've taken such good care of her for me.' Ray didn't appear to see the tightening of the muscles around Harvey's mouth, but Eleanor did.

The talk was a success, with Ray's relaxed, folksy approach putting everyone at ease. He even managed to strike the right note with trickier questions.

'Sir,' said Simon, jumping out of his seat. 'My dad says the Yanks came over here when we'd done all the hard work, then made out they'd won the war for us. Is that right?'

Ray didn't bat an eye. 'Well, son, I'd say your dad's got a point. You Brits hung on and took the worst of it, we kind of came in near the end to help out.' Simon sat, satisfied this Yank, at least, wasn't a bighead like his dad always said they were. Despite her discomfort, and the secrets that weighed on her, Eleanor felt a swell of pride as she saw Harvey nod approvingly at Ray's reply.

As Eleanor and Ray left the school, Harvey was nowhere. Miss Elmore waved them on their way, saying as they left, 'It'll be good to see you back, Miss Barton.' Eleanor smiled, but her smile vanished a moment later as Miss Elmore continued, 'When I see you and Mr. Chalmers with your heads together in his study at the beginning and end of each day, well, I feel as if we're in good hands and all's right with the world.'

Eleanor and Ray walked away from Carn Friar's in silence for several minutes.

Then he turned and gazed steadily at her. 'So, you and the boss make a pretty good team, eh?'

Eleanor picked up a tone of accusation. She tried to sound relaxed. 'You could say so, we're on the same wavelength with the children, teaching methods and so on. And we've been working together on the garden.'

Silence again from Ray, then, 'Seems like a good guy. I did wonder why he wasn't in uniform, but I guess he's that bit older. Kinda reminds me of your dad.'

Eleanor slid him a glance, searching for malice. His face gave nothing away. *Best not to reply, he'll drop the subject soon enough.*

'Honey, tell me I don't have anything to worry about, you two working so close, things can happen…'

Eleanor took a deep breath, laid her head against his chest, and murmured, 'Absolutely not, Ray.' Through the sharp shards of afternoon sun, she could just pick out a figure looking through the window of the Head's study.

Leave or Stay?

Late spring 1945

May, then June, drifted by, and the euphoria of VE Day evaporated into a flat calm for Eleanor. The war in the Pacific continued, both distant and ever-present as the Crawfords tried to conceal their desperation at Clive's continued absence.

Eleanor's conversations with Harvey were cautious and stilted, no mention of Ray's visit, no questions about her plans.

'Oh Miss Barton, I'm glad I've caught you. There seem to have been several absences in the Infants lately. I wondered if you had spoken to any of the parents.'

Harvey's comment came as Eleanor was trying to avoid his approach, ducking into an empty classroom.

'Sorry, Mr. Chalmers, I thought I had made a note on the register. Chicken pox seems to be running rampant in a couple of the families. And then, of course, it spreads.' A brief nod was Harvey's response as he continued on his way.

There was not a word from Ray, just when she felt she needed it most.

As the school year inched to its close, Eleanor did her best to concentrate on final reports, outings, and nature walks with the children. There were even trips to the beach to experience the bracing chill of the Scilly seas. On one excursion, Eleanor was watching the children explore a series of rock pools when a shadow fell across the sand. Harvey was looking down at her.

He spoke softly, unlike the clipped tones she'd become

familiar with lately. 'Eleanor, could you stop by for a bit of supper later, about seven? Something I want to show you.'

She hugged her cardigan to her against the chilly sea breeze. 'Sounds…lovely.' She cleared her throat. 'I'm intrigued.'

Later, as the sky was blazing with evening colour, Harvey opened his front door and motioned her through. 'Fancy a sherry? Or maybe even a small whisky?'

Oh dear, am I going to need extra courage? 'Actually, a whisky would be a nice change, a drop of peppermint if you have it, please.' Harvey winced. She realised that, unlike her father, he probably regarded 'whisky pep' as an abomination. 'On second thought, just a splash of water would be fine.'

Harvey brought a tray with their drinks and a small plate of water biscuits. He placed her drink on it, and gave her a blue envelope, addressed to J. Harvey Chalmers, Esq. Unfamiliar handwriting, postmarked Hull, noted Eleanor. She glanced up, unsure what to do.

'Go on, open it. Please, read it.' He took a sip of his drink as he turned to lean on the carved oak mantelpiece. She could see him watching her in the mirror as she picked up her drink and read the letter to herself.

Dear Mr. Chalmers,

I hope you understand what a shock it was to get your letter. At first, I did not know what to think and I was upset. So many years have passed, I'm now married to Eric, a nice chap who works on the docks. However, I've thought about what you wrote, and I suppose I am glad to have something more to tell Frances about her father. I will do that when the time is right.

Please do not contact me again. Frances never knew her real dad, he only saw her once when she was a baby. My Eric has

brought her up like she was his own, and he wouldn't take kindly
to being reminded that she isn't.
    Yours faithfully,
    Emma Davis (Mrs.)

Eleanor sat for a minute, imagining a dignified woman, perhaps struggling to deal with the resurgence of past grief. She looked up and saw Harvey's reflected face, then to her dismay the glitter of tears gathering in the folds beneath his eyes.

Dropping the letter, she crossed the short distance between them and wrapped her arms around his shaking shoulders. 'Oh Harvey, surely you didn't expect her to dance with joy? Look at what she says, you've given her daughter a sort of gift, even if…'

Harvey broke out of her comforting circle so abruptly that she stumbled back. 'Are you so bloody naive, don't you have any idea how I feel?' Eleanor righted herself. Of course she did. He wasn't the only one caught up in an emotional battle.

He removed his spectacles and dragged his sleeve over his eyes. For a moment, he seemed young and vulnerable. 'It's not the letter,' he said more calmly, replacing his spectacles. Before she could respond, he went on. 'I was pleased, it was more than I expected. Sydney's at peace, and I'm at peace about him.'

His attempted smile died after a twitch. 'It's you, us, really. Because I think we have something like Emma with her husband. Or we could have had.' He shook his head.

Eleanor did not contradict him.

'Too late, eh?'

She sighed. 'I don't know. When I think about it, Ray and I hardly know each other. We were together a bit, then a long time apart, then occasional short visits. But somehow, a promise has come out of it.' Harvey lowered himself onto the huge old-fashioned sofa. Eleanor could hear the rustle and creak of horsehair as he shifted on the seat.

She tried to continue. 'And yet, you and I have shared so much. You are part of my life in a different way, and I just don't know what to do.' Her turn now for tears of frustration.

He patted the seat beside him, and she slumped into it. 'Like I said, too late now.'

Without thinking, she leaned against him, reaching to touch the pulse throbbing at his neck, normally covered by a shirt and tie. He turned from her. *Oh no, I've been too forward, he's disgusted.*

But then he carefully removed his spectacles and deposited them on the pastry-crust side table. Reaching towards her, he touched her skin above the opening of her everyday summer dress.

She sighed, and he smiled, slowly tracing his finger around the points of her collarbone and up the side of her neck. 'You know, if I was a medic, I'd say you were in need of attention, your pulse is racing.'

She caught his playful mood, and murmured, 'I'm quite well, thank you, but I'd feel even better if you would…' She hesitated, her voice dropping, 'Kiss me. Please.'

Everything Harvey did felt slow and loving. Deliberately, he brushed her lips with his, before gradually parting them and touching just the tip of his tongue to hers, then drawing back, looking steadily at her.

She looked around. 'I feel a bit strange, this is your sitting room, it doesn't seem right somehow.' *And I wouldn't be surprised if that antimacassar was crocheted by your mother, I can feel her presence, I'm sure I can.* She kept that thought to herself.

'Hmm, yes, I see what you mean.' Harvey slipped his arm around her back, pulling them both to their feet.

When he faltered, getting his balance, Eleanor said, 'Harvey, I'm so sorry, I don't know what I'm doing, at least I think I know what I want to do.'

He steadied himself. 'Well, so do I.' Then, hesitantly: 'But you must say if it's not right.' Leaving her, he walked towards a closed door leading off the hall opposite. 'Coming?' he asked, looking over his shoulder and holding out his hand.

Eleanor followed, taking his hand, feeling safe. They entered a room that couldn't have been more in contrast to the rich, dark colours and strong textures of the sitting room. An iron bedstead, covered by a tightly stretched dark wool blanket. One small table. One small chest of drawers. A flecked mirror over a washstand in the corner. No doubt whatsoever he'd been in the military.

Harvey hesitated, standing by the bed, watching her taking it all in. He spoke quietly, and there was no hint of coercion in his voice. 'It's anonymous, not too fancy, maybe that could suit us?' She nodded, conscious that her breathing was getting deeper.

Not trusting speech, she perched on the edge of the bed, and then he followed. They sat, facing each other. He circled her with his arms, pulling her down so they lay together. Eleanor thought, *this is what I've wanted to do, been thinking of, even in the staff room, but...*

She pushed him away and struggled upright. 'Harvey, I can't, I'm sorry, what if I...' She'd read enough of Dr. Latz's book to know that she wasn't at the right time in her cycle.

He understood. 'Eleanor, I hope you will be pleased to

hear I haven't exactly come, well, prepared for this situation, not expecting anything from you at all. I don't have any... protection with me, a sheath, y'know.' Eleanor winced, feeling the romance going out of the situation. 'So now I'm not sure what's going to happen. Blame the whisky, but here we are.'

Eleanor lay down again, leaning on her elbow. The bed gave off a squeak of protest. 'What a mess, I know there's names for the sort of girls who say yes then no. I don't want to be like that, but I've never...' *Hang on, I can't let him think it's a moral issue for me, or I don't want him. Be honest, Eleanor.* Her voice strengthened. 'The truth is, I'm so frightened of pregnancy.'

Harvey stroked her hair. 'No bother, I don't think of you as that sort.' Eleanor's skin flushed, despite the lack of a fire in the chilly room. 'My sweet girl, there are ways I can make you happy without...' He cleared his throat, his usual self-assurance deserting him. 'That is, I promise I will not put you at risk of pregnancy.'

As he spoke, he gently undid the top buttons of her dress, paused as if checking for protest, then when she merely moved her hips slightly, he used his other hand to lift her bottom and remove her underwear. He looked into her eyes, then when she gave him a trusting, unfocused smile and a whispered 'please', bent his head and began to kiss her, starting with her lips and moving slowly down her body.

Sometime later Eleanor rolled over and leaned out of the bed, feebly trying to retrieve her lace-trimmed underpants. These were the product of her mother's determination to 'Make do and Mend', and she wondered if in their former life as a fine pillowcase they had borne witness to many a similar encounter. She couldn't believe she had somehow lost them. *They must be here somewhere*, thought Eleanor, feeling the need to regain decorum.

Harvey was dozing next to her, but as her search became frantic, he opened his eyes and smiled at her. 'Looking for these?' he enquired, holding the ivory-coloured garment out to her.

She mumbled, 'Oh, sorry, thought you were asleep. I was feeling a bit chilly.' Her jittery hands were trying to do up her dress, and he covered them with his warm ones.

Harvey assisted her as she struggled to put herself right. 'I think you've missed out a buttonhole, let's try it this way.' A blush flooded her face as she thought of abandoning herself to his dexterous tongue and warm fingers, touching and entering parts of her she herself had never explored. But her embarrassment was quickly obscured by a hot pressure in her abdomen, as she recalled the sheer joy of her response. She couldn't hold back a smile.

Slowly, Harvey righted himself. He seemed to struggle slightly to move his left leg, with its prosthesis attached under his trousers. Eleanor hesitated, then half-lifted her hand. 'Shall I?' *Would he be offended by any offer of help?*

But he grinned. 'Guess it's my turn for a bit of assistance, thanks.' Eleanor helped him shift his leg into position, and then he stood, looking down at her. 'The usual thing when one is a bit chilled is a hot drink, what do you say?'

Eleanor knew she should be going, the chances of bumping into someone who knew her were increasing as pub closing time drew closer. But it seemed wrong to hop out of bed and head cheerily into the night, and she wanted more time. So it was that one of the most sensual experiences of her life ended with the two of them staring into a warm fire, drinking cocoa, quiet and comfortable.

Eleanor was lost in thought, seeking words for what had

happened. *So sexual pleasure exists only in the service of procreation, does it?* she mused, questioning the teachings she'd tried so earnestly to absorb. *Does this mean I'm not a virgin now? Have I been unfaithful to Ray? What does 'unfaithful' mean, how can I love two people? What about Harvey's needs, what does he think?* Struggling with confusion, Eleanor was unaware she'd leaned back with a sigh.

Harvey broke the silence. 'Nice domestic scene, eh? We make love, cup of cocoa, next thing we'll toddle off to bed, perhaps read a bit, then switch out the light.' Eleanor heard something approaching bitterness. She waited.

'But it's not real, is it?' He frowned. 'No, I'm wrong, it *is* real, for tonight, but…' he took her empty cup, kissed her lightly. 'Be off with you now, while the streets are still empty,' he said, his tone at odds with the stern words.

She knew he was right and, after returning his kiss, slipped into the warm darkness. She hurried back to Crawfords', knowing she faced an uncomfortable night, wrestling with her conscience.

The following morning, she left early to face an awkward encounter with Harvey. He must have seen her arrive, because he opened his door, smiled a greeting, and handed her a cup of tea. They sat next to each other at his desk. Just as usual.

Once the door was closed, she started to speak. 'Harvey, about yesterday…'

He shook his head. 'Please. Don't. I hope you know now that nothing would make me happier than a life with you, whether digging the garden, planning a school outing, or something more, as the mood took us.' He paused. Eleanor held her breath. *What's he saying? Does he mean marriage?*

Harvey ran his fingers through his hair, looking agitated.

As if he'd read her mind, he seemed to answer her silent questions. 'But at my time in life, I can't help thinking it might be too late to find out if I'm the marrying sort.'

Eleanor stayed silent, raising her eyes to fix him with a steady gaze. *So, he is thinking of marriage. But not with any great enthusiasm or certainty.* She waited, sensing he was becoming calmer, and concentrated on keeping her eyes locked on his.

He spoke slower, hesitantly. 'I really don't know what I could offer you, or how we could be together. Or even whether we could ever be as happy as we were last night.'

But it's not even as simple as that, thought Eleanor.

Again, he seemed to sense her silent response. 'I've really got no right to even ask, you've made a promise to Ray, and he seems a decent man. But if I don't speak, I'd always wonder: could we be together? And a part of me is desperately hoping you will take that chance.'

She paused, then said, 'I know what you mean, I understand, I do love you, but breaking my promise to Ray, I just can't imagine it.'

Harvey touched her hand. 'Enough. Whatever happens, whatever you decide... you've changed me. For the better. And you've changed my life.' He stood. 'Now finish your tea, the children will be here any minute, we don't need to say any more.'

Calmer Waters

April 1945

A misty Sunday dawned two weeks later, with more than a hint of warmth in the air. Eleanor stood on Porthcressa Beach and removed her heavy jumper. Then in hurried succession, off came her vest, shoes, socks, and trousers. She stood tall in her pre-War swimsuit, with its practical short legs, and tied her hair back with an elastic band. *Not a soul in sight. Perfect.* She had not forgotten the feeling she'd had after her freezing dip on St. Martin's. *Less than a minute in the sea and my body was fizzing, yet my mind was still. That's what I need now.*

She couldn't get Harvey's words out of her head. *"You've changed my life."* There was no resolution to her predicament, but she might find respite from her turbulence in the sea.

This time, she made a less timid entry and strode out until the gentle waves lapped her knees. She was forced to stop, doubled over with the pain of cold water, whimpering through clenched teeth. As before, the pain vanished, numbness set in, and she waded out to her waist. Now the worst of it. She remembered how, as a child, her chest and shoulders resisted the last plunge, which left her gasping. No point in gradual immersion; she sprang into the air and let her weight take her under. She squatted, submerged on the seabed. She bore it for as long as she could, then pushed herself up, turning to face the shore as she descended, toes just touching the sand beneath. She launched herself off the seabed and into a strong breaststroke.

It was like pushing through a silver and blue tunnel, her

surroundings fading with each stroke. She felt warmer, went faster, and was amazed when her knees grazed the sand and stones as she landed on the beach.

Laughing, she ran up the beach to the pile of discarded clothes. She pulled the band out of her hair, seized her towel, and dried herself vigorously. *Plenty of energy and a clear head, wonderful,* she thought, as she dressed.

Out of the corner of her eye, she saw a figure approach. *Oh well, couldn't expect to have it all to myself.* The person looked more familiar the closer he got. She abandoned her plan to get dressed under her towel. Too risky with an audience.

'Good morning, Eleanor.'

'Harvey! Well, what a surprise, isn't it a beautiful day? I've been wanting to swim, just waiting for it to be a bit warmer.' *Babbling, ridiculous.* She stopped.

He gestured to the towel clutched around her. She was starting to shiver. 'Look, get your dry clothes on. Quickly.'

A furtive look around showed Eleanor that they were alone on the beach. 'All right, all right, but hold onto this towel. Wind's getting up.'

'I'll turn the other way, just in case.' He gathered the towel around her neck, checking for openings, as brisk and impersonal as he would be with one of the children.

'It's silly, really, you've seen all of me.' She stopped. It wasn't about what they had done alone. She was sure there was something so casually intimate about this scene anyone coming onto the beach would be in no doubt about their relationship. Disappearing under the towel tent, she dressed with lightning speed.

'Something warm at my place?'

Eleanor was still glowing from the sea. And, she admitted to herself, from the touch of Harvey's fingers on the back of her neck as he held the towel. 'Harvey, I'm not sure that's a good idea.'

'We'll sit at my kitchen table, the only warming up will come from a coffee, we'll have a chat, and that's it.' When she did not reply, he continued, 'I have an idea and it is a good one. I'd like to know what you think.'

Eleanor sighed. 'All right, Harvey, I'm curious now. Go on, then, I'll follow you up in a few minutes.'

They were side by side at the table in Harvey's little scullery. Eleanor set herself to listen.

Harvey scratched his chin. 'You may have guessed that we didn't just meet by chance earlier.'

'Do you know, I didn't really think anything, you were just *there*, you know, part of the picture.' She tilted her head. 'It *was* a bit of a coincidence, come to think of it.'

'I was up early, saw you heading to the beach with your rucksack, thought to myself *What's she up to at this hour on a Sunday?* So I strolled after you, saw your alfresco disrobing, and do you know my first thought?'

'Harvey, I don't want to know, please don't make this even more complicated.'

He shook his head. 'No, it wasn't that. It was fear.'

That caught her by surprise. 'But why? The sea was calm, not much wind, I always walk out and swim back, where's the danger?'

'Sorry to sound like the bossiest lifeguard at the beach, but it's really dangerous to swim alone in the open water. Rip tides that can knock you off your feet even in the shallows, hidden rocks. Not to mention that great floating glob of nasties, the Portuguese Man o' War. We get those here, the tentacles can disable you with pain, no matter how strong you are.' He stopped, breathing hard.

Subdued, Eleanor realised his worry was genuine. 'So, what's your solution?'

'You may not be here for much longer, but how about we swim together a few times? You are looking at a former Army swimming instructor.' Eleanor smiled. Something else she didn't know about him. 'Do you know half those soldiers in the Great War couldn't swim a stroke? If they were on a troop carrier and it sank, they couldn't even make it to the lifeboats if they fell into the sea.'

'Well, you are full of surprises, Mr. Chalmers, but you may not have much time to work a miracle, what do you think you can do?'

'Glad you asked.' A smile. 'I was thinking while I was watching you. I could give you pointers on keeping on course. Maybe sort out that exhausting heads-up breaststroke you use.'

Eleanor felt slightly offended. She'd won medals at school with that stroke.

Harvey hastened to add, 'Nothing wrong with it as such, it'll get you over shorter distances just fine. But how about a nice relaxed front crawl? You'll go for miles.'

Eleanor rinsed her cup in the stone sink. *From Headmaster and junior teacher, to lovers, to… teacher and pupil? If I must leave it at that, it's not a bad place.*

'All right, Harvey. We will swim.'

Swimming Lesson

July 1945

'Meet you at Watermill Cove, six am tomorrow, bathers at the ready.'

Eleanor, deep in thought as she worked on the Infants' summer term reports, hadn't heard Harvey's approach. She turned. 'You're serious, then, I'm really going to have a swimming lesson?'

'Of course. If we are going to part, at least I will not be disturbed by images of you in trouble halfway across some deep American lake.' Harvey's smile as he spoke looked relaxed and cheerful.

'Well, all right, a swim would be nice. It's been so hot lately; I imagine the water will be warm.'

Was Harvey smirking at her? 'Dear Eleanor, we can't do this under false pretences. Scilly waters are *never* warm. Bring a flask.'

Eleanor laughed. 'I've been warned. And this time I've got proper swimming goggles, if you are going to insist on the front crawl.'

The next morning, they quickly undressed in the sunshine. The cove was deserted. Harvey detached his leg, leaned it against a rock, and used a carved stick to get to the edge of the sea. With one movement, he threw the stick backwards and plunged into the water. Popping up several yards out, he shouted, 'What are you waiting for?'

Eleanor was still hopping along the sand, one leg caught in her trousers. 'Give me a chance, I'm a bit stuck.'

She managed to free herself and dove straight into a wave.

They moved out to shoulder height, getting used to the cold. And then, enjoying the cold.

Harvey swam around her. 'Now let's see your front crawl.'

Eleanor set off. She knew what her problem was, and Harvey was about to find out. Head down, two, three, four strokes, kicking energetically and all was well. She could see shells, sea glass, and waving fronds of seaweed below, the underwater landscape sliced by shafts of sunlight. But then she had to breathe. As she raised her head out of the water, she took in a gulp of salty sea, choking and spluttering.

Harvey's steadying arm gave her a chance to right herself. She couldn't help laughing.

'Okay, Johnny Weissmuller, now you see the problem, what's your answer?'

'I'll keep it simple.'

Treating me like a clumsy child, she thought.

'Two things, Eleanor. When you try to breathe, you are rearing up like a sea serpent. Consequently, your bottom goes down and puts the brakes on.'

Eleanor held up her forearm, elbow down, fingertips up. 'You mean I'm like this?'

Harvey beamed. 'Exactly, well done.'

Prize pupil, me, thought Eleanor. 'What's the second pearl of wisdom then, Sir? I might as well try to put it together while I'm at it.'

Harvey, perhaps unsure of her tone, and unable to see her expression without his glasses, replied: 'Sorry, bit too much the schoolmaster. Perhaps I should add that your bottom did look rather nice as it drifted towards the ocean floor.'

'Why thank you, Sir, but let's stick to schoolmaster for now, it's less distracting.' *Light-hearted flirting. If Annie could see her shy sister now.*

'Schoolmaster, it is then.' Once again, they had achieved a relaxed banter. 'Look, Eleanor, I've seen you at rounders, you can hit the ball a mile. But watching you swim, well, how shall I put it?'

Eleanor paddled closer. 'Don't hold back, Harvey, I can take it.'

'Well, frankly, you're just flapping your arms through the water. Use those strong muscles to catch and pull against it.'

Eleanor tried. Elbow up, fingers down, grab and pull. Not easy whilst trying to keep her balance and breathe, but: 'Oh yes, it *does* feel different.'

Another broad smile from Harvey. 'That's it. Bonus is, you don't really need your legs, just kick a bit for balance, you won't get so tired.' He stroked through the water at a steady speed, then turned. 'That's why I'm so good at it,' he shouted back at her.

With Harvey watching, Eleanor's stroke moved from hopeless to semi-competent. However, her fingers were starting to wrinkle, and she was shivering despite trying to keep active, so they headed for shore.

Harvey pointed to his stick on the beach. 'Have you got enough strength to throw that back to me?'

'I'll use that upper body strength that you've been on about.'

Harvey grinned. 'That's a thank you for the free lesson, is it?'

'Really, Harvey, I am grateful. Front crawl's always been such hard work, now I'm beginning to feel like a mermaid.'

Arms around each other, they moved through the rock pools towards the pile of clothes. Eleanor stubbed her toe and toppled, taking Harvey with her. Thrusting out her hand, she caught herself on a rock at knee height. They managed to right themselves, but Eleanor became aware of stinging pains in her wrist and hand.

She stopped, gritting her teeth. 'Harvey, something's wrong, I can't see any jellyfish, but I think I've been stung.'

Finding a larger rock, he sat and gently cradled her arm. It was covered in spines, with blue-black dots surrounding each one.

'What is it, Harvey? Feels like the worst ever bee sting.' Eleanor considered herself tough, but this pain was something different.

Harvey pointed into the shallow water, at what looked like dark purple pincushions on the rocks. 'Sea urchins, they look pretty but they have nasty poison barbs. Let's get up on the beach, see what we can do.'

Back on the beach, they stripped off their wet clothes and wrapped themselves in warm dry blankets. Harvey looked at Eleanor's wrist. 'Still hurting?'

Biting her lip, she nodded.

He rubbed his chin. 'The usual treatment is a razor blade or plastic card to get the barbs off, and vinegar to neutralise the poison. Neither available, I'm afraid.'

Eleanor was trying to pluck out some barbs, one by one. A slow and ineffective process.

Harvey gave her a sideways look. 'There is another possibility, bit of an old wives' tale, but some on Scilly say it works a treat. We've got what we need right here. Or, rather, I do.'

Eleanor was in no mood for riddles. 'Spit it out, Harvey, anything that will cool this down, I can always go along to the clinic later.'

Harvey shrugged. 'Remember, you asked.'

Eleanor, absorbed in removing yet another spiny hook,

spoke sharply. 'If you can help me, please do, or you might just be in as much pain as I am.'

'Right.' He stood, looked around the empty beach, and dropped his trousers. 'Hold out your arm and look away.'

She hadn't expected the sight of Harvey's naked lower half. 'I don't need to look away. What on earth are you going to do?'

'Urinate on your arm. And if you are looking, well, it's hard for me to go when someone's watching.'

'Are you actually going to urinate on my arm?' Eleanor couldn't help herself; she was overcome by giggles. 'Can't you use one of our cups first?'

Harvey shook his head. 'It's only sterile if it comes straight out of the body.' He shrugged. 'Never mind, forget it, maybe it won't even help.' He bent to retrieve his trousers.

Distracted from her pain, still unable to stop laughing, Eleanor shook her head. 'No, no, even if it doesn't work, it's going to keep me laughing for a very long time.' She turned her head and felt warm liquid cascading over the stinging blue marks.

Hard Choices

Summer 1945

Weeks later, towards the end of July, Eleanor returned from an after-school meeting with Harvey.

He had suggested it. 'Miss Barton, I don't think we can put off end-of-term arrangements any longer.'

'Of course, Mr. Chalmers.' Eleanor sighed. Not that she was unwilling to look at immediate plans for the children, far from it. But the dual existence was getting her down. Stiff and formal in their behaviour if there was any chance others were near, relaxed and friendly when they were sure they were alone. Which wasn't often.

They left the door to Harvey's study open, an invitation to enter. Nothing to conceal. With what seemed like unspoken agreement, there wasn't even the slightest physical contact. The subject of the future hung in the air like mist, dampening their spirits, but not a word was said.

Finally, Harvey gathered the papers with the Infants' progress reports and plans for the next year. 'Thank you, Miss Barton, I think we can leave it there for today.'

'I'll be off then. Time enough to help Mrs. Crawford with the tea.'

Eleanor opened the door to Crawfords' to see a thick envelope with the familiar APO postmark. She trudged up the stairs to her room, opening the package as she went.

She drew out a letter in Ray's familiar writing and picked up the three sheets of blank forms that slid to the floor. She set these aside. Then, scanning the letter, the irreconcilable alternatives caught up with her.

Dearest Eleanor,

Would you be willing to get married as soon as things can be arranged? We aren't really gaining anything by waiting and those prejudices I had about getting married in uniform have disappeared.

Eleanor felt a wave of anxiety. *Too soon, too soon, I can't do this.* Ray's impatience and need leapt off the page, and she almost dreaded reading on. Certain phrases stood out as the picture of her life veering off course unfolded: *I've enclosed three army forms that you must fill out and have notarised. You must also write a letter to my Commanding Officer stating that you have agreed to marry me. I've included an example of this. The length of time we'd have together would be limited. One leave, or two at the most, would be all.*

The implications of this last statement sunk in. So, they would get married, probably on a short leave, then he would go back to France to his work there. And what would she do? And for how long would she be a bride, and yet not a bride?

Still another point to be considered is the effect that marriage would have on your job and your life as a whole. I can see that you enjoy teaching, and your life on Scilly seems very happy. Whether you would want to leave all that is something you know better than I do. But my darling, you might want to ask yourself if life on an island would start to seem just a bit closed in after a while? I know I was only there a short time, and I met some fine people. It's a beautiful place, but remember, there's a whole big country waiting for you that we can share.

Eleanor sensed that this was at the heart of his urgency. She suspected that with all the love and energy he could muster, he was pulling her away from Scilly, and from the 'threat' that he discerned during his visit: her closeness to Harvey.

His closing words made his strongest argument for haste:

Just remember, more than anything in the world I want to be your husband, and I can promise you all the love and devotion it is possible for a man to give to a woman.

So powerful, so straightforward. She thought about Harvey, his complicated past, his uncertainty about marriage, something she had always assumed would happen for her. Eleanor moved to her desk and wrote. At 3am she finally turned out the light.

Hours later, Eleanor woke in the summer dawn. She usually loved this time of year when the sky was glowing with colour. But not today. She took no joy in the pearly freshness as, gritty-eyed and groggy, she dressed quietly and let herself out of the house. With her, she took three envelopes. The first was slim and addressed simply to: Mr. Chalmers, Headmaster, Carn Friar's School. The second was thick with documents, soon to be on their way to Ray's APO address. And the third would go to Mr. and Mrs. Lawrence Barton, 'Agecroft', Westholme.

It was a still morning. Accompanied by a chorus of keening seabirds, Eleanor posted the first envelope through the slot in the door at Carn Friar's. Not wanting to go back to Crawfords', knowing Harvey would soon be opening her letter at the school, Eleanor kept walking. Away from Hugh Town and its early stirrings. The clatter of deliveries, the smell of fresh bread.

Eleanor followed the path around to Porthloo, breathing in the scent of the sea and the tarry smell of the boatyard.

Without a plan, she cut across the island, past Telegraph Tower, and rejoined the coast. Out of breath after a few miles, she stopped and looked around. There was a signpost to Innisidgen Carn. A chance to connect with ancient Scilly, as she had done on St. Martin's.

A scramble up the uneven surface of the hill, and she sat alone at the entrance to the upper burial chamber. She didn't consider herself fanciful, but once again experienced a blissful sense of her own insignificance and a connection with the lives of the ancient people in these tombs.

Clear-headed and calm, she looked down on Watermill Cove below. *Remote and sheltered,* she thought. *Unforgettable memories in the water.*

She was first in the Post Office queue at opening time.

As Eleanor waited in the Post Office, Harvey arrived at the school, intending to continue preparing for the next academic year. News of the increased attacks on Japanese cities had given hope that the war there would soon be over. There was a sense that preparations for a final push were underway. The coming year could be the first time since 1939 that Carn Friar's would be free of the ever-present shadow of conflict.

He unlocked the school door and took the post from its box. Among the usual official brown envelopes he saw a white one, no stamp. And that familiar writing. Hands shaking slightly, he opened it, read a few lines, then crumpled it into the bin. Seating himself, he pulled out the Headmaster's Log, in which he had faithfully recorded daily happenings at the school from the beginning of his time as Head. He began to write.

When Miss Elmore arrived a short time later, Harvey was not in the room, and the Logbook was open. Leaning over to check the latest news, she read:

Today Miss Barton has unexpectedly given her notice. She is getting married to an American and moving to the States. She leaves on the 1st September, so a new teacher will be needed for the Infants' Room.

Miss Elmore froze, bent over the desk. 'This will break his heart,' she whispered.

Back on the mainland a few days later, Lawrence Barton walked slowly home from school. As he'd explained to his daughter in an attempt to persuade her not to go to Scilly, he was finding it all tiring lately. He would have loved to retire, but for the shortage of teachers. Now he was ready for nothing more than a nice meal with his wife, and a quiet evening with the wireless. As he hung up his coat, he sniffed the air, noting the absence of the smell of cooking. Rationing was still in place, but Madeleine usually managed to work some sort of miracle. He'd been hoping for perhaps a juicy meatloaf, involving a tiny bit of beef and a large quantity of breadcrumbs, but still tasty and filling.

He popped his head around the door to the lounge to discover Madeleine sitting bolt upright and staring ahead. A letter slid from her lap and fell to the floor as she turned. Worse than the absence of food were her reddened eyes, and the crumpled handkerchief clutched in her hand.

Lawrence rushed to her side. 'What on earth's the matter? What's happened? Is it the girls?'

Madeleine spoke in a dull voice. 'She's really going, I never thought she would…'

Lawrence pulled up a chair beside her. 'Who's going? You mean Eleanor? Going to the States?' He picked up the letter and read it through. 'Sounds as if her mind is made up.'

Madeleine burst into tears again. 'But what if he doesn't

really love her, it's just one of those wartime flings?' Lawrence tried to speak, but she didn't listen and continued, 'Why can't they live here? He seemed happy here, seemed to like us...'

Lawrence tried again. 'Listen, old girl, she's a grown woman, we have to let her go.' His voice shook as he said the words, but he pulled himself together. 'She says she loves him, and she'll be his wife, so she'll go where he goes. And if we try to stop her, we may lose her anyway.'

Madeleine was quiet, then abruptly stood. 'At least she says she wants to get married here, wants you to give her away, so I suppose that's something.' With one last sniff, she strode towards the kitchen. 'I'd better get supper on, bring me some eggs, it'll just have to be an omelette tonight.' Lawrence's heart ached for her. They'd been married so many years, but he could count on one hand the number of times she'd shown her feelings like this.

As he went out to the hen house, he stopped first at the polished oak sideboard and took out a bottle. 'Fancy a sherry?'

'Don't mind if I do,' she replied.

Another week passed and, somewhere in France, the third of Eleanor's letters arrived to a warmer welcome. The statement she'd enclosed, using the formula required by his Commanding Officer, was what Ray had been praying for:

This is to inform you that 1st Lt. Ray Miller has asked me to marry him, and I have said yes. The reason for this is that I love him.

For the first time ever, the usually immaculate Ray presented himself to the CO with his tie askew and having forgotten to shave.

The spare, gaunt man behind the desk almost smiled as he

looked at the documentation, and then at the slightly dishevelled soldier in front of him.

'Permission granted, Lieutenant. I assume you wish to apply for leave at the earliest opportunity.'

No Turning Back

July 1945

Once the letters were sent, Eleanor's actions bound her ever more tightly to her decision. She booked a seat on the plane to Exeter. She told the Crawfords of her decision and endured the sadness in their tired faces. She wrote individual notes to each of the fifteen children in the Infants Class that she would never see again, illustrating them with little drawings of activities they had shared. She made sure her files were a complete record of each child's needs and progress, leaving as much information for the new Head of Infants as she could. She laundered her overalls and bandana, placing them on a shelf in the garden shed at the school. She hoped the new teacher would support the headmaster, even though the need to 'Dig for Victory' would no longer be the inspiration.

She saw little of Harvey, only catching a glimpse of him through a half-closed door at the school as she completed her work. Miss Elmore now sat with him where Eleanor had once enjoyed her morning tea, and both displayed a distant courtesy to the departing Eleanor. She felt no anticipation at her approaching wedding, but there was relief that she had resolved the dilemma and lessened her anguish as she left Harvey behind. *You can't have it both ways, my girl,* was her bracing admonition to herself whenever she wavered. It did help.

The Rain of Ruin

August 1945

The islands snoozed towards the middle of an exceptionally warm August, and Eleanor looked daily for a letter from Ray confirming their marriage plans. It seemed as if this suspended existence would never end, when news came of bombs dropped on two Japanese cities on the sixth and ninth of August. Over a hundred thousand, possibly more, Japanese civilians died in the space of days, and it looked as if their slaughter would lead to the abrupt end of the War in the Pacific.

VJ Day was declared on 15 August, but even on the remote Isles of Scilly, joyful relief was, for some, tempered by horror at gradually emerging details of this new weapon. Standing in the Crawfords' shop as the papers came in, Eleanor read the American press release, dated 12 August 1945:

The Japanese began the war from the air at Pearl Harbour. They have been repaid many fold. We have dropped an atomic bomb. It is a harnessing of the basic power of the universe. The force from which the sun draws its power has been loosed against those who brought war to the Far East.

A chill ran down Eleanor as she read. Exultant, vindictive words. Harnessing the power of the sun? What would be left of the world if these became the new weapons of war? But seeing the incandescent delight on the Crawfords' faces as they read a long-awaited letter from their son made her realise that they saw the poison from the bombs as a pure and simple blessing.

Sitting at the kitchen table, Audrey looked up and almost babbled, 'Miss Barton, Eleanor, he's coming home, the War is over, I can't believe it, look what he says…'

She thrust the letter at Eleanor, who tried to share her jubilation. *Dear Parents*, she read, then skimmed over the details, feeling she was intruding on the young man's private message. He had been due to be part of the landing and invasion force, to take Japan as Normandy had been taken months before. He went on to tell his parents that Lt. Paul Fussell in his Division had "said it for us all" in the Forces paper. Eleanor's eye was caught by Lt. Fussell's words:

When the bombs dropped and news began to circulate that the invasion would not, after all, take place, that we would not be obliged to run up the beaches near Tokyo assault-firing while being mortared and shelled… we cried with relief and joy. We were going to live. We were going to grow up to adulthood after all.

Moved, Eleanor passed the letter back to Audrey, touching the other woman's hand. Silent, deep in thought, she retreated to the sanctuary of the room above the shop. Photographs of Ray gazed at her from the dresser. But Harvey was the focus of her reflections. She imagined that he, along with many survivors of the Great War, might have felt an initial joy and wonderment at the chance they were given. The chance to grow up, grow old, and to live out their lives. But would these surviving soldiers, full of joy in this moment, suffer as Harvey and others suffered? Were many of them destined to be living casualties, still fighting for their own peace decades later?

In that instant, Eleanor made up her mind she would not leave the following week without saying goodbye to the person on St Mary's who meant the most to her. For once she was indifferent to public exposure and hurried through the bright evening sun to Harvey's cottage.

Time to Go

August 1945

At first there was no reply to her knock, and Eleanor had to endure anxious minutes. Her courage began to desert her in the face of curious passers-by. As she was about to scuttle back down the lane, the side gate creaked, and Harvey appeared. He was kitted out in Wellingtons, a much-darned jumper, and a pair of what looked like ancient twill trousers of an indeterminate colour.

'Sorry, I've been in the garden, everything's done well this year, can hardly keep on top of it.' When Eleanor didn't speak, he held out a basket. 'Some late beans any good to you?'

Eleanor had been building herself up for an emotional encounter, and this slightly ludicrous scenario broke the tension.

She peered into the basket. 'No thanks, but they look delicious, could I take some back for Audrey?'

He smiled. 'Of course, come inside, I'll parcel them up for you.' Eleanor waited while he removed his boots in the back scullery, then followed him into the kitchen. She watched in silence as he wrapped the beans in newspaper. He shot her a sideways glance. 'I'm guessing you haven't called in on the off chance that I'd have some spare veg.'

A nervous giggle from Eleanor. 'No, of course not, it's just that I'm leaving next Tuesday, and I wanted to say goodbye properly.'

Harvey crossed to the stone sink, washed and dried his hands, then turned to place both his hands on her shoulders. 'So do I,' he said, and arm's length turned into a tight embrace.

Her face muffled by his scratchy jumper, Eleanor whispered, 'Harvey.'

He held her more tightly. 'Yes, I'm all ears.'

She took a deep breath. 'You said I'd changed you for the better.'

'Absolutely. I would say that at the moment, I'm devastated you're leaving, but oddly content. I believe, truly believe, my life will be better in the future. Even without you, but because of you.'

Eleanor sighed. 'Well, yes, and that's what I wanted to say, it's the same for me. I never told you that, and I didn't want to lose the chance.' She lifted her head, kissed his cheek, and said, 'I'll go now. I won't say goodbye, maybe I'll see you at the school before I go?'

Harvey returned the kiss. 'Hmm, not sure I want to say empty words in front of others. But yes, maybe.' Eleanor reached for the door handle as tears welled, and just made it outside before they spilled over. She started down the path, only to turn as she heard the door open behind her. A ghost of a smile played across Harvey's face as he held out the package of beans.

Monday afternoon, she would be leaving the next day, and Eleanor walked down the path to Carn Friar's for the last time. The children were on holiday, but she would say goodbye to Miss Elmore, Mrs. Thorne, and possibly to Harvey. The two women met her at the door.

Miss Elmore spoke first. 'We're so sorry you're leaving, Miss Barton, you've become a part of the school in such a short time, and we will all miss you.' She handed Eleanor a package. 'Go on, open it.'

The flowered paper opened to show a book with a colourful yellow cover: *Cooking for Pleasure*, by Sylvia Littell.

The subtitle read *Delectable Meals in Spite of Shortages.*

Eleanor was touched. 'What a truly wonderful gift. Ray will certainly get the benefit of these delicious recipes.'

Mrs. Thorne beamed. 'We didn't know if they had rationing in the States, but anyway, this Sylvia says they are for better times ahead as well, so we thought it would do for your new home.'

Unable to speak, Eleanor hugged them both, and walked towards the door. She glanced into Harvey's study as she left, but it was empty.

Miss Elmore came up behind her. 'I'm afraid he's away for a few days, Miss Barton. Gone to visit a friend on the mainland. In Penzance, I believe.' She went to Harvey's desk and picked up a package. 'But he asked me to make sure you got this.'

Eleanor looked at her colleague. Was she imagining sympathy in the woman's eyes? 'Thank you… for everything. You've been such a help and support.'

Miss Elmore made a shooing motion. 'Go on now, let's not be sad. Happier times ahead for all of us, so they say.'

Outside the school, Eleanor almost ran to her favourite bench, near the edge of Porthcressa Beach. There were a few people enjoying the August sunshine, but the beach was otherwise deserted, and she could open her package away from prying eyes. Brown paper wrapping, how like him. Nothing fancy. But what a surprise under the utilitarian wrapping. Two watercolours, the first the view of Porthcressa from where she was sitting. The second had her laughing. A portrait taken from the snap she'd sent to her parents when she started working in the garden. A bandana more or less repressing the waves of her hair, a smudge of soil on one cheek, and a large onion in her hand. A note was half-hidden under the second painting. *Knitting is not my only hobby. With fondest love, H.*

The next afternoon, Eleanor retraced her journey on the Scillonian. She stood on the deck, only moving when the last glimpse of the Isles of Scilly had faded on the horizon.

Part Three:
Back on the Mainland

Married

Autumn 1945

Eleanor and her mother huddled under an umbrella in the drizzle outside the Church of St. Bernadette of Lourdes. Mother's face was impassive as she viewed the squat brick building, completed just before the war. A small round stained-glass window and a plain rooftop cross were the muted indications of its purpose. Eleanor's parents had been taken aback by the prospect of a Nuptial Service in Latin, but they were fond of Ray, and she guessed they were trying to be stoical about her imminent departure for the States. But Eleanor could tell that the sight of this building, hunkered toad-like between houses, was too much of a let-down for her High Anglican parent. Madeleine's idea of a Catholic Church ran more to the grandeur of Lancaster Cathedral in her own birthplace.

'Ray had a look last week as soon as he got here. He thought it was quite nice, you know, not too fussy,' her voice faded nervously. 'And in any case, it's the only Catholic Church for miles, and time is short.'

Silence from Mother as she digested this information. 'Well, we will have the signing of the register and reception at the house.' She eyed the modest proportions of St. Bernadette's. 'We can fit more in at home.'

Following this display of Northern fortitude, Mother cast off the languor that had stifled her during the war years and sprang into action on behalf of her daughter. She had been a stalwart of the village Women's Institute for years, and to her own stock of silk, parachute remnants, lace, ribbons, and buttons, added favours called in from friends with spare clothing coupons. Ray managed a few days' leave at the beginning of October, and St. Bernadette's was booked. Somewhat bemused friends and family were rounded up, and on the 13th October 1945, in the dim and clammy church, they were married. The experience was nothing like Eleanor's dreams of her wedding day.

For one, before the Nuptial Mass, she was baptised, standing by a stone font in the foyer of the draughty entrance to St. Bernadette's. The letter from Father Simmons testified to Eleanor's sincere conversion to the faith. He also wrote that, as she had been baptised in the Church of England, the Roman Catholic Church did not require further baptism.

This news, coming days before they married, brought a frown from Ray. He gazed at Father Simmons's letter. 'Sweetheart, I know he means well, and what he says is, strictly speaking, current ecclesiastical guidance.' He paused and cleared his throat. 'But darling, I feel strongly that a baptism into the Roman Catholic church is essential for your new life as my wife, and not to put it too strongly, for the benefit of your immortal soul.'

Eleanor was beginning to realise how important adherence to a strict interpretation of Catholic doctrine was to him and felt discomfort at his insistence. Her thoughts raced as she stood before him, trying not to show her dismay. *What would Ray think of what she'd done with Harvey? Was that sex outside marriage? Would he somehow know that she wasn't, strictly speaking, a virgin? Was she?*

A phone call to Annie helped, as always. 'Come on, lovely Eleanor, you are marrying a gorgeous man who adores you, and getting two sacraments for the price of one. Don't take it so seriously.'

Eleanor kept her doubts to herself and agreed to the baptism.

Eleanor did feel strange, standing in her bridal splendour renouncing Satan and all his works before entering the main body of the church. However, a beaming Ray stood beside her as her forehead, chest and shoulders were sprinkled with holy water from the font, making the shape of a cross.

The priest said the words, 'I baptise thee in the name of the Father, the Son and the Holy Spirit', and it was done in ten minutes. Such a small thing, she thought, to bring so much happiness to her nearly husband.

Eleanor proceeded, blinking, into the brighter light of the central aisle. The Baptismal party was met by a group of flustered friends who hadn't known about this prelude, and who squeezed past the bride, apologising for their late arrival, thinking they had missed the main event. Eleanor quickly soothed and explained, then turned to look towards the altar, spare and utilitarian even compared to the tiny Chapel on St. Mary's. And even with the late flowers tied to the pews by Annie.

Heavily pregnant, her sister had come down from Liverpool to, as she put it, 'waddle down the aisle behind you'. The shafts of autumn sunlight carried no warmth, and there was no feeling of the joy of the occasion emanating from the cold stones. Shuffling and swivel-headed stares emanated from the early arrivals. *Everyone's wondering what's keeping me, why Ray's at the back of the church, why they are excluded.* Eleanor experienced an anxiety that had nothing to do with the excitement of a bride. She hated muddle and confusion.

Once Ray executed a quick march to his place at the altar, and the small bridal group was assembled, Eleanor's spirits lifted. With her hand through her father's arm, Annie and

Mother behind her, and Ray standing ready in front of the altar, it once again became the happiest of days. Eleanor looked down at her dress and imagined how she must appear to the guests. And most especially to Ray, whose eyes were fixed on her from his place at the sacristy rail.

Her bridal outfit was beautiful. Flowing silk, a pearl headdress and lace train, and a bouquet of late chrysanthemums. She had decided to leave her wavy dark hair loose over her shoulders under the headdress, as it had been that night of Ray's clumsy proposal. The lace veil covered her face in preparation for the ceremony. Her mother had saved scraps of silk and fashioned them into the daintiest slippers. So dainty, they just about made it down the aisle and back before falling apart, but Eleanor didn't mind. For Ray it was easy: dress uniform and a big smile.

The church organist, a sturdy woman in a tweed suit, attacked Mendelssohn's 'Wedding March' with vigour and only a few wrong notes. Eleanor and Father led the way down the aisle, his warm hand clutching her icy fingers. At the rail, the exchange of vows proceeded in a blur. Ray practically sung his responses while Eleanor, normally able to project above the clamour of a rowdy class, only managed a faint 'I do.' The Latin nuptials caused consternation among friends and relatives. As the service went on, Eleanor became aware of their puzzlement.

'What's he saying, Gladys?'

'I don't know, love, *Dom and us* something?'

These murmurings received a stern look over his spectacles from the priest, and the congregation subsided.

Finally, they were pronounced man and wife. In English, to the relief of the mystified onlookers. Ray lifted her veil, placed his warm, full lips on her cold thin ones, and she felt safe.

'Jesu, Joy of Man's Desiring' floated them gently out of the church and into the bright autumn sunshine. The happy couple and guests crowded onto the pavement outside the church, teetering precariously as cars rumbled past. Mother took charge as the photographer rushed up to begin his task. He never even got his finger to the camera shutter.

'Absolutely not, Mr. Rogers. I'm not having anyone run over on my daughter's wedding day.' She raised her voice. 'Back to the house everyone. Photographs and sherry in the garden.'

Honeymoon

October 1945

Some hours later, Eleanor and Ray set off in a taxi. Warmed and relaxed by the local West Country cider, Eleanor smiled as she straightened the hem of her going-away dress. Not that she was going anywhere. Friends of her parents kept a farmhouse B&B just outside the village and had offered the use of their finest room as a honeymoon destination. The next day, Ray was heading back to France to help with the happy task of repatriating thousands of American soldiers following the end of hostilities in Europe and Japan.

Mrs. Hall, the farmer's wife, led them up several twisting flights of stairs to a cosy room under the eaves. *At least we won't have to worry about anyone listening,* thought Eleanor. Shortage of time and accommodation had meant that they would have been faced with spending their wedding night in her parents' spare room, a simply too embarrassing prospect.

Mrs. Hall flung open the door with a flourish. 'The lavatory's next door, and there's a bathroom at the bottom of the stairs, if you fancy a wash in the morning.' Eleanor and Ray nodded, eyes averted as Mrs. Hall made her point about hygiene. 'Anyway, I'll leave you to it.' And then she was gone, leaving the couple eying each other across a sea of eiderdown on the double bed.

Eleanor fished her bridal lingerie out of her suitcase and hesitated. Ray approached, tried to embrace and kiss her. Despite herself, Eleanor flinched, as unwelcome thoughts of Dr. Williams' prescription of 'relations' as a cure for her 'neurosis' intruded into the scene. As did even more unwelcome memories of the fire lit by Harvey's gentle touch.

'Sorry, I need a minute, I'm just a bit nervous, you see.'

Ray seemed to understand. 'I'll just pop out for a smoke.' He seized his pipe and made a hasty exit. Eleanor undressed rapidly, then, more slowly, put on a beautiful sea-green nightgown. She wrapped herself in what she believed was called a 'peignoir'. Both were fashioned of sleek satin, nineteen-thirties style, another gift from Mother's past. It was hard for Eleanor to imagine her prosaic mother floating around the bedroom in these, and she smiled.

At that point, there was a soft knock at the door and Ray came in. Eleanor had been studying herself in the dressing table mirror, hoping she wasn't overdressed. She didn't realise that Ray, stepping through the door, could see her endlessly reflected in the wardrobe and dressing table mirrors. To him, she must have been a kaleidoscope of beauty in the glow of the fire, and he stopped dead.

Eleanor looked at him, thinking he might be displeased at what she had to admit was a seductive ensemble. Or by her previous reaction to his approach. But then she saw anxiety in his eyes and realised they weren't so far apart, both in their love and their fear of what came next.

She took a deep breath and held out her arms. 'Would you care to kiss the new Mrs. Miller?'

The tension went out of his shoulders, and he attempted to swing his legs over the bed in what he may have thought was an athletic and cavalier move. However, he misjudged the width, and just saved himself plunging to the floor on the other side by flinging his arms around her and pulling her onto the bed with him.

Half-stifled laughter turned to murmuring and touching as they felt the whole length of their bodies meet for the first time. Zips, buttons, and even sturdy hook-and-eye fastenings suffered as they made up for inexperience with enthusiasm and passion.

Eleanor had a fleeting, unwelcome thought that this wasn't like her experience with Harvey. But it didn't have to be, and afterwards she was exhausted and happy. They fell asleep with the bedclothes twisted and some of the discarded sea-green gown covering their legs.

The sun was shimmering through the window when she woke to see Ray observing her closely, with what seemed like a quizzical look.

She stretched and murmured, 'How long have you been watching me?'

No response to her question, but he said, 'Sweetheart, you sure are a surprise package.'

Wide awake now, Eleanor sat up, the sun reflecting off her breasts as the covers slid down.

'Is that a good thing?' She wasn't sure what he was trying to say. She thought he averted his eyes from her breasts, as if they shouldn't be revealed in the bright light of day.

'Oh yes, yes, it is, I just wasn't expecting you to respond the way you did, you really let yourself go.' Giving himself a shake, he reached for her, saying, 'You know, I haven't had a whole lot of experience, but I didn't think girls, well women, enjoyed the physical side so much.'

Eleanor put her head on his shoulder. 'Ray, I enjoy making you happy, it seems so natural.'

A big grin spread across his face. 'Well then, I guess I'm just a lucky guy.'

Marking Time

October - January 1945

Ray went back to France and Eleanor went nowhere. The ensuing weeks dragged painfully. Bored and restless, she wrote to Ray:

Dearest Ray,

(I want to write 'Dear Husband' but is that a bit old fashioned?)

I imagine your days are flying past, there must be so many details to attend to in repatriating thousands of soldiers, what a useful, satisfying task for you.

I guess they are all deliriously happy to be going home. I so envy them the bustle of departure.

However, Ray's reply some days later brought home to her that the reality was much more complicated.

My dear wife (Personally I like the sound of that!)

Darling, I know you are probably thinking we are all de-mob happy over here, but I must tell you there's another side to my job just now. To tell the truth, it's getting me down a bit.

You are right in a way, many of the guys are just plain crazy with joy, they've survived the war and can't wait to get home and get on with living.

But it's not always that simple, there's a whole lot of mixed feelings as well, and it's these others that keep me awake at night.

Like for instance, part of my job is commissioning hospital ships for the wounded. I watch the ships load up, and you know,

*I don't think some of them will ever get over their wounds,
including the ones you can't see. It makes me so sad.*

*And sometimes, guys with wives and sweethearts back home
come and talk to me, I guess because they think I will understand.
Maybe they haven't had a letter in a while, or maybe they are just
feeling scared of losing their girls (like I was after the visit to
Scilly). And they know—or suspect—that there's nothing left of
what they had before.*

*And what I find the hardest, is the fellows who've maybe got
too close to other soldiers, if you know what I mean (maybe you
don't). It's something we all turned a blind eye to, kind of under
the cloak of war. We've all been in the fight together, and they are
just as brave—or cowardly—as all the other men. The worst is
when their special pal gets killed. If anything had happened to
you, God forbid, I'd go nuts with grief, and everyone would know
about it and try to support me. But what about if a soldier's
sweetheart is another guy? Can you show your grief? Are you
going to get any sympathy? I don't think so. It's funny, the Church
tells me it's an abomination, but seems this is one teaching I'm not
so sure about.*

*Anyway, sweetheart, sorry to unload on you like this, but it
feels good to be able to share things. Which is what we will always
do, right?*

Sleep tight, darling, till we meet again.

Love, Ray

Eleanor returned this letter to its envelope, chastened by
thoughts of what others were suffering, and what a tough job
Ray had. She only had to be patient; she decided she could
manage that.

She threw herself into preparations for her last Christmas
with her family for some time. Rationing was still with them,

but Eleanor had been a primary school teacher for six years. She filled the house with homemade decorations from the end of November, despite her parents' protests that it was too early. She persevered, and her infectious enthusiasm caught hold of them all. Especially Mother who, unable to resist a creative opportunity, re-entered the kitchen for the first time since the beginning of the war. Acquiring sugar for cakes and biscuits was the biggest problem, but carrots and parsnips did the job just as well, Mother insisted. A scientist in a laboratory couldn't have achieved more than the alchemy produced by her efforts.

So, pulling together, the family assembled a semblance of a cosy, happy Christmas. In many ways it was a subdued celebration of the end of the war. The delirious joy of VE Day and VJ Day had faded, and for many people Christmas was tinged by feelings of regret at the loss and devastation endured, and relief it was over. Eleanor was haunted by memories of that Christmas on Scilly, the soft cashmere scarf, and the affectionate look in Harvey's eyes as she opened his gift. These images hung around the edges of her dreams, insubstantial ghosts she couldn't quite banish. She told herself that her current state of marriage seemed equally dreamlike, and that once she was back with Ray everything would fall into place.

Part Four:
Leaving and Arriving

This is it

January 1946

Finally, in the bleak early days of January, a letter came from the US Army Area Transport Office. Eleanor nearly obliterated the crucial instructions as she tore through the envelope and flung herself into a chair to read:

Dear Madam:

ARRANGEMENTS ARE NOW COMPLETE FOR YOUR PASSAGE TO THE UNITED STATES. IT IS VITAL THAT YOU FOLLOW THE INSTRUCTIONS EXPLICITLY. YOUR FAILURE TO ARRIVE AT THE DESIGNATED POINTS ON TIME MAY FORFEIT YOUR EARLY PASSAGE.

Movement in the UK

TRAIN TRAVEL: *Enclosed you will find a railway warrant covering your fare from your present home from LONDON WATERLOO to ANDOVER, SALISBURY, and on to TIDWORTH. You will report with all baggage to the London Reception Area at Waterloo Station on JANUARY 25, 1946, at 9:00AM. You will be met by US Army Transportation Corps Railway Traffic Officers who will assist you and arrange for your further movement.*

Humph, bossy and officious. All those uppercase letters, thought Eleanor, feeling more like a freight shipment than a cherished bride. It reminded her of the letters sent for the movement of evacuees at the beginning of the war. Terse, official, reducing the drama of parting and going into the unknown to clipped commands.

Undaunted, she set about filling the two large trunks allocated to each traveller. Her bedroom floor was soon knee-deep in items packed (warm underwear, Ray said it was perishingly cold on the farm), then removed (some woolly underwear replaced by her bridal lingerie, after all, they *were* newlyweds), then piled up as 'maybe' (would there be any use for summer frocks?). Finally, the job was done. The short notice meant there was mercifully little time for tears, final goodbyes, or regrets.

On the 25th of January 1946 Eleanor, with scores of other GI Brides, hung out of the train window and watched her parents and Annie fade into stick figures on the platform. Annie held her new baby, Elsa. As sad as Eleanor felt at leaving her sister and parents, the thought of missing her niece's early years pierced her heart. Unlike the older members of her family, the little girl would have no memory of her. She turned from the window and pushed her way through the excited throng to a corner seat.

The train chuffed out of London, heading for Tidworth Army Camp. The women had been told that it had been 'suitably repurposed' as a holding camp for the brides and their children, prior to embarkation on their transatlantic voyage. Good food, comfortable beds, hair salons and entertainment were promised.

'It's going to be like a holiday camp,' the woman sitting next to Eleanor squeaked, and although Eleanor thought *'Army camp? Suitably repurposed? We'll see,'* she couldn't resist the uncontrollable excitement that crackled through the train. She managed a smile in return.

Tidworth Camp, Salisbury Plain

January 1946

In the empty theatre, the moth-eaten velvet curtain jerked slowly upwards. A lone man sat at a table on the bright stage. White coat over his olive army uniform, stethoscope around his neck, a clipboard and a small torch held upright completed the props. His form was silhouetted and magnified against the backdrop, the stark light of the spots giving it an air of menace.

In the wings what could have been a clutch of chorus girls pressed together and awaited their entrance. Ranging in age from sixteen to thirty, naked under identical bathrobes with 'Property of US Army Tidworth' stencilled on the back.

'Well, I suppose I am their property now,' giggled Marjorie, just eighteen and nervous. 'I've got the ring to prove it.' Eleanor felt a surge of compassion. Marjorie was not much more than a child and had regaled the older brides on the train journey with tales of her 'swell' husband, who had swept her off her feet when they met at a canteen in London. Apparently he was loaded, and Marjorie would have a maid to look after her. *I wonder,* thought Eleanor. *Poor girl, how will she cope if he's been stringing her a line?*

Two Red Cross nurses were attempting to herd them into a queue, with limited success. In exasperation, one barked, 'You want to be on that ship next week, right?' Nods from the women. 'Well, you have to have a medical, and this is it. Now, who's first?'

A brief silence, then Eleanor stepped forward. This was a stage, so she would use her extensive experience of Miss

Holcombe's drama class to play the part of a teenager stepping into the communal showers, faking bravado to hide her shyness and get through the ordeal. She strode to the table, chin up, waiting until the doctor raised his head and met her eyes.

'Name, please.'

'Eleanor Mary Miller.' A mark on the clipboard.

'Open your robe, please, and step your feet apart.'

Eleanor remained unflinching while the torch probed under her arms and shone between her legs. It was less physically intrusive than Dr. Williams' probing, although just as humiliating. She could have done without the audience.

'Thank you, that's all.'

She forced her shaking knees to carry her into the wings on the other side of the stage, where clothes were piled in a row. She retrieved her soft cotton dress, lovingly made by her sister. Annie had used her own coupons to make sure Eleanor had 'something nice to travel in'.

That was the medical. The rest of the women, watching Eleanor, turned to each other in disbelief.

'What is he looking for?' said Marjorie.

'Sores,' said one woman.

'Crabs,' said another.

None the wiser, Marjorie took her turn. As she stood straddling the worn floorboards, the doctor motioned to the Red Cross nurse. A whispered conversation and Marjorie, crying and protesting, was led towards one of the cast dressing rooms.

Silenced, the rest of the women strode the stage in turn, and then dressed, relief showing on their faces. As the group left the theatre, they filed past a notice board.

TIDWORTH THEATRE FILM NIGHT
THURSDAY 8PM
MAIN FEATURE:'FANNY BY GASLIGHT'

They stared. Then, one by one, doubled over, faces running with tears of uncontrollable laughter.

When they boarded the Queen Mary the following Thursday, Marjorie was nowhere to be seen.

At Sea

February 1946

As the Queen Mary pitched, Eleanor danced upwards, her toes barely touching the steps. She raced up the staircase, her hand skimming the banister. She was trying to climb as far as possible, whilst zero gravity gave her the flight of a bird. She didn't quite make it to the top before the gargantuan ship plunged into another trough and her feet were nailed to the stairs. Just short of the top of the flight, the effort to lift a foot was too much. She waited. On the next lift, she scampered up to the main deck corridor and grabbed a rope criss-crossing what had been an open space.

After fifteen minutes of trying to traverse the heaving lounge, Eleanor reached the nearly deserted dining room and fell into a seat. Barely a day out of Southampton, the Queen Mary had been struck by a fierce February storm. The decks were off limits, and most of the women too overwhelmed by seasickness to care. Eleanor was one of the unaffected few, and she was starving, desperate for breakfast. She was also determined to bring dry toast to her cabin-mates, ignoring their protests that they were dying anyway and would never eat again.

The menu was limited; hot drinks were off, and juice came in a closed beaker with a straw. The tables and chairs were secured to the floor, and the steward was forced to execute a skilful slalom to deposit a plate of bacon, eggs, and tomatoes in front of a grateful Eleanor. She managed to finish the meal without any of its components becoming airborne, and sat back, sipping her juice and longing for a cup of tea.

There was little to see through the dining room windows. A gale-force wind blew horizontal snow into the face of the lumbering ship. The steward cleared her plate.

'Aren't you the lucky one, got your sea legs already,' he said.

Eleanor forced a smile. 'Yes, I do seem to have a strong stomach. Could I have some dry toast for the girls in my cabin? They might fancy something later.'

As soon as the steward left, her smile faded. She didn't feel lucky. Her optimism survived the humiliation and inconvenience of Tidworth but vanished on the last day there. The delivery of the final letter packets before sailing had turned her excitement to dust. Hers contained loving letters from Ray, as well as messages from her family, friends, and former colleagues. As she sat on her bed in the barracks, she heard the chatter; the letters received not only from sweethearts, but future in-laws, welcoming the new arrivals.

She had seen the letter Ray wrote to his family, describing her in glowing terms, and letting them know how happy he was. She, in turn, had written to his mother, telling her of the joy in their marriage and how much she was looking forward to being part of Ray's family. However, in the five months since their marriage, there had been nothing from any of them. And in these final packets, still not a single word.

On that cold February night, she had to face an uncertain future. And then she thought of her own parents who, despite their hurt and anger, had rallied to make her wedding joyful and her departure upbeat. But she knew that they would never get over what she had done.

Sleepless in the hours before she left, she overheard the rarest of sounds: her mother's quiet sobs, her father's harsh tones. 'What *is* she thinking? Selfish, through and through, she'll regret it. But it's too late.'

The sobbing diminished, then a whisper, 'We've lost her, Lawrence. We'll never see her again.'

That night, sleepless again on the stormy Atlantic, she switched on the tiny light by her bunk, twisting it so she wouldn't disturb the others. She rested a pen and paper on her knees, and wrote:

My dear Mother and Father,

As I leave England, I want to try and express my gratitude for all you have done for me. I have you to thank for who I am, and Ray would never have married me if I hadn't been who I am. I also want to say sorry for all the trouble I have caused, all the unhappiness I have given, and I can only hope that you will one day forgive me. Please don't worry about me, you know that I am in safe hands.

Lots of love, Eleanor

She posted the letter from New York. Once she was settled, her parents wrote regularly, but they never referred to that first letter they received from her as she sailed away from them. She was never sure of their forgiveness.

New York

February 1946

As the Queen Mary battled through the stormy voyage towards New York, the image of Ray throwing his arms around her as she disembarked remained, keeping the fear away. One huge bear hug, and her doubts about meeting her new family and leaving her old one would vanish.

She was full of hope as, presumably for the last time, she was 'processed' by US officials. In briefings on board, the women had been told that this would be 'a breeze'. Swamped by the tide of more than 70,000 war brides, the US Congress had hastily passed legislation slicing away most of the usual red tape that strangled would-be immigrants. No Ellis Island for these girls, they would not be crammed for months in miserable accommodation, stateless and forlorn. Instead, Eleanor had only to present her paperwork to a stone-faced official. She matched his impassive demeanour, as one by one, she handed him the documents declaring she was legally married to Ray, free of syphilis, gonorrhoea, and lice, and not a member of any subversive organisation. As she did so, Eleanor could see a barrier out of the corner of her eye, behind which were hundreds of young men, waving and calling. Some had brought banners, 'I love you, Beryl', or 'Welcome to the USA'. Eleanor smiled. Ray was in there somewhere.

She turned from the table to the happy crowd, scanning the faces for her tall, bespectacled husband. They were all in civvies now, which should have made it easier, but Eleanor couldn't pick him out. Would he wear something bright, to help her? Or a heavy coat, to cope with the winter cold? Would he have got out his best suit, maybe with a flower in the buttonhole?

One by one, the other brides flew into welcoming embraces, many swept off their feet and spun around as they did so. Still no sign of Ray, and the fear that she had been suppressing started to overwhelm her. Wild suppositions took root in her brain. *His parents have convinced him it's a mistake, he thought I was too bold on our wedding night, he's met someone else.* Giving herself a shake, she headed towards a table where some official-looking types seemed to be dealing with queries.

However, as Eleanor turned towards the Information desk, a Red Cross worker holding a file touched her arm. 'It's Mrs. Miller, is it?' She looked down at a sheet in her file. 'You look just like your photograph, thank goodness. Follow me.' Too bemused to speak, Eleanor trailed meekly after the woman to an area away from the main group. Pale and tired, the war brides whose husbands hadn't come to meet them stood huddled in the vast warehouse of Pier 47. A sad little gathering. To her shock, Eleanor realised she was one of them. Once there, her Red Cross guide gave her a letter with Ray's writing on the envelope. The room swam. She had been up at dawn to see the Statue of Liberty, too nervous and excited to eat and, after standing in the immigration queue for over an hour, and searching frantically for Ray, this was the last straw.

She collapsed onto a bench and the Red Cross lady handed her a glass of water.

'Shall I open the letter for you, dear?'

Eleanor nodded, her hands shaking as she passed the envelope back. 'Read it,' she whispered. 'Then tell me what he says.' The woman, whose badge identified her as Miss Johnson, drew her spectacles from her satchel and started to read to herself.

After a few minutes, she looked up at Eleanor, smiling. 'It's all right, he's meeting you in Chicago.'

'Chicago?' It didn't make sense. 'How will I get there? It's miles away, isn't it?'

Miss Johnson scanned the page again. 'He says there's going to be a special train leaving from Grand Central Station this evening. Because of the possible crowds, the Army told every man who had to come more than a thousand miles to meet the train at Chicago instead of New York. Oh, and he also says he can't wait to see you and…' Blushing, she handed the letter back to Eleanor. 'You better read the rest of it.'

Eleanor took the letter and blushed herself. Something about the matching curves of her bottom and breast. Hastily, she tucked these reassuring words into her bag to read later and squared her shoulders in preparation for yet another journey.

The 'GI Brides' Special'

February 1946

Coaches for the transfer to the train station rolled up, the women were reunited with their luggage, and everyone crowded on. Relief at not having been abandoned generated a certain camaraderie, and the atmosphere as they crawled through the busy streets was not unlike a village day out. For most brides, it was astonishing to see a city with buildings intact and shops apparently full of goods.

The driver must have caught a bit of their village outing spirit, because his voice crackled over the intercom, 'Welcome to the US of A, all you gorgeous girls!'

Suppressed giggles rippled through the coach. They hadn't felt gorgeous a short while ago, but now hats were adjusted and hair patted into place.

'Your train won't leave until tonight, so Driver Ed, that's me by the way, is going to give you a once-in-a-lifetime special deal. Your very own tour of the Big Apple like nobody's ever seen it before!'

With these cheering words, the slightly ramshackle old bus veered off the direct route to Grand Central Station and headed through the streets of the city. It was warmer than Eleanor had expected for February in New York, so she forced open the little half window by her seat. She was able to smell and almost taste the coffee coming out of what seemed like hundreds of cafés. She breathed in the scent like a drug. Real coffee, mixed with the aroma of fine cigars.

Then, as they headed down Broadway, came the billboards and the music. Billboards flashing 'Showing Now', with the show tunes blaring from loudspeakers between the theatres. Eleanor would never forget that The Majestic Theatre featured the hit musical *Carousel*, and her heart swelled to the strains of 'You'll Never Walk Alone' until the coach moved on and the music was lost in the winter air.

'Now it's getting late, but you ladies aren't gonna leave without seeing Coney Island, the biggest funfair in the whole country!' Ed was back again, and he was right about Coney Island. 'See that roller coaster over there?'

Forty heads craned out of the windows and gasped at the size of the Cyclone roller coaster, its twisting metal silhouetted against the sky. They could see the cars speeding at an unbelievable sixty miles an hour (according to Ed), up and down and around the loops. They could hear the screaming riders defying death and loving it. The sickly burnt smell of cotton candy and caramel popcorn from the stalls filled their nostrils.

The red winter sunset crept in as the coach crawled back from the beach area, back toward streets of shops shutting for the day, and apartment buildings lighting up as workers arrived home. Sensing that they were leaving the magic behind, Eleanor settled back in her seat.

But Ed wasn't finished. 'Okay, you brides, don't get too comfy, 'cause Ed's got one more trick up his sleeve. You don't know it, but we are heading down Mermaid Avenue. Like the man said, "There ain't no mermaids on Mermaid Avenue", but if we're lucky, you'll see somethin' even better.'

Quizzical glances all round, but Ed hadn't let them down yet, so everyone perked up and peered into the fading light. The coach slowed to a rolling stop outside a nondescript terraced house. Next door was a poultry shop, and Eleanor saw by the Star of David on its sign that it sold kosher chickens and other produce. Some of its wares hung naked by their feet in the windows, while eggs, oranges, pineapples, and other almost-forgotten delights spread to the steps of the attached brick house. Eleanor inhaled the faint traces of dead chicken mixed with slightly rotting citrus: it wasn't as unpleasant as she would have thought. A shoeshine boy sat on his stool, seemingly expecting trade, and a few children milled around.

Ed was speaking again. 'This here's what we call a row house, and the fella who lives here usually comes about now for a shine. *That's* what we're waitin' for.'

As Ed spoke, the door opened, and a skinny fellow carrying a guitar jogged down the steps to the street. He wore a sheepskin jacket, black lace-ups and had a black cap perched well back on his dark curls. Eleanor's eyes were drawn to that cap. Leather, she thought, with a short visor and a red leather star stitched to the side. A flashback to her history books: The Russian Revolution? Lenin? Could be, but what was it doing on the head of this Coney Island troubadour?

Anyway, the mystery man sat, stuck his foot out and passed over twenty-five cents for a shine. Then he started to strum and his nasal, compelling voice took over:

'This land is your land, this land is my land
From California, to the New York island
From the redwood forests, to the Gulf Stream waters
This land was made for you and me.'

Toes were tapping and fingers snapping in the crowd around the singer, who shifted and stuck the other foot out.

'As I went walking that ribbon of highway

And saw above me that endless skyway
And saw below me that golden valley
This land was made for you and me.'

Eleanor felt a wave of emotion swelling in her chest. This really *was* her land now, she *did* belong, and a life of promise was replacing the deprivation and fear of the war years.

They were causing a traffic jam by now, so Ed slowly pulled the coach into the main line of cars heading back into the city. Eleanor just heard the last verse:

'One bright sunny morning in the shadow of the steeple
By the Relief Office I saw my people
As they stood hungry, I stood there wondering if
This land was made for you and me.'

Every tiny muscle around every hair on Eleanor's arms tightened and tingled. She wasn't sure what he had said, or who he was, but there was something dark and deep in the catchy tune and angry words.

Ed helped them out. 'They don't let him sing that last bit in the shows. Some folks call him a Commie agitator, but we know what he really is. He's for the working man, always will be, and you girls can tell your children and grandchildren you heard Woody Guthrie sing his true song.'

Silent, thoughtful, or asleep for the next hour, the women stirred as the coach crept down 42nd Street and stopped outside what looked more like a temple than a train station. As the group was herded into the colossal building, the first thing they saw was an enormous floodlit mural encouraging the public to buy war bonds 'That we may defend the land we love'. A lump rose in Eleanor's throat. The danger had now passed, but she couldn't help thinking of what might have been if the war had turned out differently.

Miss Johnson turned her charges over to a station guard, who led them to a platform labelled '20th Century Limited: GI Brides' Special'.

The guard turned to them, raising his arms like a ringmaster, and said, 'Smile, ladies, you've got exclusive use of The World's Greatest Train, and in sixteen hours you'll be stepping down in the fabulous Windy City!'

Shuffling feet and sideways glances greeted his announcement. Then Eleanor recalled Miss Grantham's seminars on 'Cultural Integration' aboard the Queen Mary and spoke up, 'Remember what they told us on the Queen Mary,' she whispered, not wanting to offend the guard. 'In America everything is biggest, best, and most beautiful, and people won't hesitate to tell you so. What sounds to us like unseemly bragging is simply unbridled enthusiasm and confidence. Let's show him we're keen.' Eleanor nudged the girls on either side of her, and their hesitant clapping soon spread to through the group.

With a flourish, the guard directed them to the platform gate, where the 20th Century Limited was waiting, towering over them and burping steam as she waited for her passengers. Eleanor had travelled on many trains, but she'd never seen anything like this one. Made of brushed aluminium, the raised bullet-shaped nose with a central headlamp and the sweep of skirting below gave the train the look of a fantasy robot. Despite herself, Eleanor broke into a run, and she was first up the stairs and onto the train.

Part Five:
Together Again

Rolling Stone Farm

1946

Eleanor slept through the night, lulled by the music of the wheels on tracks. She opened her eyes in the grey dawn, a sharp pain in her neck preventing her from lifting her head. Out of the corner of one eye, she could see a wet patch on her friend Joan's shoulder, where she must have spent the night. A soft groan of dismay; Annie had always accused her of dribbling and bubbling in her sleep. Fortunately, she and Joan had got to know each other well on the voyage as the 'older' brides in their mid-twenties, so hopefully Joan wouldn't mind explaining the damp patch to her husband if he noticed it during their reunion. Slowly, Eleanor raised herself upright and tottered down the swaying aisle to the toilet.

A steward smiled cheerily as she passed. 'Morning, ma'am! Breakfast in ten minutes, Chicago in two hours.' He gestured towards the rear of the train. 'Dining car thataway.'

She couldn't resist and, after a quick visit to the lavatory, headed back down the train, collecting a sleepy Joan along the way. Bacon. Eggs. Real butter. Fresh orange juice and real coffee. The world suddenly seemed a much better place.

The train bustled through the Chicago suburbs and eased into Union Station. It gave a final belch as it pulled into the platform, teeming with men waving placards. Even before she stepped down, Eleanor spotted Ray. He was just that little bit taller, and looked just that bit more anxious, or so she imagined, than the others. Rushing straight to him, hair flying, she finally got the bear hug to wipe away her worries. But it didn't. She stepped back, feeling odd, awkward, and noticing that Ray's hand was sweaty as he led her to the exit.

'I've got Dad's pride and joy to pick you up—just have to find where I parked her.' He winked in response to her worried look. 'Just kidding, honey, trust me.'

There was no chance to talk as he led her through a maze of streets. As they rounded a corner, among dark-coloured Dodges and sober Chevys lining the street, Ray walked straight to a rusty red pickup.

'My dad loves this baby, I can't believe he let me use it.'

Eleanor tried to show admiration as she noted the size and the rusty body of the 'pride and joy'. The vehicle was huge, with a wide grinning grille topped by what looked like nostrils.

'She's an F-series, best workhorse we've ever had,' enthused Ray.

Eleanor's smile almost turned into a giggle as Ray helped her onto the running board and into the cavernous cab. *If my family could see me now.*

As they rumbled out of Chicago, they chatted easily enough, and Eleanor's awkwardness diminished. *It's hard enough meeting him again, he seems like a stranger, no wonder I'm nervous. And everything here is so different, I can't fit the pieces together, but I will.*

There was plenty to tell about their respective journeys. Hers in the company of excited brides, and his shepherding groups of equally keyed up soldiers home. And Eleanor was astonished by the passing scenery: endless snow, shaped into mounds, covering everyday objects, and turning them into sculptures. A huge change from the relative warmth of New York. They stopped for gas, and Ray began the ritual with which she was to become very familiar: 'putting on the chains'. This involved placing heavy chains on the packed ice, rolling the truck over them to just the right point, then hopping out to fasten them around the tyres. The chains and tyres didn't always line up first time, and Eleanor was treated to some Midwest swearing. '*Jumping Jehoshaphat!*' was about as salty as it got.

Once they were on their way, the chains produced a constant muffled clank on the packed snow as Ray drove skilfully and carefully, deeper into open country.

She wouldn't have thought she could sleep in the jolting pickup, with its agricultural smell and rough cushions. But the next thing she knew, they were pulling up to a weathered front porch wrapped around a two-storey white clapboard house. Smoke threaded up from a chimney, and lights gleamed in the front windows. Despite the cold, sweat trickled down Eleanor's armpits under her coat as she thought, *this is it. I'm about to meet the people who didn't write to me, and don't seem to want me. I've left a loving family to come to a cold and distant home. What have I done?*

Ray lifted her down from the truck and swung her over the icy steps onto the porch. The door opened, and there they were. The man she recognised from photos as Ray's father was lanky and bony—at least what she could see of him. He stood back in the shadows. Ray's mother was tall and broad, with arms twice as muscular as her husband's. Wearing a flowered cotton dress and heavy apron, she seemed untroubled by the cold. Her mouth was set in a thin line, and a large mole rested between her eyebrows, underneath a coronet of iron-grey plaits.

'So!' barked Mrs. Miller Senior. 'Here is the girl.'

Ray stepped in. 'Ma and Pa, meet Eleanor, who's made me the happiest man on earth.'

Her new mother-in-law lowered her eyes and waved an

arm. 'Bitte, kommen Sie.'

Eleanor remained rooted. She felt the blood drain from her face. She could barely pick out her reflection in the glass of the door. As icy white as the snowy backdrop.

The accent. The German words. She could hear the voices of the POWs who had been assigned to serve the departing brides in the Tidworth canteen. Many seemed demeaned by their assignment. In harshly accented tones, behind the backs of the women they served, they muttered derogatory English words they'd picked up: *GI Whore. Prostitute.*

She swung towards Ray, her voice cracking with emotion: 'Why didn't you tell me?' she hissed.

He twisted his hands. 'I couldn't risk losing you, sweetheart, lots of people changed their names when the war started, we used to be Müller, but we're Americans now. Anyway, I knew that once you met, you'd all get along.'

Eleanor's anger turned to astonishment. She felt caught in a nightmare, war memories swirling through her.

'You *knew* about Birmingham, and the prisoners at Tidworth, how could you possibly think it would all be fine?'.

He matched her whisper as his parents continued to stare from within the house.

'I thought… if you stayed on Scilly, you might, I don't know, find someone else… and I love you so much.'

For a moment, the wintry landscape faded, and Eleanor was back on the dock at St. Mary's. Another time, a very different welcome. She could see Simon, the cheeky little boy who had taken a shine to her, holding out the glowing flowers and surreptitiously wiping his dripping nose. And especially she could see Harvey, with his twinkling specs and kindly smile. What if marriage to Harvey would have been right for her? What if she could roll back time and make a different decision?

Now the four of them stood awkwardly, as frozen as the landscape. Then with an effort, Eleanor snapped herself back to the present, to the life she had chosen. She pulled the soft cashmere scarf more snugly around her neck, its soft fibres reminded her of Harvey's touch, and everything they had shared.

Put the past behind you. Eleanor stepped forward with her hand extended and forced a determined smile onto her face.

Spring Thaw

1946

Late March, nearly six weeks since she had managed to get through that dismal frozen day. Eleanor woke on an early spring morning and couldn't believe she was still in America. There had been moments when she plotted her escape, back to small, damp England, back to her family. Back to Scilly, and Harvey. Then hour by hour, day by day, she inched her way into life at Rolling Stone Farm. *An apt name indeed for this farm of immigrants*, she thought, grimly at first, then with wry amusement as time passed and the pain of homesickness eased somewhat. The dull ache never completely went away, but she found a muted pleasure in the novelty of her life on the plains. And in a steady stream of letters from Annie, complete with photos of baby Elsa, and of Janusz, her Polish husband, whose moustache was as wide as his face.

Padding across the warm wooden floor, she pulled the plain green hand-stitched curtains back from the little window overlooking the fields. Eight in the morning, Ray had already been gone hours, helping his father on the farm. Eleanor looked around their bedroom, where shafts of warm sunlight replaced the icy spears that had pierced the room in the early weeks. Outside, the sun had drawn back the blanket of snow that greeted her. Now only remnants of the deepest patches could be seen, looking dirty and defeated by the coming of spring.

Eleanor stepped across the hall to the bathroom. Everything was so big, the bedroom enormous, the bed would have comfortably accommodated four, and the bathroom cavernous though never quite warm. The newlyweds had their own rooms on the second floor of the farmhouse, a consideration for which Eleanor was deeply grateful. Not to mention surprised at the apparent sensitivity shown by her stern-faced in-laws to the newlyweds' privacy.

Eleanor didn't linger in the chilly bathroom, she hurried back to the sunlit bedroom to pull the quilt over the bed. Mother Miller, as she'd been told to address her mother-in-law, had made the quilt as a young bride. She was newly arrived in America and trying to learn the customs and crafts of a strange land. Eleanor remembered hearing this story, as she was feeling alone and adrift herself on that first day. Hilda—Mother Miller's given name, although never used out loud, even by her husband—had shown her the room and, after a slight hesitation, explained the history of the quilt. She traced the pattern with her fingers as she spoke. To Eleanor's surprise, her English, although accented and occasionally sprinkled with German expressions, was perfect.

'You see, here is my journey. We had a little farm in Germany, we were very poor. Walter thought we should make our way to this New World; people were needed to farm the land. After we got here, I cried every day until I started to make this quilt. I joined the two countries.'

As tired and lost as she felt, Eleanor believed that the woman was trying to tell her something. Something about her understanding of what it was to be a stranger, to be uncertain of a welcome. Maybe even to mitigate the brusqueness of her initial greeting.

Weeks later, Eleanor gave the quilt a final pat and a tug, then hurried down two flights of creaking wooden steps to the warmest room in the house. She had already come to love the kitchen, with its mammoth range, scarred pine table and armoire displaying the Millers' prized collection of imported Spode tableware. However, she was in no doubt that this was Hilda's domain, as her early offers of help were met with a firm 'Sit. And eat.' It was clear that, in this part of the house, Eleanor was a visitor, who had yet to be allowed beyond the end of the kitchen table. She was best tolerated in a seated position, fuelling herself for the day ahead.

The wound inflicted by the loss of the familiar began to heal. Ray's part in this was immense. It was becoming apparent that his love for her was no wartime romance. Living out the early days of marriage in view of his parents was a challenge neither of them could have prepared for. However, Ray rose to the task, pulling her with him. Without being demonstrative, he made it clear to the older couple that Eleanor was everything to him. He ensured that she was included in conversations, and he kept her informed of his comings and goings.

'Just going to plant up in the north field, honey, we'll be back for lunch,' he would call out.

At first, his parents would exchange bemused glances, but as time went on, they accepted that she was the centre of his world. For one thing, they stopped speaking to her through him. 'Would she like another cup of coffee?' became 'Would you like anything else, Eleanor?' Progress indeed.

In the quiet and peace of their room, they could nurture their closeness. At first, Eleanor felt an awkwardness that had nothing to do with the presence of parents two floors below. Then she realised that, some months after their marriage, this was the longest time that they'd spent together. As well as the gigantic bed, their room contained lamps, tables, and two cosy armchairs. To begin, the journey from reading peacefully, curled up in the chairs, to lying together on the bed seemed impossibly long and difficult.

One evening, Eleanor spoke up. Thanks to the early end to the farming day, it was only eight o'clock, and she wasn't in the least tired.

'Ray.' Warm brown eyes peered up at her over his spectacles. 'Do you remember our honeymoon B&B, how the bed was so small you nearly fell off the other side?'

He put his book aside. 'I sure do, that could have been a nasty accident.' A wide grin at the memory.

Eleanor returned the grin and rose to her feet. 'Well, I don't think there's much risk of injury here. And you know, I really need a cuddle.'

From that point, they rediscovered the enthusiasm of their wedding night, interrupted only by their adherence to the advice of Dr. Latz. His scientific publication resided in the drawer of a bedside table. For reference, and reassurance.

Now, as Spring showed itself noisily and colourfully on the farm, Eleanor came down to breakfast determined to break out of the 'honoured guest' role she felt Ray's parents had assigned to her. This polite exclusion had led to spending long hours in her room, feeling lonely and useless. Milly and Dot, Ray's sisters, had married Canadian brothers and moved north, so any chance of a sisterly bond died before it could get started. There were only so many letters she could write her parents and Annie, only so many books she could read, and only so many solitary walks she could endure.

'Good morning, Mother Miller,' she sang out as she entered the kitchen.

Before Hilda could instruct her to sit for her breakfast, Eleanor spoke again. 'It's such a lovely morning, would you mind if I collected a few eggs?'

Hilda frowned. 'I have enough for your breakfast, there's

no need.'

Eleanor tried again. 'You know, we used to keep chickens, I looked after them and collected the eggs to make up our quota for the war effort.'

A resounding silence swallowed the conversation as both women thought of the reasons for the quota. Eleanor could have kicked herself.

Then Hilda spoke. 'Huh, you? Fancy schmancy schoolteacher, what do you know from chickens?' She snorted, but it didn't sound unkind to Eleanor.

'You'd be surprised,' said Eleanor, 'I even used to, um, get them ready for the pot when they'd finished laying. And look,' she indicated her sturdy trousers and work shirt. 'I'm already dressed for it.' Another silence ensued, but a less awkward one as Hilda presumably contemplated the image of Eleanor wielding an axe and plucking feathers.

Grunting softly as she bent, Hilda reached into a cupboard. She handed Eleanor a wicker basket with what might have been the smallest twist of a smile. 'Okay then, Miss Chicken Girl, see what you can do. But mind you, they don't always lay in the hen house, watch where you step.'

Eleanor returned after a short while. The basket had become too heavy to carry, and she didn't want to be disgraced by any breakages.

Hilda, however, assumed the worst, and greeted her with, 'Humph, not so good as you think you are, Missy. Good thing I've got enough anyway.'

Wordlessly, Eleanor handed over the basket. Hilda peered in, to see almost two dozen glowing chestnut-coloured eggs, some still warm, with under-feathers clinging to them. *That's okay, no need to apologise,* thought Eleanor sarcastically. But the older woman did something that felt even better.

She handed Eleanor an apron and set a bowl and whisk on the countertop. 'Wash your hands and get a few of these ready to scramble. If you know how to scramble eggs.'

Eleanor, who had been chief cook for the family in England, decided now was not the time to defend her roast chicken dinner and apple crumble, or to show her knowledge of the need for economy in domestic science. She held her peace. 'I'll certainly have a go, just let me know what you want me to do.'

So it was that Eleanor found herself elevated to assistant chef, part of the family rather than an onlooker. Her acceptance took another step forward when she cautiously revealed her interest in gardening. Both the senior Millers were devoted to their kitchen garden, and visibly brightened as Eleanor asked questions about the crops. Especially when she expressed admiration at the size of individual vegetables (local prize-winners, she discovered).

It wasn't long before the horticultural equivalent of being allowed to scramble eggs took place. Walter Miller, noting her presence at his elbow as he set some early peas, handed her a hoe and a paper packet of seeds. 'Here you are then, let's put another row in here. Take your time, though, it'll all go crooked if you rush.'

Eleanor felt that she'd been handed a sacred implement and steeled herself to carry out the duty imbued in it. Over the weeks, she'd come to realise that this gaunt-faced, taciturn man was consumed by love. Not necessarily of his family, or his dog, but of the earth and the rhythms of the farming year. She could tell, because the three conversations she'd had with him had been about ploughing, planting, and harvesting. As he spoke, his sallow cheeks flushed and his gaze, usually trained on the middle distance, turned directly to her face.

She became a person to him in those moments, and was determined to make the most of her chance. She was no stranger to the security of a bond with a father.

Ray, who was working nearby, said later that his father's face was an absolute picture when, after a short while, he turned and saw the dead straight row. Eleanor had even garnished it with pea sticks in readiness for future growth.

The older man turned to his son as they gazed at Eleanor's work together. 'You've got a good one there, son.'

For Eleanor, this 'victory' over her in-laws' scepticism was bittersweet. Sometimes she wearied of having to tread carefully, second-guessing their reactions to overcome what she felt was prejudice against her 'strangeness'. She still yearned for another garden, thousands of miles away, planted and harvested with easy companionship.

A Turn for the Worse

Summer 1946

The extremes of weather that flung Midwest farming communities from one season to the next took Eleanor by surprise. No sooner had Spring released Rolling Stone from ice and snow, than Summer blasted in like an over-heated furnace. High temperatures, combined with moist and muggy air, meant Eleanor was soaked in sweat and exhausted before she even reached the early ripening peas. She'd done the hard work of planting them with such ease, but the mere picking of a few pods often left her wilting under the searing sun.

A scorching morning in late June and Eleanor forced herself out to the garden, on this occasion intent on getting beans. She knew that unpicked beans would soon become tough and stringy, whereas Hilda was always happy to have any surplus for canning and preserving while they were tender. She felt tired and weak. The blazing days were usually followed by thunderstorms in the night, and the crack and flash of each storm shocked her into nightly wakefulness, heart pounding as she relived the flash of the antiaircraft guns and the thumping strike of bombs.

Eventually, broken sleep and disturbing dreams took their toll. On this particular morning, she found it harder and harder to see as she walked, the dark closing in even as the sun's brightness increased. The last thing Eleanor was aware of before she lost consciousness was the lazy buzzing of bees, or was that a ringing in her ears? She twisted as she fell among the bulbous beefsteak tomatoes, her wide-brimmed hat blew away, and she was left exposed to the penetrating rays of the sun.

In the kitchen, Hilda paused in her preparations for putting up the expected beans. The girl—as she still thought of Eleanor—should be back by now. One thing you could say about her, she didn't dawdle. A few minutes passed, and she worried. Grabbing her straw hat and a flask of water, she hurried towards the kitchen garden. She broke into a run as she recognised the floral pattern of Eleanor's everyday summer dress, its owner motionless on the ground.

Eleanor had little memory of being dragged into the shade by Hilda's strong arms. She didn't witness the sturdy figure of her mother-in-law breaking into a sprint as she ran into the house to telephone an ambulance, then sprinting back again to sit and wait with her, cradling her head and trying to force sips of water between her parched lips. She learned all this later from Ray, who had extracted the details from his taciturn parent in an effort to understand the emergency.

The next time Eleanor opened her eyes, she flinched. She was surrounded by dazzling white: reflected light onto white sheets and walls, and, close to her face, the white coat of a man wearing a stethoscope.

'Glad to see you're back with us, Mrs. Miller, I'll let your husband know. He's driving the nurses crazy out there.' He started towards the door.

Eleanor cleared her throat. 'Wait,' she croaked. 'What happened? Who are you?'

He turned back to her. 'Sorry, I should have explained. I'm Dr. Tellerman, and when you were brought in, I thought you had a touch of heatstroke.' He folded his hands over his substantial belly and beamed at her. 'But when we took a look at you, well, it looks like you're expecting a happy event.'

Eleanor stared. He seemed puzzled, and spoke slowly, as if he thought she wasn't quite all there. 'A baby, Mrs. Miller. Congratulations!'

Underneath the blotches of sunburn, Eleanor felt the colour drain out of her face. 'But that's impossible!'

Dr. Tellerman paused, as if trying to make sense of this unanticipated reaction.

He patted Eleanor's hand. 'I'll just get your husband, my dear, you have lots to talk about.'

Pregnant

Autumn and Winter 1946

Weeks later the reality of pregnancy sunk in. Eleanor had put the absence of her periods down to the turbulence of recent months, the sea journey, the loss of her home, the stress of a new environment. In fact, the same thing had happened to her during the Blitz. Perhaps she'd failed to tune into her body as she should have, and they'd abstained at the wrong times. She put these points to Ray.

'Obviously,' was his brief reply.

Although he expressed sympathy with her shock, he couldn't conceal his delight.

'Look at it this way. We've always said we wanted children, we're young and healthy, and we've got my parents on hand to help. It couldn't be better if we'd planned it!' He paused, his face arranging itself into a less gleeful and more righteous expression. 'And, of course, we'll be doing our bit to get the numbers up, you know, all those poor lads killed in the war, they say the population's right down.' His voice trailed away, perhaps gathering from the look on Eleanor's face that this appeal to patriotism might not have entirely succeeded.

Oh yes, doing our bit to produce more bodies for the next war. Well, I hope this one's a girl and she stays out of it. Eleanor kept her views to herself and smiled weakly. 'You're right, and I am getting used to the idea. I just wish I didn't feel so sick and dizzy, I hope it will pass.'

Only to herself did she admit that pregnancy tied her even more closely to Ray, making it even harder to return to England. *Not that I want to, of course.* Pushing the thought to the back of her mind.

In fact, as weeks turned into months, the sickness and dizziness did ease. However, Eleanor was astonished at the weight she put on. People who saw her when the February due date was still three months away assumed the baby's arrival imminent. When she had headaches and swollen ankles, Ray called the doctor out. Dr. Goodman had to battle through drifts of December snow and spent some time stamping and shaking the white stuff from his suit before he could even examine Eleanor.

Ray held her hand as she waited in the darkened bedroom. 'Ray, what if I'm ill when the baby comes in February? How will I ever get to the hospital?'

Ray squeezed her hot, swollen fingers. 'Now then, my dear Mrs. Miller, I've been driving these roads in winter since I was fourteen.' Perhaps he remembered the loose interpretation put on the legal driving age by farmers, because he corrected himself. 'Well, sixteen.'

A faint smile appeared on Eleanor's face at the image of a very young Ray, barely able to see over the steering wheel, peering through swirling snow as he drove the old truck into town.

Ray leaned over to hug his shaking wife. 'That's better. After all, I did manage to get tons of supplies to thousands of men on the front line during the war. Shelling all around. So you can trust me to transport one pregnant lady to the hospital, when it's only snow falling, right?'

As it turned out, Eleanor needn't have worried, at least not about getting to the hospital in a February blizzard. Dr. Goodman, drawing on years of practice as a country GP, checked her blood pressure and asked to use the telephone. Puzzled and frightened, Eleanor and Ray tried to hear what he was saying, but his words were indistinct. What was clear was his urgency.

He came back into the room. 'Sorry to rush out like that, Mrs. Miller, but I'd like to get a few more tests done, and I wanted to make sure the hospital was geared up for it, what with Christmas coming up.' His tone was calm now, and his gentle voice soothing. 'I think you may have something called Pre-eclampsia, it happens sometimes, your blood pressure goes up and your kidneys don't do so well getting rid of fluid.'

Ray spoke up. He might have been trying to match the doctor's calm tones, but his voice shook. 'Doesn't sound good, doc, can you treat it?'

'Oh yes, especially if we catch it early on and keep an eye on you in hospital until the baby's born. And we can always get this little one out a bit early if necessary.'

Eleanor gasped, horrified at the implications. *A Caesarean? A dead baby?*

She didn't speak, and the doctor continued, 'I know it's easy for me to say, but please, please try not to worry. I've seen many cases like this in my time, and, once the baby is safely born, the mother feels better almost right away.'

Eleanor tried to digest this. She heard the doctor's reassuring words about her condition, but nothing at all about how these weeks in hospital were going to be paid for. Her parents had written to her about the excitement generated by the advent of the British National Health Service, healthcare to be free for all. However, as far as she knew, everything in America had to be paid for by the patient, or by Blue Cross or Blue Shield insurance payments, and she knew they weren't in those schemes.

'Dr. Goodman. Ray.' Both men swung around to look at her, as if surprised to hear her speak from her prone position.

'I just want to know, how are we going to pay for all this time in hospital?'

Ray beamed, seeming to feel he was on firmer ground. 'No need to worry a bit about that, sweetheart. We've got the GI Bill. Veterans' families get the best care in the world.'

Out of the corner of her eye, Eleanor noticed that Dr. Goodman was trying to get Ray's attention.

The doctor interrupted at this point. 'That's certainly true, but, ah, it has to be at a Veterans' Administration leased hospital.' Puzzled looks from the couple. 'And in fact, I believe the nearest one that does maternity care is in Winona.'

Ray looked dismayed. 'Sixty miles, doc? Can't she go anywhere closer?'

Dr. Goodman shook his head. 'I'm afraid not.'

It began to dawn on Eleanor that her first Christmas away from England was going to be in hospital, miles from the home and family she was only just getting used to, presumably with the few other sad cases who had to stay over the holidays. Longing for her mother, and especially for her sister, she tried to put on a brave face.

Dr. Goodman must have spotted the lip wobble. 'It won't be as bad as you might think, Mrs. Miller. We make a bit of an effort, you know, with decorations and a Christmas meal. Well, of sorts. And the priest comes in for Christmas Mass, plus we always have the carollers singing their hearts out. Mostly in tune.' He turned to Ray. 'I'll have a word with the senior nurse, make sure that you can visit pretty freely.'

Hibernation

Winter 1946

Eleanor spent the next three months in hospital. Her world shrunk to the bed, a small table and locker beside it, and a wooden chair for visitors. Women on either side of her came and went, trailing threads of friendship and promises to keep in touch. Venturing out to the shared lavatories was an epic journey, not undertaken lightly. Sometimes, when her headaches and discomfort permitted, she sat and read, or knitted baby clothes. *If I have triplets, they won't go short* she thought. Her family wrote regularly, and she provided them with a somewhat censored account of the situation.

Dear Mother and Father

I was so pleased to get your last letter, but sorry to hear you are having such a terrible winter. Fancy only being able to see the tops of cars!

I am well, just having to rest a bit. Doctor's orders. I'm in the hospital, only because we have a lot of snow here too, and the farm is a long way from the hospital if there are problems.

So don't worry, your grandchild will arrive safe and well, everyone here has been so kind.

No reply from her parents, who probably took her at her word. Which is what she wanted. Annie, however, was not so easily fooled:

My dear sister,

Do I detect that things are not exactly as smooth as silk? They don't put pregnant women in hospital for nothing, and I don't buy that 'long way from the farm' story!

I've looked into it, and I could get passage on a freighter, so at least I could come and hold your hand. And bring you some English mags, how would that be?

I haven't told you my news, I'm about twelve weeks gone, so there's going to be a double baby bonanza this year. My lovely doc says I'll be fine to travel (although I may not have mentioned the freighter) so how about it?

Eleanor was tempted. A few years ago, she might have taken Annie up on her offer without thinking. But the news that a baby was on the way made the journey risky, if not impossible. Even for Annie, who seemed to sail through experiences that left her twin floundering.

Strangely, though, Eleanor found that she adjusted to this gentle prison once the initial frustration wore off. She didn't feel the need for anyone other than Ray and, less essentially, his mother. Above all, she felt safe and cared for by Dr. Tellerman and the hospital team. Waiting for the winter to pass.

Warning Signs

Winter to Spring 1947

February 20th, and Eleanor looked down at the squirming infant. She could see that she was holding a baby, which she had been told was her baby. However, the skin of her arms felt numb, as if she was watching someone else hold a baby. She looked around. She was in a private room, but wished she was back on the ward with the bustle of staff and the friendly faces of the other women. The door opened. Ray, carrying flowers, and Hilda, carrying a knitted baby shawl, entered the room. Both looked a little nervous. She learned later that they had been told that Eleanor was 'taking a bit of time to adjust, it's not unusual after such a difficult labour'. They had also been told that 'Baby isn't too keen on the breast, but we've got her on an excellent formula, she's doing well.'

Eleanor had tried to freshen up for Ray's first visit. Having seen herself in the cracked hospital bathroom mirror, she was shocked at her thin face, almost as white as the pillows that cradled it as Ray later entered the ward. She couldn't miss what she was sure was a look of concern as he bent to kiss her. Turning from her, he cupped the tiny head of his daughter, who made a sound like a rusty gate and waved her miniature fists.

He adopted what sounded to Eleanor like a forced jollity. 'Well, I thought we were going to have a Valentine's baby, but she sure took her time getting here. Almost two days of labour, what a trooper you are, and no wonder you look a bit... washed out.'

Dreamily, Eleanor contemplated the image of the baby

'taking her time', wending her way down the birth canal, pausing maybe for a bit of shopping or sightseeing. While outside that warm and cosy tube, her mother was being gripped and flung about by a storm of pain.

She tried to explain. 'Ray, it was awful, I hated every minute, thought it would never end.'

He looked helplessly at his mother, who moved to the bedside, lifted the baby, and wrapped her in the newly knitted shawl.

Hilda touched her daughter-in-law's hand, a brief feather of a touch with her roughened fingers. No words were spoken, but in her touch and expression Eleanor heard: *Let me take her, I will look after her, don't worry.*

She lifted her head. 'Dr. Tellerman says I need a few more weeks rest, my kidneys aren't working properly yet.' Exhausted, she fell back, closing her eyes and whispering, 'Please, take her. I can't do it, not now.' As she drifted off again, she murmured, 'Ray, we talked about names…'

Ray nodded, 'We sure did, sweetheart, what do you think now she's here?'

Eleanor whispered, 'I want to call her Sarah. Such a gentle name, I love the sound.'

Ray's furrowed brow smoothed as he produced a broad smile. 'Great choice, sweetheart, and we can call her Sadie for short, a real all-American name.'

Eleanor heard his words from a distance. *A real American girl. I guess so.*

Into Spring

February 1947

The weeks went by, Eleanor cocooned in her hospital bed, willing her still inadequate kidneys to do their job so she could leave. At first, she wondered if she should mark the days on her bedstead, as prisoners did, in case she lost track of time. However, Hilda and Ray brought Sadie to visit every Tuesday, Friday, and Sunday without fail, giving her something to track the days against. And, eventually, something to look forward to.

Almost without realising, she felt a bond with the tiny infant. Little rituals that had once seemed beyond her became routine: changing Sadie's nappy, which she learned to call a diaper, feeding her, checking to see if her nails needed trimming, even giving her a bath.

One Sunday in March, Sadie slept in her mother's arms through most of the afternoon visiting hours. When Hilda reached out to return the baby to the newborn nursery, Eleanor clung on.

'It's all right, Mother Miller, let's not disturb her. I'll get someone to take her back later.'

Hilda stopped. 'Don't get ahead of yourself, Missy. If you keep her with you, you've got to look after her, it's the rule here.'

Eleanor was sure that Hilda was trying to protect them both, but she was also sure that it was time. To put her foot down, to be a real mother. Her mother-in-law loomed over her as she sat on the bed with Sadie.

Straightening her spine to meet Hilda's eyes, she said, 'You can tell them I won't trouble them for so much as a clean diaper.'

'Suit yourself then.' What could have been dismissive words were cancelled out by the twitch of Hilda's mouth. A smile passed between them.

From that point, Eleanor wanted to eat, to get out of bed, and to get better for Sadie. She took an interest in the world outside the ward, listening to the radio in the patients' lounge and keeping up with the news. On a Sunday, she even glanced at what Ray called 'the funny papers'. These broadsheets featured brightly coloured comic strips that had Ray roaring with laughter, although Eleanor struggled to raise a smile at Dagwood and Blondie or the Katzenjammer Kids.

At the beginning of April, Eleanor was curled in the lounge waiting for Ray's Sunday visit. She was cradling Sadie and glancing at the day's paper as the baby slept. She spotted a comic strip she had not seen before, featuring a hillbilly character in dungarees called 'Li'l Abner'. *Reminds me a bit of Walter*, she thought. The episode featured a determined-looking young woman pursuing Abner with a pitchfork, captioned "Sadie Hawkins gets her man!"

When Ray arrived clutching a bouquet of early flowers, he settled in the chair opposite. Eleanor, unsmiling, picked up the newspaper and roughly exchanged it for the flowers, which she cast onto another chair without admiring them. Ray looked up, bewildered by her frosty greeting.

'Ray Miller, you've nick-named our daughter after a man-chasing floozie in Dogpatch, USA, what on earth were you thinking?' Eleanor glared at him. 'I love the name Sarah, and now everybody calls her Sadie and I feel like we're stuck with it.'

Ray looked distinctly sheepish. 'Tell you the truth, honey,

Li'l Abner's my favourite comic, and…' He took a deep breath, '…and anyhow, I always think Sadie's a real sassy girl, goes after what she wants, like I hope our girl will.'

A silence fell between them. To her surprise, Eleanor felt a bubble of laughter growing in her chest. She looked down at Sadie, who was beginning to stir and kick her blanket off.

'Okay Ray, maybe I'm overreacting because I like the sound of Sarah. But if she turns out to be a strong American woman who stands up for herself, I guess Sadie will suit her.' *But she'll still be Sarah to me.*

Eleanor took the paper and put it back on the table. She gave the baby to Ray and picked up her flowers, enjoying their scent.

'I think Sarah wants a cuddle with her daddy.'

As spring came around again, Eleanor packed her bag and emerged blinking into the chilly sunshine, holding her daughter, ready to start life as Sadie's mother.

Back at the farm, Eleanor was absorbed in looking after the baby. Hilda, with what may have been some effort, withdrew from Sadie's care and stayed in the background. Her role was partially overtaken by Bonzo, the family mutt.

He was always on hand to assist in his way, according to Hilda. 'That dog, one minute chasing the rabbits outside, then next thing under my feet. No clock needed, time to feed die Kleine.' *She sees the funny side, she's loving this*, thought Eleanor.

Eleanor looked at Bonzo. He could not be called handsome, with a crooked overbite, stumpy bowed legs and mismatched eyes showing his mixed ancestry. A bit of border collie in there somewhere. 'Well, Mother Miller, he's obviously an intelligent dog, wants to make sure we're doing our job right. Or maybe he feels he has to herd us, keep us together?'

'Humph. More like a chance to get in the warm house.'

Whatever the reason, he knew when it was time for Sadie's bottle, and where the diapers and lotions were kept, and would nudge the correct drawer in the right order. And his gimlet-eyed supervision of bath times made Eleanor laugh.

'Bonzo, what on earth are you doing?' The dog was pushing a wooden box around the bathroom floor. 'Trying to trip me up?' He fixed her with a brown eyed, blue eyed stare.

She put Sadie in the bassinette while she tested the bath water. Bonzo didn't move, short legs planted, head cocked in a way that seemed to say, 'Will you *please* listen to me?'

'All right, what's in here then?' Eleanor opened the lid to reveal a collection of rubber ducks, and a soap dish in the shape of a tortoise. 'Oh, I get it, she likes a toy in the bath, right?'

She reached for a green duck, only to find Bonzo blocking her way, holding a small yellow one gently in his jaws. 'Oh, right, thanks Bonzo, she likes this one, does she?'

Chuckling, she gave the duck a surreptitious clean before popping it and the baby in the bath. *Hope you're not offended, but dog drool and babies, yuk.*

Sadie caught sight of the toy and splashed enthusiastically. If a dog could look smug, Eleanor imagined that Bonzo did.

However, there was one member of the family who found it difficult to adjust to life as a family of three (plus dog and grandparents). A few weeks after Eleanor's return, when the air was softening into spring, she put Sadie to bed and settled to read a book.

Ray came into the room, smiling, and opened his arms.

'How about a cuddle for the proudest Dad on the planet?' As Ray embraced her, she could feel his erection through their layers of cold-weather clothes and drew back.

Seeming to think that reassurance was called for, Ray murmured 'It's okay, honey, the doc said any time after six weeks, and we're well past that.'

Eleanor smiled weakly. 'I know, but he also said I shouldn't risk another pregnancy for at least a year or so.' Ray was silent, stepping back, the smile gone from his face. *He did remember, of course*, thought Eleanor. *He was there when the doctor advised them that another pregnancy too soon could lead to possible kidney failure, and even death.*

Eleanor reached out to touch his hand. 'You know how much I enjoy making love. It's so important to both of us.' A shadow of a smile returned to Ray's face. Eleanor took a deep breath. 'But I'm not sure this "rhythm method" is the answer for us anymore, not when the risk is so great. Please, Ray, couldn't we talk to the priest? Surely there must be some allowance made. Some more reliable form of contraception we could use?'

Chill in the Air

Spring 1947

Two weeks later, Eleanor and Ray stood on the path as the Rectory door shut firmly behind them. Father Anselm had been pleasant, and sympathetic in his way, but firm in his advice. If conception could not be risked, they did indeed have a choice, it seemed. Abstinence. Eleanor could not believe her ears. A loving young couple, in this fix through no fault of their own, must give up the physical side of marriage for as long as the risk remained. *I should have expected it,* she thought. *Here's a man who, we are told, has cheerfully given up sex in the service of God, has presumably never watched his wife suffer and nearly die, and yet he's the one who gives the orders.*

Eleanor was furious and turned to Ray to let him know, but he shook his head. 'Not now, sweetheart, wait till we're on our own at home.'

So ensued a long and awkward silence. The truck rattled along the back roads, seeming to take a lifetime to make the journey back to the farm.

Once or twice, Eleanor tried to speak, to burst the boil of anger, but Ray's reply was curt. 'I said *not now.* I just want to concentrate on the road.' So Eleanor spent the journey thinking. And remembering the many and surprising ways physical love could be expressed.

Into the Deep Freeze

Late Spring 1947

They entered the farmhouse, walking straight past enquiring parental looks and up to their rooms. They sank wearily into the armchairs, angled gazes crossing in the gloom as they avoided each other's eyes.

Eleanor's anger subsided, she felt shocked and drained. 'Ray' she began, hesitantly. No response. 'Ray, please.'

He turned slowly towards her. His voice was cold and distant, unlike anything she'd ever heard from him. 'No sex, that's what the man said. Could be months, maybe years. What kind of marriage is that?'

Eleanor was stunned. Was he saying he couldn't—or wouldn't—tolerate giving up sex? Or was he giving up on their marriage?

Eleanor took a deep breath, aware she might be about to risk everything. 'Ray, please listen to me.' He did at least raise his chin from his chest and turn his gaze towards her.

Her voice wavered, but she wouldn't turn back. 'Ray, I was thinking… I know you probably think I was a pretty innocent virgin bride…' His eyebrows snapped up to join his hairline, and she hastened to add, 'I mean, I was, but I did read a bit about married love, I found a book under my parents' bed.' She felt herself flush at the thought of her parents' activities. Ray's expression did not change. *In for a penny*. Her words tumbled over each other as she rushed towards what felt like a cliff edge.

She came to the crucial point, which she had thought of on the silent journey back from the priest. 'And of course, those days at Tidworth, a real eye-opener listening to some of the girls. I had no idea about the, um, variations, ways of reaching a climax, you know. What I'm trying to say, is that there's other ways to give each other pleasure, not risking pregnancy, not committing a sin.' *God forgive the lie about Tidworth*, she thought. *And Harvey, forgive me the lie about us.* Her voice subsided in the face of Ray's continued silence and her own embarrassment at the word 'climax' hanging in the air between them for the first time.

Ray stood and looked down at her from his considerable height. 'That. Is. Disgusting.' His mouth looked ugly, twisting with the words. 'You have understood nothing about the Church's teaching on this, or you wouldn't even consider it.'

Seeing the mortification she knew must show in her face, he may have slightly regretted his tone, because his voice softened. 'Darling, we have the priest's word, and if you want to keep our marriage, and meet this test of our faith, we must refrain from sexual activity until the doctor says the possibility of pregnancy is no longer a risk to your health.' Perhaps taking her continued silence as acquiescence, he moved towards the door, closing it behind him, leaving her alone in the gathering gloom.

When he returned a short time later, he opened the door to a completely dark room. He switched on the light, and Eleanor raised her hands against it.

He knelt beside her, pulling her hands down to reveal swollen red eyes and damp cheeks. 'I'm sorry, my love, I was just surprised and shocked at what you were saying, but I know you spoke out of love for me, and you want to make this work.' She locked her eyes on his but did not speak.

He cleared his throat. 'Anyway, I've just talked to Mom and Pop, explained to them that what with the baby not sleeping so well and all, and me needing my energy for planting and working at the school, I'm going to move into the spare room down the hall.' Still nothing from Eleanor. 'I mean, it's not forever, just for a little while. We will still be together, loving each other and Sadie, it'll just be easier if we don't have the temptation.'

Finally, wearily, Eleanor spoke. 'That's fine, Ray, you do as you please. I'm going to get Sadie's bottle ready.' She rose and left the room, with Ray still crouched awkwardly on the floor beside her chair.

Dreams

1947

Months later, Eleanor realised her marriage had become like sharing digs when she was in training, although with the addition of a baby, and without the excitement of a new boyfriend or two among the housemates.

She and Ray met for meals, went for walks and excursions on the weekends, attended church and poured their love into Sadie as she began to stagger about on chubby legs. After less than a year, this was marriage for Eleanor and Ray, a stale and dried out thing that barely rustled between them. Something had been sucked away, leaving a sort of civilised friendship. Ray often brought her a cup of cocoa at bedtime, leaving the room with a polite 'goodnight, my darling' and switching out the light. Eleanor always got up and turned it back on, sometimes to continue another long and severely edited letter to her family, or just to put off the darkness.

Summer rolled around, Sadie was moving around well, and Ray came into the room one morning.

Unusually, he perched on the edge of the bed, cleared his throat, and reached for her hand. 'Sweetheart, let's go somewhere. I mean, for a little vacation.'

Eleanor withdrew her hand. 'This is a bit out of the blue.' Her voice sounded flat to her ears.

'I know, but I saw in the paper there's going to be a Railway Fair in Chicago, July time. It'll be at Union Station, where I met you after the Queen Mary. I've got a special feeling for that place.'

Eleanor thought. 'I suppose I can't see a problem with

that. Sadie will love to see the trains.'

Seemingly relieved, Ray continued with enthusiasm. 'And the Freedom Train will be there, you'll get to see the original Declaration of Independence, the Bill of Rights, it's a-once-in-a-lifetime opportunity. We could stay in a little boarding house I know.'

The rust red pickup took them back to Chicago. Eleanor was awestruck by the grandeur of Union Station, which she hadn't appreciated as she waited anxiously for Ray so long ago. Pushing Sadie in her stroller as Ray fetched sandwiches, she caught sight of a shop front within the station concourse: American Express Travel Agency: Book US and Foreign Travel Here. On a whim, she pushed open the door and stepped inside. Then stopped, seeing the racks of pamphlets and the posters of the great liners on the wall. *What am I doing in here? What's come over me, are those ships my way home?* She approached the front desk, hoping she'd affixed a look of casual interest to her face, but feeling sick with the yearning to see her family.

She emerged after half an hour, clutching several pamphlets for the Cunard White Star Line to Europe ('Getting there is half the fun'). Heart pounding, she looked around to see a frantic Ray rushing towards them.

He stopped abruptly, seeing the brochures. His face turned pale under his field tan. He snatched the pamphlets. His lips tightened as he read the first one. 'So exactly when were you going to tell me you're going to leave me?' She could tell he was barely suppressing his shock.

Eleanor did not know what she was planning and answered without thinking. 'No, no… I was just hoping maybe I could visit my family. I'd really like them to see Sadie before she gets too much bigger, and her passage is free till she's two.' She stopped, her stomach churning. Had he no idea of the day-to-day misery she felt? Didn't he realise she missed her family and England with a pain that never went away, with little joy to balance it?

Ray's tone was stern. 'Well, I won't be able to come. I'm teaching summer school, and Dad needs me on the farm. Anyway, we can't afford two fares.'

Eleanor shrugged and stuffed the pamphlets into her bag, bending to hide her tears. 'I don't know, it was just an impulse, let's eat and then go see the Freedom Train.' *He's right, just for that moment, I wanted to leave. I long to be back in England. Was I even thinking about going back to Harvey?* She tried her best to control her thoughts.

Ray wasn't appeased. 'Doesn't look like you're very interested in American heritage. I thought you might even want to become a citizen, but I guess not.'

Eleanor looked down at the chubby face of her daughter, framed by curly, soft brown hair and dusted by matching freckles. Sadie adored her father, and Eleanor adored Sadie, so that was an end to it.

She put her arm through Ray's. 'Well, of course I want to be American, I've got an American daughter and husband, why wouldn't I?'

The family set off to the Freedom Train. No more was said about travel.

A special delivery letter from Annie came weeks later.

Dearest sister

I don't know where to start or how to write this letter. So I'll just plunge in.

Two weeks ago, Father slipped off a ladder in the garden, hit his head on a stone. He wouldn't go to hospital, said he was fine.

You've probably guessed, but I wish I could make the shock less. He didn't wake up the next morning, blood clot on the brain, they said. By the time you get this, the funeral will be over (Mother's wish to have it quickly).

I didn't want to send an impersonal telegram, especially when you wouldn't have been able to get here (I did check, even freighter passage is hard to arrange, especially for a winter sailing). I hope you understand.

Father was looking through the photos you sent of Sadie just the night before, he was laughing at her playing with the dog. It made him so happy to know things were working out for you. I hope that's the image of him that you keep with you. After all, he wasn't a great one for bursts of laughter, and Sadie seemed to do the trick.

I still can't believe he's gone.

Our family sends love to yours.

Eleanor folded the letter and went to her room. *I could have been with him, said goodbye, if I'd stayed at Carn Friar's.* She sat holding the letter, staring ahead. She wasn't aware Ray had entered the room until she felt his hand on her shoulder. She passed him the letter to read.

'Darling, I'm so sad for you, he was an amazing guy.' Eleanor didn't reply. Ray bent to embrace her. 'Did you, I mean, would you want to maybe go see your family? I'm not too sure about the money and all, but…'

Eleanor interrupted. 'It's all right, Ray, there probably wouldn't be anything till summer, I found that out when I was in the travel office in Chicago.'

'Oh, well.' He removed his arm from her shoulders. 'But don't forget we all love you and want to help.' He gently lifted her chin, seeming to find inspiration. 'I know, would you like me to ask the priest to remember him in prayers at Mass? For the repose of his soul?'

Eleanor held back a sharp refusal. *After all we've endured because of the Church and its rules? Absolutely not.* Then she realised that Ray was doing everything he could to comfort her. Awkward and uneasy, he was taking risks out of love. She took his hand. 'Please do, then I would feel I'm doing something, at least.'

Part Six:
Heading South

Winter

1948

It didn't get any better, it didn't get worse. Eleanor lived a dual existence: contented wife and mother on the outside, wispy grey shadow of a grieving daughter inside. She felt the Millers watching over her, caring for her, unable to express their sympathy. Walter frequently sought her opinion on horticultural matters, and Hilda produced a regular supply of dumplings. Sometimes she stood over her daughter-in-law, arms folded, until Eleanor finished the substantial fare. 'Got to keep your strength up, I'm getting too old to manage on my own in the kitchen, you know.'

Eleanor maintained a place in family life, getting bolder in the kitchen with Hilda's encouragement. A cake. Some soup. Praised highly by all, astonished at her talents.

Sadie helped to make the difference, as she was what they called 'forward' in her development. Barely a year old and she could walk and make some sense with words. She loved to imitate grown-ups. She stirred batter, emptied cupboards onto the floor, and swept the dirt around in circles, delighted with the patterns it made. She was irresistible. Bonzo was her constant companion. He would sit patiently, sometimes wearing a doll's bonnet, while Sadie babbled earnestly at him. It was as if from her birth, he'd taken on the job of carer and playmate, occupying the space that might never be filled by a brother or sister.

As spring fought its way out of the northern winter's icy grip, Eleanor's growing equilibrium was shattered by a telegram. The fear generated by the ochre envelope had not

271

diminished in peacetime. Eleanor left the house to read Annie's words.

Mother unwell won't eat STOP Says don't come STOP Letter follows STOP

At first, Eleanor ignored her mother's order. *I didn't say goodbye to Father, I must try.* She endured despair trying to book a passage, her efforts ultimately futile. Long-distance telephone calls to shipping companies in Chicago and New York had to be booked in advance, and the lines were poor. The Mauretania, The Queen Mary and the Queen Elizabeth were newly recommissioned following war service, but the first sailings would be later in spring. The United States Lines' America, also refreshed after the war, did not call at Southampton, meaning a further journey to England from France.

Eleanor exhausted all the possibilities and succeeded only in exhausting herself. She was about to telegraph her failure to Annie when the promised letter arrived from Mother, written in shaky copperplate.

My Dear Eleanor

Since your father's passing, it has been difficult to find meaning in life. As I imagine you are aware, we were very close, and I feel lost without him. I have no appetite for anything I used to enjoy, including food. Annie has been to stay, she's had the doctor in. He says I am depressed, and that it is normal when a couple have been so close for so long. Eleanor, it is more than that. I just want to be with Laurence again.

Before I go, I wish to say how proud we always have been of you, and how happy that you have made a good life for yourself. It was a hard decision for you, but it seems to have been the right one. We never replied to your letter from the Queen Mary, asking for forgiveness. That may have been cruel, perhaps punishing you for leaving. So, this letter is your answer now.

I wish we could have seen little Sadie, but you brought her to life in your letters and photos. She must be such a joy to you, as you and Annie have always been to us.

As Eleanor finished the letter, two thoughts came into her mind: *I believe her, I can't remember when she's spoken to me with such emotion* and *Thank God I never told them about the troubles in my marriage.*

A short time after, a telegram from Annie arrived.

Mother at rest beside Father STOP

A Kind of Harvest?

September 1948

Harvest time rolled around again. Walter's carved mahogany face softened as he watched his granddaughter and daughter-in-law doing their bit in the garden. He showed an unexpected understanding of small children, giving Sadie little tasks, praising how she carefully separated the pea pods from their stalks, and ignoring the disappearance of some of the more tender peas into Sadie's mouth.

'Look, Opa, is empty!' she lisped around a mouthful of sweet little green globes as she held out an open pod.

Walter solemnly inspected the empty pod. 'Never mind, Schatzi, some of them are like that, we'll put it in the bucket for the pigs.'

He reached down and picked up Sadie's bonnet, which spent more time on the ground than on her head as she dashed between the rows. 'Get this on you now, I reckon you've got two million freckles from running around in the sun today.'

He smiled as Sadie's blue eyes almost crossed in an effort to see, and count, the freckles on her nose. He picked her up and swung her into the August sky.

Eleanor was more at ease with Walter than any other member of the family. Although so different from her own Father, his quiet, steady acceptance soothed her pain.

He gradually opened to her, and it was a great day when he leaned on his hoe and said 'Nellie, I'm getting on a bit, and to tell you the truth, I don't know what I'd do without you, girl.'

For the first time in many sad months, Eleanor experienced genuine contentment. She even forgave him for his insistence on calling her Nellie. Sign of affection, she told herself.

Towards the end of August, Ray came back from a buying trip. He had been away three days, looking at new equipment for the farm. As usual, Eleanor was relaxing with a book after putting Sadie to bed. Ray entered and bent to plant a kiss on her forehead. He perched on the edge of the other armchair and took the book from her hands. Eleanor looked up in surprise. He rarely disturbed her quiet moments, so she gave him her attention.

He cleared his throat. 'Sweetheart, I know you aren't happy.'

Eleanor opened her mouth, then decided to seize the chance for honesty. 'No, Ray, I'm not. I wouldn't exactly say I'm *un*happy, but I guess this is far from what I thought our marriage would be like. What *any* marriage would be like.'

All the feelings that had led her into the travel shop at Union Station came surging back. Her voice rose with anger. 'Ray, just think about it for one minute.' He flinched, which she ignored. 'Of course I'm bloody unhappy! Anybody would be! I'm away from home, my parents never got to see Sadie, *you* stopped me from even trying. You got all hurt, like I was rejecting you. I miss my friends, I really miss my work, I love your parents, they've been wonderful to us. But I don't want to go on living here forever. And I get more affection from Bonzo than I do from you.'

He dropped his head, his hands hanging loose between his knees. After a few moments, he looked up. 'That's pretty much what I thought, but it sure does hurt to hear you say it.' A deep breath. 'So anyway, I've gone and done something, and

I need to know what you think.'

Eleanor sensed he was struggling, so she tried to calm down and look encouraging, although what she felt was trepidation. Their drift had taken them so far apart, it was hard to imagine what positive steps Ray could take.

He seemed to steel himself, then it all came out in a rush. 'Okay, I lied to you. I wasn't buying equipment this week, I applied for a job. Small university down in Virginia, place called Stony Point, nice little town.'

Eleanor was too stunned to speak. 'You did *what?*'

Ray reached out and took her hands. 'Just hear me out. They want an assistant professor in music education and composing so I went down there, had an interview, and they want me, what do you think about that?'

Eleanor didn't know what to think. 'Ray, you're a high school music teacher. A very good one, of course. But Assistant Professor at a university?'

He didn't seem offended by her candid remarks. 'Well, that's true, I didn't think I had the right qualifications either, no PhD, but they really liked my music. And my ideas for teachers, having been one myself. And they say I can study for my post-grad qualifications on the GI Bill, same as when we got free health care, because I'm ex-Army.' Having ignored her splutters as he produced this bombshell, he stopped abruptly.

'So, did you accept?' Eleanor's mind was racing. *How far did he go behind my back?*

Ray looked horrified. 'Of course not. I told them I'd have to talk to you and let them know. I only kept it a secret because I didn't really think I'd get it. Didn't want to get your hopes up.'

She nodded.

'But Eleanor, it could be a chance for us. To get past the tough times, to love each other properly. Mom and Pop have been great, but I feel like if we live like this much longer, we won't have anything left.'

He waited for a reply and when it didn't come, tried again. 'And it'll soon be two years since Sadie was born, maybe we could start to, you know, make love, in our very own home.' Ray gave her a pleading look.

Eleanor was still getting over her astonishment. She couldn't ever remember having a conversation like this with Ray. He tended to gloss over the negative, silence her with breezy optimism, or shut his mouth in a thin line. Now he was hitting the nail firmly on the head, understanding her deepest misery. She rose and crossed the short space between them. It was a sad reflection on their relationship that a look of apprehension crossed Ray's face. Seeing this, she settled gently into his lap, forcing him to snap his spread-out legs together so she wouldn't land on the floor.

As they lay back in the chair, chuckling at the near mishap, Eleanor put her lips to his ear. 'Let's go.'

It was surprisingly wrenching to leave. Not physically hard, they didn't have much. All they needed was to buy a second-hand Plymouth and trailer, fill it with their few possessions, make a nest of blankets in the back of the car for Sadie, and they were set. The worst part for Eleanor turned out to be tearing up the fragile roots of her bonds with Hilda and Walter. These had been hard to nurture, were nearly killed by her loneliness and illness, but flourished because of a determination she hadn't thought she possessed. Over a thousand miles of long, mostly empty road would now come between them, and Hilda's 'Be sure you come visit' rang hollow.

They left, one hot, silent early September morning, taking the road south, enduring Sadie's pleas to take Bonzo. Hoping for the best. Hilda and Walter stood in the door in their summer clothes, a sad echo of that first meeting in the snow.

Trying Hard

Autumn 1948

As they travelled, the dry dusty heat of the plains gave way to a clammy hot blanket covering the mid-Atlantic states. Even violent storms didn't clear the air as they did in Rolling Stone. To their relief Sadie was a good traveller, although endless games of 'I-spy' tested her weary parents. They broke their journey after about five hundred miles, and Sadie was enchanted with the delights of sleeping in a motel. There was a small pool for an evening dip, and afterwards the vibrating bed thrilled her (only ten cents in the slot). She was unbothered by the noisy air-conditioner trying to rattle its way out of the window frame. She made a princess crown from the strip of paper on the toilet seat: 'Sanitised for your protection'.

As they drove deeper into Virginia, Ray pointed out tobacco plantations and other evidence that they really were entering 'The South'. But the most startling evidence came as they headed down back roads through the Appalachian Mountains. About twenty miles outside Roanoke, feeling hungry, Eleanor was on the lookout for a roadside cafeteria. Spotting a sign saying 'Real Home Cooking' outside a ramshackle clapboard building, she pointed it out to Ray.

'Let's pull in, it might not be so easy to stop in a big town.' As they slowed to turn in, Ray indicated a painted sign on the roof.

'COLORED' was spelled out in large letters, and he swerved back onto the main road.

Eleanor twisted around. 'That place didn't look so bad,'

and Sadie wailed 'Hungry!' but Ray drove on.

'There'll be a better one in a minute.'

Sure enough, twenty minutes later, they pulled up outside a smartly painted building, with a sign that proclaimed: 'Welcome to Grits 'n' Gravy!' Puzzled, Eleanor got out of the car, enjoying the chance to stretch her cramped limbs. She looked up at the restaurant, and there was a different sign on this roof: 'WHITES ONLY'.

Ray followed her gaze. 'That's what I meant, down here the law says the Negroes and the Whites can't mix, so they get what they call 'separate but equal' places, close together but not too close. Restaurants, schools, railway cars and so on. Water coolers, even, all with signs.'

Eleanor's jaw dropped. '*Really?*'

Ray nodded. 'Called the Jim Crow laws, after an old minstrel show by a white guy making fun of Negroes. Means they can get arrested if they go into Whites Only places.'

Eleanor realised that what she was looking at was pure bigotry, enshrined in law. She shook her head. The two restaurants were separate, certainly, but they didn't appear to be equal.

Not that Eleanor was so naive as to think prejudice didn't exist in England. Class, accents, skin colour. People judged others, but it was covert, done in code. 'I'm so sorry, Mr. O'Rourke, I don't think we've got room for your big family here, try Doyle's Boarding House down the road.' Eleanor knew that the message of rejection to Irish customers, even if it was not emblazoned on rooftops, was rooted in the same prejudice. But she remembered the Black American soldiers in England, seen as 'exotic', good dancers, good fun. And popular at the village hall dances she and Ray attended. In 1940s Virginia, it looked like these same men would be seen as… what? Dangerous?

'Ray, we just had a terrible war because one lot of people hated another, this feels like we've travelled backwards. I don't know if I want to live with that.'

Ray sighed, reached to pick up Sadie with one arm, putting the other around Eleanor. 'I know, but honey, that's just how it is down here in the South, we sure aren't going to change it.'

Eleanor was silenced.

Clean Break, Fresh Start

Stony Point 1949

Ray studied the map. 'Okay, this looks like Cleveland Hill, it's a development the university keeps for its staff. This is the apartment I told you about, we'll just be here till we can buy our own place.'

They pulled out and drove up hill, past rows of low grey wooden huts, each sliced like a loaf cake into apartments. '11-R, 11-R,' he muttered as they crawled along, finally reaching Building 11.

Eleanor stared at the buildings, set around a central square covered here and there with tufts of wispy grass. The earth between was a deep rusty red, cracked in places like an old terracotta pot. A deflated beach ball was blown to and fro by the warm wind. Her heart sank. She was pretty sure she knew disused military housing when she saw it.

Ray, however, had switched back to optimistic mode. He opened the door into the living/kitchen area, furnished with utilitarian pieces and dominated by an enormous brown oil stove. Two bedrooms and a bathroom completed their quarters.

His smile sailed over her sour face. 'Well, this'll do fine till we save up to buy. Look, Sadie, you've got your own little bedroom, and Mommy and Daddy have got one too.'

Eleanor peered into the larger bedroom, noting the faint musty smell and the dismal sludge-coloured decor. Not to mention the twin iron beds, with their striped ticking mattresses showing ghostly traces of the activities of previous occupants. She sighed, unable to imagine their suspended sexual relationship bursting into life in these surroundings.

Four weeks passed. Ray was immersed in his new job, and Eleanor was beginning to look on the bright side. They managed to have sex once, taking care not to roll off the narrow twin bed, feeling as awkward with each other as strangers.

An unsatisfactory experience, after which neither had the energy to push for more than a quick kiss and cuddle in the evenings. 'It'll be better when we get our own house,' they agreed as they focused on getting to know their new surroundings.

Although the accommodation was spartan, the facilities on Cleveland Hill reflected a legacy of its former use by military families. There was an outdoor children's pool, a community centre, and a pre-school. By taking Sadie to activities, Eleanor got to know other mothers, and the change from the isolation of the farm lifted her spirits. Despite not having played with other children, Sadie soon lost her shyness and made friends. In fact, having her previous communication limited to adults and a dog seemed to be an advantage.

She could often be heard encouraging and praising other children, just as she had been nurtured by her parents and grandparents. 'Don't worry, Beau, try again, look, Sadie will show you how,' brought comfort to a distressed playmate and a glow of pride to her listening mother.

Furthermore, despite the austere living arrangements, each little unit housed various members of the university staff, with whom Eleanor and Ray had much in common. Eleanor became a member of the ladies' bridge group, an opportunity for an evening out each week. At sunset on Tuesdays, she joined the well-dressed ladies emerging from rusty screen doors and stepping gingerly down the splintered wooden steps in their high heels.

One by one, many of her new friends moved off the Hill into their own homes. After nearly a year, Eleanor, Ray, and Sadie made the same move, swapping the camaraderie of the Hill for the suburban elegance of a three-bedroom bungalow near the university.

Stepping through the door for the first time, Eleanor closed her eyes in bliss. Furniture polish and Ajax cleaning powder filled her nostrils, along with the scent of a rambling honeysuckle outside the window. A few days of hard work saw their belongings more or less arranged, a new play school found for Sadie, and quite a few casseroles enjoyed. The latter were gifts from the neighbours, as the Millers were taken to the hearts of other families in the winding tree-lined road.

One Monday morning, Eleanor was initiated into the newly established ritual of the Tupperware Party at their neighbour Margaret's house. Apparently, a chap called Tupper had started the whole thing. Housewives selling food storage to friends in their own homes rather than shops. The excitement generated by plastic containers was a mystery to Eleanor, but the overtures of friendship were welcome.

During Margaret's demonstration, Eleanor felt an overwhelming, cramping need for the toilet. Embarrassed, she hastily excused herself and almost sprinted from the room. Sitting on the toilet, she felt a rush of fluid, and looked down to see a pan full of clotted blood. Eleanor went weak, and for a while was unable to figure out what was happening to her. *Is it my period?* She was pretty sure it was more than that, she was late this month. In a daze, she rested her head on the cool porcelain of the sink. She didn't know much about miscarriages, or 'losing the baby' as she'd heard them called as if in reference to the carelessness of women. Whispers and headshakes, carrying a hint of shame, of failure. She had to get home, away from these women she didn't even know well. *How sad,* Eleanor thought, dabbing at her eyes. *Ray only travelled a couple of times between those squeaky old beds and look what's happened.*

She did her best to clean herself, splashed water on her eyes, and returned to the party. 'I'm so sorry, Margaret, I'm not feeling too well, it's, well, you know.' She gestured towards her abdomen.

Margaret understood and put her arm around Eleanor. 'I know, honey, I get it so bad each month I can't even get out of bed. Want me to carry you home?'

Eleanor was no longer surprised by the local expression for "do you want a lift?" and shook her head. 'It's fine, thank you, I just need a bit of fresh air.'

Still shocked, she let herself into the house. Thank God Ray was picking Sadie up from play school. Packing pads between her legs, and holding a hot water bottle to her stomach, she drifted off on the sofa. She dreamed of the child she could have held. Sadie's little brother or sister. When she woke, the cushions were soaked with her grief.

Eleanor, in an emotional fog, barely heard the clipped tones of the doctor after he had examined her the next day. The words came at her like grenades. Miscarriage. Fibroids. Haemorrhage. Urgent hysterectomy. She was breathing in anaesthetic, then her womb was no longer a part of her before the sadness begun to lift. So shockingly sudden she was left feeling detached, as if the loss and the surgery was happening to someone else.

Days later, the expression on Ray's face as he sat with her after the operation filled her with guilt. At the loss of the child that could have been, and of the future children they would never have.

'I wanted more children, honey, I can't help being sad about it. A little brother or sister for Sadie.' He sighed. 'We've been so unlucky.'

Listening to him, Eleanor hugged her secret thoughts to herself. *I can never get pregnant. I will never have to go crawling to a priest, begging for permission to avoid the risk, and I won't have to be terrified of sex.* She managed to hide her relief behind a downcast expression, which also concealed her anger. *Isn't Sadie enough in herself? Are we really that unlucky?'*

Trying, and Settling

1951

It was a big day for Eleanor and Ray. February in Virginia could be bitterly cold, and their breath made frosty clouds as they climbed the steps to the Stony Point University Hospital. Eight weeks since her surgery, the GP had referred Eleanor to the gynaecology clinic to check that all fibroid growths had been removed and that sex was no longer a threat to life.

On instruction, Eleanor had consumed copious amounts of water. She had to grit her teeth and clench every pelvic muscle during the x-ray, terrified she would suffer the embarrassment of wetting herself.

Once she had submitted to the slimy heavy pressure of the x-ray, Eleanor leapt off the table, leaving her underwear behind. She went half ran down the corridor, looking around frantically.

Spotting a sign for the women's toilets, she barrelled into the first door, pushed the three occupants aside with 'Sorry, I'm bursting,' and sighed as the painful pressure was released.

At that point she became aware that the lively chat of the other women had ceased.

Peering out of the cubicle door, she went to the basin, saying, 'I apologise, I just had one of those x-rays, you have to drink...'

Looking into the mirror, she was struck by the contrast between her pale winter face and the warm dark brown faces of the other women. Well, their colour was warm, but their expressions seemed closed and unfriendly.

One woman opened the door, pointing to the sign that said: 'Colored Women Only'. 'Yours is down there,' she said, pointing to another door.

Eleanor was embarrassed. She remembered seeing the restaurants and realised what she'd done. 'I honestly didn't know, didn't expect, I mean...'

The stern look dissolved. 'You don't sound like you're from around here, but you need to understand how this works.' Her tone was bitter, maybe she wasn't liking this reminder of Jim Crow any more than Eleanor. Or worse, was she filled with cold anger at Eleanor's unthinking assumption that everything was open to her white skin?

'If we did the same, we'd be in big trouble.'

Chastened, Eleanor scuttled out of the rest room, back to the clinic to retrieve her underpants.

An expanse of polished mahogany desk spread between the couple and the doctor as they awaited what felt like a verdict. *Are we on trial?* Eleanor thought.

The doctor cleared his throat and pronounced, 'You will be pleased to hear, Mr. and Mrs. Miller, that the x-ray was clear. My examination reveals that the internal wounds have healed, and you can safely resume marital relations.' He got hesitant smiles in return. 'Do you have any questions?'

Eleanor seized the moment. 'Doctor, I'm relieved that I can't get pregnant, not that I didn't want more children, but the risk...' He nodded. 'But now I'm worried that, well, nothing will work anymore, I won't feel anything...' A surprised look from Ray. There was a slight frown from the doctor, scribbling a note as she spoke, not meeting her eyes.

After a few moments, he held out a piece of paper. 'That sounds like quite a worry for you.' He paused, as if considering his words. 'I'm going to refer you to a colleague.

You will see that he's a psychiatrist. That doesn't mean I think you are mentally ill, of course, but he may be able to help you with your anxieties.'

Eleanor took the paper. *Maybe it will be alright, I won't have to see anyone else, I just want things to be normal.*

That evening, Sadie sound asleep, they turned to each other. Ray tried. Eleanor tried. She was able to relax just enough, but there was a tightness, discomfort and fear that distracted her. Afterwards, they agreed that they were a bit rusty, they would not give up, everything would work out.

So commenced weeks of increasing anxiety for Eleanor. Excuses to stay up late finishing a book, or tidying. They knew what was happening but stopped themselves from speaking. Finally, without telling Ray, Eleanor made the appointment, then kept it a secret through three more uneasy months.

The Diagnosis

1952

The day of her appointment with the psychiatrist finally arrived and this time Eleanor hoped to keep her clothes on. Apart from that, she felt the familiar clamminess, a sense that her body and life would be scrutinised, and that she was about to fail a test. The door opened and, to Eleanor's dismay, the man who settled himself behind the desk was blond, fresh-faced, and probably not much over thirty.

Dr. Franks looked over gold-rimmed spectacles. 'So, Mrs. Miller, I understand you are having some difficulties with marital relations.'

No pleasantries then. Straight to the point. Something to be said for it.

Eleanor sighed. 'Well, yes, it started with contraception, being ill when I was pregnant, I thought I might die. Now I'm just not interested. More than that, I'm scared.'

Eleanor realised she wasn't giving a very good account of herself.

The doctor gave what was probably meant to be a kindly smile. 'I wonder, Mrs. Miller, if you are one of those ladies who has never particularly enjoyed the physical side of things, do you think so?'

'No, that's not true, when we were first married, it was wonderful, I enjoyed sex, I really did.' She stopped, seeing the dubious expression across the desk.

The doctor looked at the notes in front of him. 'I see that your womb had to be removed, so there's no danger of pregnancy now. And yet, you are still having difficulties.'

Eleanor tried again. 'It's just that something that seemed so straightforward... well, I now connect it with pain, and the fear of dying. It seems such a long time ago that sex was... joyful.'

Even longer than I will ever say. She wondered if things would have been better with Harvey, no issues with contraception, having some control over how many—or few—children they had. Too late now.

The doctor spoke again. 'Mrs. Miller, I can see that this is a difficult subject, I won't put you through any more embarrassment.'

I might have been wrong. Young doesn't necessarily mean insensitive.

'I think that my diagnosis would be that you are in fact what we would describe as under-sexed. In my experience, it's possible that this will change, just by giving it time.' Now it was Eleanor's turn to look doubtful. 'But I can assure you that many couples have warm and loving marriages even though their sexual needs are different.' *So, he's saying I'll have to settle for something far less than I'd hoped for.*

Remembering Harvey, Eleanor could contain herself no longer. Under-sexed? She burst into peals of laughter and was still chuckling as she left the room. She learned later from her GP that the psychiatrist's report, in addition to describing her as 'under-sexed', concluded that she had experienced a 'hysterical episode' on being given the news. Dr. Franks considered that she was 'emotionally fragile and might benefit from psychotherapy'.

Part Seven:
Tabu

Judith

1952

As she drove home, Eleanor decided not to say anything to Ray about her visit to the psychiatrist. She was older now, understood herself better, and wasn't prepared to accept this damning assessment from someone who only knew her as a 'case'. What's more, the visit reminded her that at one time she'd delighted in the pleasure her body could give. With two different men, for that matter. Surely it would be possible to reawaken these feelings.

She felt the stirrings of hope.

Eleanor parked the car, and walked up to the back door, humming. To her surprise, Ray was there to greet her.

She smiled. 'This is nice, I wasn't expecting to see you. I've just been out getting a few things Sadie will need when she starts kindergarten.' She held up the bag of school supplies she'd bought as a 'cover' for her visit to the psychiatrist.

Ray returned her smile. 'Well, darling, there's someone I'd like you to meet.'

Eleanor followed him into the living room, then stopped, puzzled. A hint of perfume, sweet, spicy, and sensual. *I know that scent.*

A young woman, perhaps in her early twenties, sat on the sofa. Because of the light streaming through the window behind, Eleanor couldn't see her face well. The sun reflected off blonde waves and picked out her full breasts under a navy sateen jacket. The elation that had floated Eleanor into the house evaporated.

Oblivious, Ray introduced them. 'This is Judith Whitlock,

one of my MA students. We've stopped by to get a few files, um, Judith has kindly offered to be my part-time secretary, to help me get my research papers sorted out. I never seem to have time, what with my teaching load.'

No reply from Eleanor, at which point Judith rose and extended her hand. As she took it, Eleanor made out dark eyebrows over blue eyes, and a full red mouth against alabaster skin. Out of the young woman's mouth came a strong Southern drawl.

'Why, Miz Miller, I can't tell you how pleased I am to meet you. Ray, I mean Dr. Miller, has said so much about his family, I think he must be the luckiest man alive.'

Eleanor got a grip on herself and shook the other woman's hand. 'A pleasure to meet you, Miss Whitlock, and thank you for helping my husband. His work does get a bit overwhelming at times.' She plastered a smile onto her face. 'Can I get you some coffee?'

Judith patted the chair next to her. 'Now, I reckon you'll be a bit tired, all that running around and shopping. How about I fix us a cup of coffee, and you can rest yourself a bit.'

Eleanor remained standing. 'You don't need to do that, Miss Whitlock, I can manage.'

'Oh *please*, Miz Miller, I always help out at home, especially when Mama has a bad day.'

Not willing to argue, but still slightly uneasy, Eleanor sat. *Maybe I'm being oversensitive.* She recalled how she and Annie took over domestic duties when Mother was unwell during the war. *Women in America do seem to get busy in other people's houses.*

Judith breezed into the kitchen, leaving a trace of perfume.

I've got it now, she's wearing Tabu, thought Eleanor. *Advertised as the 'come hither' perfume.* She remembered being

296

shocked by her colleagues in Birmingham. 'Hey, Eleanor, want to come out with us tonight? Splash on a bit of Tabu, you might get lucky.' She could recall the lingering scent in the staff room the next day, with its suggestion of the previous night's encounters. 'Taboo' indeed.

Judith's head appeared around the kitchen door. 'Dr. Miller, how about you show me where things are, and we'll give your poor wife a chance to catch her breath.'

What does she mean, 'poor wife'? I can't be more than ten years older than she is, yet she's talking about me like I'm decrepit.

Judith sashayed in with a tray of coffee and cakes. 'Here you are, Ma'am.' She set the tray down with a big smile.

Ray trailed behind her, looking, in Eleanor's opinion, sheepish.

'I brought the sugar bowl, don't take it myself.' Judith patted her curvaceous hips. 'Got to watch my figure, you know. But Dr. Miller said you like it.' She looked at Eleanor, who was surprised to see something like anxiety in those blue eyes.

Maybe she's nervous. He is her professor. Eleanor smiled. 'Thank you, Miss Whitlock, that's fine. Now you sit down and relax as well.' She gestured to a chair on the other side of the room. Judith settled with a rustle of starched crinolines, their white netting visible to Eleanor.

Ray cleared his throat. 'I'll keep on sorting out those papers.'

Judith half rose from her seat. 'Let me give you a hand.'

Looks like I'm not the only one who gets the overly helpful treatment, thought Eleanor. *Maybe she just wants to please. Nothing for me to worry about.*

Ray shook his head. 'It's okay, I'll leave you girls to get to know each other.'

A brief silence, broken by Judith. She leaned towards Eleanor, reducing the distance between them, and dropped her voice. 'Now then, Miz Miller, I hope you're feelin' better. I was so sorry to hear about your...' she dropped her gaze, '...troubles.'

'What troubles would those be?' Eleanor was aware that her tone came across as stiff. *What's he told her? Has he been talking to her about our problems? The miscarriage?*

Judith either didn't pick up the change in Eleanor's tone or was undeterred by it. 'Why, I meant losing that baby, having an operation...' She gestured downwards. 'I just can't imagine what that must be like, and I'm not surprised you look kind of tired.'

'I'm well, thank you Miss Whitlock. Now, I'd love to hear about your studies, have you just started a Master's degree?'

Ray came back into the room, interrupting Eleanor's attempt at diversion. Before anyone else could speak, Judith said, 'Now listen, you two, I've just had a real good idea.'

Ray and Eleanor looked at her. *I wonder if he's dreading what she might say next,* Eleanor thought. *I certainly am.*

Judith turned to Eleanor. 'Now then, Miz Miller, how about I fix supper and watch little Sadie for you, maybe a couple of evenings a week? That would give you a chance to rest, I could do a bit of studying once she's in bed, and you two could maybe even go out to the movies or something.' She looked delighted.

Ray spoke before Eleanor could reply. 'That's a mighty kind offer, thank you, we might just take you up on it.'

Eleanor looked at her watch and stood. 'You'll have to excuse me, it's time to pick Sadie up.' As she left the room, she called out, 'Thank you, we'll let you know if we need a sitter.'

Later that evening, Ray returned to the subject of their

visitor. 'Seemed like you and Judith got on okay, she's a nice young lady, works really hard.'

A pause. 'Yes, she seems very helpful and kind. I expect she's been a godsend to you with your research.'

'She lives all on her own in a rented room, doesn't seem to have many friends. And I know she likes kids. To tell the truth, I wouldn't feel so bad having to work late if I knew you could get out and have fun.'

Eleanor felt she was being pressured into something. *What happened to us going to the movies together?* She told herself not to be suspicious. 'All right, Ray. A couple of the other mothers at Sadie's nursery school asked me to go for a swim on Tuesday nights, maybe Judith could help out then.'

Ray planted a kiss on her cheek. 'That's my girl, I know you need something like that, to help with, you know, the emotional problems the doctor talked about.'

Eleanor's face fell. *Do I really have emotional problems? Is that what everyone thinks?*

Ray didn't seem to notice her change of expression. He opened the newspaper to the sports page. 'I'll check with Judith tomorrow.'

This was the beginning of what Eleanor thought of as 'The Reign of the Princess.' Judith was with them for Sunday dinners, as well as looking after Sadie at least once a week. Sadie seemed to like the young woman, and Eleanor had to admit Judith was good company in many ways.

However, she sometimes felt overshadowed by Judith's self-assurance, and she would have liked to have one relaxing Sunday with just Ray and Sadie. Whenever Judith joined them, it was painfully obvious Judith and Ray had a shared enthusiasm for their work, from which Eleanor felt excluded.

Who is Eleanor?

1960

Eleanor crouched at the end of the lane. *Why did I let Bobbie talk me into this, I'm going to look like a fool.* Her plain black swimsuit hugged her tightly. The implausible blue of the water stretched twenty-five yards ahead of her. Coach Simpson stood on the side of the pool with a stopwatch, Eleanor's friend Bobbie was ready in the lane next to her as the command came: 'On your marks...'

Eleanor hadn't competed at sport since school, but the buzz came back to her. So did Harvey's exhortation, 'Keep your bottom up, Eleanor!' She powered down the pool and was astonished to touch just ahead of her younger friend.

Coach Simpson waved the stopwatch. 'Twenty-five seconds, Eleanor, not jet speed, but plenty fast enough for your age group in the Masters.'

Eleanor could hardly believe it. Bobbie had persuaded her to try out for the University Masters' Club, but she really didn't think she had the stamina or technique. And she told herself she was happy plodding up and down the pool on a Tuesday.

Coach Simpson came up to her as she hauled herself out of the water. 'So, we'll see you for training Wednesday evening then?'

Eleanor put her sports bag down and went into the living room. Ray and Judith sat side by side on the sofa, books and papers scattered. She hesitated. 'I thought you had orchestra practice tonight, Ray?'

'Hi, sweetheart.' He rose and kissed her forehead. 'It was

cancelled, so as Judith was here to look after Sadie anyway, we decided to do a bit of work. How was the swimming?'

'Fine, I guess. I tried out for the Masters' club at the university.' Blank faces greeted this news. 'I got in, so I'm going to start training with them on Wednesdays.'

Ray frowned. 'Honey, is that a good idea? What about your health, the stress of the extra training?'

Judith interrupted. 'What I think Ray's trying to say is, maybe it would be too much for you. I don't swim myself, but wouldn't you say it's a young person's sport? We care about you; we wouldn't want you to do too much.'

Eleanor's pride collapsed like a pricked balloon. 'I don't know, I hadn't really thought about it, maybe I shouldn't. Anyway, I'm tired, I'm off to bed.' She left the room, but not before she caught a look between Ray and Judith.

The next morning, Eleanor rang Bobbie. 'Listen, I've been thinking, I'm not sure I'm cut out for the Masters' group.'

'What's changed your mind?'

'Well, you know I've had a few health problems. Ray thinks it might be too much for me. And my friend Judith, she thinks it might be more for younger people, like you. I wonder if I'm fooling myself.'

Silence at the other end of the line, then, 'So, Ray and Judith, they're qualified doctors, are they?'

'No, of course not, but I just don't seem to have the confidence to argue with them. Or with you, to tell the truth.' Eleanor sighed.

'I'll tell you what I think, then I won't say any more and you can make up your own mind,' said Bobbie. 'You were great, and what's more, I'm pretty sure you'd enjoy it. There's plenty in the group who are older or less fit than you are. You could come along for a couple of sessions, see how it goes.

301

And you don't have to do competitions if you don't want to. Maybe just a relay now and then. As a bonus, we all go out sometimes for a beer or a pizza. They're a nice crowd, Eleanor.'

'Okay, I'll think it over.' *She's right, why am I letting them tell me what's good for me?* 'Anyway, bye for now, Bobbie, see you Tuesday.' Eleanor put the phone down slowly. She approached Ray, sipping his mid-morning whisky in his study. He looked up at her.

'Ray, if you've got rehearsal next Wednesday, you'll need to ask Judith to look after Sadie. I'm going to Masters' training.' She left the room before he could reply. Her heart was thumping, and she felt shaky. *I don't know who I am anymore*, she thought, *in the water I'm strong, but in this house I'm a weak, sickly person who can't do anything. Is that really me?*

As time went by, Judith's parents were also frequent visitors, and it became the custom for the Millers and Whitlocks to spend Christmas and Thanksgiving together.

When Eleanor questioned the family's constant presence, Ray's answer surprised her. 'Honey, I feel like Judith and her folks are part of our family. In fact, I wish my own parents could be a bit more like them.'

Eleanor tried to understand this, knowing the buttoned-up characters of the senior Millers. However, she remembered their painfully stilted efforts to accommodate the daughter-in-law who must have seemed so alien to them and felt a rush of affection. *He's being unfair.*

Disintegration

1965

With precision, Ray set the tray on Eleanor's lap as she sat up in bed. A cup of weak tea, two pieces of plain toast. *Invalid's breakfast*, thought Eleanor. *A spoonful of jam wouldn't kill me.* However, she knew it wasn't worth the hassle to get him to change.

The last time she tried, Ray had taken offense. 'I'm just trying to look after you, my dear. Too much sugar is bad for you, especially as you get older.'

Ray sat on the edge of the bed. Eleanor looked past him, through the window at the wind blowing the autumn leaves into swirls of colour.

'Sweetie, let's talk about arrangements for Thanksgiving and Christmas. Judith's parents are starting to make plans; we need to figure out a date.'

Eleanor was expecting this, and steeled herself to reply. 'Ray, I know we usually spend family holidays with the Whitlocks, I just wondered if we could maybe go see your parents this year.' She held her breath. His face looked sorrowful. She continued, although she felt like she was up against a brick wall. 'They're getting on, Sadie will be off to university soon, this could be a last chance to be all together.' His face turned more thunderous, and she faltered.

'Eleanor, sometimes I just don't understand you. You know how much Judith does for us, and Sadie enjoys getting together with MeeMaw and PawPaw.'

That did it. Eleanor found strength. 'That's just it, they are *not* her grandparents. Nor are they your parents, for that matter, no matter how much you might wish they were.' She stopped, horrified at the words coming out of her mouth.

Ray rose and looked down at her. Controlled anger in his voice. 'We'll talk again when you are able to be more rational. Meanwhile, I'll tell Judith we will head up to Fluvanna the Wednesday before Thanksgiving.'

Eleanor heard him go into his study, heard the slam of a cupboard door, then the sound of liquid flowing into a glass. *It's getting earlier, he'll be drinking before breakfast next thing.*

Later that day Eleanor, on her knees, dug out a dandelion with fierce jabs into the sticky red soil. Then another, each one a small victory earned in the veg patch she had carved out of their backyard. Her rutabagas (she'd laughed when she first heard what swede were called in America) needed breathing space. A shadow fell over her.

'Hello, Miz Eleanor, look at you digging away out here. Still mighty hot this time of year.'

Eleanor looked up, shading her eyes against the autumn sun. Judith was crisply turned out in navy slacks and a boxy red jacket. 'Hello Judith, I'm catching these weeds before they overrun the winter vegetables. What can I do for you?'

'I just thought we could maybe have a little chat, a cup of coffee? I'll go make it; let you finish up here.'

Eleanor was pretty sure she knew what the 'little chat' would be about.

The two women faced each other over the kitchen table. Judith reached forward and touched Eleanor's hand. 'Now, honey, you know how much I admire you, the way you keep going even though you're not that strong.'

Silence from Eleanor, which Judith seemed to take as agreement.

'I feel we've gotten real close over the years, and you know how much I care about you.'

Still no reply from Eleanor.

'That journey up north, it's a good three days, and can you imagine how hard that would be for you? And another thing, Mother and Daddy are looking forward to seeing you *so* much, I know you're too kind-hearted to let them down.'

Eleanor sighed. Years of experience had taught her that there was nothing she could say that would make Judith see her point of view. *I never knew what people meant by 'Steel Magnolia' until I met this woman,* she thought, *sweet and pretty on the outside, cast iron on the inside. Always gets her own way.*

'Fine, Judith, we'll go to your folks this year. Maybe we can visit the Millers in the Spring when the weather's better.' *Is that a triumphant look? Oh well, I haven't got the energy to push back. One of these days, maybe I'll just give up and leave. Make it easier for everyone.*

'Well, I'm so excited about that, we'll have us *such* a good time.'

Thanksgiving

1965

Eleanor looked around the table. Daddy Whitlock at one end, Ray at the other. Sadie and Eleanor on either side of Judith's father, Judith and her mother similarly surrounding Ray. An enormous turkey gleamed bronze in the middle of the table, with colourful side dishes dotted around the bird.

Mr. Whitlock led the blessing, and when everyone was sitting with a plateful of food, he set the conversation rolling. 'So, little Sadie, what are your plans now you're nearly finished high school?'

Caught in the glare of the spotlight, Sadie turned pink. 'I'm not sure yet, I only just got my SAT results, I'm hoping to go on to college.'

Eleanor couldn't help herself. 'Sadie's being modest, she got great results, she got into UCLA.'

Around the table, forks paused halfway to mouths.

Mrs. Whitlock was the first to speak. 'What, go all the way out to California? When we've got good colleges right here?'

Ray reached for the Jack Daniels, pouring so much into his glass there was only room for a splash of coke and a couple of ice cubes. 'Sadie, Sweetie, I didn't know...'

Feeling the tension, Eleanor wished she could disappear. *Why did I have to bring it up? Poor Sadie, I've landed her in it.* Then Sadie was speaking, her voice calm and resolute.

'I'm sorry, Dad, I know you wanted me to go in-state, but they've got a great social work programme at UCLA. And anyway, I want to spread my wings.' She gave her parents what Eleanor thought was a cheeky smile. 'After all, that's what you two did.'

Ray didn't appear to be charmed. 'What about the money? With your mother not able to work, I'm not sure we can afford it.'

Not able to work? thought Eleanor. *So, I'm the problem. Well, you've got a surprise coming.*

Sadie seemed undeterred. 'Don't worry, they've got job-finding programmes for students, and anyway, apparently I might get a scholarship for some of my fees.'

Judith had been watching Ray, but now she turned to Sadie. 'Sweetie, I sure do understand, UCLA is a great school, and California must be an amazing place to live.'

'Hippies, draft dodgers, drugs,' came a mutter from Daddy Whitlock.

Judith ignored her father's rumblings. 'But one thing I'm not sure about… have you thought what it might be like for your poor mom, if you can't come home at the weekends? Specially if your dad's away working sometimes?'

Eleanor saw an uncertain look cross Sadie's face for the first time and felt a surge of anger. *This is* not *going to happen.* She took a deep breath, and said with a laugh, 'Sadie, if you make a decision based on what Judith thinks are my needs, you could be spending some lonely weekends.'

Everyone, except for Sadie, looked amazed. It was as if the turkey on the table had reared up and joined in the debate.

'Some of us in the swimming group are planning to drive up to Lake Shenandoah most weekends for a bit of swimming. For a change. It can get a bit boring, plodding up and down the pool, you know.' She smiled sweetly.

Sadie looked pleased. 'Sounds great, Mom, it's beautiful up there in the mountains.'

Eleanor felt everyone else fade away, only the two of them

now in the conversation.

'And I've been meaning to tell you good news. I've applied for a job at the private Special Needs school up on Cleveland Hill. Just as a part-time teaching assistant, but they've said if a full-time post comes up, well, who knows?'

Sadie smiled at her mother, who beamed back and said, 'You go on and take up the UCLA offer, what an opportunity for you. And I quite fancy a trip to California at some point.'

Sadie laughed, relaxed and confident again. 'Okay, Mom, I'll see you out there. That is, if you can fit it in.'

The meal finished, Daddy Whitlock settled to watch the football. 'Eleanor, you help Mother clear away, Sadie, you come watch with me.' He patted the sofa beside him.

Ray stood and stretched. 'Judith, how about you and I freshen up the drinks, then we'll all get settled.' The two of them disappeared into the den and could be heard opening up the drinks cabinet.

Mrs. Whitlock heaved herself onto a stool at the sink. 'I'll rest myself here and wash, you can dry, you know where things go.'

Eleanor didn't mind. Going back and forth to cupboards meant she wouldn't be expected to chat much.

The older woman passed her the crystal drinking glasses. 'These can go in the bar, in the den. Take care, now, they belonged to my mother.'

Her hands full with two of these treasures, Eleanor kicked open the door to the den. And nearly dropped the glasses onto the oak floor. Right in front of her, Ray and Judith were wrapped in a close embrace. Judith had her back to Eleanor, but her heaving shoulders suggested she was crying.

Suddenly, Ray spotted Eleanor over Judith's shoulder. In one smooth movement, he let go of Judith and stepped forward to face his wife. 'I'm glad you came in, honey, Judith is really upset because she thinks you are angry at her. Now you can tell her yourself that it isn't true.'

Her mind racing, Eleanor set the glasses down on a table.

'Well, it's true that I didn't agree with what you all were saying to Sadie, especially that she should miss out on such a great chance. I just wanted to make sure she knew that.'

Judith turned and raised her reddened eyes. 'Felt like you were telling her not to pay any attention to me.'

Eleanor was struck by the woebegone expression on the younger woman's face. *Have I got this all wrong?* 'Oh Judith, I know you meant well, of course I'm not angry. And I hadn't had a chance to tell you all about the job and other things.'

Moving from Ray, Judith rushed to hug Eleanor. 'I'm so glad, I just don't know what I'd do if we weren't friends anymore.' Turning back to Ray, she reached out her hand. He seemed to know what she wanted. Out came his handkerchief, Judith dabbed her eyes and blew her nose, and her face brightened. 'Now then, Ray, let's you and I make sure everyone's got a drink.'

Eleanor went back into the kitchen and resumed drying the dishes. *I wonder what she was really crying about.*

Making the News

1967

Eleanor's hair was still damp from swimming as she entered the new pizza restaurant on Main Street. The air conditioning hit her with a blast, and she shivered. She spotted Bobbie and the rest of the Masters' swimmers in a corner booth and squeezed in.

'Hot chocolate, please,' she spoke to the waitress as she sat.

Bobbie pushed a pan containing a pizza the size of a wagon wheel in her direction.

'Help yourself, honey, we were just talking about you.'

'Oh dear, what have I done?' Eleanor's reply resulted in a burst of laughter around the table.

Phil, one of the small group of swimmers who was older than Eleanor, punched her lightly on the arm. 'Listen to that accent, don't we just love it?'

'Honestly, you lot, I've been twenty years in this country, and you still think I talk like the Queen.'

Bobbie laughed. 'Well, you sure as hell don't talk like us, but we love you anyway.'

Eleanor joined in the laughter. 'I know you do, I'm happy to give you something to joke about. So, what's going on?'

Bobbie shot a glance at Phil, then spoke up. 'Now then, Eleanor, we know you've always said you don't want to do any competitions, but we've got a big, big favour to ask.'

Eleanor started to speak, but she didn't get a chance. Bobbie talked right over her.

'Hold your horses there, girl, and hear me out. What it is, is Lizzie, Ronnie Mae and me want to enter a relay team in the County Championships, but our ages have got to add up to 160 years.'

Eleanor waited. The 'big, big favour' was coming.

'We need someone over forty-five to make it up to 160, and we've looked through all the club lists, and guess what?'

'No, what?' Eleanor shot her friend a suspicious look.

Bobbie was undeterred. 'Now, don't you cut your eyes at me, I'm offering you the great opportunity of joining the Stony Point Women's 160 Years Relay Team, how about it?'

Eleanor took a sip of her hot chocolate. And another. Then she nibbled at a slice of pizza. She wasn't going to admit it, but after going along to a few of the club competitions, she'd been thinking she'd like to give it a try. Everybody got so excited about the relays, lots of jumping around and hugging. It reminded her of her netball days.

'Fine. I'll do it.' She had to chuckle at the astonished looks around the table.

'Wait a minute, you didn't even give me a chance to make all the arguments, you're no fun!' Bobbie pretend-pouted. She beckoned to the waitress. 'I reckon this calls for something stronger than hot chocolate.'

Two months later, Eleanor and Sadie dragged themselves into the house and deposited half a dozen shopping bags on the floor in Sadie's bedroom.

Sadie had protested at first when her mother suggested a pre-university clothes buying spree. 'Mom, it's California. They don't have seasons out there like we do, and they sure don't wear fancy clothes. I just need plenty of shorts and t-shirts, a few pairs of jeans, and I'll be all set.'

'Humour me, Sadie, we can have lunch and spend some of the money I'm going to earn when I start work at the school.'

As they looked through their purchases, they heard Ray

coming upstairs.

'Hey Dad, come and look at all the hippie clothes I got for California,' Sadie giggled as she called out.

Ray appeared in the doorway, glass of whisky in one hand, the Stony Point Daily Sentinel in the other. He smiled at Sadie. 'Very funny, you can't get me going like that. You've got too much sense to turn into a hippie out there, I bet my life on it.' He turned to Eleanor. 'Honey, can I talk to you downstairs?'

Ray put the newspaper on the dining room table and opened it to the sports page. He stabbed his finger on a headline: 'Local Masters Top the Table at County Championships'. Puzzled, Eleanor looked at the article, then she began to sweat as she read. "Another success was the women's 160+ years relay team. With the help of newcomer Eleanor Miller, they triumphed in both events and added maximum points to the team tally."

Ray shook his head. 'Honey, I don't know what you were thinking. Putting yourself through that stress, risking your health.'

As he spoke, Eleanor could tell from the bourbon fumes that the whiskey in his hand was probably not his first of the day. 'Ray, I don't understand why it bothers you so much. It's fun, I like the people, it keeps me fit. But you seem to think it's harmful.'

Ray's voice trembled. 'I know you're physically fine now, but don't you remember when we first met? You'd had a breakdown, you were scared of your own shadow, and you had to go back to Mommy and Daddy. And I don't want to see you end up in a mental hospital.'

'Ray, that was a long time ago, and having bombs dropping all around was completely different, surely you can see that?' Her voice dropped. 'You know, for a long time it's felt like you… that you and Judith… want me to be weak, not to do things, not to have other friends.'

His face went a deep red. His hand shook so much he had to put his drink down. He was almost shouting. 'She's your *friend*, I'm your *husband*, and we love you. How can you say that?'

'Stop it, you two!' Sadie stood in the doorway. Her face was pale, there were tears in her eyes. She picked up her backpack and slammed out of the house.

Eleanor looked at Ray for a long moment. 'Okay, Ray, no more competitions.' *For Sadie.* She followed Sadie out of the house, leaving Ray alone with his drink.

Treading Water

June 1967

Seven o'clock on a Saturday morning. Eleanor heard Bobbie's car horn sound down in the street. Ray and Sadie were still sleeping. She'd heard Ray stumbling around his study till late the night before. He often fell asleep on a folding bed in there. She would find the empty bottles the next day, in a neat row by the trash can, for disposal. Not a word was said between them about his escalating alcohol consumption. And, after a few rebuffs, she no longer tried to persuade him to come to bed with her. To get some rest, or for any other reason.

Eleanor stuffed a pack of sandwiches and a thermos of coffee into her swimming bag. This would be her first lake swim.

She pushed her sadness about what was happening to her marriage to the back of her mind and smiled at Bobbie. 'I'm excited, I feel like a child going on vacation.'

'I think you're gonna love it. Let's get going!'

As they drove out of town into the mountains, Eleanor felt the air change. They left the stifling heat and humidity behind them, rolled down the windows, and let the breeze blow through their hair.

After about an hour, they pulled into the lake entrance and paid the ranger at the gate.

Lizzie, Ronnie-Mae, and Phil were already there, and led the way through the trees around to the beach area. A wide stretch of sand, the lake waters lapping up to it, and a tree covered island a few hundred yards offshore. *It's heaven*, thought Eleanor.

Phil gestured. 'Ladies changing cabin thataway, mine's this way, see y'all in the water.'

Eleanor started to strip, her suit underneath her clothes. 'No need, I'm prepared.' She pulled on her goggles, and was first in. All the pool training she'd done for the past years stood her in good stead, and before she knew it, she saw the rocks and submerged logs at the edge of the island.

Carefully putting her feet down, she waded to a small bank and pulled herself up. Mud squelched between her toes.

'You okay, Eleanor?' Phil was right behind her. 'I know some folks don't like lake swimming, what with the muddy bottom and the fish, and all.'

'Phil, there were a lot worse things in the sea where I used to swim, a long time ago. I don't mind this a bit.' For a moment, Eleanor was back on Scilly, smiling as she remembered Harvey, remembered the sea urchins, and the two of them laughing at his improvised treatment of her stings. She realised that Phil was speaking.

'Looks like you went a long way away just then, kiddo.'

Eleanor nodded. She must have had a dreamy expression. 'Happy memories.' She pointed to the water. 'Here they come, maybe we can swim round the island, what do you think?'

Later that afternoon, Bobbie dropped Eleanor at the bottom of the drive. She couldn't have driven up it, Judith's car was parked in the way. Eleanor went to the line and hung out her wet clothes. *How am I going to play this? Sadie was so upset when she heard us arguing, can't let that happen again.*

Eleanor walked calmly towards the house. Her daughter would be at university in months, and until then she could just tread water, wait it out, refresh herself in the lake at the weekends. *I can do this for now, then we'll see.*

'Hello, everyone!' she called out. Judith was in the kitchen,

Ray on a chair, reading the paper as she worked. *Lovely domestic scene* thought Eleanor.

Judith waved an oven glove. 'We weren't sure when y'all would get back, so I just fixed a bit of fried chicken and mashed potatoes, I didn't think you'd feel like cooking after all that exercise.'

'That's very kind of you.' Eleanor realised she wasn't forcing herself to put on a sunny face, she really did feel relaxed. And hungry. 'Smells great, when do we eat?'

Two months passed. On an overcast, thundery day, Ray and Eleanor helped Sadie to pack the last of her belongings into the Anstey's car. The late-August heat was oppressive, and Eleanor was glad to see the air conditioning controls in the car. Rick Anstey had just finished a PhD in Ray's department. His wife Stella had a job at a hospital in Los Angeles, and he had been offered a junior post at UCLA. They'd been the answer to the Millers' dilemma: how to get Sadie, and everything she needed for university, nearly three thousand miles across the country? The Ansteys were happy to have the extra money for petrol, and Sadie was thrilled to be taking a classic road trip.

'Will we be going on Route 66? *Please?*'

Eleanor laughed. 'From what I hear, only if you want to take a couple of weeks to get there. And you've got to turn up for Freshman Orientation, so I guess it'll be the interstate pretty much all the way.'

Eleanor and Ray gave their daughter a last hug. Then, loaded to the roof, the Ansteys' car rolled slowly down the drive.

Eleanor followed Ray into the kitchen. Despite the August heat, she shivered. All the warmth had gone out of the house.

Back to School

September 1967

Eleanor looked at the curved corrugated shape of the Cleveland Hill Special School. The building reminded her of the Quonset huts that had welcomed visitors to St. Mary's Airfield. Given the ex-military use of the housing on the Hill, this had probably served a similar purpose. None of the granite permanence of Carn Friar's.

As she walked down the corridor, some children greeted her. 'You the new TA?' asked one, a girl of about ten. Her honey-coloured hair hung in plaits, which swayed as she shifted her walking frame to accompany Eleanor.

'That's right, I'm Mrs. Miller. And you are?'

'Cheryl,' came the reply, 'I'm in your class. Our TA got pregnant. Principal's office over there.' She pointed to a chipped door which was still painted military grey.

'Thank you, Cheryl, I kind of remembered from when I was here in the summer, but I wasn't sure.' She knocked on the door. 'See you in class, thanks for showing me the way.'

Emily Rogers, the Principal, opened the office door. 'Nice to see you again, here's Patsy Thomas, she teaches the third grade, you'll be helping her out.'

'Hi Eleanor, good to have you with us, the kids are looking forward to meeting you.'

Eleanor was no longer surprised by the American way. Jump straight to first names. Although it was going to take some getting used to in a professional setting.

'Let's go face the music, they're always kind of hyper at the start of term.' Patsy led the way into a classroom that showed evidence of efforts to erase the military shadows. Bright curtains, paintings on the walls, stacked craft boxes on shelves.

'What a happy place!' Eleanor couldn't wait to start.

Patsy grinned. 'Can't even feel the ghosts of the soldiers anymore, can you?' She pulled out a sheet of paper and handed it to Eleanor. 'How about you take the attendance, good way for you to get to know the children. And vice versa.'

'Great, I'll do that. And, uh, what should they call me?'

'Well, they call me Miz Patsy, this is the South, after all. But they usually just call the TAs by their first names if that's okay with you. I guess it's different in England.'

'It's been so long since I taught, but I think it's still Miss for all the women teachers over there, married or not.'

Patsy looked at her thoughtfully. 'Yeah, I forgot, you're a qualified teacher. Hope this don't seem like too much of a comedown for you.'

'Absolutely not! I haven't taught in years, my qualifications aren't recognised here anyway, and I'm just so glad to get this opportunity.' She paused, remembering the crowded classrooms and strict rules of her early teaching days. 'We had all ages and abilities at my last school, but I've never had the chance to work with children with learning disabilities. There's so much I can learn here.' *And maybe one day I can go back and get my qualifications, who knows?*

'Well, I think we're going to be just fine, then. Let's get started.'

Sunday lunches with the Whitlocks continued, a weekly torment for Eleanor. The loss of her daughter's companionship left her isolated at the family table. Excluded from Ray's bond with his 'true family', merely tolerated by them.

Yet something was different. Instead of dragging a lump of dread from one weekend to the next, the ordeal of Sundays was diminished by the days in between.

It was still warm enough to go to the lake most Saturdays, and sessions in the pool kept her going through the week. As did the pizza afterwards. Eleanor kept her promise to Ray and declined offers to make up relays. She'd done this to spare Sadie the distress of arguments, and her loss had served its purpose. Smooth sailing through the summer. But now Sadie was no longer there, Eleanor's mind wandered, *I'm free to take it further. No more sitting on the side-lines for me, wishing I was part of the excitement. Maybe a charity event?*

Eleanor now had an enjoyable social life and satisfying job. Ray never asked her how she was getting on at work, but neither did he make negative comments. Working mornings only, she was always home when he got back anyway, so she guessed her job hardly existed for him.

In any case, she didn't need his approval. Every day at the school was absorbing, and she got plenty of positive feedback from colleagues. Each time she responded to a challenge another piece of her confidence returned.

There were only twelve children in the class, but their extensive needs meant Patsy and Eleanor were kept busy making sure that each child had chances for success and progress. Cheryl hoped to get a job one day. Mason, who didn't always speak, was learning to sign and write his name.

Eleanor loved the ethos of the school. It was a strong and happy place, but there was one area that seemed a bit lacking, and that was exercise. Several children had physical impairments, but Eleanor didn't see why these should be a barrier. Cheryl, who was able to walk, had bad days when she used a wheelchair. *I know better than some that disability doesn't mean no ability.* Eleanor thought wistfully about the kinds of exercise she'd enjoyed with Harvey and smiled at the memory.

Her journey into work took her past the little outdoor swimming pool where, many years ago, Sadie had learned to swim. Eleanor decided there was nothing to lose.

'Patsy, I want to try out an idea on you before I say anything to Mrs. Rogers.' They were tidying the classroom at the end of the day.

'Fire away, I usually like your ideas.'

'What about swimming for the children? The pool's only across the way, it's not deep, and it's heated. We couldn't use it in the winter, but what about when the weather's warm?'

Emily Rogers was not one to dither. A proposal to the governors, and before Eleanor knew what hit her, she was enrolled on a swimming instructor's course. Patsy, grumbling, signed up to train as a lifeguard, and the Cleveland Crayfish Swimming Club was born.

Sitting on the sand at the lake in early October, Eleanor thought back to the previous Thanksgiving and her cheerful announcement that had freed Sadie to take up the UCLA offer. *I was speaking more in hope than expectation about going to the lake, having a job. Looks like I've been my own fairy godmother.*

Another advantage of Eleanor's more balanced life was its effect on her relationship with Ray. He stopped trying to convince her that she was weak and incapable. *Overwhelming evidence to the contrary,* she thought.

Bobbie nudged her. 'Liven up, Eleanor, it's our last time here till spring, no daydreaming.'

Slowly, Eleanor got to her feet, then broke into a run. 'Race you to the island!'

Shocking

December 1967

A Sunday morning. Ray had gone to early Mass, saying he didn't mind going alone, and that Eleanor should relax and enjoy a lie-in. She didn't argue. She was happy to have a bit of a laze before getting the roast ready. The Whitlocks would arrive around twelve, as usual.

It felt to Eleanor as if she and Ray had reached a truce in a battle that had exhausted them both. Maybe they would even go to the movies, do things contented couples did? At least Eleanor was content, but Ray? Ray was quiet. And most nights, he drank until the early hours.

Still in her dressing-gown, Eleanor picked the newspaper off the front porch. She decided to try the Sunday crossword. She was sure Ray kept a dictionary in his briefcase, so she made herself a cup of tea and had a look. The first item she found was a thick folder, with a small hand-drawn crucifix in the corner. She knew Ray was working on pieces inspired by biblical quotes, wondered how he was getting on with it, and opened the folder.

On top of various typed items was a bound bundle of what looked like handwritten letters, except that they were on lined file paper. Odd. Eleanor untied the string and spread them out on the desk. She picked up the first one.

"I dream of those kisses under the dogwood tree. My heart beats faster whenever I know we are going to meet."

At first, Eleanor was amused. So, Ray was secretly writing light romantic fiction, under the cloak of a worthy religious effort. Curious, she read on, leafing through the closely written pages. She didn't recognise the handwriting, and gradually she realised that these were letters addressed *to* him, not fiction *by* him. Written by Judith, detailing their meetings at conferences, snatched kisses in hotel rooms, and longings for a future together. The smile disappeared from Eleanor's face. *I've been such a fool.*

She swept the folder and letters across the desk around the room, onto the floor. Then, measuring her steps, regaining control of her actions, undressed and packed. *All along, they were together. I should have known.* She halted her packing briefly. *But I did know, it's just I believed them instead of myself. Never again. Let them wonder where I've gone, I need to think.*

Eleanor looked at the pile of library books by her bedside. *Better take some reading, no telling how long I'll be gone. Rosemary's Baby* joined the neatly folded nightdress, underwear, and casual clothes in her case. "A compelling and disturbing story, in which a seemingly caring and well-meaning couple assume control over the mind and body of a young woman." Eleanor shivered as she read the jacket blurb. *Maybe not for late-night reading.*

She checked to make sure she'd left everything ready for the meal. They would only need to cook the vegetables. Ray and Judith would almost certainly see her disappearance, no matter what the cause, as further evidence of her frailty and instability. However, leaving everything well-prepared for a meal that she would not share might at least undermine that assessment. *Lunch might be slightly delayed,* she thought, *but there'll be plenty to talk about while they're waiting.*

As she closed the door behind her, she imagined Ray returning from Mass and finding that she and her little Toyota runabout were gone. How long would it take him to find the folder on his desk, the letters crumpled and scattered? What would he think when his search of the house revealed that her overnight bag, hat, and coat had vanished? And how would he explain her absence to the Whitlocks?

She decided not to leave a note.

Part Eight:
Renewal—1968-1972

Back to the Farm

Christmas 1967

Eleanor did not go far. Straight up into the mountains. Her little car objected, but she urged the ancient vehicle up each hill, keeping the windows open for relief from the uncontrolled blast of the heater, stuck on high.

This time of year, most of the rental cabins at Lake Shenandoah were empty. One would be a place to gather her thoughts, decide what to do. Billy the caretaker lit a fire in the cabin, looking sideways at her as she stared out of the window, through the bare trees to the silvery lake.

"'Scuse me, can I get you anything from the store, ma'am? Maybe some food, few more logs?' Anxious tone, furrowed brow. 'You plannin' on stayin' long?'

He probably doesn't know what to make of me, poor chap. Eleanor smiled, hoping to reassure him. 'Why, thank you, maybe a loaf of bread, a couple cans of soup, some coffee, eggs. Whatever you think might keep me going for one or two days.'

He nodded and moved rapidly towards the door.

'Oh, is there a phone I can use?' *Better call Ray. That would be the sane, considerate thing. I need to know how he is going to react, to prepare myself.*

'Pay phone outside my cabin, down that track.' He pointed back away from the lake. 'Help yourself.'

She heard Billy's pickup roar into life. The store was a few miles down the road, she had time. Pulling her warm coat around her, she fished coins from her purse.

'I'm so glad you troubled yourself to call.' The words were said slowly.

Oh dear, he's drunk. Never slurs his words like most drunks, gets more precise. No point trying to talk.

'I wanted to let you know I was safe, but I don't know when I'll be back. I found the letters from Judith, I need to think, and I need to do it away from you.' She let out a breath.

'Thank you very much for letting me know.' He hung up.

Eleanor rested her head on top of the payphone. Ray sounded so cold, detached. But he must be angry. What would he do when, if, she returned? Fear overtook her, as sweat trickled from her armpits despite the cold. *You hear about husbands putting their wives away, would he really do something like that?* She took a deep breath. *You haven't done anything wrong.*

Eleanor was shivering, but there was one more call to make. She shoved a pile of silver into the phone, and dialled Sadie's number in California.

'Hi Mom, what's this? Early Sunday morning call, are you okay?'

'Yes, I am, Sadie, but I'm taking, well, a break, I guess you could call it. Some time away, er, from your father.'

A brief silence. Then, 'That's not the biggest surprise I've ever had.'

'You knew? That there were... problems?'

Eleanor heard Sadie's sigh down the line. 'Of course I did. Made me miserable for a while, Dad pickled most of the time, tension you could slice, the Whitlocks always there. But time and distance have given me a chance to reflect.' A pause. 'Maybe you need the same. Things don't always work out, do they?'

Eleanor was surprised by these words of wisdom, and the

hint that Sadie accepted that her parents might split up. And that she'd seen and heard more than they had realised.

Eleanor relaxed. 'I think you've just said what's in my mind.'

A plan started to form. *Time and distance, eh?* 'Sadie, I'm staying at the lake for a day or so, trying to think what to do. This might be a crazy idea, but what if I just kept on driving up to Rolling Stone? I've been dreading spending another Christmas with Judith and her parents, and I'd love to see your dad's folks.'

She braced herself, expecting Sadie to be horrified at the thought of her mother making the thousand-mile journey north. On her own. In the winter. Again, her daughter surprised her.

'Great idea!' Eleanor could hear the enthusiasm in Sadie's voice. 'Tell you what, Mom, I get a long holiday at Christmas, why don't I join you for a bit? I could get the train out from LA, I'd love to see Oma and Opa, and Christmas on the farm,' Sadie's voice wobbled, 'would be wonderful.' She ended with a sniff.

Touched, but unsure how to comfort her daughter over the phone, Eleanor spoke briskly. 'Right then, love, I'll maybe give them a call tomorrow, see what they say. Better go now, it's freezing out here and we're going to get cut off any second.'

Eleanor spent a peaceful evening, reading *Rosemary's Baby* and dozing in front of the little acorn stove. Billy had provided soup and rolls, and two bottles of Pennsylvania Rock ale. Perhaps he felt she needed calming. Eleanor was familiar with this students' favourite, which turned out to be drinkable, even though she wasn't fond of beer.

From time to time, Eleanor put down her book and imagined driving to the farm, waiting for her inner sensible person to talk her out of it. After three hours, it still seemed like a good idea. She decided to sleep on it.

Early the next day, she fished out the remaining change from her purse and hurried to the phone. Hilda would never answer, so she had to make sure to ring before Walter went out to check the animals.

She heard his gravelly voice, still with a slight accent after so many years.

'Rochester 2571, Walter Miller speaking.'

Oh dear, what am I doing? Eleanor panicked, nearly hung up. Ray rang his parents about once a month, and sometimes called her to the phone, but she never called them herself. And they hadn't visited in years, was she a stranger to them? *But what's the worst that can happen?*

'Father Miller, it's… it's Nellie, how are you?'

She heard his quick intake of breath, then a wheeze set off a coughing fit. 'Nellie, what's wrong? What's happened?' He managed to catch his breath.

How awful, she thought, *his first thought is of disaster.* 'Everything's fine, don't worry, it's… well, I was wondering if I could come and visit for a few weeks, it's been such a long time.' She stopped and there was a pause before Walter spoke..

'Of course, we would be so happy to see you. And Ray? Sadie?' His voice had gone from distressed to puzzled.

'Actually, Ray won't be coming, I will explain when I get there. But Sadie would like to join us for Christmas.'

'Hilda, it's Nellie, she and Sadie are coming to visit! For Christmas!' Walter had probably turned from the phone to shout to his wife, but there was no mistaking his joy.

Snow had begun to fall as Eleanor pulled up to the farmhouse. *Whew, just made it. No snow tyres, I'd have been in a pickle if it started to pile up.* The front door was flung open, and two figures stood in the doorway, just as when she'd first arrived. But this time, moving a bit slowly, the older couple stepped onto the porch with their arms outstretched. First Hilda, then Walter enfolded Eleanor in firm hugs that belied their years. She realised that the dampness on her cheeks was not melting snow.

In the midst of all this emotion, Eleanor felt something hairy against her legs. A small terrier, tail in near full rotation, was demanding instant attention.

She looked up from scratching the rough fur on its head. 'This can't be?'

Walter shook his head. 'Oh no, Bonzo is long gone.' He pointed out of the window to a small, engraved stone, half covered in snow. 'But this is Bonzo's daughter, we call her Lucy, I don't know why.'

Hilda spoke up. 'Silly old man, you know it's my favourite programme, "I Love Lucy". That's why.' She took a long look at Eleanor. 'So, are you hungry, travelling girl?'

'I certainly am, I'll just get my things, freshen up a bit, if that's all right?'

Hilda led her through the dining room to the spare room at the back of the house. *Thank goodness, not our 'honeymoon' suite. I won't be haunted by memories.*

After a substantial farm supper, they sat round the table. So much to catch up on. Conversation had flowed around her journey, the contents of Sadie's letters (giving her parents what were probably edited versions of university life), Eleanor's teaching, the success of the farm crops, the farmhands they'd hired to help out. Lots to talk about. And not a single mention of Ray, nor a question raised about why she had come.

Silence fell. Finally, Walter spoke. 'Nellie, Ray called us.'

Uh-oh, let's see where this goes.

Hilda leaned forward. 'He said he made mistakes, he upset you, but you maybe took it the wrong way?' Her tone was hesitant. 'He said he was very mixed up.'

It sounded as if Ray was trying to be honest with his parents. 'Yes, it's true, we've had problems.'

Walter was bracing himself. His fists balled, he leaned as close to Eleanor as the table would allow. 'Nellie, you know we love you, and we love our son. This is real hard for us.'

'I know, and the last thing I want to do is make you feel that you have to take sides. You don't, and that's not why I'm here.'

Walter's fists unclenched a bit. 'Mother Miller and I, we had a talk after he called, and this is what we think.' He took a gulp of water. 'We sure don't want to know any details. Ray said he loved you, but there is someone he's got close to, and that's more than we want to know, right there.'

Eleanor waited. Eventually he continued. 'I guess these days people get divorced at the drop of a hat, but we wanted to ask you…' He stopped and put his head in his hands, as if it was too much for him to go on.

Eleanor touched his arm. 'I think you understand something about what's happening. It's true that divorce is a possibility, but I know that goes against everything that the two of you believe in, am I right?'

He nodded. 'We want to ask you to maybe give it another try, see if the two of you can make it work?'

Eleanor looked at the couple, who'd been so kind to her, who were suffering almost as much as she was. And she suspected that they didn't even know about Ray's drinking.

'I'll tell you what. I'd like to stay with you for a few weeks, till after Christmas. I won't speak any more about any of this unless you want to ask me something. I just want to enjoy being with you, and Sadie when she comes. Then when I get back, if Ray's willing, we'll maybe go see someone, get help, see if we can make things work.'

The Sunday before Christmas, Eleanor drove to the train station in Chicago, feeling a twinge of sadness as she recalled the last time she'd been there. The beautiful building was alive with sparkling lights, and the sound of a brass band playing carols. Sadie almost ran down the steps of the Southwest Chief into her mother's arms. They sobbed as the rest of the passengers eddied around them.

Eleanor blew her nose. 'I am so, so happy to see you!'

Sadie was busy with her own handkerchief. 'Mom, you look wonderful!' She scrutinised her mother's face. 'Not a bit like a woman in the middle of a marriage crisis, I would say.'

'It's done me so much good to be at the farm, I guess it shows. Getting away from the problems.'

'Well, fine, but I want to know, what tipped you over the edge? What happened? Last straw and all that.'

'It's a bit tricky, I know your dad loves you, and I guess you're fond of Judith. In fact, so am I. We're friends, in a way. And I don't want to…'

Sadie interrupted. 'Yeah, okay, I love you all, but just tell me the facts. I will work my own way through it.'

'We've got a four-hour drive back to the farm, we'll probably stop for a bite, so plenty of time to talk on the way. Once we get there, let's have a peaceful Christmas with your grandparents. They know roughly what's going on, but they told me that all they want is to enjoy the time together.'

Sadie planted a kiss on Eleanor's cheek. 'It's a deal.'

Hours later, Sadie sprinted up the steps to embrace both

waiting grandparents at the same time. 'Oma, Opa, I can't believe I'm really here!'

Eleanor remembered being horrified by Hilda's German words when they first met. *Funny, hearing my own daughter using childhood German names doesn't bother me a bit now.*

Hilda led them through into the family room where a roaring fire greeted them. Spicy smells hung in the air, mingled with pine scent from the Advent wreath.

Hilda indicated the fragrant circle with its four candles. 'Now is the fourth Sunday, we will light the candles, but first, a drink.'

Eleanor and Sadie flung themselves into overstuffed green armchairs.

'Same furniture, I do believe.' Sadie rubbed the worn chair arms.

'Built to last,' said Walter, 'no need to change.'

Hilda disappeared into the kitchen and returned with a tray of steaming cups. 'You like Glühwein, of course?'

Eleanor could sense the effort that had gone into their welcome. She felt a glow that had nothing to do with the wine.

She raised her drink. 'Frohe Weihnachten!' Glasses clinked, smiles all round. Eleanor looked at the beaming faces, as Hilda and Walter heard her give a traditional German greeting. *No-one knows that those are the first German words to pass my lips. My gift to you, dear in-laws.* Sadie, post-War baby, seemed oblivious to the undercurrents.

They finished their wine, and Hilda herded them into position around the wreath. Using a taper, she lit the first candle. 'The prophets foretold the coming of Christ.'

She passed the taper to Walter, who spoke confidently, 'The child in the manger brings love.' He lit the second candle.

Eleanor could see that Sadie looked worried, as it dawned on her that she would be expected to speak.

Eleanor took the taper from Walter and lit the third candle, remembering her earlier Christmases at Rolling Stone. 'The shepherds brought joy at the birth of the child.' She turned to Sadie, mouthing 'peace', and Sadie improvised: 'Peace to all at this blessed time.'

Hilde took charge again. 'So now, we sing. Stille Nacht. But we are in America.' She raised her head, and her voice was thin but true: 'Silent night…'

The rest joined in; their faces lit by candle flicker as they sang.

Suspended

1968

'Ray, there's a bit of a thaw, I'll start the drive back to Stony Point tomorrow.'

Mid-January, and Eleanor was ready to keep her promise to Hilda and Walter.

'All right, I was beginning to wonder if you would ever come back. Anyway, drive carefully.'

Eleanor thought his voice sounded different. Unsure of himself, maybe shaken by her weeks away. She knew he'd spent the holiday with the Whitlocks. *I'd like to have been a fly on the wall at that little gathering.*

He spoke again. 'Eleanor, I'm so sorry about what you found, I can explain…'

She stopped him. 'Not now. We'll talk when I get back.'

The day after her return, talk they did. About 'till death do us part', and the marriage vows. About his confusion at the all-consuming love he felt for Judith, mixed with feelings he still had for Eleanor. About her annoyance with his need to see her in a negative light.

'It's almost as if you have to think of me as weak and frail, so you could be a carer for me and a lover for Judith.' At the farm, Eleanor had plenty of time to think, and now Ray was getting the benefit of her conclusions.

'I promise you, Eleanor, Judith and I never did anything. I mean, our relationship wasn't physical. I was never unfaithful, that would have been a mortal sin.'

Eleanor sighed. 'I believe you, Ray. Following the rules of the Church is important to you, even if our marriage isn't.

Although I've never been so sure what "unfaithful" is.'

'I didn't mean it to sound like that,' he protested. 'It's just that you and I, we seem to have grown so far apart. With Sadie gone, we don't have much left.'

Eleanor sat in silence, hearing the truth in his words. She noticed his hands were shaking. *He's held off drinking today*, she thought. *What a picture of woe. Better get this over with.*

'Ray, I really don't want to give up on us without trying, to see if there's anything left.' She reached out to touch his hand. 'We loved each other so much, in the beginning.'

'We did, but trouble is, all I can think about is how much I want to be with Judith, and I don't know if I can stand it much longer.'

Eleanor wanted to hide her hurt. 'And drinking helps you cope with the misery of being married to me?'

'No, no, it takes away the pain of not being with her.' He stopped, perhaps realising that this was the first time he'd acknowledged his drinking.

They were side by side on the sofa, and Eleanor couldn't bear sitting next to him any longer. She stood. 'Look, Ray, do you want to try to repair our marriage, to get some help?' *There you are, Walter and Hilda, I said I'd try.*

The long pause wasn't promising, but at last Ray said, 'Eleanor, I do. I reckon this is the first time we've talked honestly, and I feel a bit better already.' He stood, putting his arms around her in what felt to her like a brotherly hug. She clung to him, realising how starved she was for affectionate touch. She promised herself if it didn't come back into their marriage, she would not spend the rest of her life without it.

'Then I'll see if I can find anyone who does Catholic couples' sessions.' She kissed his cheek, and they parted in peace.

Irretrievable Breakdown

1969-70

Eleanor thought it would be easy. In America, there were so many therapists. Or so it seemed. However, finding one who was able to counsel Catholic couples proved frustrating, disheartening. She rebuffed Ray's attempts to explain away the letters from Judith, wrapping herself in a cocoon of silence on the subject.

Finally, they crept far enough up the waiting list of a Catholic counsellor to at least get an assessment. Michael Jarvis was about fifty or so, Eleanor thought when they first met, but he never divulged even a crumb of personal information so she couldn't be sure. He wore a suit and tie, favoured a nice lemony aftershave. A firm handshake, direct eye contact and what Eleanor thought of as 'American teeth'. Rigorously straightened at some point in childhood.

Michael made it clear to them he saw his role as that of an enabler. 'I'm here to make it possible for each of you to give your views, and then help you decide if there's any way the marriage can continue. I'm not here as a judge, to determine who's right or wrong.' His gaze moved from one to the other. No objections received. 'And I will be looking to help each of you identify what you might have contributed to the breakdown.' *Food for thought, that.* Eleanor wasn't sure she welcomed quite such a balanced approach.

Another six months, then finally they began monthly sessions. It started well. Ray and Eleanor agreed afterwards that while sympathy from the counsellor was in short supply, understanding was not. Eleanor thought they managed to use

Michael's approach to take tiny steps forward. With no prompting, Ray promised not to contact Judith, and Eleanor promised not to check up on him.

However, the empty bottles continued to pile up in the trash. After a few months, Eleanor spoke up at the beginning of a session. 'Ray, I'm really worried about how drinking is affecting your health.' *There, I've said the forbidden word.*

Ray gripped the chair arms, white knuckled. 'You may not have noticed, but I've cut down.'

He's gone on the defensive, it's no good, thought Eleanor.

Michael turned to Ray. 'Does what Eleanor says make any sense to you?'

Ray's tone was despairing. 'Sorry, everyone, but I can't make this choice. Save our marriage and lose Judith. It's just too much.' He put his head in his hands.

At that moment, Eleanor understood. Their improved behaviour to each other was like a kindness that might be given to a sick or dying person. But maybe it was only on the surface, as Ray still seemed to need alcohol to treat the pain of separation from the person who mattered most.

A month later, just as they were getting ready for their next session, he stopped at the door. 'Look, can you tell Michael something's come up at work. I just can't do this; I feel torn in two.'

Eleanor went on her own, and she settled into her usual chair in Michael's office. But she did not pass on Ray's lie.

Instead, she told her own truth. 'Michael, I'm not sure I want to carry on. Ray didn't want to come today, his heart isn't in it. I feel like I ought to keep trying because when we made our vows, I believed I loved him, and that we were joined for life.' She sighed. 'You know, looking back, when Judith came into our lives, I started to lose my confidence, I guess.' She glanced at Michael, who remained still, a look of intent listening on his face. 'Somehow she and Ray started treating me like I was mentally or physically ill, and I began to believe I must be.'

Michael leaned forward slightly. 'Tell me if I'm wrong, but I'm getting the impression you're starting to question that view.'

Eleanor shifted in her chair. 'I've made friends, started to enjoy myself with them.' Her speech was halting. 'Sorry I'm taking so long with this. It's as if up till now what we've been telling you has been all about our history, we know it by heart, and today… it's like I'm figuring out a new story.' A pause.

'Which is?' said Michael, his voice gentle.

'That maybe I need to change my life, that in some way I need to get away from Ray as much as he wants to leave me.' She twisted her fingers in her lap. 'Oh my God, I don't believe I've said that.' She straightened her shoulders. 'I can't keep watching him drink himself to death because he simply doesn't love me anymore. Or he loves Judith more.' She sank back, exhausted. 'Is a divorce the worst thing that could happen?' Almost in a whisper, she answered her own question. 'I think we've reached the end.'

'You know, sometimes what happens is that couples find a way to say goodbye without tearing each other apart,' said Michael, 'and it's not wrong to count that as a kind of achievement. Next time we meet, maybe that's what could happen for you and Ray.'

As she left, Eleanor felt numb. Not distraught, as she might have been even a few months ago, but free of pain.

Two weeks later, the insistent ringing of the phone woke Eleanor from a sound sleep. She felt for the receiver beside the bed, knocked the phone onto the floor, and finally managed to answer it, lying half out of the bed. 'Eleanor Miller here,' she mumbled. She squinted at her watch. One o'clock in the morning.

'Mrs. Miller, I'm calling from the Emergency Room at the hospital.'

Eleanor was wide awake now. 'What's happened? Is it my husband?'

'Yes, I'm afraid he's been taken ill. Don't panic, he's stable and not in any immediate danger, but we can't discharge him. Would you be able to come in? We can fill you in on the details when you get here.'

Ray lay stretched out in the ER. Hooked up to an intravenous drip, rolling back and forth, mumbling, sometimes banging against the rails pulled up on each side of the bed. As she watched in alarm, he became still. His eyes were open, but he seemed to be staring into space, stupefied.

I've never seen him like this. Eleanor looked at the doctor who'd shown her to the cubicle. 'What's the matter with him?' She thought she had a pretty good idea; she could smell the booze.

'We think he's had way too much bourbon, way too quickly. Alcohol poisoning, you could say. In a stupor.' Eleanor looked sharply at the young medic. There was no sign of judgment on his face, or in his tone. He checked Ray's pulse, adjusted the IV, and continued. 'He was pretty much unconscious outside the 7-Eleven, couple of the guys he was with got someone in the store to call the ambulance.'

The image sickened Eleanor, Ray slumped outside a convenience store with other drinkers as customers came and went. She had convinced herself he mainly drank at home, clattering around in his study at night. Or occasionally at cocktail parties, where he presented as a 'professorial drunk'.

A bit too friendly with the ladies, a bit unsteady on his feet. Nothing unusual for those occasions.

This, however, looked like a catastrophic slide into oblivion. It was as if he didn't care about anything other than the bottle. She noticed he was wearing a hospital gown. Had he soiled his clothes?

'What happens now, what should I do?' She imagined she sounded as lost as she felt.

A small smile from the doctor. 'To tell you the truth, there's not much you can do till he comes round a bit. We may need to give him further treatment and keep an eye on him overnight. If he vomits, there's a danger of choking.'

Eleanor put the bag she had hastily assembled on the floor by the bed. 'There are a few of his things here, maybe someone could put his pyjamas on?'

'We'll look after him, don't worry. You get some rest and come back tomorrow.'

Eleanor couldn't get the key in the car door; her hands shook too much. *I'm not safe to drive.* Finally, she managed to open the door and slump into the seat. Looking out of the window, she could see people coming and going in the rain-slicked hospital car park. Worried-looking relatives, hospital staff arriving for their shifts or perhaps on a break. A busy night-time world, which she was reluctant to leave for the eerie solitude of home. A better idea came to her as she waited for calm. She edged her way past the other vehicles and out onto the road.

It was 3am when she pressed the doorbell of Judith's Colonial-style duplex. After a few minutes, an upstairs window opened. Judith peered down at her, blonde curls framing her sleep-flushed face. *How lovely she looks*, thought Eleanor. *And I'm about to shatter her serenity.*

'Eleanor,' hissed Judith. 'What on earth are you doing down there? Do you know what the time is? Heaven's sake!' She slammed the window shut.

Funny, she doesn't even sound worried, doesn't ask about some sort of emergency, she's just annoyed. Eleanor wondered what it must be like to live in a world where everything usually goes smoothly for you. The door opened. 'Come on in, sit yourself down, tell me what's going on. I'll make us some coffee.'

Eleanor perched on a bar stool in the kitchen. 'Judith, Ray's in hospital.'

That got a reaction. 'Oh, my Lord, what happened? Is he all right?' She was still bustling around with coffee cups.

'Well, yes, he's going to be. I think. They told me to go see him in the morning when he's, um, feeling better.' Eleanor hesitated. She wanted an honest conversation; this wasn't a good start. 'I should have said, when they've got him sobered up. The ambulance picked him up outside 7-Eleven. Alcohol poisoning.'

Eleanor saw Judith's back stiffen. When she turned back to Eleanor, holding two cups of coffee, her face looked strange, wiped clean of all expression. 'So why exactly are you here in the middle of the night, telling me this?'

Eleanor gripped the edges of the bar stool. 'Because I want you to come with me to the hospital in the morning. But first, I want to tell you why.'

Judith sipped her coffee. Impassive still. 'Go right ahead.'

Now that the moment was here, Eleanor wasn't sure how to begin. 'I don't know how much Ray's told you, but I know you and he are, ah, very close.'

Judith's expression turned wary. 'Well, of course, we've been good friends for years.'

Eleanor's next words came out in a rush. 'No, I mean he loves you, wants to be with you, and he's drinking himself to death because he feels trapped with me. We've tried to do something about it, but it's no good. I still care about him, and I don't want him to die.'

Judith sat as if her knees had given out. For the first time since they'd met, she was speechless, and Eleanor felt in control.

I'm going to make the most of it. 'What I want to know, though, is, do you love him just as much?'

Judith did not hesitate. 'I tell you, from the first minute I laid eyes on him, never been anyone else for me.'

No mistaking the honesty there. Eleanor was reassured. She nodded. 'I just wanted to make sure he wasn't going to end up losing you if we split up. I wondered if you would run away once you knew you could actually be together.'

Judith shook her head. 'Miz Eleanor Miller, you are amazing, talking to me like this.' She took a deep breath. 'I want to say, I don't get on all that well with most women, so you are, well, a precious friend.' She looked at Eleanor. 'Maybe that's hard for you to believe. But I don't want you to hate me.'

'Judith, I don't think you're some kind of monster. Truth is, I can't help but like you too. I just wish we'd never met you. You know, I was in a situation a long time ago where whatever I did, someone would be hurt, including me…' She stopped. Judith was the last person she wanted to tell about Harvey. 'Anyway, I don't want to spend the rest of my life unhappy, and it's not too late for any of us. I got a terrible shock, seeing Ray like that. I guess it made me face reality.'

Judith moved forward, as if to hug her, but stopped. Eleanor turned away.

'Visiting hours 1100, see you there.'

New Chapter?

May 1971

The two women stood together by Ray's bed. He'd been moved to a single room, and he was wearing his own pyjamas. There was evidence of a wash and a shave, not just in the way he looked, but in the absence of the smell of sweat and whisky.

However, underneath the superficial improvements, his appearance was shocking. Closed eyes, sunk into their sockets, thread veins on his nose, his skin a mottled grey. Eleanor stole a look at Judith, whose face had lost its colour. Eleanor cleared her throat; Ray opened his eyes.

Eleanor pulled two chairs up to the bedside. She spoke gently. 'How are you feeling?'

Ray struggled into a half-sitting position. 'Fine, fine, slept pretty well…' Two disbelieving faces greeted this statement. He slumped back. 'In fact, worst hangover ever,' he croaked. 'Don't remember much.'

Judith, unusually subdued to this point, spoke up, 'Eleanor told me what happened. Looks like you pretty near drowned yourself in bourbon, you fool.' The harsh words were belied by the touch of her hand on his cheek. Ray looked at Eleanor, alarm in his eyes. Judith quickly withdrew her hand.

Eleanor decided it was time. 'Ray, I'm here to say I want a divorce. I think you are going to kill yourself if you don't stop drinking. And I just can't bear to watch.' With that, Eleanor couldn't keep calm. She sobbed, quietly, while Judith stroked her arm, looking helpless.

'Eleanor, honey, I'm so sorry, we never set out to hurt you...'

Carefully, Eleanor moved her arm away. She wiped her eyes. 'I know that. And don't think I'm being a saint; I'm doing this for me as well. I don't want to spend my life trying to fix something that's totally broken.'

Eleanor could see a thin sheen of sweat on Ray's forehead. *Quite a few hours since he had a drink, must be getting pretty uncomfortable.* 'I think I've said enough. I've been thinking about this for a while, but I guess it's a bit of a bombshell for you. I'm going home to get some sleep. You two can talk, but I've had enough for now.'

She went home and fell onto the bed, sound asleep in her clothes.

Taken Apart

June 1971

Eleanor wasted no time setting their parting in motion. She and Ray both knew quite a few lawyers from their university contacts, but she chose to look through the phone book and pick one almost at random, leaving him to select his attorney as he wished. She found Priscilla Smith, Attorney-at-Law, who turned out to be a no-nonsense woman with a 'not much I haven't seen' manner.

'Now then, Mrs. Miller, we're suggesting the new "no-fault" divorce. Based simply on a breakdown of the relationship. Some states haven't got it yet, but we do. Every state has different procedures, but it's quicker, easier, and definitely cheaper. That's if you both agree.'

Eleanor had been dreading trying to establish Ray's 'unreasonable behaviour', which she thought was required. So shameful for them both. 'Yes, please, if he agrees, I imagine that would be the least... painful.'

Everything moved so quickly. Two weeks later, she walked through an empty house. Ray was living in a bachelor colleague's spare room, having agreed to pursue the 'no-fault' option. The twelve-month legal separation clock was ticking.

Eleanor considered the people she wanted to inform. Annie, Sadie, Ray's parents. Anyone else could make do with the grapevine. She sat on the floor by the phone and dialled.

'Rochester 2571, Walter Miller speaking.'

Eleanor thought his voice sounded weak. 'Father Miller, it's Nellie.' No response, so she went on. 'I wanted you to know... I tried, we tried, but...'

Then he spoke. 'We know. Ray called, said you were getting divorced. But we still don't understand. He said he was fond of you, but in love with someone else and couldn't live without her.' Eleanor heard an exasperated snort. 'What's that supposed to mean? He will die if he's not with this special woman? Ridiculous, I told him, there would be so many dead people if it was fatal not to follow your passion. I could tell you…'

Eleanor cut him off, fearing unwanted revelations. Evidently Ray hadn't mentioned the drinking. Keeping her voice gentle, she said, 'In fact, I think for Ray it's true. He's been drinking more and more for years now because he's so unhappy not to be with her. The doctor has told him he'll be dead soon if he doesn't stop.' Silence on the line. 'I still care for him, very much, and I just can't let that happen.'

'What is he, crazy? Nellie, can't you fight for him? I can't believe he's done this to you, wonderful girl like you.'

At least Walter's voice sounded stronger, but Eleanor didn't want him to condemn his son. 'In fact, it was my decision in the end. I hope you don't think I'm selfish, but I want more out of life than this, can you understand that?' Eleanor thought she could hear Hilda in the background, trying to find out what was going on. 'Please explain to Hilda, and I promise that Sadie and I will still be part of your family, no matter what.'

There was a pause. 'Well, thank you for trying.' Then a sigh. 'Goodbye. For now.'

Eleanor collapsed back against the wall. She had intended to ring Sadie straightaway, but she felt drained after her conversation with Walter. And overcome with sadness at the blow that this would be to them. She called Bobbie. 'Hi, fancy a trip up to the lake? I need to clear my head.'

Just over an hour later, they were running through the cool mountain air into the refreshing water.

'Usual swim, round the island?' Eleanor called out as she splashed through the shallows.

Off they went. Eleanor was full of repressed energy and swam full tilt until she flung herself onto the beach half an hour later. Rolling over, she looked up to see Bobbie just emerging from the water.

Bobbie sat on the towel beside her, panting. 'So, what are we calling you these days? The Royal Rocket?'

Eleanor laughed. 'I guess I really did need to let off steam, this whole divorce thing, you know.'

Bobbie looked at her. 'Yeah, I do know. Mine was a few years ago now, but I can still get het up thinking about the hassles.' She trickled sand through her fingers, thinking something over. 'Okay, I've got a stress-busting idea for you.'

Eleanor stretched, enjoying the feel of the early September sun. 'All ears here.'

'Well, here's the thing. How about you do the swim leg of the Veterans' Triathlon Relay at Green Lake next year?'

Muffled laughter from Eleanor. 'Yes, of course, a triathlon, why not?' She hoped Bobbie realised she was being sarcastic. 'Never done one, not even sure what it is, I'd make a fool of myself.'

'Well, I reckon you've just done over twice the distance, beat the hell out of me. It's not until May, plenty of time to train. What do you say?' Bobbie played her trump card. 'And it's for charity, the March of Dimes. You could get the school involved, quite a few of those kids have congenital conditions, research funding is really important, right?'

Eleanor nodded. 'But don't *you* want to do it? You've done triathlons before.'

Bobbie grinned. 'Well, apart from thinking someone else should have a go, unfortunately I'm not old enough. Gotta be over 50.'

Eleanor imagined lightening up the dreary months of legal separation and the process of divorce with a focus that involved her work and friends. 'All right, I'm convinced, although I'll probably regret this in a few months' time.'

Bobbie pressed home the advantage. 'I bet there's plenty of people at the school who would sponsor you, maybe the kids would like to be team cheerleaders?'

'Careful you don't oversell it. I'm in. And thanks.'

Later that afternoon, Eleanor wrote to her sister.

Dear Annie

I'm writing to let you know Ray and I are getting a divorce. He is in love with someone else. We've tried counselling to see if there was a way to be happy together, there just isn't.

I imagine this will be a shock. I haven't told you how bad things were, because what could you do from thousands of miles away? I'm sorry, maybe I should have, I hope you understand.

In a way, I'm glad Mother and Father can never know what has become of the marriage they had such reservations about. I think they forgave me in the end. Although it's been harder to forgive myself.

Sadie seems to be accepting the divorce. She was more aware of our troubles than we realised, and she loves us both. She also gets on well with Judith, Ray's—what do I call her?—girlfriend? Surprisingly, so do I. Sort of. It's a long story, that I might bore you with one day. Sadie is making a good life for herself in California, although from time to time she talks about wanting to get a job in England! Funny how the pendulum swings.

All my best wishes to you, Janusz, and the girls. They must be so grown up Maybe we can get together when this all settles down.

Eleanor looked at her watch. Late morning in California, a good time to ring Sadie. To ring Sarah.

'Hello, love, I'm ringing with some news. Although it might not be news, I don't know if you've spoken to your father, you might already know…' *Am I gabbling?*

'Hi Mom, he tried to call me at work last week, which was a bit weird. He hasn't called back, but unless someone's died, I'm guessing this is about the two of you?'

Eleanor took a deep breath. 'We're getting a divorce.'

'Well, as I said before Christmas, it's not the biggest shock I've ever had. I know you were going to try to work it out, but am I right that you couldn't?'

'We did try, um… Sarah,' *that just came out, will she mind?*, 'we really did, but your dad loves Judith, she loves him, and I want to get my life back on track rather than picking over the bones of this dead thing.' She stopped. *A bit melodramatic?*

'Very colourful turn of phrase, Mom, but you've made the point. And I suppose what I want to say is that, in a funny way, I'm happy for you all.'

'You really mean that?'

'Actually, I do. I feel a bit sorry for myself, to tell the truth, because at any age it's nicer to be a child in a happy family. And I can't quite get rid of the voice of the Church you brought me up with. But I love you and Dad, I can see that he and Judith are good together, and I like her, although I don't know if I will ever forgive her. If that makes sense. And by the way, I like being called Sarah. Only by you, of course.'

Eleanor was touched by her daughter's honesty and, not for the first time, wished there wasn't a continent between them. She pressed her fingers into her eyes to stop the tears.

'Love you, Sarah, we'll speak again soon.'

A New Year

January 1972

New Year's Day. Eleanor opened her eyes, blissfully hangover free. *Unlike some of the others at Phil's party, I'll bet.* She smiled at the thought of her friends. They'd all seen in the New Year together. She'd limited herself to a couple of glasses of wine and fizz at midnight, but quite a few of the 'finely tuned athletes' (Bobbie's description of the Masters' swimmers) would be waking up feeling less than perky, she imagined.

Shoving her feet into fleece-lined slippers, she padded to the window and opened the curtains. She couldn't see much in the winter dark, but an eerie white glow in the garden told her there was fresh snow on the ground. A few flakes continued to drift downwards.

It had taken awhile to feel comfortable waking up in an empty house, but now she liked it. She had breakfast to suit her routine, put jam on her toast if she fancied, and if it wasn't a working day, dressed when it suited her.

At the beginning of this year I was married, at the end of it I won't be. Eleanor had mixed feelings as she prepared her breakfast, brewing her coffee first. Sadness at the failure of her marriage, the loss of the love that she and Ray had once felt. Mixed with a kind of nervous anticipation, almost an impatience to get started again. *This calls for a festive outfit,* she decided. Nice pair of trousers and a Christmas jumper. A present from Bobbie, the jumper featured Santa diving into a pool. Red hat and Speedos, just the thing to banish the gloom. *Well, where else am I going to wear it?*

The doorbell rang. At first, Eleanor thought she must have

misheard. Eight o'clock, New Year's morning, who on earth would visit? She peered through the spyhole in the door to see a face, distorted by the concave glass. Swirling wind blew snow around the ghostly figure. *Judith? Am I seeing things?*

Chain unhooked, key turned, bolt slid back, then she opened the door to her visitor. The glass wasn't the only reason for Judith's distorted appearance, her eyes were red and swollen. Dark circles underneath. She started to speak, but Eleanor gently laid her fingers on Judith's lips.

'Wait, come and sit down.'

She switched on the gas fire, wrapped a throw around Judith's shivering shoulders and poured her a cup of coffee. The icy cold and dark seemed to have seeped into the room despite the fire. Eleanor shivered.

'Now, tell me what's wrong.'

Judith hesitated. 'Ray… I… that is, we went out for a meal last night, New Year's Eve, I thought he might finally be planning to give me a diamond. Small, of course.' A shaky laugh. 'We were having a nice time, but I thought he looked distracted, like he was waiting for the right moment to propose.' A sip of coffee turned into a gulp. 'Boy, was I wrong. He finally got around to what was buggin' him. Turns out the new Bishop has told all the local priests not to allow divorced Catholics to marry in the Church.'

Eleanor was puzzled. 'But you two can get married somewhere, right? There's nothing stopping you.'

Judith shook her head. 'There is if you're Ray Miller. He's got his heart set on a Catholic church wedding. Specially as the university chaplain told him it would be okay, before this new rule came in. Ray being Ray, he's started to have a drink or two more because he's so upset. He'd been doing really well, going to meetings…' Her voice tailed. 'All that to say, I told him I wouldn't marry him anyhow, anywhere, if he didn't quit drinking, and he says he can't. Sure is a mess.'

Here I am, providing sympathy to the woman who wants to marry my husband. Do I need this? Eleanor's thoughts must have shown in her face.

Judith spoke, her voice pleading. 'Eleanor, I'm so sorry, I shouldn't be dumping this on you, you're the last person who should have to put up with hearing about my troubles with Ray. It's just that his boss at work has given him a warning. And now Edwin, you know, the guy he's staying with, he wants Ray to leave because he wants his own space. I couldn't sleep, came out here on impulse.'

Eleanor didn't pretend. 'You and I might get on all right but talking like this drags me back to where I don't want to be.' *Ease up a bit, Eleanor, she can't hurt you.* 'Anyway, I can't think of what I can possibly do.'

Judith sat up a bit straighter and drained her coffee. 'You are so right, I guess I figured you would understand better than anyone, I didn't think about how you'd feel, I'm so sorry.'

'Stop apologising, please. It's certainly made for a different start to the new year for me, anyhow.' She paused. *It won't kill me to be a bit helpful. Put her at a distance, in a way.* 'The only thing I can think of is, well, have you talked to the chaplain? Father John… somebody? He thinks the world of Ray, and if there's any way to arrange things, he might be the one to do it. I think he's moved on to some higher post now, but the university would be able to put you in touch.'

Judith brightened and gathered up her belongings. 'I might give that a try. I'm going to leave you in peace and say sorry again.'

'Happy New Year,' breathed Eleanor, as the door closed behind her visitor. But the icy cold remained.

Celebrity at Last

May 1972

Eleanor reached the end of the pool and flipped over, facing the dazzling ceiling lights. How many yards had she put in? Her arms felt like they were going to fall off, her back was killing her, and she was grinning. *Last indoor session before the triathlon, it's warm enough to train in the lake, I can't wait.* Her doubts when Bobbie first suggested the event had turned to excitement, bolstered by support from Cleveland Hill School.

'So, Eleanor, what's this I hear about you doing a charity swim?' Emily Rogers had appeared at the classroom door a few weeks before as Eleanor was tidying art materials.

'Oh hello, Mrs. Rogers.'

'Emily.' The Head was reminding her of the school's informal approach between colleagues. Eleanor struggled with it.

'Right, Emily, yes. Well, I'm part of a swimming group and we've decided to do the Green Lake Triathlon Relay to raise money for research. Two of our other members are doing the run and cycle, I'm the swim part of the team.'

'I am truly impressed. Especially as… well, how to put this… y'all aren't exactly teenagers.'

Eleanor laughed. 'We certainly aren't. We're in the Veterans' category, and would you believe, we're almost the youngest.'

'Where's your sponsor form, then?'

'Oh, actually, I just happen to have it here in my bag.' Eleanor blushed, although asking for money for a good cause wasn't too embarrassing. Emily handed the sheet back to her. Fifty dollars!

'Thank you, so generous, really appreciate it,' Eleanor stammered.

'You're welcome, now let's see if we can get the whole school behind this.'

The day arrived, and the Stony Point Masters were supported by a busload from Cleveland Hill School. Green Lake sparkled, the course was clearly marked, and a nervous Eleanor waited at the start. She'd been warned by friends about the rough and tumble of open water competition and was expecting a scramble as everyone ran down the beach. However, it was still a shock. Elbows out, legs flying, the pleasant people she'd been chatting to on the shore turned into demons the minute the horn went.

It's only a swim, you just have to finish, you don't have to be first, Eleanor chanted to herself as she strode into the water. Out of the shallows, shutting out the other swimmers, she got into her stroke. Looking around as she went, she kept the fluorescent turn buoy in her sights. To her surprise, she realised she was gradually moving through the field. A breast stroker with a kick like a frog caught her leg with a strong blow. *I'll have a bruise there tomorrow*, she thought. But it didn't slow her down.

Turning at the buoy was mayhem, with every swimmer trying to shave their distance as much as possible. She popped out of the roiling crowd, then, head down, sprinted for the end. As Eleanor ran up the beach to hand over to Phil for the cycle leg, she could hear the children cheering 'Go, Crayfish!' and see the banners they'd made waving in the sun.

Two days later, Eleanor picked up her copy of the Sentinel and turned to the sports page. Nothing. Not even a couple of inches. Disappointed, she tossed the paper onto the table. As she did so, she noticed a photograph on the front page. 'Stony Point Vets Top Fundraisers for March of Dimes' shouted the headline. And there they were, the three of them looking bedraggled but delighted. She read through the article and her satisfaction was complete. They had won the Veterans' category as well.

August, and a relaxed Eleanor stretched her legs and spread her toes in the dappled sunshine. The garden was mainly a flat stretch of manicured lawn (easy for a ride-on mower), but since Ray left, she had created a shady, secluded area with flowerpots and small shrubs. It had become a favourite, private place. The serenity it brought made it the perfect spot to open the brown envelope with the Court stamp.

She held the final divorce decree in her hand. No young children, no pets, therefore no living creatures to be painfully divided. The house would be sold, they would have equal share of the profits. *How strange*, Eleanor thought, *that's what our lives together have come down to. Real estate.*

She went inside, picked up her sports bag, and went straight to the pool.

Just a Bit of a Blip

May 1977

Eleanor watched as the children laughed and splashed in the little pool. *Look at that, every one of them can swim in some fashion. None of them will drown because they can't make it a few yards to the side.* In all her years of teaching, this was one of her proudest achievements.

Patsy came up beside her. 'I never thought the Crayfish would keep going, but just look at this.' She put her arm around Eleanor and gave her a squeeze. 'Good job, coach.'

Eleanor laughed. 'I was watching them swim just now, thinking this is something I'll remember when I'm old and grizzled. Funny what makes us happy.'

Patsy blew her whistle to get the children out of the water. 'How about a drink tonight, usual crowd?'

Eleanor smiled. The school staff had all become friends over the years, and often got together to unwind after work, celebrate a birthday, any excuse, really.

'Sorry, I've got training tonight, but let me know next time.'

'Oh yeah, forgot about that, Miz Super-fit. You put us to shame.' Patsy chuckled.

Later that evening, Eleanor hauled herself out of the university pool with a grunt of satisfaction. *That was a mile. Not bad for an old girl.*

There was something about the after-swim shower that brought back memories of her school days. Naked bodies, all shapes and sizes, attempted conversations over the hiss of the water. Fun, in a strange way.

'Sorry, Bobbie, I left my shampoo on the shelf by you.' Eleanor reached up to get the bottle. Putting a blob on her hands, she shut her eyes and gave her hair a good scrubbing. *Get those chemicals out, my hair's dry and frizzy enough already.*

Later, Eleanor and Bobbie sipped their post-training wine. They had long since given up beer in favour of the less calorie-loaded chilled white. Eleanor thought Bobbie looked subdued.

'What's up?' She nudged her friend gently.

Bobbie stared into her glass for what seemed like an age. Finally, she looked up. 'Listen, I'm probably being silly, but you know when you reached past me for the shampoo?'

Eleanor was puzzled. 'Yes, but surely that's not upset you?' She started to laugh, but Bobbie's unsmiling face didn't encourage levity.

'Eleanor, there was a lump. On the side of your right breast. It kind of stood out when you stretched.'

Without a word, Eleanor slid out of the booth and walked in a dream to a stall in the restroom. Yes, she could feel it. Buried in flesh, but probably uncovered when she reached for the shampoo. About the size of the cat's-eye boulders she used to play with at school, it seemed to move around a bit. *How could I not have noticed?* The shock was powerful, so she sat on the toilet seat and took deep breaths until she felt calmer.

She returned to her seat. 'You're right, there's something there. I'm so glad you told me. Glad you were staring at my breasts.'

Some of the anxiety went out of Bobbie's face. 'Couldn't help but see it when you practically stuck your boob in my face. I had to tell you, even if you're mad at me for being a fusspot.'

'Which I'm not. And you're not a fusspot.' Eleanor managed a shaky smile. 'Don't worry, I'll make an appointment right away.' *Thank goodness for the school's health insurance.*

After a needle biopsy, 'most likely to be a cyst' turned into 'a few cancer cells in there, but it's at a very early stage.'

Eleanor absorbed the news. 'So, if I must have breast cancer, this isn't the worst it could be?'

Dr. Waddell smiled. His freckles and russet hair reminded her of Father Simmons. 'That's it exactly, Mrs. Miller. At this stage, the outlook is good, but we do need to discuss treatment.'

Eleanor frowned. She'd done a bit of reading to prepare herself, but then given it up as it made her more anxious. 'I believe that the surgery is pretty drastic, very disabling.' She was trying to be brave.

Dr. Waddell shook his head. 'We tend not to do such radical surgery these days. Most patients opt for a removal of just the breast. The results are good, the healing is much quicker, and a prosthesis will give a natural appearance under your clothing. Or some surgeons now offer a removal of the lump only, although the research on that procedure is in its early days.'

He stopped, probably thinking that this was more than enough information for her to take in. 'Think about it, and I'll see you in a week or so. My receptionist will give you some leaflets to look through.'

After a week, the leaflets were still unread. Every morning, Eleanor woke, got up, had breakfast, went to work if it was a weekday, came home and sat at the table, surprised to see the leaflets there. She simply could not believe that this was real.

Finally, at the end of the second week, she woke up feeling

as if she'd been hit by a sandbag. *Cancer. I've got cancer.* She cried into the pillow, then sobbed in the shower. After calling in sick, she decided to clean the house, sobbing as she did so. She fell asleep in the afternoon, worn out with keeping the bad thoughts back.

Later that day, she stood naked in front of the mirror. She pulled her right breast under her armpit, leaving a flat surface on one side. *Hmm. Not hideous, but odd. It's my smaller one, lots of women are different sized, so maybe it wouldn't look too strange.*

Eleanor's breast was removed, leaving muscle and glands in place. In her mind, this gave a better chance of 'getting it all', and the research on lumpectomy couldn't tell her differently yet. Once the drains were out, she was almost overwhelmed with calls from Sadie and a stream of visitors. *Never thought I'd be glad of the limited visiting hours,* she said to herself after she'd made particularly exhausting efforts to keep smiling.

She expected to see her swimming friends and her school colleagues but did not expect to see Judith slipping into the room a few days after the operation. It was after evening visiting hours (*typical Judith, does what she wants to do when she wants to do it*), and Judith looked furtive as she checked her surroundings before entering.

She thrust a huge bouquet of creamy, fragrant magnolia blossoms into Eleanor's hands.

'These won't last but a few days, anyway they smell so good, I figured it was worth it.'

Eleanor wasn't sure about how pleased she was to see Judith. However, the flowers banished every antiseptic smell from the room. *She couldn't possibly know I've always called her "The Steel Magnolia". Could she?* 'Thank you, that's so kind of you, it's good to see you.' An awkward pause. *I'd better ask.* 'So how are you doing?'

Instead of answering, Judith pulled a brown paper bag from under her jacket. It contained a bottle of wine, a corkscrew and two plastic wine glasses. She poured them each a glass, then settled on the edge of the bed.

Then she spoke. 'I guess I'm kind of okay. Well, Ray's kind of okay, in case that's why you're asking.' *It is*, thought Eleanor, *are they ever going to get married?*

Judith rubbed her forehead. 'He's still waiting on Father Jack to figure something out. But I guess he's making an effort. Most times we go out, have a good time,' She stopped, maybe realising she was talking to the person who used to share those good times. 'Anyway, every once in a while, he just goes on a bender, and I won't put up with that, so I break it off. Then he's sorry, wants me to promise we'll get married, I won't promise, and it starts all over again.'

Eleanor took a sip of wine, glad she'd been able to cut down on her pain medication. Probably wouldn't be good together. 'Well, it's a shame, I hope things get sorted out.' Which, to her surprise, was true. She was, if anything, a bit bored, had no interest in hearing about their troubles. *Is this what they call 'moving on'?*

After a week in the hospital, Eleanor was ready to go home. No driving for a while, so Patsy gave her a lift and took her case upstairs to the apartment. There was a package outside the door.

'Swimsuits,' said Eleanor. 'I ordered some from the Sears catalogue, I need to see what works best when I've had my fitting for a permanent prosthesis in a few weeks.'

Patsy hesitated. 'Eleanor…'

Eleanor looked up from removing the brown paper wrapping. 'Mmhm?'

'Are you, well, okay? I mean, you seem so practical about all this, the cancer I mean, I'm just worried…'

'Thinking I should be crying all over the place? I can tell it's hard for you to even say the word, and I don't know how I want people to be with me. So yes, I'm sticking to the practical at the moment, making out this is just a bit of a bump in the road. Until I figure my life out. Can you understand that?' She stopped. *Have I been too harsh, ungrateful, unkind?*

Patsy didn't seem put out. 'Actually, it makes total sense. And you're right, I didn't know what to say, how to be your friend.'

Eleanor relaxed. 'But that's it! If you're not sure, say you're not sure, it's so much easier. For me, anyway. Can't say for other women.'

She pulled the swimsuits out of their packaging. Nice patterns. And one had a ruched front, so she wouldn't have to wear her prosthesis in the water for a balanced look. 'And don't forget, I'm still English, and we don't emote all over the place like you Yanks.' A teasing smile in case Patsy thought this was a criticism. 'Nothing like living through a war to stiffen your lip forever.'

Thinking about Patsy's words later, Eleanor was struck by how different she felt now, compared to the fear and loneliness following her hysterectomy. *Something's changed, I feel stronger. Complete. How strange.*

Part Nine:
Under Attack

Fighting Back

September 1982

Five years ticked by, mostly serene, modestly content. The first day of the new term was over. Eleanor sank into a chair, reached down the front of her dress, clasped the prosthetic breast, and transferred its gelatinous weight from her body to the half-filled fruit bowl. There its translucent perfection nestled among the wrinkled apples. She laid her hand gently over the scar that covered her heart and took a deep breath.

The prosthesis had done its job for the day. They had moved through the hours together, greeting the children, meeting their parents, and presenting a vision of mature composure. With her permed hair and a cap-sleeved floral dress covering her body, Eleanor was sure she looked just like all the other middle-aged women caught between their hippie kids and ageing post-war parents.

Now she was alone in her tiny apartment, everything except the bathroom in a ten by twelve-foot space.

During their separation, Ray's GP had told Eleanor that Ray found it difficult to live away from the family home, even on a temporary basis. He was so fragile that he might drink himself to death if he had to leave permanently. No consideration of what the effect on her might be. Eventually, they agreed to hold off on selling the home, and he agreed to contribute towards a rented apartment for her until he could save up to give her the money for her half of the house. She was still waiting for that, ten years and counting since the divorce.

Her friends chivvied. How could she let him string it out?

Why couldn't he save up enough? *Truth is, I feel safe here. Enclosed, protected, and, not to mention, financially secure.* She looked at her swimsuit, drying on a rack. *Thank God for the lake.*

Her hand curled around a tall glass containing a carefully assembled mixture of gin, ice, tonic, and mint.

She took a swallow, then another, giving a quick glance towards the letter half-hidden behind the fruit bowl. The drink tasted medicinal, pleasantly bitter. She wasn't ready to pick up the letter, with its Diocesan stamp; she needed to control the dread that was clutching at her and find the courage to read it. Why was she hearing from the Church after so long? Was this the outcome of whatever Ray had done to make it possible to marry Judith in the Church?

Darkness brought no relief. To move some air in the small room, Eleanor had opened the only window protected by a screen. It was already thick with the corpses of insects fatally drawn to the dim light of the lamp by her chair. The orchestral harmonies of cicadas and tree frogs rose and fell, and she could just catch a whiff of ozone from a coming storm.

As she sipped the drink, isolation enveloped her. The peace she'd felt after her mastectomy was nowhere to be found. There was no one to talk to, to ease her fear. She thought about ringing Sadie, always so level-headed and good-natured. It would lift her spirits just to have a chat. She reached for the phone, then stopped. What time was it in England?

Sadie had just started her job over there, Eleanor had been so pleased when Sadie told her. 'I've got a job in London, Mom, can't wait to live in the land of your birth. And the approach to hospital Social Work is so different, it's not so much about finding out if someone can afford the medical fees, like it is here.'

Now Sadie seemed so far away, separated in distance and time. Another thought: Sadie had been accepting of the divorce, understanding that it had been coming for a long time. But this was different. How to convey the threat she was feeling from the Church over a crackly transatlantic line, when she might have woken Sadie from sleep?

Eleanor sighed, and her sips turned to gulps. She could picture the scene in her small corner of the garden, when Father Sebastian had come to see her sometime after the divorce. He'd written, saying Ray wished to remarry in the Church, and needed her help to look at the best way forward. Then all had gone quiet, although she assumed some sort of turgid ecclesiastical procedure was lumbering on in the background. Or maybe not, maybe he'd given up. But now, here was this letter, glowing in the electric dusk, almost certainly the promised follow-up from that conversation with the priest.

Sometime later, she put down the glass, now containing only water and soggy mint. Her hand seemed a long way from her body; she watched it gleam in the dusk as she retrieved the envelope. She was conscious of the heavy parchment as her fingers traced the raised Diocesan Seal, leaving sweat-slick on the pristine surface. She read:

From the Office of the Diocese of Shippington, Potomac Basin, Maryland.
September 4, 1982
Dear Mrs. Miller
I write as the final step in our work to let you know that our Tribunal has rendered an Affirmative decision in the case that

your former husband has presented to us, and granted a Decree of Nullity with respect to your marriage. This decision means that he and you are free to remarry in the Catholic Church in the future should you wish to do so.

As I mentioned when we met earlier this summer, I write today to let you know the final outcome of the case. I again want to express my deepest appreciation of your very gracious hospitality. I hope that this letter finds you in good health and a bit cooler than everyone here is at present!

Sincerely yours in Christ,
Reverend John P. Sebastian

Eleanor crumpled forward, and the long scar contracted, sending sharp pains across her chest where the stitches had held. Perspiration and tears rolled down her face, washing powder into the lines around her eyes. She could hear again the words said by the priest. She could remember the light glinting on his round spectacles and especially her hot flush of embarrassment as, at his request, she doggedly provided details of the frequency and quality of her and Ray's 'marital relations'. Amongst other things.

As a convert, she hadn't fully understood the local interpretation of the Church's position on remarriage after divorce. That a divorced person could remarry, but not in the Church, and that's what Ray was determined to do. However, if it could be established that theirs wasn't a true marriage, the way was clear for him.

Eleanor was bewildered. How could they have concluded that she and Ray had never been truly married? Twenty-five years and a child? The baby who never was? It made no sense. *I've got no-one to blame but myself. I was the one who suggested to Judith that Ray could get in touch with that priest.* And this was the result.

At the time of their meeting, she thought that Father Sebastian had also seen it that way. 'I still have to speak to your former husband, Mrs. Miller,' he had said, 'but I simply cannot see that there are even any grounds to bring the case before the Tribunal.'

His words had given her the impression that Ray's request would be turned down. It would never even get to the Tribunal. What did Ray tell him that had changed the priest's views? A chill crept over her. As she'd so helpfully suggested to Judith, Ray had pleaded for help from the priest. The priest, so fond of Ray, who might do anything to help him. Eleanor began to understand. She could imagine that, seeing Ray's desperation, the priest had set about constructing an 'escape' for his friend. What really hurt was that he seemed to have convinced himself that this was a good outcome for her as well.

A few blocks away on the University campus, Father Sebastian ("call me Father Jack") was sitting in a leather chair in his study, smiling at the letter he had sent. He thought he had struck just the right note by emphasising the liberating consequences of the Tribunal decision, plus a few breezy social comments, and his work was done. She should have the letter by now; he was relieved to have extracted himself from what had seemed an impossible situation. He allowed himself another glass of a rather nice red, a birthday present from Ray.

In the former Miller family home, a mile and a world away from Eleanor's efficiency apartment and the priest's study, Ray was sweating in the same evening heat on his screened veranda. He held a glass of iced tea in one hand, and a copy of Father Jack's letter in the other. A recording of the university orchestra's D.C. concert played in the background. As the music washed over him, he felt renewed satisfaction at his climb from small-town teacher to moderately successful conductor. The university had put its faith in an under-qualified former soldier, and he felt he had repaid this belief by solid achievement.

He raised his glass in a toast to the priest. Father Jack, who, after witnessing Ray's decline, had delved into the obscure topic of ecclesiastical nullity. He had constructed a basis for Ray to marry in the Church, presenting the argument that Ray's naivety and immaturity, exacerbated by the stresses of war, resulted in a 'lack of due discretion of judgment'. Therefore, he was not psychologically capable of the vows of marriage. A Declaration of Nullity would allow him, as a divorced person, to marry the love of his life with the blessing of his Catholic faith.

Much later that night, Eleanor moved and straightened her spine. The storm had broken, and the air was lighter. She picked up her Basildon Bond writing pad—a cool blue, just the right colour, and wrote.

Dear Father Sebastian,

Your letter is cleverly expressed, but it is iniquitous that it skirts around the most salient points. Firstly, I already consider myself free to remarry in the catholic (meaning universal) church. You seem to assume that this will be good news. It is not.

I believe you deceived me as to the purpose of your visit. You have contrived to 'nullify' a true marriage. This I cannot forgive.
Eleanor Miller

The following Tuesday Father Jack opened the blue envelope as he walked into the rectory's Formica-bedecked kitchen. He stopped mid-stride, tight-lipped and frowning. However, he did not have a minute's doubt. He had entered the priesthood to give expression to his gift for bringing lost souls to God. He had saved Ray from the scourge of alcohol, the mortal sin of adultery, and the torment of a marriage to the wrong woman, entered into under the duress of war. Mrs. Miller, who until now had shown commendable adherence to ecclesiastical advice, was overreacting. His response would have to be guarded. Ray's talent must continue to flourish, unimpeded by alcohol and spiritual pain.

The battle began. Shots were fired in the weeks ahead, with no quarter given on either side.

Dear Mrs. Miller,

I presumed you would realise that when I referred to the Catholic Church, I was referring to the Roman Catholic Church. I am a Roman Catholic priest. I am sorry that you misunderstood.

Dear Father Sebastian,

You do not state in so many words that our marriage has been annulled. Perhaps this delicacy means you have some understanding of the devastating effect that this decision has had on my health?

Dear Mrs. Miller

I feel that I must state outright that we have issued an ecclesiastical Decree of Nullity. Before the Roman Catholic Church, your former marriage has been declared null.

Null. Eleanor reread the previous week's letter from the priest and turned the word around in her mind. She hadn't eaten breakfast, but the partly digested remains of last night's sandwich flushed up into her mouth. Sour liquid trickled down her chin, increasing the stains on her nightdress and giving off a stale smell. She imagined she could hear the tinkling of glass as every part of her life was shattered: her well-groomed and collected image, her memories of herself with her handsome husband, of her lovely home and child, her hard-won recovery from divorce and illness.

She was supposed to be getting ready for Mass, but that was now impossible. Her marriage had been annulled by the Church whose comfort she deserved. She wanted no further part of its ceremonies and judgments.

Later that week, as she sat with her hands flopping over the arms of her chair, the phone rang. Eleanor's head turned towards the sound. It was one of those modern phones: curvy, all in one piece. Sadie had given it to her for Mothers' Day a few years back. She waited, but the ringing didn't stop. She counted each ring up to twenty. *You win*, she thought, and lifted the slippery plastic to her ear.

'Eleanor, it's Patsy—why didn't you answer sooner? I saw Mrs. H. at the store, she said you called in sick all last week. I've been so worried.'

Now Patsy would come over, as a best friend would. Eleanor knew she must not let anyone see her in this state. Dropping the phone, she snatched the priest's letters. No one must see those either. Coat over her nightdress, car keys clutched, down the rusty staircase and into the car she went. Shoes. She had forgotten her shoes. No time to go back, she would manage without.

The sun was coming over the horizon as Eleanor accelerated the car up the hill. The rays of the sun pierced her eyes, hitting the back of her throbbing skull. She had forgotten about the sharp bend at the top. She saw it too late and tried to brake.

A sharp stone on the brake pedal dug into her soft bare sole, and she recoiled. That was the last thing Eleanor remembered until she looked up and saw smooth tiled walls and was conscious of the smell of disinfectant. Her chest hurt as she tried to breathe.

Anthony: A Turn for the Better

Late September 1982

She heard a cough and looked towards the sound. A figure stood by her bed, silhouetted against the too-bright neon strip light: black suit, white priestly collar. Father Sebastian? Where was she, and why was *he* here? She felt frantically for her spectacles, desperate to see properly.

A pale freckled hand came into view, holding her spectacles out to her. Fighting down the fear and nausea, she peered through the lenses. At a complete stranger.

'Sorry, Mrs. Miller, I hope I haven't frightened you?'

English accent, she thought. *Safest to say nothing.*

'Mrs. Miller, I'm Anthony Evans—Catholic chaplain to the Army Hospital here in Tidewater. Your doctor said you've been very disturbed since the accident, and I've come to see if I can be of help.'

Accident? Eleanor stared back at him, frozen with fear and confusion behind the smoky glass panel that seemed to float between them, muffling his voice. She would not utter a word to this middle-aged stranger, with his kindly face and soft speech. She had been fooled before.

Father Anthony waited, and then reached for a chair. 'May I sit down?' Eleanor gave the briefest of nods.

'Mrs. Miller, I can see that this is all very strange for you, so maybe if I explain a bit more about who I am, and then fill you in about what's happened to you, things might fall into place.'

He seemed to take her continuing silence as permission to go on. 'To start with, you've probably picked up that, like you,

I'm not American.' He stopped, twisting his fingers as if unsure what to say next. Eleanor moved to turn her back to him. 'Wait. Hear me out.'

She sighed and halted her turn halfway. He was evidently not easily deterred.

'I was an army chaplain in England during the Second World War; I've been seconded over here because I saw a lot of men who were, let's say, not just physically wounded by combat.'

Eleanor lifted her gaze towards the clock on the wall. Would he get the message and leave her alone?

But he persevered, to her annoyance. 'Some of the Vietnam vets have come back in even worse shape, and I've been advising the medics here at the army hospital and talking to the men themselves.'

Father Anthony paused, and she peered sideways at him. Was he trying to judge the effect of his words? She still couldn't speak, but her eyes remained fixed on his face. She felt the muscles in her own face tighten as she tried to concentrate. She desperately wanted him to tell her where she was, and why she was there.

Perhaps he sensed her need. 'In case you were wondering, you had an accident three weeks ago, on the Lower Road in Stony Point, near the university. You were taken to the local hospital, but once you were stabilised you were brought here, to Tidewater.'

It still made no sense to Eleanor, which must have been obvious to the priest.

'Because of your ex-husband's service, you are entitled to get care at a military hospital, and it was felt that the situation was a bit delicate, as you are both so well known in Stony Point.'

377

Eleanor gave a tiny nod. She began to understand.

Father Anthony let out what might have been a relieved breath. 'Anyway, transferring you to Tidewater seemed like the best solution, so here you are.'

Eleanor drew in a deep, painful breath, and her eyes widened in terror.

'You can't remember any of this?' he asked.

She blinked, and tears welled in her eyes.

'Well, you weren't badly hurt, but you haven't said a word since. The doctors think you are in some sort of shock, but as you haven't spoken, they've come to no conclusion about treatment.' He paused, then continued even more gently, 'And I think I might be able to help.'

She felt the blood drain from her cheeks. She looked down at her hands, at the veins showing through her skin.

The priest leaned forward. 'Please, Mrs. Miller, don't be frightened. I don't have any mystical knowledge. It's just that the police found letters in your car, and yes, I did skim through them, to see if they might help me to help you.' He paused. 'Maybe I shouldn't have done.'

Her hands came up to cover her face and she turned.

'Listen carefully, Mrs. Miller, there is absolutely nothing to be embarrassed about, and you have done nothing wrong. If anything, I have, reading your letters, but the medics were getting desperate. I'm sorry.'

Her hands came down. This priest was saying something new.

'I believe the stress of the process you've been through, and the outcome, were major causes of the accident, and your loss of memory. Which your doctor says may be temporary.'

Once again, Eleanor heard shattering glass, but this time it was the glass wall as she broke through. She straightened her shoulders and turned to face the priest. She was still only able to catch a few of his phrases.

'…some experience of Tribunals since coming to the States… incorrect procedures… grounds for appeal…'

She was not taking this in. She cleared her throat and forced herself to speak.

'Excuse me, Father, I'm afraid I didn't quite get what you've been saying.' Her own voice sounded rusty.

The priest looked up with a slight smile, then continued as if they'd been chatting for weeks. 'I was saying that, under church law, you have the right to appeal. I think this could be on the grounds that procedures were not followed correctly. Specifically, you were not given the opportunity to defend your position.'

Eleanor saw him take a deep breath. She guessed he was trying to be careful. 'Obviously, it's not possible to predict the outcome, but could it be beneficial to your health to fight back? And I would be willing to support you. I would not be able to do it *for* you, of course, but I could act as your consultant. Perhaps on points of law and process.'

There was a long silence. Flies buzzed around the strip light in the dingy side room as she looked away from him. Why was he doing this? It was the first time someone had held out a hand to her, and it wasn't easy to trust. Her mind went back to the early days of Ray's courtship, to their whirlwind marriage, then the loss of everything familiar, the loss of love. And how strange that she was now on the brink of challenging Ray through ecclesiastical courts, how had it all come to this?

Father Anthony waited, possibly seeing the play of emotions over her face, not wanting to force a decision.

After a few minutes, she looked directly at him. 'Yes,' she

said firmly, the croak gone from her voice. 'I want to try to defend my position, as you say. We had a true marriage, and I will not allow them to just wipe it out without a fight.'

He returned her gaze, nodding slightly. That was all Eleanor needed, 'I can't think straight now, I need time, could we meet again? Somewhere outside this hospital, to discuss how I might go about it?'

'Of course. Now rest.'

She was asleep, exhausted, almost before he left her side.

Returning Fire

October 1982

Three weeks later, unaware of what had happened in the hospital, Ray and Father Jack met in the priest's study at the university. It was 4pm, their usual time, and the setting November sun fought through the grime on the windows to illuminate rows of ecclesiastical texts. These meetings had given Ray the spiritual support and counselling he had needed throughout the divorce and nullity proceedings, and the happy occasion of his recent marriage to Judith. Now the two men were reflecting on Ray's achievement of a state of spiritual and emotional peace.

They sat in cracked leather chairs facing each other. The younger man had changed from his priestly collar and suit into a soft flannel shirt and dark slacks; his glasses reflected the light from the setting sun, emphasising the very few lines on his 45-year-old face. At sixty-five, Ray seemed less at ease in his clothes; his well-pressed trousers rode some way up his shins, and now pinched at the waist. This was probably the effect of substituting too much food for too much drink as he struggled along the path to sobriety. He was aware that, even now, his face showed traces of the struggle.

But this was the time for a quiet celebration. Thanks to Father Jack, he was sober, and he was composing again. During the latter years of his unhappy marriage, Ray had just about been able to stand in front of an orchestra and interpret someone else's work with the aid of bourbon. But now he felt released to create his own pieces and had returned to the joy of the musical and spiritual work that he and Judith had begun. Father Jack would say modestly that he was merely an instrument of God's grace, although he was happy to have played even the smallest part in Ray's renewal.

As the men celebrated on one side of town, Eleanor slowly tidied her apartment on the other. The meetings with Father Anthony after her discharge had opened her eyes to the possibilities of legal process, and of rights of appeal within the Church. Armed with this, she was ready to fight back. The steamy summer heat had given way to a mild autumn. A cool breeze blew in and cleared her sense of defeat and hopelessness from the room.

Eleanor settled in front of the ancient Underwood, loving the smooth feel of the coated keys under her fingertips. It was a beast of a typewriter: heavy cast-iron, with levers and rollers, manufactured sometime in the 1930s. She could barely lift it. But she had been able to afford it, which pleased her immensely. It was her weapon in the next round.

Dear Father Sebastian,

You may be surprised to hear from me and may have assumed that I have accepted the 'Decree of Nullity'. If so, you would be wrong. I was prepared for my ex-husband to remarry, because I knew that only this would make him happy, but I am not prepared to be completely painted out of the picture as if our marriage had never existed.

Please could you answer the following:

First of all, why was I not notified that I could appeal the decision of the Tribunal?

Secondly, why was I not offered the services of an Advocate?

Respectfully,

Eleanor Miller (nee Barton)

She folded the letter, running an angry fingernail along each crease. Her heart was pounding as she hurried to the Post Office before she could lose her nerve. Once the letter was out of her hands, she felt no fear, no regret. Elation flooded through her and took her almost skipping back along the street.

Days passed, then weeks, but Eleanor remained serene. She walked and swam, continued her recovery, and met twice weekly with Father Anthony to plan their approach.

Finally, a response.

Dear Mrs. Miller,

Indeed, I was surprised to hear from you, as some time has passed, and I had hoped that both you and Mr. Miller had moved on with your lives, secure in the knowledge that the Tribunal decision had been made regarding the spiritual welfare of all concerned. However, I will respond to your questions.

1. The case was not appealed because, by virtue of our procedural norms, the obligation to appeal may be dispensed with by the National Council of Bishops. In this case, it was.

2. You were not encouraged to enlist the services of an advocate because, following your gracious testimony, there was no need for it.

You may not challenge the local Tribunal decision; any appeal must now be made to the Court of the Second Instance in Baltimore.

Father Anthony had warned her to expect a dismissive response, but nothing could have prepared her for her anger. She had always thought the expression 'a red mist descended' to be hyperbole, but it was happening to her as she read this letter.

'*Obligation to appeal dispensed with?*' She had never been told of any right of appeal, which had then been 'dispensed with' by the shadowy Bishops, with no indication of the grounds.

'*No need*' to encourage her to seek an advocate, following her '*gracious testimony*'? So that cosy visit from Father Sullivan, which he had requested to 'have a chat' about Ray's petition to nullify their marriage, that had been considered 'testimony'?

Eleanor rose, sending papers and ornaments flying as she set off to pace the room. Time was, when she would have collapsed under the weight of such a lofty brush-off. She had always been considered the weaker of the twins; she was seen as prone to anxiety and inclined to defer to authority, and to her stronger, more assertive (and five minutes older) sister. But no more. She had an advocate now, and while the legal information might come from him, the anger and determination were hers.

Anticipating a negative response, she and Father Anthony had already drawn up a statement for the Baltimore court. Eleanor found their notes in the scattered papers, took a deep breath, and settled again in front of the trusty Underwood.

To whom it may concern,

I am challenging the decision to grant a Decree of Nullity on the grounds that my right of defence has been denied (American Procedural Norm 22). It is also my hope that others can learn from the consequences of my treatment at the hands of the Roman Catholic Church.

Eleanor Miller

No trepidation this time as she approached the Post Office;

she strode, shoved the letter through the 'Outgoing Mail' slot and marched back again, scattering squirrels, dead leaves, and a startled woman with a baby stroller as she went.

Her new-found certainty that *now* her story would be heard left Eleanor ill-equipped to deal with the ensuing delays. Someone was sick, someone else had retired. The file was passed back and forth for months. And then Father Sullivan raised questions about Father Anthony's involvement on the grounds that he was seconded from the UK, which took more than a month to resolve.

More time passed in debate, and Eleanor felt stretched to breaking point, and so alone.

Her regular meetings with Father Anthony were helpful, but narrowly focused. He was a busy priest with extensive duties. He advised her against confiding in friends, as most of them either could be, or already had been, approached as witnesses. She had been made to swear not to discuss the annulment with anyone else, and she wondered if the purpose was to protect the Church from the indignation others might express at the one-sided ordeal she was forced to undergo. Or perhaps in the hope that isolation would weaken her spirit.

And then there was Sadie. With her own career progressing in London, she had reacted calmly to news of the divorce some time earlier. But when Ray rang Sadie to let her know that he was seeking a Decree of Nullity, apparently he'd had a shock.

In an indignant phone call, Sadie told Eleanor, 'You would not believe it, Mom, he had his spiel all worked out! It was just a religious formality, it wouldn't make me illegitimate, blah blah blah.'

Eleanor could imagine Sadie steaming.

'Do you know what I said?' Sadie didn't wait for Eleanor's answer. 'I said "*bullshit!*" and hung up on him.'

Would have loved to have been in the room when Ray had that conversation, thought Eleanor. But she contented herself with a noncommittal, 'Oh dear.'

So, no chance to unburden herself to Sadie; her desire to protect her daughter was too strong. Eleanor felt her determination ebbing as she battled to keep up a pretence of normality, suffocated by loneliness.

She had almost decided to abandon the effort, fearing it would destroy her, when she received another letter.

Office of the Tribunal
Archdiocese of Baltimore
October 24, 1982
Dear Mrs. Miller,
In reply to your statement, I agree with you that your questions regarding your rights in the petition are just. If you so desire, you may still challenge the decision on the grounds that your right of defence has been denied (American Procedural Norm 22). It would mean that the process must be corrected by supplying the omitted steps, and then the decision itself updated accordingly.

If you wish to undertake this challenge, please complete the enclosed questionnaire concerning your marriage, and return it at your earliest convenience.

Respectfully yours,
(Rev) Gerald F. North

Inquisition

1983

Eleanor had to reread the letter to make sure she had understood. The woman who had so often backed down in the face of opposition cast a resolute eye over the list of questions sent from Baltimore. She hauled the Underwood to its place on the kitchen table.

Question 1.

Where, and in what circumstances, did you first meet Raymond Arthur Miller?

She began to type.

Eleanor shifted and stretched, surprised to see that two hours had passed. Surprised, too, at the intensity and detail of the memories called up by the question. Wartime romance, tea parties, rationing. She wrote it all down. She was even more surprised that a task she had feared would destroy her with the raw pain of memory instead diminished her hurt. It was easy to recall that first meeting, the awkwardness, the attraction she had squelched, thinking it would come to nothing. So wrong.

Question 2

When, and how, did your courtship begin?

The details were equally easy to recall. Affection triggered by gratitude for a lift from the village shop. As she told the story, it occurred to Eleanor that maybe Ray had been looking at her all along. And that her assumptions about Annie being more attractive, more fun, grew out of her shaken confidence after the Blitz. Delighted with this new insight, she raced through the story of their courtship with ease.

As days and weeks passed, Eleanor fell into a routine. Between answering the questions, she sat in the garden, walked, met with Anthony (first name terms as they worked intensely on her appeal), and contacted the 'witnesses' she was required to produce. Her colleagues and friends agreed to be interviewed in support of the validity of her marriage. Although for the non-Catholics among them, it took considerable explanation to make sense of the request. They were baffled by what they saw as an arcane process, which bore no relation to modern life.

There were two potential witnesses who might have been more perturbed than most, despite their Catholic faith. Walter and Hilda Miller were no longer alive to be pursued by priestly investigators. Both had lived well into their eighties, Walter dropping down suddenly while feeding the animals, Hilda dying several years later in a nursing home. Eleanor was glad they would not suffer the distress of being approached. In fact, she probably wouldn't have put them through it. And yet, they had been the truest witnesses to the early years of her marriage. A photo of them standing in front of their farmhouse graced her dressing table. Side by side, they gazed at her living quarters with what Eleanor fancied was stern disapproval. She often smiled with affection at the image. *American Gothic. All they need is a pitchfork.*

She returned to work and was touched by the welcome from colleagues and the children at the school. No one quizzed her about the circumstances of her disappearance, and she even received a homemade card from the children in her class: "We missed you, Miss Eleanor, and we're so glad you are back because we are fed up of supply teachers." It was embellished by drawings of birds, flowers, and an unflattering portrait of what she assumed was the long-suffering stand-in.

Question 3

Before the marriage, were you together frequently enough and under such circumstances that you could get to know each other well?

Pulling her dressing gown more tightly around her, Eleanor gazed through the window at the falling snow. It was only afternoon, but darkness was descending, and the temperature dropping. Her image in the cold glass bore no resemblance to the dancing girl, swinging around the parlour with Ray, banishing his demons. Now there were dark shadows under her faded blue eyes, sharp collarbones showing above the robe, and lines of pain visible. Snowflakes, spectral tears, floated down her reflected face.

Finished, she reread her response. Get to know each other well? They were so close, so melded into each other's minds and bodies. A half-smile eased the lines of pain on her face at the memory of it, and she thought, *I can do another one before dark.*

Question 4

During the year preceding your marriage, did you discuss your plans for the future life you would lead with each other?

Eleanor sighed. Whoever had devised these questions had no knowledge of what it was like to live with long separations, short, intense times together, and the possibility of sudden death hanging over their 'plans for the future'. Still, she would have to make her case. She closed her eyes and took herself back. *When had their plans come together?* She had a vision of her surprising (to everyone, including herself) decision to take a job on the remote Isles of Scilly. 'Yes,' she whispered to herself. The answer was in those months on the islands, when she was free to think and act for herself, and what started as dreams became plans for her future life.

An hour later, Eleanor arched her back and moved her cramped fingers. As the deadline approached, she was using every spare minute to construct her responses and was encountering surprises along the way.

She remembered now how disconcerted she'd been to receive Ray's letter as she nestled into life on Scilly and the warm friendship with Harvey. Looking back nearly forty years, she felt again her—resentment?—at being rushed into actions that would turn the course of her life.

Had the wave of Ray's passion knocked her over, and driven out any considered thought? What if she hadn't found the priest on St. Mary's and converted to Catholicism?

She had kept all of Ray's letters, and, looking again at this one, realised how much it revealed about the man as she knew him through the years. She could imagine him sitting upright at his desk as he wrote. He would never write any document, even one so intimate as making plans for marriage, curled in a chair with a drink, as she often did. And the letter itself. At times his gift for understatement and tortuous expression was astonishing: 'A bit of a jar'; 'the biggest angle as far as you are concerned'.

But then, he was brought up to keep a tight rein on his emotions, especially the more sensuous ones. Eleanor sighed. In a way, the reality of his love came through more powerfully when the dam broke, and urgency overwhelmed him. 'Loving you so much... wanting you so desperately,' he had written. Strong, mutual love.

That was the foundation of their marriage. Wasn't it?

Midnight. Eleanor stared at her watch in disbelief. She had been lost in the dizzy happiness of her time on St. Mary's. Had she said enough? Too much? The 'planning in the year before her marriage' had mainly been condensed into one intense week, followed by the whirlwind triggered by Ray's letter suggesting they marry right away, in England. And all against the background of her unsettling feelings for Harvey.

Father Simmons was dead now, but she still had the Holy Card he had given her when she had been received into the Church. He had praised her diligence and sincerity over the long months of study. A kindly man, who unknowingly led her into the trap that threatened to squeeze the life out of her now.

Eleanor's fingers were hurting from pounding the keys, and she switched to the smoothness of a fountain pen. Bitterness and regret, distractions she could not afford. The pressure was on. The tribunal demanded her responses by the new year, with no thought to the Christmas she would like to have, the full-time job essential to her single survival, or the cancer that never quite left her side from one check-up to the next. She looked at the next question and sighed. Well, this answer wouldn't take long, so just one more tonight and then she could sleep.

Question Five:

Was your wedding day a happy day for you both? Was there a honeymoon?

Eleanor felt a wave of fondness for her long-dead parents. Not a single word of criticism or reproachful remark had passed their lips in her hearing. Although Mother had insisted that the wedding photos be taken at the house, claiming that the wedding party would risk death stepping out from the church straight onto the busy main road. For the first time in years, Eleanor looked at those black-and-white photos. Her bridal outfit was beautiful, even by today's standards. Flowing silk, a pearl headdress and lace train, and a bouquet of late chrysanthemums. She couldn't remember now what colour they had been. So yes, it had been a happy day for them both. The happiest of days.

Eleanor realised she had left out the second part of the question, was there a honeymoon? A wry smile as she recalled the time at the farmhouse bed and breakfast: clumsy, inexperienced, embarrassing, delightful, exhausting, and she started to write.

Abruptly, she put the pen down. She had been assured that her responses would be treated in confidence. Really? She knew that, in addition to her advocate, the questionnaire would be seen by at least three clerical judges. Not to mention the typists who prepared the documents. The blood rushed to her face as she experienced the reality of the power that these celibate men had over her. What did they say—and feel—as they read over and discussed intimate details contained in questionnaires such as hers? But was she in too deep, had she too much to lose, not to submit herself to this debasement, not to tell them what they wanted to hear?

Just this once, though, she would protect what had been their last uncomplicated, joyful time together. Picking up the pen, and with a firm hand, she wrote:

Yes, there was a honeymoon. It was also a happy time. And left it at that.

Question Six:

Give an account of the first years of married life, the communication and cooperation between you, and any quarrels or difficulties.

It was early morning the following day, and for the first time, Eleanor was at a loss. 'The first years of married life' had started apart. They had married, spent three days together, and then didn't see each other for five months. During that time, she had been hurled into a series of events removed from her previous existence (and so little resembling the conventional marriage her inquisitors may imagine). One shock after another, constant adjustment required. Life on the farm, the unexpected pregnancy, the terror of Sadie's birth. As well as what she realised now was the death of physical union, loving touch, and all that these meant to her. No quarrels, not really. Just surviving, one day at a time.

Question Seven:

When did trouble first affect your married life? What was it?

Eleanor started to give an account of how she had found the romantic letters in Ray's case, how she had packed her bags and left. Then she stopped, trying to remember why she had not waited to confront him, why she had fled, giving him no chance to explain.

'That wasn't it,' she whispered. A submerged truth surfaced, shaking her decades-long belief that it was Ray's obsession with Judith which had destroyed them. For the first time, she faced another possibility: that the trouble with her marriage was there almost from the start. It lay in her feelings for Harvey, tangled up with the power of sexual pleasure. The pleasure that had been destroyed by the priestly edict forbidding contraception, and her subsequent terror of pregnancy. The decision to go through with marriage to Ray despite her doubts had, in fact, been when the trouble started.

It was painful, this stripping away of self-deception. Did this mean that there never was a true marriage after all, because she'd gone into it loving another man, not fully accepting the teachings of the Church? Eleanor had always prided herself on her honesty, on her willingness to acknowledge her failings. Was now the time to do so?

She grappled with these questions, her self-inquisition far more probing than anything the court had asked of her.

'No,' she whispered again, 'it was not my fault.' Steeling herself, she mounted her defence. Many people have other sweethearts before they marry. In fact, Ray told her he had dated another teacher. And for a celibate priest to tell a young couple that the only way they could reduce the risk of death was to abstain from sex... well, that was cruel, wrong, perverted even. Furthermore, it was Ray who rejected any thoughts of other ways to give each other pleasure.

Eleanor made her decision. Straightening her spine, fiercely hammering the keys, she continued: *Trouble first affected our marriage when I found love letters from Judith to my husband.* Looking at what she'd written, she felt no regret, and no guilt. Let them work with what she gave them. She had been a true wife to Ray.

Peace on Earth

Stony Point, December 1983

Three months later, it was done, and she was satisfied. One last discussion with Anthony, then she gave him the document to submit as her advocate. She sent a copy to Father Sebastian. Maybe he *would* learn. Anthony sent her written confirmation of her achievement:

Dear Mrs. Miller,

In submitting my Advocate Brief on your behalf, I pointed out the statements in favour of marital validity from you and your witnesses. I stressed that the length of marriage between you and your former spouse certainly verified commitment, which both parties maintained (until Mr. Miller had a change of heart).

We must now leave the final decision to the 2nd Instance Judges. You can be reassured that you have followed your conscience to the best of your ability in providing the Church Court with a more complete picture of your previous marriage. May God bless you with peace of mind and a joy that only He can give.

Sincerely yours in Christ,
Rev. Anthony Evans

Yes, thought Eleanor as she ran her fingers over a lump on her neck, *that is exactly right*. She leaned back in the chair and closed her eyes. Clinic tomorrow.

Three days later, the autumn light was fading as Father Jack opened the thick envelope at the bottom of the morning's post. Beads of sweat broke out on his forehead as he read through the contents. He forced himself to pay attention to Eleanor's story, as she laid out every detail of the joy she had first experienced with Ray, their happiness at the birth of their child, and the love which had formed the foundation of a valid, if doomed, marriage. He sat for some time in the dark and the cold, this man with his gift for reaching out to troubled souls.

Part Ten:
Return to Scilly

To St. Mary's

December 1983

Unaware that she had won her battle with Father Jack, despite his devotion to Ray, Eleanor too sat in the cold and dark. She had hardly eaten or slept since her clinic appointment. Time had passed, and while her body was outwardly still, her brain was filled with electricity. Flashes, crackles, burnt connections left her almost unable to think or plan. Until she opened her mind to the implausible.

It started with the shock of the clinic, the scans, x-rays, and blood tests. The few malignant cells in her breast, hopefully disposed of along with the breast itself, had snuck unobserved into her blood, her bones, her liver, and were soon to mount an assault on her brain.

In shock, she'd managed to ask, 'How much time?'

'It's always hard to say, but you should be able to enjoy this Christmas, spend it with friends, family, or whatever takes your fancy.'

Eleanor stared at her fingers, twisting the handkerchief she held into corkscrews.

The oncologist spoke again, gentle, compassionate, compelling. 'Look at me, please, Mrs. Miller.' Eleanor raised her eyes and met a kind of challenge. 'You do have some time, we can't say for sure what will happen, or when, but it is sadly no longer possible to cure your cancer. There is treatment to manage the symptoms. Come back next week, you are bound to have questions, and we can discuss the next steps.'

In fact, Eleanor never did speak to the oncologist again. However, she was forever grateful for those few words.

Because of them, she didn't return to the clinic the following week. By that time, she was 30,000 feet above the Atlantic, on her way back to St Mary's, gin and tonic in hand. Because it took her fancy.

What surprised Eleanor most was how little St. Mary's had changed in nearly forty years, although the manner of her arrival certainly had. With even the new Scillonian III unable to sail in the winter, she had no choice but to make her way from Newquay on a little Twin Otter aircraft. Eleanor had treated herself to a first class seat on the transatlantic flight, but this final leg of the journey to St. Mary's lacked any such luxury. The flight was not much smoother than the original Scillonian would have been, although mercifully brief.

Descending from the plane onto the landing strip, Eleanor gasped at the wind cutting into her face. No wonder the flight had been turbulent. Dragging a small case, she headed for the shelter of the terminal building. The terminal, thanks to recent refurbishment, was an improvement on the quasi-military hut in which she had waited for Ray's arrival so many years ago. The weather changed Eleanor's mind about walking into Hugh Town, and the lone taxi driver was glad of her custom.

As they made their way slowly along the coast road, Eleanor twisted in her seat. A road sign: 'Lower Moors Site of Special Scientific Interest'. She caught her breath. She had forgotten how close the nature reserve was to the airport, but she hadn't forgotten the picnic. When she first planned the trip, she had convinced herself she was returning to Scilly because of all the happy associations the islands had for her. Her time there had always signified recovery from the trauma, enjoyment of the beauty of the beaches and unspoiled countryside, and the renewal of her career after its interruption by war. But once she'd booked her flights, she admitted to herself that the faint hope she might somehow meet up with Harvey was impossible to ignore.

Her memories were interrupted by the taxi driver as they edged up the steep drive to Tregallen's Hotel. 'Here you are, madam, I'll just get your bag out.'

Eleanor was glad of his hand helping her out of the taxi. It was the time of day when she felt weariness pressing down on her. No pain, just such an effort to move her feet. 'You've chosen well, it's the oldest hotel on Scilly, very elegant.'

Eleanor's smiled. 'I know, I used to live here, many years ago.'

In her room, she drank in the view. Even in the early dark of winter, the sparkling lights on the harbour and the silvery fading clouds took her breath away. A few moments of peace and beauty, and she knew she'd made the right decision.

Still trying to resist jet lag, Eleanor ordered a sandwich, then slid into fresh smooth sheets. She woke to see the sun climbing into the sky, already almost as high it would go on this winter day. Feeling an unaccustomed pang of hunger, Eleanor layered herself with warm clothes and made her way to the dining room.

From her table near the harbour side of the room, she was almost blinded by sunlight bouncing off the waves. Eggs Benedict, rarely found on any menu in Virginia, glistened in front of her. Her appetite roared into life, and she had to restrain herself to enjoy the taste. A small dribble of Hollandaise trailed briefly down her chin, before she furtively wiped it away. Eggs Benedict it would be for the remainder of her stay.

Eleanor's plan was to walk down to the school, then back into Hugh Town, maybe see if Crawfords' Newsagents was still there. Beyond that, she told herself, she would see where the impulse took her. She knew she would be tired in the afternoon, ready for a sleep, so she wasn't going to push herself, that wasn't the point.Would the school still be there? Eleanor held her breath as she came round the Strand and saw the rocky headland that gave the school its name. There it was, recognisable still, although disfigured by carbuncles of later additions. Including what seemed to be a toilet block. Eleanor had to admit that this was a good thing, as she recalled the horrors of the wartime facilities. The original granite building was unobscured, its bell tower reaching above the hotchpotch of late 20th century folly surrounding it.

Eleanor's approach was cautious. She could see an official-looking sign outside the door. She read: THE COUNCIL OF THE ISLES OF SCILLY, CHILDREN'S SERVICES AND YOUTH CENTRE. No longer a school, then. She saw a few bicycles in the rack outside, but no other signs of life, probably because the Christmas holidays were about to start. *Would anyone mind if I looked around the outside?* Eleanor slowly crept round the original building, which had housed the school hall. Peering through the salt-encrusted windows, she saw a room with the shape of the original hall, and she could make out the herringbone pattern of the well-worn parquet floor. There seemed to be a snooker table at one end. Not a feature Harvey would have approved. Harvey again. Eleanor sighed. Had she really thought she could return to St. Mary's and not be accompanied by Harvey, every step?

Throat-clearing behind her, and Eleanor jumped. A man stood there, maybe in his late forties, clad in brown from head to toe: brown-framed spectacles, a beige shirt and darker tie, over which he wore a yellowish-brown overall. Even his hair and eyes were brown, setting off his pale, chapped skin. He was leaning on a stiff-bristled brush.

'Can I help you, Madam?'

Eleanor gathered herself. 'Sorry, I used to teach here when it was a school, I'm visiting Scilly and thought I'd have a look round.'

To her surprise, he did not respond immediately, but leaned forward and peered at her. Finally, hesitantly, he spoke. 'It's not Miss Barton, is it? Sorry, you have a look of her.'

It was Eleanor's turn to peer. At the badge on his overall, which proclaimed: Simon Wilson, Caretaker. 'Simon, what a wonderful surprise!'

Simon was almost as tongue-tied as he was when, as a boy, he and Harvey welcomed her to Scilly. Finally, he found his voice. 'Miss, I mean Madam, I'm just about to brew myself a tea. I don't suppose you'd like to join me, then you can have a look around if you like?'

'Thank you, Simon, how kind.'

In Simon's cubbyhole off the main hall, they beamed at each other, but conversation was slow to start.

Eleanor sipped her tea and decided she'd better get things going. 'Do you know, Simon, one of my happiest memories of my time here was seeing you at the dock when I arrived, welcoming me with flowers.' *Harvey standing behind him, a bit forbidding at first, if I recall.*

Simon seemed to lose some of his initial shyness. 'And you turned out to be the best teacher I ever had. It's funny, I remember you helping me with my reading, you never shouted, just made me feel like I could do it.'

Eleanor didn't trust herself to reply. She was deeply touched.

403

'But do you know what I remember the most?' Eleanor shook her head. 'Well, we used to come to you to get the splinters out, remember?' Eleanor nodded. 'And it really hurt, but you used to start telling us stories before you dug around with the needle, by that time, I'd be so interested in what happened next, it didn't hurt so much.'

Eleanor felt the beginnings of tears. *I'm lucky to find out how I will be remembered.*

She put down her empty cup. 'I'd love to have a look around, if I may? I want to see all the new additions.' She grinned. 'Especially the toilet block, it has to be an improvement on the old one.'

Simon laughed, and she followed him back into the main building.

Looking for Harvey

Later that day

As they started out, Eleanor wasn't sure she should have taken up the offer to have a look around the school, maybe it was better to leave the memories as they were. But with Simon at her side to provide a bridge to the past, she enjoyed the tour. They passed Harvey's study (now an office crammed with social workers' desks), and in an instant, her plans changed.

Instead of turning back towards the centre of Hugh Town after her tour of the school, Eleanor continued in a loop to St. Mary's Old Church, the site of the main cemetery. After all, Harvey would be well into his eighties, so maybe she'd better try to find out whether he was alive. On her tour with Simon, Eleanor had seen a collection of plaques dedicated to former heads, including Harvey. She'd hesitated to ask her guide about his old headmaster, fearing he would read too much into her interest. From the plaque, Harvey seemed to have retired in 1967, and she couldn't imagine he would have left the Isles in his retirement. If he was dead, he would probably be resting in the churchyard. Heart pounding, she wandered the gravestones, realising too late that Simon wouldn't have been in the least surprised by a casual inquiry, and she could have saved herself a fair bit of trouble. Now she felt at a loss. Where to begin?

However, Eleanor soon figured out that the graves closest to the church were the oldest, so she moved out towards the edges. She walked slowly and respectfully around the stones, studying the names, and pausing to look down through the palmettos to the sea. Once her anxiety subsided, it was a surprisingly relaxing and enjoyable exercise, requiring just enough concentration to keep her from tripping over half-buried stones. Suddenly, there was the name:

> *Beatrice Chalmers, beloved Mother of Harvey*
> *Called to rest 1 June 1938.*
> *At Peace.*

Eleanor caught her breath, reaching out to touch the moss-covered memorial. She looked around and discovered that Beatrice was not the only Chalmers there.

A small stone that looked newer, plainer, was inscribed with:

> ### CHALMERS
> *Here lies Lucy, dear wife and companion of Harvey*
> *Called to rest 2 April 1972*

Eleanor had to put a hand on the stone to steady herself. Why shouldn't Harvey have married? She hoped it had brought him the happiness that she had chosen not to. But who was Lucy?

Eleanor wandered a bit further around the two graves, thinking Harvey would have wanted to be buried with his wife. No sign of him. *So, I can't be sure that he's alive, or even still living on St. Mary's. But I don't know that he's dead either. Keep looking.*

By this time, Eleanor felt the familiar afternoon lethargy creep over her. Better not try his cottage yet. And what if he and Lucy had children? They might be living there. How arrogant and stupid she was to assume that he would never find anyone after she left.

Instead, she continued back around the town centre and along the seafront. Although the weather was mild for late December, she didn't think there would be many at Porthcressa beach. She would rest on one of the sheltered seafront benches, then see where curiosity took her.

As she approached the curve of the beach, with most of its wartime fortifications now gone, she was disappointed to see that all the benches were taken. People shielding their sandwiches from the gulls, couples entwined, workers possibly taking a mid-day break, and several solitary individuals, their faces lifted to the pale sunshine. At the far end of the beach someone had set up an easel, intent on capturing the panorama. As Eleanor approached, wondering which of these she might disturb with a request to share their bench, she looked again at the artist. A few more hesitant steps, and she raised her hand to shield her eyes. An elderly man, she concluded, but there was something about the squared-off shoulders that caused her to inhale sharply. Furtively, she crept around the back of the bench, positioning herself to see his painting. Now she was right behind him, and had her story prepared if a stranger turned and saw her. Visiting St Mary's, interested in local art, that sort of thing.

Turning slightly, the artist lifted his hand and touched her arm. 'Did you think that you could be here for twenty-four hours, and I wouldn't know?'

For a brief second, Eleanor considered a pretence of surprise. However, under the circumstances she abandoned any thought of dissembling about her motives for popping up behind a bench on the beach.

'I've been looking for you. I had a look in the churchyard first, otherwise I would have been here sooner.' She realised how this might sound. 'I mean, I didn't actually think you'd be dead, I hoped you weren't, but I thought I'd better...' Flustered, wondering if she should tell him that she had seen Lucy's grave, she ran out of words.

Harvey turned, smiling, and patted the seat beside him. 'Well, as you can see, I'm not ready for the cemetery yet.'

They sat, face to face for the first time in nearly forty years. Eleanor thought he looked much the same, sharp features, deeply lined skin, perhaps fewer strands of hair, but instantly recognisable. She knew the years and illness had not been kind to her appearance, but she lifted her chin and returned his gaze.

He seemed to know what she was thinking. 'Never forgot you, never thought I'd see you again, but I'd know you even if the local telegraph hadn't already spread the word.'

Slowly, he lifted his hand to her face, stopping, then continued when she didn't flinch. 'Still haven't quite got the knack of keeping those curls under control, I see.' Carefully, he tucked a wayward strand of grey hair back under her scarf. 'I've about finished for the day, fancy a drink back at my place?'

Eleanor stopped at the door of Harvey's cottage, looking around her. He seemed to be the only occupant, but there were unmistakable signs of a softening. Cushions where there had been none, furniture that wouldn't stiffen the spine, and colours that reflected the turquoise and grey of the isles.

'Harvey, I love the colours here now. And the furniture.' She ran her hand over a cream sofa.

He paused, looking around with a half-smile, perhaps seeing the changes through Eleanor's eyes.

'That's Lucy's doing. In her opinion it looked like a stage set for a murder mystery with all that heavy dark furniture.

She was right.' Eleanor waited for him to explain who Lucy was. He gave himself a slight shake and opened a sleek pale oak cabinet. 'Now, what's it to be? Still a sherry drinker?'

There goes my chance to ask about Lucy. 'Not really, it's gin and tonic these days, I don't suppose you've got any?'

He rummaged amongst a jumble of bottles. 'Sorry, my love.' He stopped. 'Oh dear, that sort of slipped out.'

Eleanor wanted to reassure him. 'Old habits. No need to apologise.'

He sat back on his heels, and Eleanor marvelled at his flexibility. He followed her gaze.

'I walk miles every day, rain or shine. Bit of swimming as well. And you can't keep a garden going without bending.' He pulled out a bottle. 'Tell you what, if you'll settle for a whisky this evening, when you join me for Christmas dinner, I'll make sure to get some gin in.'

Eleanor's heart pounded. More quickly than was entirely polite, she knocked back her whisky. 'Christmas. Well, yes, I'd love that.' She stood carefully, her feet starting to feel detached from her body, her head swimming with exhaustion. 'And now I've really got to get back to the hotel. I usually have a sleep in the afternoon. Old age, you know.'

Harvey dropped a light kiss on her cheek as she left. She turned back as he closed the door, and thought she saw concern shadow his face.

Later that evening, Eleanor sat up in bed at the hotel, watching through the window as the lights danced along the harbour wall below. *How on earth do you make a connection, even have a conversation with someone you've loved so much, hurt so much, and haven't seen for so long?* There were great stretches of the lives they had lived squashed between them, with the eruption of old feelings trying to break through. Or so it felt. And it wasn't just about Eleanor and Harvey, there was her beloved Sadie, now with a permanent UK work permit and settled as a social worker in London.

She sighed, reaching for the phone to do what she should have done earlier. Sadie answered, and Eleanor braced herself to deal with her daughter's reaction.

'Hello, love, Mother here.'

'Mother, I've just been thinking about you, how wonderful.' *Sadie sounds pleased. Good*, thought Eleanor.

Sadie continued, 'How are you, how is the treatment going? Come to think of it, *where* are you? You sound like you're in the next room.'

Eleanor hesitated. She had told Sadie about the cancer, visited her after the operation, and explained that the outlook was positive. As it was then. Recently, she had told her daughter that she was having a few recurrences treated, but it was nothing to worry about. 'Well, my love, I'm not exactly in the next room, but I am on holiday. On the Isles of Scilly.'

Silence at the other end of the line.

Then Sadie laughed. 'Mother, you never cease to amaze me. You should have let me know; I could have taken time off. Wait a minute, I might be able to take a few days at Christmas, let me think. Oh no, I promised to swap duty with a friend so she could visit her mom over Christmas.'

Eleanor broke in. 'Actually, I may be staying with an old friend over the holidays. But could we meet up afterwards? I'd love to see you, hear about how things are going, have a proper chat.'

Eleanor heard a sound at the other end of the line, then a dog burst into high-volume barking, and her daughter said, 'Oh dear, there's the door, Bonzo Two is always on guard, looking after me. Better go. We'll speak soon, this is fantastic!'

Her mother chuckled. 'Just like his namesake when you were little, back on the farm.'

Eleanor rested back on the pillows, exhausted. She had managed not to answer Sadie's question about the cancer treatment.

Another St. Mary's Christmas

December 1983

Three days later, Christmas Eve, and Harvey was true to his word. They sat by his fire, Eleanor cradling a gin and tonic, complete with a slightly withered slice of lemon and a single ice cube.

She smiled to herself, but Harvey noticed. 'Something wrong, Madam?'

'I've lived in the States for so long, ice comes in handfuls there, you know. So I had to laugh at this lonely ice cube, wonderfully British.'

Without a word, Harvey reached for a brown plastic ice bucket, lifted the lid with a flourish and plopped four more cubes into Eleanor's glass. 'There you are, Madam, diluted gin and tonic, hope it's to your liking.'

By the second drink, they were telling stories bridging the forty-year gap. Starting cautiously with careers, Scilly news over the years, Sadie and her growing up. Then beneath the personal histories to the pain and loneliness. Hers among strangers, in an alien culture, with the devastation of a dying marriage. His as he struggled to recover from his grief when she left, his retirement.

There was a pause. 'Harvey, I saw Lucy's grave. You did marry then?'

He seemed unperturbed. 'Do you remember that I said you'd changed me, that being with you had lifted the guilt I'd carried around for so long?'

'I do. And I remember thinking it was such a generous way to say goodbye. I mean, I was so torn, I felt awful about the harm I had done, would do. You eased that guilt.'

A slight frown on Harvey's face. 'Well, I wasn't intending to be generous, I meant it. And the proof was the contentment I found with Lucy. We had ten happy years before, sadly, she died.' He sighed. 'And yet look at me, I just seem to go on and on.'

Another pause, as Eleanor adjusted. 'I was wondering… how did you and Lucy meet?'

Harvey stared at her for a moment. 'Eleanor, she taught at the school for thirty years. While you were there, and after you left.'

The light dawned. 'Miss Elmore? You and Miss Elmore?'

Harvey nodded. 'I suppose you and she weren't on a first-name basis but, after you left, she came to mean a lot to me. In a quiet sort of way, she was perfect. She understood everything. She told me that she had always cared about me and had always known about us.'

Eleanor was embarrassed. Harvey took her hands. 'No need to look like that, it was fine. I had such affection for her, very different from what I felt for you, but genuine, and we were very happy.'

Eleanor searched his face. She believed him and opened her mouth to speak.

Harvey shook his head, passed her a drink, and lifted his own. 'That is more than enough about me, you will remember that I am not my favourite subject of conversation, so please, no more. I want to show you something.'

Subsiding, Eleanor followed him out of the sitting room. He opened the door of the bedroom. Eleanor peered into the room, softly lit by a bedside lamp. The austere single bed she remembered was gone, replaced by a comfortable double bed, covered with a quilted satin eiderdown. 'You are welcome to stay if you wish.'

Eleanor drew back. Apart from her reluctance to sleep in Lucy's bed, she didn't want Harvey to see the array of medication that ended her day, or the prosthesis that hung heavily on the side of her chest.

'No, no thank you. It would seem too strange, and anyway, I've nothing with me.'

He put his arm around her. 'Sorry, totally failed on sensitivity, didn't I?'

She rested her head on his shoulder for a moment, then murmured: 'No, *I'm* sorry, it's just too much, I guess. But Christmas dinner tomorrow, is that still on?'

'Of course. Hopefully an improvement on an elderly wartime hen, eh?'

They walked back to the hotel, hand in hand, almost at ease. But Eleanor knew there was one more story to be told. Tomorrow she would have to tell it.

Christmas Day, cold and sunny. Eleanor felt the warmth of Harvey's cottage envelop her as he opened the door. She peered into the little dining room, delight to see the sturdy gate leg table was groaning with Harvey's efforts. A large turkey reposed on one of Harvey's mother's Delft platters, its bronzed skin reflecting the glow of the fire.

'Oh Harvey.' Her voice choked as she realised the effort he must have put in.

He took her coat and pulled out a chair at one end of the table, ignoring her half-spoken comment. 'You'd better be hungry; I think I should have invited another half a dozen people.'

He disappeared into the kitchen and returned with two bowls of soup.

'Hope you like mushroom, I've only given you a small

serving, there's plenty more if you want it.' He leaned and spoke in a semi-whisper. 'It's tinned, there are limits to my skills, you know.'

Eleanor waited for him to sit opposite her.

He picked up a shiny red Christmas cracker. 'Right, let's get into the spirit of things.' With only two of them, pulling the crackers and extracting the contents involved considerable physical contact, with their arms wrapped around each other as the years fell away and they laughed like children.

The remainder of the meal featured produce from Harvey's garden to go with the turkey. When they'd finished, Eleanor pushed her chair back with a sigh. The table was littered with the remains of the turkey, as well as china serving dishes containing varying amounts of leftover sprouts, parsnips, carrots, and swede. The roast potato dish was empty.

'Delicious, Harvey, best meal I've had in so long. Including at Tregallen's.'

He stood, piling plates. 'Let's clear, then maybe pud a bit later?'

Eleanor joined him. 'My idea of a perfect day. A doze in front of the fire, dessert, followed by fresh air.'

As they sat in the fireside chairs, Harvey pulled out a bulky package, wrapped in Christmas paper.

This time Eleanor was prepared. 'Let me go first, Harvey, I don't think I've ever given you a gift. My turn.'

Her present for Harvey was wrapped in red and green tissue paper, the best that could be obtained at the little gift shop on Hugh Street. Harvey carefully dismantled and folded the tissue paper, setting it aside, presumably for future use.

Once a teacher, always a teacher, thought Eleanor, amused.

He held up a burnished pewter flask in a leather case, inspecting it, a look of delight on his face. 'Eleanor, it's beautiful, I don't have a decent flask, and I do like a tot while I'm painting.'

'Take it out of the case.'

He obeyed, and saw the inscription: "From Eleanor, Christmas 1983. All Clear Now".

He gazed into the fire, rubbing his thumb along the letters. 'Perfect. Just perfect.' He took her hand. 'We have waited a long time; didn't think we'd ever be together again.' He held her hand to his cheek for a moment, then cleared his throat. 'Now, here's a little something, not as elegant, but I hope you'll like it.'

He reached down and handed her a package wrapped in what was probably previously used glittery paper.

Eleanor carefully removed the wrapping, looking sideways at him as she did so. 'I'm folding this so you can re-use it.'

He laughed. 'Fair enough, I think that's the 1970 vintage, but good quality, you know.'

It was Eleanor's turn to chuckle as she drew out a beautifully knitted scarf in seaside colours: turquoise, grey, gold. 'Harvey, this is stunning, reminds me of the Scilly beaches.' She noticed a few typical dropped stitches adding to the scarf's charm. 'Surely you didn't have time to…'

He looked rather pleased. 'Well, I didn't have to unpick one of Mother's jumpers this time, I managed to get the colours I wanted from Mrs. Drummond's shop and put the painting aside for a couple of days. Thought it was about time you had a new scarf.'

'I still have the mauve one, you know. It's more or less grey now, but…'

Harvey waited.

'I was going to say, it's very dear to me, and this one will be too.'

Silence fell. Eleanor wanted to tell him, to explain why she'd come, but couldn't find the words. 'Let's walk,' she said.

The December wind cut through them. Harvey pulled her arm through his.

She braced herself. 'Harvey, I want to tell you something.'

He turned to her. 'Well, that's fine, but there's something I want to say first, so you will just have to wait.'

His tone was, she could only think, 'headmasterly'. As if he were quelling an unruly morning assembly, even though amused by their antics.

'I want you to stay,' he said. 'To live with me, to enjoy whatever time we have.' Eleanor opened her mouth to tell him about the cancer, that time was shorter than he might think. But he cut her off. 'Don't forget how well we knew each other. That hasn't changed. I can sense that something is wrong, and I might even venture to say that you are on a farewell tour to a place where you were happy. Would I be right?'

Eleanor settled for a nod.

He squeezed her gloved hand. 'So, let's make it even happier. I could do with some help in the garden, for a start.'

She finally found her voice. 'Harvey, I'm not sure you realise… there's medicines, my body, well my body looks different.' She stopped as he continued to gaze at her with what appeared to be an undaunted expression. 'I had breast cancer, Harvey. A mastectomy, then got the all clear, but a few weeks ago I found out…' She sighed and turned slightly away when he reached for her. 'Let me think about it. I go back on the twenty-seventh; I'll decide by then. And you will have a chance to reconsider.'

She was shivering, and not just from the cold.

Harvey opened his coat and pulled her to him, wrapping her inside. This time she didn't resist. 'I don't need to reconsider but thank you. I suspected something like that, and I can tell you it makes no difference to wanting you with me. But I do understand, lots to think about, Sadie especially.'

Eleanor stayed as she was, reluctant to leave the warmth and comfort. Since her operation, she'd never allowed herself to be pressed up against anyone, thinking they would feel the cold tension of her prosthesis. Harvey was unflinching, and her body revelled in warmth, and something more sensual.

Harvey moved her even closer with a hearty squeeze. 'Now, I'll walk you to the hotel.'

As they approached Tregallen's, he stopped and turned to her. She leaned forward, closing her eyes, then felt him kiss each eyelid. 'Boxing Day turkey leftovers for us tomorrow. And bring your night things, it's about time we woke up together.'

Another Decision

December 1983

The winter sun cut through ice crystal patterns on the window. An unusual Scilly frost. Eleanor poked her nose out into the freezing air. Clearly Harvey had not embraced central heating, so she retreated under the covers. His side of the bed was empty, and she peered around the room. His lower leg leaned against the far wall. He must have taken his crutches to make the trek to the semi-detached lavatory. Although she hadn't heard the swoosh of the high-level chain pull that usually resounded through the house.

Her prosthesis rested on the nightstand, next to a bottle of liquid morphine and a packet of tablets. She'd wanted to put it in the drawer, but Harvey objected. 'I've got no intention of trying to force my leg into a cupboard, so why shouldn't your breast join the display?'

The bedroom door creaked. A couple of thumps, then Harvey entered, managing to balance himself on one crutch while pushing the door open with the other.

A teacup and plate on a wooden tray lurched precariously, but he righted himself. 'Breakfast in bed?' he suggested. 'Whew, I should have put the leg on first, didn't want to wake you.' He set the tray down on the bed.

Eleanor rescued the teacup and accepted the pink quilted bed jacket he offered. It smelled faintly of lavender. 'Goodness, Harvey, I haven't seen one of these in a while.'

'Mother's. She'd be delighted to see you in it. As am I.'

Harvey slid back into bed and gently put his arms around her. 'Sleep well?'

'Like a log.' She replied. 'And I've decided.' She felt his arms tense around her and hurried to speak. 'Harvey, my time is really short—maybe weeks, perhaps a few months or more, I don't know for sure. But if you are okay with that, then yes, I'd like to stay with you. But I…'

He fell back, closing his eyes with a sigh. 'So that's a yes to my proposition then?'

'What proposition?' Eleanor was thrown off track, her solemn speech about not wanting to burden him flew out of the window. 'Harvey, I have no wish to get married, I'm done with that.'

'Not *proposal*, dear Eleanor, I'm talking about a *proposition*.' She thought he winked. 'The sex might not be quite as lively as I recall,' Eleanor gave him a push, but it didn't stop him. 'But I think the spark is still there, hmm?' He pulled her to him.

The next day she cancelled her return flight.

Stretching Time

January 1984

January seemed to last years. Instead of feeling weighed by the doom hanging over her, Eleanor experienced each day as if they had all the time they wanted to make a life together. But far from being full of emotional intensity, their days consisted of mundane events. Peeling veg, side by side at the sink. Spotting the early bulbs, braving the cold in the Scilly sunshine. And Eleanor's favourite, sitting together in the bath like spoons, Harvey washing her hair and stroking her skin.

The sea provided their one big adventure. As February began, once again Eleanor felt the warmth of the returning Spring, much earlier than on the mainland. *I wonder if it's warm enough.*

She reached under their bed, pulling out a sports holdall. Harvey came in as she undid the zipper. 'Well, I'm glad to see you doing some more unpacking, sometimes I look at you and think you're about to take flight. What have we got here?'

Slowly, Eleanor opened the bag. Harvey peered over her shoulder. At first, all that could be seen inside was a quantity of black rubber, which was revealed to be a full-length body suit.

Harvey chuckled. 'Good heavens, I suppose I'm just as partial to skin-tight rubber as the next man, but Eleanor, there was no need to go to such lengths to spice up our relationship, it's fine as it is.'

Eleanor shut the bag firmly. 'Very funny, Harvey, it's a wetsuit, for the cold Scilly water.'

He looked at her, the smile gone from his face. 'You kept

up the swimming then.'

'More than kept up, swimming got me through the worst of times as well as being my delight all the time. You will be pleased to hear I never forgot what you taught me.' She ducked her head, attempting a look of modesty. 'If you promise not to laugh, I might show you my press cuttings, I was a bit of a local celebrity at one point.'

Harvey shook his head. 'As always, you are a wonder.'

Eleanor pulled the wetsuit out and held it up to her body. 'I'm glad you think so because I have a big favour to ask.'

'Which is?'

'We're going for a swim, Harvey, a swim I promised myself when I spent time on St. Martin's. Do you remember?'

'Of course. Rather eventful time, as I recall.' He paused, and she thought he was remembering the U-boat, the little school, maybe even the effect on her of Miss Billings' sherry decanter.

'I know the water's not very warm yet, but with a wetsuit… surely you could borrow one from a diver? And we will go for a swim on St. Martin's. Please.'

Harvey held up his hands. 'You win. I'll ask one of the chaps at the harbour. But it'll have to be a short suit, otherwise the empty leg might be a bit of a drag, don't you think?'

St. Martin's

Eleanor wondered what any watching islanders thought, seeing what appeared to be a rubber-clad elderly couple wading into Great Bay, his arm around her neck. If anyone looked more closely, they might have noticed that the tight rubber only swelled over one side of her chest, and only one leg protruded from his wetsuit.

She hoped no one would think much of it. Year-round diving, snorkelling, and fishing were part of Scilly life. As were older people in various states of disrepair.

Even with the wetsuits, the temperature wouldn't allow more than a short dip. Eleanor's face burned with cold as they swam steadily out from the shore. She looked down through the forests of kelp, where fish played in and out of the sunlight. Then a dark shadow blocked the sun, and she realised they were not alone.

'Harvey, look!' A whiskery nose popped up in front of them, joined by several others.

Harvey followed her gaze. 'They probably think we are some weird sort of seal cousin. Just swim gently by, they won't bother us.' Harvey took Eleanor's hand through the water, then pointed back at the seals from a short distance. 'Selkies, people call them, plenty of legends told.' He looked at Eleanor with a grin. 'They can turn into humans and mate with us.'

Eleanor thought she saw intelligence in the eyes of the seal. 'Nice story, but you'll do for me.' She moved closer to him in the water.

After a few hundred yards of swimming near the seals, the

cold forced Harvey and Eleanor back to the shore. Wrapped in blankets and warm jumpers, their wetsuits drying on the rocks, they devoured sandwiches and dozed in the sun.

Eleanor sighed and rolled into the crook of Harvey's arm. 'So happy,' she murmured, as he held her close. She began to doze. *But did I cheat us both of the life we should have had?* She answered herself before she slept: *Leave it be. Seemed like the right choice at the time. And this is the right choice now.*

Back to the USA

A lawyer's letter broke the peace of daily life on St. Mary's. She could almost hear Mr. Murray clearing his throat and speaking to her. Dry but essentially kind, he wrote as he spoke. Her 'precipitous departure' for Scilly had meant that her Will remained 'somewhat incomplete'. Changes were needed to ensure Sadie, her sole beneficiary, would be dealt with expeditiously even though she lived abroad. These must be signed and witnessed, and he was concerned that some weeks would pass if this was attempted by post.

Eleanor knew she needed to go back to Virginia, to pack up her apartment and 'put her affairs in order'. She hated that phrase. Her affairs *were* in order, here on St. Mary's, and she resented having to waste precious time away from what had rapidly become her home with Harvey.

She pulled herself together. She had to go, to make everything right for Sadie. She knew that her daughter would be deeply affected by her mother's death and making one last journey might reduce legal tangles for her beloved child. This was enough to take Eleanor away from Harvey. Nothing else could, but the thought of even a few days away from her contented life on Scilly dragged her down.

Yet when Harvey asked if she wanted him to come with her, she thought about it, then refused. 'Harvey, I need to see this as a trip to wrap up the last details of what you could say is a failed business. To set the scene for future success.'

He mulled this over. 'I see. Then you will return to the firm of Miller and Chalmers, onwards and upwards.'

Eleanor smiled but thought the business comparison had gone far enough. 'That's the idea, but the main thing is that I can't bear the thought of questions, explaining us to curious friends and neighbours. I just want to close the door on Virginia on my own. Quickly and firmly.'

Harvey's arms crossed behind her back as he held her for a few seconds. 'Then I will be waiting.'

Still feeling resentful (at the law, never Sadie), she booked her flights for the second week in February. She was feeling better than she had in ages and was taking far fewer swigs from the morphine bottle. She did hope that, once she'd done what she had to in Virginia, she and Harvey could continue the rhythm of their days together in peace.

Harvey watched her pack, as she stuffed various items into her case with a mutinous look on her face. 'Eleanor.' She carried on with her petulant packing.

He spoke again. 'Eleanor, stop.' She obeyed, scowling. He pulled the case towards him, then upended the contents onto the bed. 'What on earth are you doing?'

Eleanor knew she was being unreasonable, taking her anger out on the person who least deserved it. She couldn't help herself.

He began carefully folding her clothes, laying them gently in the case with the other necessities she'd set out, until it was nearly full. Eleanor slumped beside him, laying her head on his back as he packed, enjoying the feel of his muscles moving smoothly beneath her cheek. She was impressed with the neat result, no doubt a legacy of his military background.

'Sorry, I simply don't want to spend a minute away.' She managed a laugh. 'But I must remember that none of this is your fault.'

'I know.' He finished the task and reached under the bed

to extract a brown paper bag.

'I needed to make sure there was enough room for this.' He handed it to her.

Eleanor drew out a magazine. The cover featured a square-rigger in full sail, and underneath was the title, "The Scillonian Magazine, Winter 1983". She gave Harvey a quizzical look.

He leaned over and showed her the table of contents: "World Pilot Gig Championships Set for May Bank Holiday", "Scillonian Ready for 1984 Season", and similar items.

'A bit of light reading for your journey. We don't have a daily paper, but there's enough local news in here to pass the time.' He turned his face away, his voice rough. 'And to make sure you remember what you're coming back to.'

As Eleanor leafed through the small publication, a photo slipped out.

Harvey picked it up and passed it to her. 'Oh, and here's your bookmark.' A photo of the two of them, taken a few weeks ago by a passing stranger at their request. Holding hands, turned towards each other, walking in lockstep, and laughing as they braved the chill on the beach.

Eleanor looked up from the photo. 'Harvey, I need to say this.' A quizzical look from Harvey. 'I'm really feeling quite well now, just getting tired easily. But it is possible that... I might not be able to come back, you know?'

He cleared his throat, and spoke haltingly, looking straight at her. 'Yes, I do. And losing you, whenever and wherever it happens, will be a terrible blow. But it won't break me, Eleanor, because of these past weeks. So don't worry about me, do what you must. And if you aren't knocking at my door on the first of March, then I will know.'

Leaving Sadie

February 1984

After another lively flight from Scilly to Newquay, Eleanor took the train to Waterloo. Descending cautiously onto the platform, she searched the waiting faces. There was Sadie, just as they had planned. Her curly brown hair stylishly cut, she was wearing high waisted cobalt trousers and blue enamel earrings to match. She rushed to hug her daughter.

She couldn't stop hugging her, until Sadie, laughing, peeled her arms away. 'Okay, Mother, I'm glad to see you too. But I am desperate to know what you are up to.' On the phone, Eleanor had told her a somewhat edited version of the truth. That she had decided to extend her stay on Scilly, that she needed to go back to Stony Point to close up the flat and sort out a few things, that she would explain when they met for lunch on her way to the airport.

Sadie looked around. 'No luggage, I see. So, let's go straight to the café, it's quiet, and only five minutes away. You can get a cab from there to the airport, my treat.'

Food ordered, they faced each other across the little table. Sadie leaned back and folded her arms. 'Okay, so what's going on? I don't know whether to be worried about your health or pleased that you're going to be nearer.'

Eleanor took a deep breath. 'Maybe both, love. I told you I've had a recurrence of the cancer.'

Sadie nodded, 'And you were having some treatment? You never said how it was going.'

This was so hard. Much harder than telling Harvey. 'Sarah, it turns out that the cancer can't be cured. And the treatment is, well, to give me time to enjoy myself.' The smile, and most of the colour, disappeared from Sadie's face.

Eleanor reached out for her daughter's hand. 'Please, don't be sad, enjoying myself is exactly what I'm doing, and that's really what I want to tell you about.'

Sadie was silent. Eleanor, her throat dry, sipped her coffee, feeling waves of shock coming from Sadie, who recovered herself to ask, 'How much time?'

'I really don't know, it could be weeks, months, no one can say exactly. I'm feeling pretty well now, and I've been quite busy.' Eleanor's heart ached as she watched the effort with which her daughter pulled herself together.

Sadie managed to produce a look of amused interest. 'Busy doing exactly what, I wonder?'

Eleanor, still full of the joy of her time with Harvey, smiled, and didn't find it difficult to match Sadie's tone. 'Well, I won't go into all the details, but I can say I've been in touch with an old friend, visited places where I was happy during the war, and it's been absolute bliss.'

Eleanor didn't feel ready to tell Sadie any more about Harvey. Would her daughter think her mother was being disloyal to Ray? She recalled that Sadie, even as an adult, had been saddened by her parents' divorce, and even more by the few details of the annulment battle Eleanor had shared with her. The subject of meeting someone else had never come up. *When I'm gone*, thought Eleanor, *it's enough for her to know that I was happy, and doing what I wanted to do.*

It seemed she was right. There were tears in Sadie's eyes, as she leaned over the table to hug her mother, but she did not pursue the subject of the 'old friend'. 'I'm still in shock, but I can hear you loud and clear. You're telling me that things are not good with your health, but that you don't want to make a tragedy out of it.'

Sadie sat back down and passed some sandwiches across the table. 'And you don't want me to do so either, so let's have a bite to eat, the taxi will be here soon.'

March 1984

Stony Point: What was left behind

Sadie peered through swollen eyelids at the faded, curling label tacked to an anonymous brown door in a row of similar doors, each distinguished by varying patterns of peeling paint. 'E. Miller' was written in plain letters. So, this was where her mother spent most of her final years.

Sadie stood with the key in her trembling hand, apprehensive at what she might find behind the cracked brown surface. She almost wished that she had not persuaded Mr. Murray, the executor, to let her have access to the apartment before she went back to England. She turned the key and stepped in. She bent and retrieved an envelope lying on the mat. 'Archdiocese of Baltimore' was embossed on the heavy vellum. A fleeting thought: *Maybe one of those church charity things Mom got involved in.* She placed the letter on a side table to look at later.

Sadie surveyed the scene. Thin cold sunshine picked out showers of dust in the air and fell on a haphazard collection of boxes on the floor. Most were cardboard, the corrugations beginning to show where the sides had sagged and split. Seemingly random contents spilled out: glassware, jewellery, clothing, varicoloured files, and anonymous plastic bags. There were also a few wooden tea chests. These were larger, sturdier, and half-full of equally random items. She wondered if her mother had been preparing for her return to Scilly but ran out of time. There was the same smart new case that she had brought to their lunch in London, splendid among the dusty disarray of the rest of the room. It looked as if she was ready to leave.

Moving cautiously across the cluttered beige carpet, Sadie perched on a low footstool and gazed around the room. She had promised Mr. Murray that she would let him know her wishes about the 'disposal of your mother's possessions.' She felt too raw for the task, but the thought of strangers pawing through Eleanor's life felt worse. She steeled herself. Where to begin?

For a start, Sadie wanted to get rid of the impersonal paper bag she'd brought from the hospice, stamped 'Patient Property'. She shook the contents onto the crazed veneer of a coffee table: a plastic box containing an unused luxury soap, a packet of tissues, a pair of stylish tortoiseshell spectacles, a wallet, and some gold earrings bound together with surgical tape.

Then Sadie stared. Landing on the coffee table, the prosthetic breast wobbled slightly, translucent and glowing in the weak sunshine. For the first time since the funeral, Sadie's face softened as she was taken back through time, to just after her mother's surgery.

Three years before, having been pronounced clear of cancer, Eleanor had visited her daughter, 'to celebrate getting the All Clear,' she said. It was one of those surprising Junes in England. The sun beat down on the roses in the little courtyard outside Sadie's flat. Eleanor stretched out on a deck chair with a gin and tonic while her daughter read through government guidance on proposed changes to mental health legislation. Sadie's career as a social worker gave her huge satisfaction, but little time to deal with 'boring admin'.

Bonzo Two, her dearest companion, indicated a need for a moment outside. Sadie took a break and glanced through the window to see Eleanor, swimsuit rolled down to her waist, her remaining breast bared to the warmth of the sun.

Back in the drab apartment, revitalised by this heart-warming memory, Sadie tackled Eleanor's new suitcase. She drew the zip around and flipped the lid open. She couldn't have been more astonished if a bird had flown out.

A pair of rose-coloured French knickers and a matching camisole lay gleaming on top of the case. They were new, still carrying their tags but, Sadie suspected, also carrying Eleanor's belief in herself as a woman with a life to live. Another surprise as she lifted the underwear; velour lounging pyjamas, also new, expensive, and suggesting luxurious afternoons in front of a cosy fire in a country cottage. *Well, well*, thought Sadie. *Who exactly was that friend on the Isles of Scilly that she was going back to stay with?*

Before moving on to the other possessions, Sadie checked inside the hospital bag. Stuck at the bottom, she could see an airmail envelope. The address read H. Chalmers, Glebe Cottage, 6 Moorwell Lane, Hugh Town, St. Mary's, Isles of Scilly, UK. Eleanor's writing, and she must have had quite a bit to say to H. Chalmers. The envelope was thick. Curious, but eager to continue sorting the boxes, Sadie placed the letter on the table with the one she had found earlier. She put the contents of the hospital bag into the smart new case and labelled it: 'For shipping to Sadie Miller.'

On to the nearest cardboard box. There was a brown envelope at the top. It contained Eleanor's brief three-page Will, and a handwritten sheet dated February 12, 1984. A quick look at the Will confirmed that she was her mother's sole beneficiary and Mr. Murray was to act as Executor. There was some sort of codicil, signed by Eleanor, to do with UK/US cooperation. Sadie set the Will aside, not caring. Mr. Murray would have the original.

Picking up the handwritten sheet, she saw a list of individual bequests to friends and family. Eleanor had obviously taken great care with this; it included such instructions as: 'Make sure Bobbie gets the new goggles in my sports bag. I haven't worn them, they were very expensive' and 'Annie can have the bronze horses, she's always liked them. Tell her to mind her toes, they fall over easily and are very heavy.'

The list was so personal Sadie could almost see Eleanor frowning in concentration as she put it together. Reading it was too much, Sadie sobbed in the empty flat with the anguish of uncovering fragments of a life lived with determination to its end. Eleanor had known she was dying, but there was plenty of evidence that she did not wait passively to go. The list of bequests joined the Will.

Sadie's tears were also of anger at herself for settling in England, oblivious to Eleanor's misery. Should she have looked beyond the cheery letters to sense her mother's pain? When Eleanor returned to Scilly, and they met for lunch on her way back to Virginia, should she have probed more deeply, maybe even gone home with her?

Sadie wiped her eyes. What to do with this list, when she was due back in England in two days? She would never locate all these items, and it didn't seem like a task for the solicitor, even if he could distribute them once found. She remembered that she had seen the bronze horses on top of one of the boxes, and remembered also that Mr. Murray's mother had been a friend of Eleanor's. A solution came to her. She placed the horses next to the new case, sliding a note under the heavy base of one of them: 'Would your mother kindly locate the items on this list? And then could the two of you do the best you can to locate the recipients?'

Sadie sat back, satisfied, and again lost herself in contemplation of the events that had led her to this dusty room.

The call from the hospice had been a shock, so convinced was Sadie that she would see her mother on St. Mary's before long. In a daze, she flew to Virginia, arriving in the chilly southern spring to attend Eleanor's funeral instead. A Requiem Mass, in whose anonymity she detected no trace of her mother. The priest obviously hadn't known Eleanor, and Sadie thought it could have been anyone's funeral. She sat stony-faced and dry-eyed, unable to connect the solemn ceremony with the mother she had known. At the end of the service, she rushed out, brushing aside the freckled hand held out to her by someone in the congregation. Another priest. Sadie set her face against him and didn't stop. She cried in the taxi, all the way to Eleanor's flat.

Letters I

March 1984

Now, as Sadie sat amongst the boxes and dust, every item she touched was bringing Eleanor closer. Her eye was caught by a folder labelled: "Appeal against Decree of Nullity".

The watery sunshine faded almost to dusk as Sadie read through the correspondence in the file. The documents detailed what at first seemed to be Eleanor's lonely battle against the Church establishment, a fight to reclaim the validity of her marriage even as Ray appeared to be trying to obliterate it.

Sadie paused, enraged. No wonder Ray was absent at Eleanor's funeral. Despite her fury at her father's pursuit of a Decree of Nullity, she loved him and wanted to believe that he was a decent man. Maybe he had felt remorse at Eleanor's suffering? She remembered his drinking, the evidence of his torment. He also had suffered. Throughout his life, he had been an obedient child of his faith, with a child's fear of eternal punishment should he defy the priests, Christ's representatives on Earth. Sadie looked again at Father Sebastian's letter to Eleanor, announcing the Decree of Nullity. *This decision means that he and you are free to remarry in the Catholic Church in the future should you wish to do so.* She caught her breath, and the anger at her father dissolved, replaced by a new way of looking at her old hurt. She realised now that Ray must have believed that he had been given a way forward, out of his agony and self-destruction. At the same time, Eleanor could now find happiness with someone else, which may have eased his regret at the hurt she had felt.

And he had been able to marry Judith in the Church. *Even so,* she thought, *couldn't he imagine the pain he would cause?* Although it was possible for Sadie to begin to understand, it was harder to forgive.

Judith. Sadie had happy childhood memories of Judith looking after her. Sadie's grandparents and other relatives lived in the northern states and in England, so Sadie had no family nearby. Judith was like a favourite aunt, who brought fun and a whiff of naughtiness into her life.

As time went on, and the nature of Judith and Ray's relationship became clear, Sadie had felt guilty about her fondness for the woman who could be said to have destroyed her parents' marriage.

When Sadie moved to England, Judith occasionally remembered her birthday, wrote from time to time, and never uttered a word about what must have been her own despair during the aftermath of the Millers' divorce. Looking back, Sadie wondered: *How had 'the other woman' felt when, instead of marching up the aisle, she found herself a helpless observer of Ray's struggles with his demons as her own youth passed?* From what Ray had shared with his daughter in stilted transatlantic phone conversations, Sadie knew Judith's refusal to marry him while he was drinking had forced him to choose. Really, she had Judith to thank for the fact that he now seemed happy, sober, and productive. Not to mention alive.

Sadie had fallen into a reverie and shook herself in the chill of the room. She continued to read through the 'Decree of Nullity' file with a new calm.

Although the cold, dismissive tone of most of the correspondence from the priests sickened her, the determined style of Eleanor's responses inspired pride. Her mother didn't give up, but made her case right to the end.

Along with the formal correspondence, the file contained letters from someone called Father Anthony Evans. Some of these appeared to be legal advice and encouragement. There was also "a copy of my Advocate Brief on your behalf", in which he confirmed that she had done all she could to appeal the decision.

Other items from this priest seemed friendly, almost intimate. "Thank you for the beautiful tailored shirts from your last trip to London. The size was perfect, and I love relaxing in them when I take the dog collar off."

Sadie wondered about Eleanor's relationship with Anthony. Reading what he had written, she sensed true friendship and strong support, maybe even something like a mother-son bond. Eleanor had not fought her battle alone. *I can't judge all priests by the way she was treated by some.* Sadie recalled the hand she had brushed aside, the kind face at the funeral above the clerical garb. Could that have been Anthony?

Letters II

March 1984

Mulling over her discoveries, Sadie remembered the letter on the mat, perhaps something to do with Eleanor's appeal. She picked it up from the table where she had placed it, and hesitated. Opening her mother's post still felt strange.

The letter was formal and, to Sadie, cold as ice.

Case: Miller/Barton
On Appeal
To: Mrs. Eleanor Miller, Respondent
Date: 6 March 1984
This is an official notification that the formal opening of your case will take place on 6 March 1984. This is a formal judicial action, and you need not attend.
Sincerely in Christ,
Rev. Gerald North
Presiding Judge

Furious again, Sadie grabbed a piece of writing paper from a box on the floor. The paper started to tear under the pressure of her pen as she wrote.

Dear Reverend North,
Regarding what you call the 'Miller/Barton case', I am writing to inform you that you will receive no further correspondence from my mother.
She died on the 16 March 1984 and will obviously never know whether her appeal was successful.

I see that in her submission to the court, she stated that one of her reasons for putting herself through this gruelling process was 'so others might learn from my treatment at the hands of the Catholic Church'.

I can only hope that they will.

Sadie Miller

Pleased with her effort, feeling slightly better, Sadie made a space on the hall table for her salvo next to Eleanor's letter to 'H. Chalmers'. She would post them as soon as she left the flat. One more box, then she would stop for now. She noticed a small wooden chest next to the suitcase. Unlike the more utilitarian boxes and crates, this one looked decorative and solid. She turned the small brass key in the lock and lifted the lid.

At first glance, the box appeared to be full of knitting. Some looking greyish and faded, perhaps originally a lilac. She pulled it out. A scarf? Underneath was a much more vividly coloured one, and as she lifted it, a note fell out.

Darling Eleanor, forty years is far too long to wait for a new scarf, but I hope this will keep you warm on the chilly days. With love always, Harvey

Sadie's mood changed in an instant, from indignation at the injustice of her mother's treatment, to surprise and something like delight at the implications of what she had found. Intrigued, she continued her exploration of the contents of the box with a lighter heart.

At the very bottom she found a couple of small watercolours of a beach, and a sketch of a young Eleanor, with her hair tied up and… was that an onion in her hand? The artist's initials were H.C. And finally, she found what seemed to be a recent photo. The photographer had caught Eleanor walking hand-in-hand with a smartly dressed older man along an almost deserted beach. They were laughing, carefree and happy.

The apartment no longer seemed inhabited by the spirit of a lost soul. Sadie realised that she was smiling, soothed by her own reflections on the past. The final piece of the mystery of 'staying with an old friend on St. Mary's' fell into place. Sadie decided to look again at the letter to Mr. H Chalmers she'd found in the hospital bag. Now that she was sure who he was, she opened the envelope with tender care and read.

Dearest Harvey,

I know you will have understood when I didn't appear, but I wanted to write and let you know that, although it seems I won't be able to come back to Scilly in the flesh, my thoughts are all of you. Also, I enjoyed the look on the chaplain's face when he leaned over my bed and, in a concerned voice asked what I was doing. "Writing to my lover", I replied, "could you see that it gets posted?"

Sadie hastily replaced the letter in its envelope without reading further. Much too personal. Obviously, the chaplain had not posted the letter. Sadie slipped it into her bag. She would make sure it was delivered. She could, after all, do something for her mother.

Sadie put the wooden box next to the new case and marked it: 'For shipping to Sadie Miller.' She felt that she had a precious inheritance, which was all she wanted. She would ask Mr. Murray to donate the rest of the furniture and other possessions to charity.

Sadie left the flat smiling. What a contrast between the

evidence of Eleanor's painful struggle to overturn the annulment, and the warmth and happiness that came out of the last box.

Back in England, Sadie did not immediately return to work. She felt caught in limbo, grieving for her mother, but filled with wonder, not to mention curiosity, at the turn Eleanor's life had taken.

Several days after her return, another official-looking letter from the Archdiocese arrived.

Dear Miss Miller,

Please accept my sincere sympathy at the death of your mother. She had told me about the cancer when we last met, and I have remembered her in my prayers.

Her case was about to receive a final decision from the Judges. In accordance with Roman Catholic law, the death of a spouse terminates any procedures whereby a marriage can be declared valid or invalid. Or, more accurately, your parents' marriage is considered valid since the contrary has not been decided by two concurring judgments.

Sincerely yours in Christ,
Rev. Gerald North

"Your parents' marriage is considered valid". Sadie had to re-read the logic behind this conclusion. She was used to dealing with legalese in her work but had never come across an ecclesiastical version. As the meaning of the words became clear, her first reaction was anger. What Rev. North was saying was that Eleanor's appeal had 'stopped the clock' on the Decree of Nullity, pending a decision by the court. However, by dying Eleanor had achieved her goal. But, thought Sadie, Eleanor was denied the chance to have her case properly reviewed. Would she be dissatisfied, feel that her story was incomplete? So terribly unfair. Sadie crumpled the evidence of injustice and was about to throw it away. Then she remembered the last time she had seen her mother. What had struck her as they sat in the café was a sense of peace and happiness. Far from being bitter, Eleanor had glowed. It was making sense.

Moving slowly, Sadie put the crumpled missive into her bag. Thoughtfully, she looked at the letter to H. Chalmers, pinned to a noticeboard in her kitchen after her return from the funeral. It needed a stamp if she was going to post it, but there was an alternative.

Sounding the All Clear

April 1984

Just over a week after her return to London, Sadie staggered slightly as she descended from the Scillonian at St. Mary's.

'You're in luck,' the travel agent had said, as Sadie's face showed her dismay at the price of a flight to St. Mary's. 'You could get the first sailing of the season on the ferry, it's much cheaper.'

Sadie now knew the reason that the price was 'much cheaper'. Feeling lightheaded after nearly three hours on a rolling sea, she found a bench and consulted the tourist map she had picked up in the travel agency.

Half an hour later, she knocked on the door of Glebe Cottage. Her heart pounded as she waited, wondering if this had been a good idea. What if he was annoyed at her, thinking she was merely inquisitive? She now knew about the relationship and felt that, in a way, she knew Harvey. But would she be a stranger to him, intruding on his grief? Just as she was about to leave, the door opened. A slim figure peered out at her from under a battered sun hat. She judged he was in his eighties, dressed in worn gardener's overalls and a baggy beige jacket. A contrast from the well-turned-out gentleman in the photograph, but recognisable.

'Sorry, I was in the garden. Can I help you?'

Sadie took a deep breath. She'd faced far more daunting doorstep introductions as a social worker. 'I'm Sadie Miller, Eleanor's daughter. I'm looking for Mr. Harvey Chalmers.'

She expected him to be taken aback, perhaps worried, but his face lit.

'Of course.' He peered at her for a long moment. 'You couldn't be anyone else. You are so like her.' He held out his hand. 'Harvey Chalmers, and I'm delighted you've come.'

Sadie breathed a sigh as she shook his hand. 'Mr. Chalmers, I hope you don't mind, I've come on impulse because...' She stopped, dismayed. What if he didn't know Eleanor was dead? How stupid and cruel to just turn up like this.

He seemed to read her expression perfectly. 'Please, don't worry. Eleanor told me that if she didn't return on the day we agreed, I would know that she had died. And that day came and went.' There was a suggestion of moisture in his eyes, but he pulled himself upright and gestured to the side gate. 'Can you stay and talk for a little while?'

Sadie nodded. 'I'm booked on the afternoon ferry, so I've got a bit of time. And yes, Mr. Chalmers, I'd love to stay for a bit. I only began to understand what you meant to her when I went through her belongings... afterwards...' She couldn't go on. But once again, Harvey knew why she faltered.

He opened the gate. 'Then please, do call me Harvey. Let's sit in the garden, the spring flowers are putting on a typical Scilly show.' He gestured towards a pair of well-worn garden chairs. 'And you might think it strange, but I would actually like to hear what happened after she left in February.'

Sadie reached into her bag and drew out Eleanor's letter. 'I can do better than that. She can tell you herself.'

Slowly, Harvey took the letter, turning it over in his hands. He took it out of the envelope. An enquiring look at Sadie indicated that he was aware that it had been opened.

She squirmed under his gaze. 'Yes, I did start to read it, but, well, as soon as I realised how personal it was, I put it right back.'

The beginnings of a smile from Harvey. 'It's fine, really. And it brought you here.'

Relieved, Sadie went on. 'Yes, obviously the chaplain hadn't sent it as she'd asked, and I didn't want to put it in the post, although I suppose it would have reached you.' She hesitated. 'Actually, I was curious, I wanted to meet the man who meant so much to her.'

For the first time since Sadie's arrival, Harvey looked shaken. He reached for one of the chairs and sat heavily, taking off his glasses and wiping his eyes with a grass-stained cloth. Sadie waited, strangely at ease as she stood there.

Finally, he spoke. 'Do you know, I think I might just sit on my own in the sunshine with this. I feel as if it's the last conversation I will have with Eleanor and…' He stopped. 'Sorry, bit fanciful.'

Sadie shook her head. 'Not at all, it makes perfect sense to me.' A slight pause. 'I'm going to leave you to read.' Opening her bag, she took out a scrap of paper and scribbled her telephone number on it. Bending slightly, she handed it to him. 'I don't know if we'll meet again, but I'd like it to be possible. So, here you are.'

As Harvey reached for the paper, his hand continued up towards her face, where the windy walk had blown her hair across her cheek. He stopped, gave himself a shake, and took the paper. 'Thank you, Sadie. I too would like to think it's possible.'

Sadie closed the gate softly behind her.

Slowly, Harvey removed Eleanor's letter from its envelope. Six closely written pages of it, on thin airmail paper. A smile crossed his face as he read the exchange with the chaplain, who had probably been startled by her cheery reference to 'writing to my lover'. He looked up. A trick of his imagination, maybe, but he could almost see Eleanor's mischievous grin at these last words. After a moment, he continued reading.

Sometimes they ask me here if I've slept well. I don't, really, but I do have amazing, vivid dreams. It's probably the morphine, but they usually feature you and our time together. It's another way that you are with me, and we certainly have some adventures.

I have so much to say to you, I want to fill you in on every thought, action, feeling I've had since we said goodbye, so I hope you've got the stamina to read through all this. Although I may not have the stamina to write it. I suspect my thoughts will be a bit random, incoherent even. I seem to sleep so much lately.

The sun tracked across the sky and the garden faded from view, leaving only soft light and Eleanor's voice.

Here in this peaceful haven, I haven't so much to do. There are nurses, assistants, and doctors everywhere. They even bring the drinks trolley round at cocktail hour, so I hope you will picture me enjoying a G&T to the end.

I don't have—or want—many visitors, but I did have the most welcome surprise not long after I was admitted. Annie turned up—I'd written explaining time was short, and she hopped on a plane and was by my side days later. Ever the creature of impulse and action. But it was as if we were still in our little bedroom at home, sharing secrets and forgiving any words spoken in anger. All the bitterness I felt when Ray stated before our divorce that 'he'd married the wrong twin' left me. It was always like a noxious gas that had poisoned and lessened my relationship with the dearest person on earth (next to you and Sadie, of course) and after a few hours together, that bitterness was gone.

I've been enjoying (is it the morphine again? It gives the gloomiest thoughts a lift) looking back on the decisions I've made. Sometimes I think that if I'd been more courageous in the Blitz, I wouldn't have come to stay with my parents. I wouldn't have met Ray, but then what if I hadn't been driven by restlessness and boredom to take the job at Carn Friar's? I wouldn't have met you.

Now comes the hard part. What if I hadn't chosen Ray, gone to America, which resulted in living a big part of my life away from England, unhappy and lost? Well, I wouldn't have Sadie, and I don't think I'd have the peace I'm feeling now. But it's been hard-won, and the cost has been the life I might have had with you. If I have regrets, my love, it's the loss of those years we could have had together.

And what if I'd just decided to curl up and die when I got The Very Bad News? Coming back to Scilly, back to you, was the best choice I've made, and has brought me a lifetime of happiness. A short lifetime, and I have some sadness about that, but truly, more than enough for me.

Hang on, I'm getting to the best bit. To me, our love is a thread, stretching from the dock at St. Mary's in 1944 to this bed. It's tied us together through the years, even though I didn't realise it. I'm holding the end of it now and I won't let go.

Must finish, they are coming with the drinks. Is it that time already?

All love, Eleanor

Afternoon shadows crept across the garden, taking the warmth of the spring sun. Harvey closed his eyes and remained still, holding the letter, unwilling to let Eleanor's voice fade with the light.

For a few minutes more she was with him.

She shimmered inside his eyelids, a new arrival to Scilly,

emerging bleary-eyed from the Scillonian on a late October day. Her worsted skirt twisted, and she was weighed with her belongings. Even so, she freed an arm and summoned a smile as she gathered the daffodil bouquet presented by one of the children.

That first image disappeared. Then Eleanor strode towards him, resplendent in her Land Girl trousers, a basket over one arm, the other raised to show off her bicep. 'Could you do with a bit more muscle in the garden, Mr. Chalmers?'

Now he saw Eleanor in a serviceable swimsuit and rubber cap splashing water into his face as she swam from him, veering sharply to race him back to shore. The sun turned water droplets to jewels as she drew alongside, throwing her arms into the air. 'Harvey, isn't this the most beautiful day?'

Finally, there she was, curled in his bed wearing nothing at all. He could almost feel her soft skin under his touch and hear her laughter. She held out an empty glass. 'G & T with plenty of ice, please.' He half rose to mix the drink, but she blew him a kiss and was gone.

Harvey opened his eyes. The late afternoon breeze had dried the tears on his cheeks, no need to reach for a handkerchief. He put Eleanor's letter back in its envelope and stood, arching his back to ease some stiffness. As he made his way into the house, something white caught his eye on the ground. He picked up the paper scrap, noting the hastily scrawled numbers. With a smile, he tucked it into his jacket pocket.

Acknowledgements

Waiting for the All Clear is inspired by the experiences of my mother and some of the more than 60000 GI Brides who left the UK for America at the end of World War II. I can only imagine the courage and optimism it must have taken for them to launch themselves into the unknown. I am particularly grateful to Michele Thomas of the website uswarbrides.com for permission to use material from the site.

My thanks go to Carole Smith, who encouraged me to keep writing when my motivation had waned. She introduced me to the Wimborne Writing Group, whose members provided valuable criticism as I painfully put together the early chapters.

Amanda Martin (formerly Curator of the Isles of Scilly Museum) was extremely helpful during my visit to the isles; I was able to learn much about primary school life in wartime, as well as the daily experiences of the Scilly population.

Alan and Sophie Whitehead used their extensive experience of Scilly to provide me with an illustrated report about St. Martin's (they even managed to locate some old photographs of the school). Thanks to them for taking time out of their holiday to become a research team. Helpful reports were provided in the earlier stages of the manuscript by Katherine Mezzacappa (through Joe Sedgwick of The Literary Consultancy) and Neil Broadfoot (via Keirsten Clark of The Writing Consultancy). I have greatly appreciated the patient support and clear guidance I have received from Jan Fortune and the Leaf by Leaf team at Cinnamon Press. As a first-time author, I would have been lost without this.

Finally, I want to express my gratitude to Sarah Barr, who has been my mentor throughout. Her gentle but firm guidance enabled me to achieve my goal of completing the book and provided me with so much more in terms of developing my understanding of myself and my writing.

Further Reading

I discovered many print and online resources while writing this book. For readers who may be interested in some of the topics addressed, here is a selection of further reading:

Goodbye, Piccadilly: British War Brides in America by Jenel Virden

GI Brides: The Wartime Girls Who Crossed the Atlantic for Love by D. Barrett and N. Calvi

What God Has Joined Together: The Annulment Crisis in American Catholicism by Robert Vasoli

Shattered Faith: A Woman's Struggle to Stop the Catholic Church from Annulling her Marriage by Sheila Rauch Kennedy

www.saveoursacrament.org – a website dedicated to reforming the annulment processes

www.uswarbrides.com – Michele Thomas, coordinator of this website, kindly gave permission for the content to be used.

About the Author

L.B. Gray is the daughter of a G.I. bride and spent much of her early life in the American South. She now lives in the South of England and draws on her experience of both cultures in her writing. Her study of psychology at university informs her writing, as does her subsequent career practising as a counsellor and lecturer in the subject.

Despite an enjoyment of writing at school, nearly sixty years passed before she attempted to re-awaken this pleasure by joining a writing group. She has had two short stories published, and *Waiting for the All Clear* is her first novel.

Author photo by Lucy Gray